Before the Rain

Also by Karen Hayes

SUMMER POEM
LETTING GO

Before
the Rain

Karen Hayes

SIMON & SCHUSTER

LONDON · SYDNEY · NEW YORK · TOKYO · SINGAPORE · TORONTO

First published in Great Britain by Simon & Schuster Ltd, 1995
A Paramount Communications Company

Copyright © Karen Hayes, 1995

The right of Karen Hayes to be identified as author of this work has
been asserted by her in accordance with the Copyright, Designs and
Patents Act, 1988.

Simon & Schuster Ltd
West Garden Place
Kendal Street
London W2 2AQ

Simon & Schuster of Australia Pty Ltd
Sydney

A CIP catalogue record for this book is available from the
British Library

ISBN 0-671-71868-1

Typeset in 13.5/15pt Perpetua by
Palimpsest Book Production Limited, Polmont, Stirlingshire
Printed and bound in Great Britain by
Butler and Tanner Ltd, Frome and London

For Nigel, who was there

Acknowledgements

I would like to thank Elsie Browning, for both her companion-
ship and the sharing of her house while writing this book, and
for encouragement on all the others. Other people I should
like to thank are Joanna Frank, for sowing the seeds; Helen
and Chris Shaw of English Nature for many of the details;
the residents of the Palace Gate Hostel in Exeter for sharing
their stories; and my children, Julia, Jacki, Adrian and Jeremy
Boreham – and their friends too numerous to name – who
sparked off so many ideas.

Chapter One

She wills herself not to cry as she walks along the Embankment. The unexpected surge of memory forcing her out into the street at Charing Cross instead of catching the train for Kent has shaken her, disoriented her. Opening her eyes wide to keep the unexpected tears back she stands facing the river, watching a sightseeing boat crammed with tourists meandering along the still, opaque water, seemingly at random like a leaf tossed carelessly into a familiar stream.

'*Emmeline! Em, look at the boats — shall we go on one? Shall we be tourists, just for today, just for once like we used to? Please, Em, don't do that. Don't cry, for God's sake . . . can we for one day forget everything, just enjoy London?*'

She had hoped to do that now, have a little diversion before going off to Canterbury, enjoy some pleasant if banal reminiscing. See if the pigeons were still in Trafalgar Square almost thirty years later, that sort of thing. But instead of amused recollection, the sight of those grandiose lions, the cascade of water, the clusters of tourists gathered in ethnic coachloads and dispersed like pigeons themselves amongst the bored, greedy birds, has stunned her with a sense of loss so deep, so profound, she feels displaced, derailed.

'Look, Emmeline — no pigeons! I told you I'd take you here when there were no pigeons and no tourists. Isn't it worth getting drenched? God, I can hardly see you, it's like standing in a waterfall. But it's a warm rain, a warm night too. What a day it was, before the rain began!'

What a day it was, before the rain . . . Emmeline stands on Waterloo Bridge and tries to remember, but the eighteen-year-old girl she was then eludes her. She's no more a part of Emmeline now than the long, straight, pale-lemon hair she had, or her appendix — which was ruthlessly removed and disposed of years ago. The long hair, the appendix, the girl Emmeline at eighteen — none are part of her now; each has been carefully sliced away and discarded.

She walks along Waterloo Bridge as in a time warp. The memories burst in her head like bubbles from a cheap champagne, intoxicating her but not pleasantly. The bridge, the boats, the Thames itself . . . the Embankment where she ate her first fish and chips, wrapped in a tabloid newspaper . . . It is all still here but the girl is gone, and Emmeline can only see her fleetingly in a shadow, a certain turning of the light, the reflection of sun on water.

She walks and walks. Along the river, towards the Royal Festival Hall, amongst the stalls selling second-hand books, past the buskers, the jugglers. Finally, because her overnight bag is getting heavy, she sits on a bench in the late August sun, facing the river and facing the sense of loss that still permeates her like a persistent dampness, making her ache, making her sad. This is no more than a ridiculous nostalgia for the past, she thinks as she looks over the brown, slightly turbulent water. She understands that this introspection is triggered by the sudden burst of England, of London, exploding into her vision, into her senses; it has made her look at herself, made her recall that she was not always this person, this mature woman with the enamel-slick hair, the confident walk, the assured, elegant clothes still unruffled even after a night flight from Atlanta.

A moment of uncharacteristic panic overcomes Emmeline as she sits facing the river, watching gulls following a squat barge floating nonchalantly past. How did she become who she is now? When did this metamorphosis take place? She feels a sharp stab of regret for that gawky, vulnerable, hopeful girl she left behind here all those years ago.

The river flows and flows, and Emmeline watches — like the old Bob Dylan song we used to sing then, she thinks sadly. Dazed by the long flight, the unexpectedly hot sun, the flush of memories, she feels the river enveloping her, carrying her away to the past, and she closes her eyes and flows soporifically with it.

*

'Oh, look! The Statue of Liberty! I shall quite miss America back in England, won't you?'

Em, hanging over the railing with the other passengers, watching the sea widening between herself and the country she was born in, grew up in, said shyly, 'I've never been to England, but I don't think I'll get homesick.'

The boy next to her turned and smiled. 'I thought you were English, like me,' he said. 'I didn't realise you were American. What a country you have! I've been hitch-hiking all over it for the past six months.'

3

Emmeline nodded, unable to think of anything else to say. The boy must have been about her age — eighteen — yet he seemed impossibly travelled, sophisticated. Together they looked towards the receding skyline, and Emmeline, in her excitement, her soaring anticipation of the year to come, felt that the boat was carrying her away from her childhood and into real life and adulthood at last.

'Are you going to London?'

The question broke into her reverie and she turned to the boy beside her. He looked like a young Peter O'Toole in *Lawrence of Arabia*, she thought with awe — with that long lanky body, those deep blue eyes, that tousled blond hair worn slightly longer than the boys back home in North Carolina.

'Yes,' she replied gracelessly, suddenly tongue-tied. There was a pause, then, in a rush: 'I'm going to drama school there.'

The boy looked at her with sudden interest, amused by the pride with which she said those last few words. 'Do you have a place somewhere?' he asked, wondering if she were just another of the hundreds of starstruck Americans hoping to invade the British theatre scene without any thought of how to go about it.

'Yes, of course,' she said indignantly, her shyness forgotten. She had auditioned in New York with great trepidation, after the long train journey to the city from the small southern town where she had grown up. To everyone's surprise, except perhaps her high-school drama teacher who had directed Emmeline in countless plays and who had initiated her application to the drama academy, she had been offered a place.

She mentioned the name of the school and the boy,

startled, said, 'What an odd coincidence. I'm starting there too. I should have begun last year, but I had the chance to act in a company doing a short tour of the States so I jumped at it. When the tour finished I stayed on, wanting to travel around a bit before going home. I take up my place this year.'

'Then we'll be there together!' She looked at him with such simple undisguised pleasure that he grinned widely, warming to her at once.

'I'm Hal,' he said, basking in her shy smile. 'Henry Allen, on the theatre programmes.' He bowed extravagantly, mocking himself. 'And you?'

'Emmeline. Emmeline Lake.'

'Great name, much better than mine for those programmes. Is it your real name?'

'Sure is. Do you think I'd make that up?'

'Well, Emmeline Lake, welcome to England. Though of course we're not quite there yet,' he added, seeing the bewildered look on Em's face. He offered her his hand, which he intended her to shake, but not understanding, she clutched it clumsily instead, then got embarrassed and tried to pull away. Sensing her distress he held it gently, then took it to his lips where he kissed it in a flamboyant, theatrical gesture which broke the awkwardness and made her laugh, then look hesitantly at him. His eyes, she thought, were bluer than the skies of her childhood, and she wanted to fly in them like a bird flying away for ever from her outgrown nest. The whimsy of her feelings startled her.

'I suppose I'd better go back to my cabin and unpack,' he said, breaking the spell but not, to Emmeline, the enchantment. 'Are you travelling alone?'

'Yes. I'm in a cabin for four, but I haven't met my roommates yet.'

'I'm travelling on my own as well. My three cabin-mates are German and speak very little English. We had a hilarious time trying to get acquainted, my German being hopeless. I lapsed into very bad mime, but it seemed to work.' He started to walk away, but something, perhaps the shy, eager look on Emmeline's face, prompted him to say, 'Maybe we'll meet up later this evening?'

This evening. There were ten evenings ahead, ten days, on this student boat taking a thousand-odd young people, either Europeans returning home after back-packing in the States, or starry-eyed Americans following in the footsteps of the Beatles and the Stones, across the Atlantic. Emmeline, dazzled, promised to look for Hal later and made her way euphorically across the deck and downstairs to the cabins, where she got lost several times before finally asking a short, sturdy Italian sailor with grizzled black hair and hot steamy eyes where Cabin Number F 28 was.

The Italian shook his head, shrugged his shoulders eloquently. His grasp of English was poor, although he had been on the boat, the *Castel Felice*, for several years now, usually on the England to Australia run, bringing out optimistic emigrants seeking a new life in a new country. The passengers of those crossings were mostly families with small children, and a sprinkling of earnest young men off to seek their fortunes. This riotous passenger list seemed to Giorgio to be made in heaven: at least half appeared to be young single girls, Americans off to Europe on a lark, or pale-faced English roses returning home after being liberated in the States.

This English or American rose standing in front of him now was speaking, but since he couldn't understand he stared at her instead, taking in her long pale hair, bleached like the sun at the end of summer, and her astounding legs, daringly poking out from a blue cotton skirt that barely covered her knees. Emmeline, feeling wicked, had bought the skirt in Bloomingdales the day the boat sailed, having just arrived in New York to spend the night in the YWCA before setting sail for Europe. As she wandered through Central Park, along Fifth Avenue, she was filled with a profound sense of change, of adventure. The skirt, shorter than any she had ever worn before, was a symbol of that change.

Giorgio, finally noticing that the girl had stopped talking and was looking at him expectantly, shrugged his shoulders again and said, *'Non capisco quello che dice.'* I can't understand you.

'Cabin F 28?' Emmeline repeated, emphasising each syllable.

'Why honey, that's my cabin,' a deep husky voice growled between Emmeline and Giorgio and they both looked up at a young black woman with Amazonian legs and buttocks and shoulders. The legs were bare, the buttocks covered with the shortest red leather skirt Emmeline had ever seen, and the shoulders were draped with a blouse of some kind of see-through muslin, leaving both Em and Giorgio eye-level with two fat, unencumbered nipples.

'Che carina!' Giorgio exclaimed.

'Get lost, sailor,' the young woman said. And then, to Emmeline, 'Come on, I'll take you to our cabin.'

Emmeline followed at what seemed a breakneck speed through a maze of corridors to Cabin F 28. There, still lugging her small suitcase which she hadn't got around to depositing in the cabin with all the excitement of embarkation, she rather hesitantly followed the black girl inside.

'This is Daisy, she's got the top bunk over there. We just met a few minutes ago.'

Emmeline nodded her head at a tiny figure sitting on the edge of the bunk, kicking her small feet like a child over the sides. She looked about twelve, with her small bones and her straight, shoulder-length hair, a rich deep copper, parted straight down the middle like a white highway going through an autumn forest. Her features, small and salient like a thorn, softened when she smiled, and then she became a rose, Emmeline thought, with all that thick copper hair tumbling like petals around her face and neck.

'Hello, I'm pleased to meet you,' Daisy said, reaching down her hand to Emmeline.

'Don't you guys just *lu-u-rve* that British accent?' the black girl exclaimed. 'And who are you, honey?'

'I'm Emmeline Lake.'

'Hi, Em. I'm Sojourner Truth Wilson.'

'Excuse me?'

Sojourner Truth Wilson laughed. 'It's a bit of a mouthful, huh? But don't worry, everyone calls me Sojo.'

'Oh. Well, hi, Sojo.'

'My momma named me after Sojourner Truth, the black slavewoman who became a suffragette. She was some woman, that Sojourner. I got one helluva lot to live up to.' Sojo laughed, and shook her head, and her thick hair, dyed red and standing a foot straight out in all directions, swished the air in the cabin like a great fan. Daisy and Emmeline stared, mesmerized.

'Well now, I was just on my way out to get some sea breezes, and to check out the talent on this here boat. It don't look like there's anyone over twenty-five on it, 'cept me, of course.'

'You?' Daisy gasped.

'Honey, I'm twenty-seven, but don't you go telling

nobody, ya hear? I'm on this ship to find a man, sweetie, and settle down, preferably in some little but expensive country shack in England or mebbe one of them cha-toes in France. I've had enough of the good ole U. S. of A.; there ain't much here for me, let me tell you.'

Emmeline, who had recently been fired up by the strong emerging Civil Rights movement which had, to her joy, even infiltrated the redneck area in which she had grown up, was moved to protest, but Sojo was out the door before she could begin.

'Well,' Daisy said admiringly, after Sojo had left the cabin. 'What an amazing woman.' She hopped off the bed, straightening the tie of her high-waisted yellow dress, her pale arms in the sleeveless frock as fragile as petals. 'You're American too, I take it?' she said. 'I come from England, the North. I've just spent ten months in the States, visiting friends, looking around. Taking a year off between A-Levels and going to university. My parents had a fit, but I couldn't bear any more academic work without a break. What about you, are you having a holiday?'

Emmeline explained for the second time why she was going to London. Gratifyingly, Daisy had heard of the drama school, even knew someone who went there.

'Uh, excuse me, but is this Cabin F 28?' A rather nervous voice floated through the open door, and Emmeline and Daisy both said at the same time, 'Yes, it is.'

An extremely pale girl wearing a brown suit, with matching A-line skirt and severe jacket, entered cautiously. 'I think that I belong here. Oh yes, there's my suitcase. One of the stewards said he'd bring it down for me. I was sick, you see. Seasick.' She shuddered.

Daisy and Emmeline made sympathetic noises which,

instead of soothing, appeared to terrify the newcomer. 'I'm Marsha Krukchek,' she said apologetically, as if needing to explain herself. 'I've never been on a boat before. I've never even been out of New Jersey before, except for my three years at the Catholic University in Washington.' She suddenly clutched her stomach, and the two other girls held their breath. Then, as if more explanations were expected from her, she burbled on nervously: 'I'm going to France, to be a governess. I graduated in French, you see, just last summer. Father Jerome, the Department Head, found me this job. He knows the French family – a good Catholic family, very devout. I wouldn't have taken the job if it weren't a good Catholic family.'

Marsha trailed off, wringing the white gloves in her hands as if they were the family wash about to be put on the clothes-line. She looked desolately at Daisy and Emmeline through severe brown-framed glasses, her dark hair pulled back in a no-nonsense, old-fashioned pony tail.

Emmeline, her own gaucherie forgotten when face-to-face with someone worse, introduced herself and Daisy, and showed Marsha the bunk that was hers. Daisy, bouncing around the cabin, tried to put Marsha at ease by explaining where she was going, and what she had been doing in America. Marsha listened, trying to look polite and interested as she had been taught to do, but after a moment or two she said dolefully, 'I'm sorry,' and bolted off to the bathroom.

'Oh dear,' Daisy said, crestfallen. 'Did I bore her?'

Emmeline smiled. 'I think you made her dizzy. I guess she's seasick again.'

'But we're hardly out of the harbour.'

'Poor Marsha. She's going to have a real bad crossing.'

They rolled their eyes ruefully at each other.

'Come on,' Daisy said, buoyant again and ready for adventure. 'Should we go up on deck and explore?'

'Sure,' Emmeline said, thinking of her lanky blue-eyed boy.

Because the late afternoon sun was still hot and sultry, all the decks were swarming with people drinking beer, dozing in deckchairs, clustering in small effervescent groups sizzling over with laughter, with shouts, with the occasional burst of song. At the back of the ship a dozen young men and women were sitting on the floor listening to a bearded youth playing an old guitar and singing. Emmeline, intrigued by the song, by the refrain *'The times they are a changing'*, stopped to listen. 'What a great song,' she said.

'Mm, it's fab, isn't it! Dylan wrote it, of course.'

'Who's Dylan?'

Daisy looked at her quizzically. 'You've never heard of Bob Dylan?'

Emmeline shook her head. Daisy linked arms affectionately with her and she said, as they walked on, 'It's a good thing you met me, Em. Such a pity I'm not going to London. You'll need me there, to show you the ropes.'

Em looked out over the sea, where America had been but no longer was visible. 'I can't wait to get there. I just can't wait.'

'I hope it's all you expect it to be, Emmeline. I hope it's every bit as good.'

'It will be. I know it will.' Crossing her fingers for luck she looked again out to sea, but this time towards England, towards her shining, sunlit future.

*　　*　　*

Emmeline stirs, feeling chilled on her bench even though the sun is warm, the air still and serene. She watches the Thames for another moment or two and then gets up and begins to walk slowly towards Charing Cross Bridge. On her way past the Royal Festival Hall she sees, huddled on the steps, a young woman with long tangled fair hair and a pallid face. As Emmeline walks by, the girl holds out her hands, but not until she is halfway across the bridge does Emmeline realise the young woman is begging. Distressed, exhausted, Emmeline makes her way to the British Rail station and catches the next train to Canterbury.

'Em! Em, at last! I can't believe it.'
  'Nor I. How long is it, Daisy – five years or is it six?'
  'Nearer seven or eight. I flew over there for your fortieth birthday party, remember?'
  'Oh my, has it been that long?'
  The two women pull away from their embrace, appraise each other. Daisy's copper hair is variegated now, flecked with white and grey. It falls pleasantly behind her ears and is tied back with a green headband which matches the bright green sloppy jumper she wears over leggings. Her little pointed face has softened over the years, blurred, but Emmeline thinks this has made her much more attractive now than she was at nineteen.
  'I can't believe you're here,' Daisy is saying. 'It's taken you all these years to come back.'
  'I know. Thank goodness you visited me occasionally in Georgia.'
  'And France, we met there twice. Visiting Marsha.'
  'The last time was about twelve years ago.'
  'No, truly?'

'And Italy. We stayed at Sojo's.'

'Yes.' The two women pause, shake their heads at the passage of years, embrace again. Though they have lived apart they have remained close through long and frequent letters, transatlantic phone calls, intermittent meetings in other countries.

The door of the farmhouse slams open and a slight, slim figure in a long white crocheted skirt, a patched, many-coloured velvet top, comes running out into the garden where Emmeline and Daisy have met. Her feet are bare and around her ankles are tiny bells which tinkle harmoniously as she runs, and her long fair hair, loose and tangly, has coloured ribbons and beads plaited all through it. For a moment Emmeline, glazed over after the flight, the diversion in London, and then the lengthy train trip to Canterbury, thinks she has found *herself*, the girl she has lost, the girl of eighteen she was looking for in the shadows and crevices of London.

'Aunt Em!' the girl cries. 'Don't you recognise me?'

It is Gemma, of course, Daisy's youngest daughter. The last time she saw her was in Atlanta, when she had come out for a holiday with her mother. She couldn't have been more than ten or eleven then.

'You've changed,' Emmeline says inanely.

'You haven't,' Gemma says tactfully. Then they all laugh, and arm in arm make their way into the farmhouse.

'What do you think of your Mum's American friend?'

Gemma, having left her mum and Emmeline over tea and scones in the large comfy kitchen, is out in the old barn next to the house talking to a young man named Ronald Basildon, whom everyone calls Baz. Baz is washing down and cleaning out an ancient but still serviceable gypsy caravan, a proper horse-drawn Romany caravan which belongs to an elderly man called Jonnie. Jonnie, in hospital recovering from pneumonia after a hernia operation, will be living in a house for the first time ever this winter, and has lent the caravan to Baz and Gemma.

''Tis because I cannot bear it to be empty,' he told them when they went to see him in hospital. ''Tis a proper home, not an antique as some would like to have it.'

As soon as the caravan or *vardo* — its Romany name — is cleaned and painted, and a newer wood-burning stove installed, Gemma and Baz are going to move into it, much to the chagrin of Daisy's parents, who have grudgingly agreed to let them use the orchard next to the barn as their winter camping site. In the summer they plan to travel.

'Emmeline?' Gemma says, kissing Baz briefly on his forehead and running her fingers through his stiff wiry hair which stands up around his head like the mane of a dark, dangerous beast. 'You want to know what I think of her?'

'I want to know if she'll be on our side. Help get your mum off our backs.'

'Oh, Baz!'

'She still hasn't forgiven me for leading you astray, you know. Nor has your dad. They still think that if it weren't for me, you'd have stayed on at the farm.' He puts down a plastic bucket full of soapy water and dries his hands on his trousers, which are made of a heavy wine-coloured fabric, baggy and tied at the ankles. He wears a black collarless grandad shirt and has two gold loops in his left ear.

'Don't be too hard on them, Baz.' Gemma winds her slim, slight arms around his waist and looks worriedly into his eyes. 'I'm the last one to go, out of five of us. I knew Mum would have a crisis when it happened. She's got nothing else, you see. Just us and the farm, and the farm was always Dad's.'

Baz runs his hands up and down her back, loving the feel of her, the softness of her. 'Were you really going to be a farmer?' he asks teasingly. 'A shepherd, a pig-lady – you?'

'I was always the one most interested, the one who wanted to be outside all the time, helping Dad. I loved the sheep, still do.'

Looking at her serious face, the frown on her forehead, Baz moans, 'Oh love, maybe I *am* taking you away. Maybe your dad *is* right. Maybe if you hadn't met me you'd have done the right thing by them.'

He looks so concerned that Gemma smiles, touches his face. 'I'd have left one way or another,' she says gently. 'There're so many things I want to do, so many places to see. I can't wait until spring, when the weather's warm enough for us to get on the road. Oh Baz, what fun we'll have!'

*

'*What fun we shall have!*' Daisy, skipping up and down the deck of the *Castel Felice*, was electric with energy. 'What fun it will be! Ten whole days on a boat like this.'

'I know. I feel we've lived a lifetime here already, and we've only been sailing a few hours.'

'Do you think we should go and eat dinner now? Don't they have different sittings?'

'I don't know, I've never travelled before.'

'I came over on a plane; I've never been on a boat. Somebody told me about the *Castel Felice* sailing in early September and it was so inexpensive, I jumped at it.'

'Me, too. And the thought of going over on a boat seemed

so much more romantic than a plane.' Emmeline rolled her eyes, mocking herself at this confession.

Daisy, unable to contain her exuberance, gave a little whoop of excitement and began to run along the deck, pulling Emmeline with her. 'Shall we explore the ship a bit more before we eat? It's like being in a strange new town, so much to see, so much to do. Oh Emmeline, I never want to go home! The thought of starting university bores me to tears.'

'Then why go?'

'My parents would kill me if I didn't, especially after taking a year off and running to the States. But I loved the travelling, the exhilaration of it all, the bustle. Oh, I shall miss it, Em, all the places I haven't seen, the things I haven't done!'

Emmeline thought of the many more things *she* hadn't done, coming straight from a small-town high school on to this boat. But Daisy was nineteen, a whole year older than her: she had plenty of time to catch up.

They spent the next hour exploring, finding the cinema which was playing a Peter Sellers film, investigating the disco at the front of the boat, now fairly empty and quiet but with a jukebox ready for use and flashing its lights in the corner. They found a deck with table tennis tables and another with a swimming pool, and several bars and lounges, and a huge ballroom at the back with a proper stage, already set up with a piano and some other instruments.

'We're not going to do ballroom dancing, I hope,' Daisy giggled.

It was late when they finally found the dining room. They had been assigned a long table in the middle of the huge room, but by now there were only two or three people sitting there, Sojourner Truth Wilson amongst them, her long curvy arm wrapped around the neck of a dishy Scandinavian boy.

'Well hi, you two,' Sojo called as Emmeline and Daisy sat down. 'I was wondering where you were. Meet Nöjd.'

'I am happy to make your acquaintance,' Nöjd said stiffly, obviously not relishing company.

'I think I met our fourth cabin-mate,' Sojo said. 'I went back to the cabin after you left and found someone throwing up in our little sink. Looked real bad.'

'That was Marsha. We just checked her before we came here. She's resting now.'

They ordered food, something gorgeous and Italian, and soon Daisy and Sojo were chatting away, ignoring Nöjd's body language which was obviously stating that any more than two was definitely a crowd. Emmeline, not hungry in spite of the tempting food, ate what she could and soon excused herself, telling Daisy and Sojo she wanted to get out on deck again.

What she really wanted was to find Hal. That sweet face, that longish yellow hair, reminded her of the guardian angels in her old childhood prayer books and Bible stories, the archangels with their slim, powerful bodies, their strong caring faces, their profound and deep and sad blue eyes—

'Emmeline?' She jumped guiltily as Hal leaned next to her against the railings.

'What're you thinking about? You looked miles away.'

'Uh, nothing, much.'

'What a sea, look at it. And the moon – thin, hungry, lean. Like Cassius.' He laughed ruefully. 'I played him once, in the sixth-form production of *Julius Caesar*. I was dreadful, but it was all sour grapes. I wanted to be Mark Antony, you see, and was determined to be a rotten

Cassius to prove the director wrong. It was a bloody awful thing to do.'

They both were silent, Hal brooding on his youthful misdemeanour, Emmeline not knowing what to say. They stared at the moon and the stars and the sea for what seemed to be a long time, until Hal turned to her and said, 'And you? How did you get involved in the theatre? You seem fairly sane, but perhaps you're not what you seem.'

'Well, I—'

'But who is what they seem? Not me, not you — not even the deceitful moon up there, looking pencil-thin and starved to death when we all know she's round and fat.' He stared belligerently at the moon for a moment and then produced a tobacco tin and cigarette papers from the pocket of his jeans. 'Here,' he said, handing her the lit, rolled joint.

Emmeline, mistaking it for a cigarette, said politely, 'No, thank you. I don't smoke.'

Later, she was grateful to Hal for not saying anything, for not even smiling. Instead, he silently inhaled, turning to the sea again. After several moments he said softly, 'Maybe you are what you seem. Should we go somewhere and find out? C'mon, I'll buy you a beer. Or don't you drink?'

'Of course,' Emmeline said tightly, wondering if he was making fun of her.

He wasn't, or at least not by the end of the evening. She had three Budweisers and fell in love; he had only two, but finished his joint as she talked and talked. They left the bar and ended up on the deck watching the sea again and then Hal spoke, and she listened. By the time he had walked her to Cabin F 28 they were old friends, and as he briefly, tentatively, kissed her good night, Emmeline knew that she wanted much, much more.

'Back at last?' Daisy said as Emmeline shut the door behind her. 'It's very late.'

'You sound like my mother.' They both laughed, quietly so as not to awaken the sleeping Marsha. 'Why aren't you asleep?'

'It seems like such a waste of time! I've not been back that long myself.'

'Isn't Sojo in yet?'

'Not likely. Nöjd was following her all around the boat like a heartsick puppy.'

Emmeline laughed again, and kicked off her shoes to join Daisy who was sitting up in her top bunk. 'I've been waiting up for you,' Daisy said mischievously. 'I passed you on deck with that beautiful blond lad. I don't think you even saw me, you were both so engrossed in conversation.'

'You're right – I didn't. Oh Daisy, we talked and talked! About everything under the sun – about the theatre, about the war in Vietnam, about ourselves . . . I've never ever talked to anyone like that.'

'Come on, who is he? Tell Auntie Daisy everything.'

Emmeline giggled. 'Do you have any food? I'm starving.'

Daisy handed her some apples she had taken from the dining room and they began to munch. Then, to the easy rolling of the ship, the pale light of the skimpy moon outside the porthole, Emmeline and Daisy, bonding like two siblings, began to talk, hesitantly at first and then with increasing confidence and familiarity, so that by the time the first streaks of dawn lightened up the porthole, they had laid the foundation of a friendship that would last a lifetime.

*

Daisy is showing Emmeline around the old Tudor farmhouse,

which hasn't changed that much since Em saw it last. 'I guess something that's been around five hundred years or so isn't going to alter in three paltry decades,' she said, grateful that at least some things stayed the same.   According to local legend, the house had once been a hunting lodge belonging to Henry VIII, and Emmeline could well believe it. It was craggy, timbered, unsymmetrical and fascinating, with extra wide door-frames reputedly installed so that the King did not have to bother to dismount before entering but could ride his horse inside.

They are upstairs, in the room Emmeline will be using for the year she is staying at Woodland Farm with Daisy and her family. 'I've put you in your old room, Em,' Daisy says. 'It used to be Paul's, but he was the first to go so we turned it into the main guestroom.'

The room has a new carpet, deep and patterned red, but the big brass double bed, the one she slept in with Hal, is still the same, as are the leaded windows facing the woods and the granite fireplace filled with dried flowers. 'Central heating now,' Daisy says with a grin.

'I'll miss the fires.'

'The fireplace downstairs is still functioning. We use it often.'

The farmhouse is on a hill, and through the open window Emmeline can see the ten-acre wood which belongs to the farm. The trees are still green but beginning to lose some of their summer freshness. 'I remember those woods in autumn,' Emmeline says. 'The first time I visited you here was in the fall.'

'They were always such fleeting visits. Now at last we shall have you for a whole year. What fun!'

'I shall be working, Daisy.'

'You always are. When it's not term-time and you are free of your university commitments, you are writing papers, or theatre reviews, or books—'

'It's all part of my job. Besides, I enjoy it.'

Daisy, wandering around the bedroom as she talks, flicking off some imaginary dust here, straightening a picture on the wall there, says, 'Well, I shall enjoy having you here, and the university is going to have to make use of you term-times only. The rest of the time we shall play.'

Emmeline, relaxing on the bed, smiles and says: 'Do sit down, honey, and stop flitting about so. You haven't lost any of your bounce, I see.'

Daisy stops in the middle of rearranging the bowl of fresh sweetpeas on the dressing table. 'No, that's the trouble,' she says. 'The energy's still there, but there's nowhere to put it. Not any more.'

'The kids?' Emmeline says gently. She knows through Daisy's letters that it has been hard for her to handle the departure, one by one, of her five children.

Daisy nods, suddenly unhappy, the restlessness in her small frame momentarily stilled as she joins Emmeline on the bed. 'Gemma's leaving, as you know. All these years we were so sure she'd stay on, take over the farm, and now she's leaving.'

'You can't force her to stay, Daisy. You of all people should know that.'

'She wanted to, Em. For years she wanted to. Her father was so pleased.'

'But then she grew up. We all do.'

'It wasn't that. It was Baz.'

'Who?'

'Her boyfriend. I haven't told you about him yet. She met

him this past year, doing A-Levels, and it was after that she suddenly changed. All she wants to do now is go off with him in a gypsy caravan and be a scissor-grinder, for God's sake, selling her homemade candles and his didgeridoos.'

'His what?'

'A didgeridoo is an ancient Aboriginal instrument, carved out of a long piece of wood. He not only makes the ridiculous things, he plays one. And gives workshops on them.'

Daisy looks so crestfallen that Emmeline laughs. 'Oh Daisy, it sounds wonderful, wonderful! You'd have been in your element on that boat if you had fallen in love with a maker of ancient Aboriginal instruments.'

Daisy concedes the point with a smile. 'Well, I didn't. I fell in love with Leo.'

'And I with Hal. You know who the lucky one was with that one.'

Daisy, brooding, says darkly, 'Sometimes I'm not so sure.' Then, seeing the questioning, troubled look on Emmeline's face, continues more cheerfully, 'Anyway, I've got lots planned for us when you're not up at the university. We'll see plenty of theatre in London, for a start. Did you know that Hal's just opened in a new play, *Volcano*? Would you like to go and see him? In the play, I mean.'

Emmeline is stunned. Hal, in London? She had read in the *New York Times* not very long ago that he was in Paris; he did a great deal of work with a theatre company there and indeed, his second home was in France. Emmeline has not seen Hal since she left London nearly thirty years ago.

'You're not enthusiastic about the idea,' Daisy says.

Emmeline shakes her head slowly. 'No. Not at all. Coming back here was bad enough, you know.'

'Still?' Daisy says sympathetically. 'Still?'

To Emmeline's distress the tears well up in her eyes again, run over her cheeks. 'Oh damn, I'm sorry. This is nothing but exhaustion, Daisy. I'm perfectly all right.'

Daisy, looking at her perceptively, says, 'Oh my dear,' and then, 'I shouldn't have kept you chattering away when you are desperate for sleep. There's plenty of time before dinner, why don't you nap for a couple of hours?'

Emmeline agrees that this would be a good idea and Daisy leaves the bedroom, promising to wake her up in plenty of time for dinner. Emmeline crawls tremulously under the duvet in the big brass bed and feels it rolling beneath her, as one does after a long journey. For the next couple of hours she drifts in and out of sleep, dreaming she is on a boat, feeling the sea lift her, treacherously gentle, and then plummet her down, down, down into the depths of something dark and familiar and hazardous.

When she wakes she cannot remember where she is. The room has gone grey with a storm pelting wind and rain on the windows, and in her confusion she hears someone's voice calling out to Daisy but she cannot discern whose it is. She lies there listening to the voices as they mingle with the sound of the wind and the rain and she is not sure whether they are past or present or, frighteningly, in her head. The erratic beating of her heart echoes the drumming of some loose tarpaulin or canvas going slap, slap, slap against the tiles of the roof and Emmeline listens, hypnotised, spellbound, as a man's voice sings tunelessly in the bathroom next door and the world shifts and sways and rolls, like the sea, beneath her.

Chapter Two

'*Emmeline, come on, you're getting soaked! Here, come under my coat if you want to stay out on deck. There, is that better? I can hardly see you, it's so dark . . .*'

But I can see you, Emmeline thought, huddling under Hal's long black coat. I can see you with my heart which is beating like the rain against yours; I can feel you, touch you.

It was the second night out at sea and the *Castel Felice* was rolling in the swell, the aftermath of a storm that had begun that afternoon. The winds had calmed down considerably by evening but now the rain was pelting the decks with great heavy drops. Emmeline and Hal had come outside to escape the crush of people, obviously not put off by the pitching of the boat, who were crowded into the immense ballroom for what was whimsically called the 'Get Acquainted' dance. An Italian band was playing, its members struggling manfully with a medley of Beatles songs when it was obvious they would have been happier with Cole Porter. Nonetheless the dance-floor was packed with high-spirited revellers, and the band was soundly applauded after each number.

Emmeline, snug under Hal's coat, was oblivious to the

storm, happy to be out of the crowd and alone with him. But suddenly a man's voice, deep and exuberant, was singing: 'By the sea, by the sea, by the beautiful sea . . .' while a lighter, giggly voice said, 'Hush, Leo. There's somebody else out here, look!'

'I love . . . to be beside the sea, beside the seaside, by the beautiful seeaaa . . .' The song dissolved into more laughter.

'Daisy, is that you?'

'Oh, my goodness.' More giggling. 'Emmeline? I thought you had gone to the cabin ages ago. Is that Hal? Oh, what a night. We had to leave the dance-floor, it was so crowded. Did you see Sojo? She and Nöjd are the hit of the evening; they're wild together on the dance-floor. And even innocent Marsha got over her seasickness long enough to get out there to do a two-step with a clean-cut American boy from a Baptist College in Alabama. She's gone back to bed now, but at least she surfaced for a bit.'

A sudden gust of spray, as the ship pitched heavily, poured over them.

'Hey, I'm soaked.'

'The wind is up again.'

'Exciting, isn't it!'

They all laughed, ready for anything.

'Oh,' Daisy said, 'this is Leo, by the way.' She was hanging on his arm as if on to a bag of treasure: greedily, possessively.

They talked for a few moments and then Hal said, 'It's getting wetter and colder out here by the minute. I fancy a good strong warming drink, what do you think? Shall we all go inside?'

Though many of the passengers were still at the dance,

the bars were also crowded, the air reeking with the pungent scent of beer and marijuana, mingled with the salt smell of the sea. They drank coffee and whisky carelessly, saying they would all be frugal tomorrow.

'There's no tomorrow,' Hal said, his fingers tapping on the table to the music coming from the jukebox, the Beatles singing jauntily *'Can't Buy Me Love'*.

'This boat was so cheap, we can afford to be a bit extravagant,' Leo said. 'My cabin-mate's mother was convinced that the fare charged couldn't possibly include food, so she packed him a trunk full of tins: baked beans and tuna fish and all sorts of edibles.'

Leo was a few years older than the others, a stocky, broad-faced man with dark curly hair and an appealing crooked smile that drew others to him like a steadfast beacon. After agricultural college he had left England to travel, first to Australia and then on to New Zealand where he spent several years on a sheep station working up to manager of the 5,000 acre farm. Now he was on his way back to England, via a six-month break in America travelling around the country with a mate, to begin work on his father's farm in Kent.

'How do you feel about going back?' Hal asked.

'Mixed. I loved New Zealand – I might go back there, who knows. But England's my home and I'll stick around for a while, see what happens.'

It was four in the morning when Hal and Leo walked Emmeline and Daisy to their cabin. The wind had abated, leaving a disappointing drizzle which would obscure the sunrise they had hoped to see. 'It's only the second night on board,' Hal said softly when Emmeline expressed her disappointment. 'There will be other nights, other sunrises.'

This casual comment elated her out of all proportion, as did his gentle good-night embrace.

Marsha was asleep so they tiptoed in and fumbled around in the dark so as not to awaken her. Sojo was nowhere in sight, nor did they expect her to be. Stifling giggles, Emmeline and Daisy hoisted themselves on the top bunk and stared out of the porthole, watching for a sign of morning.

'I'm starving!' Emmeline said suddenly.

'Again? Don't you ever eat at the proper times?'

'We should go and find Leo's cabin-mate, with that trunk of food.' They both laughed, trying to stifle the sound with their hands.

'Have an orange, that's all I've got tonight.' Daisy threw one to Emmeline and then said thoughtfully: 'I really like him – Leo, I mean. I've been with him all night, and I can't wait to see him tomorrow.'

'Great.'

'Not really. It's daft, actually. He's not my type. I mean – a farmer, for God's sake! Me?' She chewed contemplatively for a moment, like the cows of the countryside she was visualising. 'God, no!' she screeched at last, causing Marsha to stir slightly in her sleep. 'I'm the complete city person, through and through. I'd be bored witless in the country.'

'Daisy,' Emmeline said kindly. 'You've only met Leo tonight. You're not marrying him.'

Daisy looked at Em as if she had uttered great words of wisdom. 'True.' She grinned. 'Do you know what my mother wrote to me before I left New York? "Never have a shipboard romance; they never amount to anything."'

'I hope you're going to take her advice.'

'Like hell I am. Would you? *Would you?*'

'Nope,' Emmeline replied, staring at the porthole and

wishing desperately for morning, so as not to waste a moment of this voyage. 'Never.' She thought of Hal, of his angel's smile and clear blue eyes, of his entrancing English accent, and felt so wise, so sophisticated, and so terribly, terribly in love that she didn't think she could bear it.

'Let's go to sleep,' she said suddenly. 'I want it to be morning.'

She moved down into her own bunk, threw off her clothes, and fell into a dreamless sleep, eager to awake to another rapturous day.

*

In the Kent countryside thirty years later, Emmeline wakes to dark rain. The curtains are drawn and the bedside lamp is on, and Daisy is there sitting on the bed with tea in a China mug. 'Are you all right, love?' she asks, face soft with concern.

Emmeline sits up, props herself on the fat feather pillows. 'Oh, tea. Thanks. For a moment I didn't know where I was; I was dreaming of the boat. Our second night out, when you met Leo. I'm not even sure if I was asleep or not.'

'"Don't have a shipboard romance; they never amount to anything",' Daisy quotes. They both laugh.

'You've been happy, haven't you, Daisy? No regrets?'

'You ask me that every time you see me. No. No regrets.' But her face looks wistful somehow, Emmeline thinks, as if there are things she will never have, and has stopped asking for.

'Anyway, dinner will be ready soon. Come down when you feel like it.'

Twenty minutes later Emmeline comes into the kitchen. It is a huge beamed room where the family eat all their meals, except for special occasions when they branch out into the main living room which is more like an Elizabethan hall than a modern sitting room. As she goes in she is embraced by a strong pair of arms, and the voice she heard singing in the bathroom says with pleasure, 'Em, you've finally made it. At long last.'

'Leo, I don't believe it. I never thought I'd see you again. You wouldn't go to the States and I wouldn't come back to England.'

'There was never any time, somehow. So much to do on the farm.'

'I guess it's fifteen or so years since I've seen you — in France, that time Daisy dragged you off the farm to visit Marsha. You're looking good.'

'And you.' They stand back and openly appraise each other. Emmeline hasn't changed very much, he thinks, for when he saw her last she had already cut her long lemon-coloured hair, let it go back to its natural light brown. She looks more assured now, he decides, but also slightly wary, on guard, like a friendly dog uncertain whether its bone is going to be snatched away.

Leo *has* changed, Emmeline thinks: his face and body are heavier and his hair is no longer dark but salt and pepper. But the wayward smile still has the power to warm, to evoke an answering smile. He looks reassuring and solid and wonderful, and she marvels that after all these years, he and Daisy are still together, still seemingly happy.

It was exactly four months after the night they met that they married. Daisy, without a qualm and despite the fact that her parents refused to speak to her for years afterwards, abandoned her plans for university and moved straight in with

Leo into this same farmhouse on the hill where she has lived ever since.

Her parents, solicitors in Manchester, were used to persuasion and tried it all: gentle coercion, subtle indoctrination, blatant blackmail and even bribery. Nothing worked: Daisy gave up her place at Manchester University, where she was to study law, packed her books and her Rolling Stones albums, and headed South, stopping first in London where she bought a white leather mini-skirt in Carnaby Street and a flowing Victorian shawl in Kensington Market to wear on her wedding day. Leo, meanwhile, had returned to the farm, where, after the sudden death of his father, he was faced with the sole responsibility of running the extensive pig enterprise that his father had meticulously and with great pride built up over the years. His mother, never quite satisfied in the South, very quickly moved back to Leeds where a profusion of brothers and sisters in socially-acceptable professions clustered around her and re-introduced her to the refined society she felt she had missed since her marriage to a farmer. Leo's sister, older by many years, had fled the farm ages ago and now lived abroad, so Leo was truly on his own, and the responsibility weighed heavily on him.

But he had his Daisy. After a riotous wedding at the registry office in Canterbury, attended by all their acquaintances from the boat, Daisy and Leo and their friends celebrated with a glorious weekend at the farm, eating and drinking and playing guitars and singing, rolling joints and grooving to the music of the Who and the Stones, listening to the protest songs of Joan Baez, taking long walks in the January snow. They helped Leo feed the few sheep he had bought when he took over the farm, throwing out bales of sweet-smelling hay on to the icy fields; and on their wedding night, stayed up with him and Daisy in the pig-shed because his prize sow, Bella the Beautiful, was about to farrow. She produced ten magnificent progeny that night, and each one was cherished and given a name by the proud assortment of godparents. Luckily, by the time the piglets were sold off for pork chops, everyone had gone home.

Leo, totally baffled at first as he had been on the ship by these strange exotic creatures bursting with the excitement of the times, with their own promise, went along with the flow, and indeed quite got to like it, though he never puffed a joint or went on a peace march. Not that he was against either pot or peace: the one he just didn't fancy, the other he never had time for. The farm was hard going, but he loved it. In New Zealand he had both worked and socialised with no one but farmers – down-to-earth, solid, conservative people – and Daisy and her colourful friends with their love beads, their fringes and feathers, their voracious passion for what they called truth, freedom, peace, captivated him. He grew his unruly hair long – well, longer than usual – suffering all sorts of indignities when his mother came to visit. Sometimes he wore the Indian shirts Emmeline or Hal would bring him from London, gifts for his hospitality, for the old house soon became a kind of meeting place where one could always find like spirits, excellent home-brew, and plenty of countryside in which to attune oneself to the spirit within, should that be on the agenda.

'Henry VIII would have turned in his grave,' Leo's mother Alma once said, her visit unfortunately coinciding with one of Emmeline and Hal's and some of the others.

'Nonsense, Mother. The old rake would have loved it,' Daisy replied, her eyes barely off the book she was reading. It was Helen Gurley Brown's *Sex and the Single*

Girl which someone on the boat had passed along to her.

Spotting the book, Leo's mother cried, 'Daisy! How can you read that rubbish?'

'Oh, is it rubbish? Have you read it?'

'Of course not! The *Daily Telegraph* said it is a symptom of a sick society for a book like that to be written and published.'

'Well then,' Daisy said triumphantly. 'I told you you should change newspapers.'

Leo, listening to this exchange, smiled and said nothing. He thought Daisy rather brave for standing up to his mother; he himself had never been able to do so. Instead, he had opted out, escaping her by going as far away from her as possible, and staying away as long as possible. He often wondered how his gentle, unassuming father, an outdoor man who communed with the trees and primroses long before it was fashionable to do so, could live with such a woman, but such are the mysteries of love, he told himself.

Which of course made him think of Daisy. He loved her deeply, as his father loved the great thousand-year-old oak tree in the field in front of the house: with reverence, awe, and a determination to protect her from the hatchets of life, however sharp or cruel they would turn out to be. In New Zealand Leo had gone out with one or two farmer's daughters, and one he had even considered marrying, but his apparent lack of passion was soon obvious even to her and the relationship dissolved with the same lack of intensity as it had begun. Meeting Daisy had turned his preconceived ideas of what he wanted in a woman upside down: from that first night on the *Castel Felice* he knew, irrevocably, what he needed.

And Daisy? She jumped into Leo's arms and into his life with the same abandonment she had shown when she defied her mother and father and went off to America for a year, deferring her university place. Born and brought up in Bristol, then in London, and finally in Manchester, she had anticipated living in cities all her life and was totally bemused to find the country charmed her. She fell profoundly in love with everything: the woodland leading up to the farm with its profusion of wild flowers, the golden fields of barley, the animals, especially Bella the Beautiful, Leo's best sow, and indeed Bella was never sold but allowed to live her life out peacefully in the apple orchard long after her days of fertile glory were over. Leo, the son of a farmer and a farmer himself, was amused, exasperated, and secretly loved Daisy more because of her daft affinity with his animals and with his land. She softened him, smoothed the edges, and though it frightened him sometimes, he knew it was good.

Regrets? Daisy had none, not then, and when the children came, five in all, she was even more blissful, doing the earth mother bit with the Rayburn-baked bread and the homemade jams and pickles: the lot. She crooned protest songs to her infants, breastfed them for a year each, and carted them off to demonstrations in London and, years later, to Greenham Common when she thought it necessary and appropriate. Regrets? She didn't have time for that sort of thing. Nor the inclination.

Now in the farmhouse kitchen, the beams tinged with red as the sun sets beyond the fields and reflects through the old lead-paned windows, Daisy looks at her husband and her oldest friend and says, with a smile, 'This is like old times, isn't it?'

Emmeline nods. Almost, she says to herself. Almost.

She can still see Hal, locked in some time warp of her memory, still young and golden and apart: forever separate, forever gone.

'Emmeline? I'm Clem Todd. Welcome to the Theatre and Drama Studies Department.'

The man, who is wearing jeans and a striped shirt resembling an outspoken deckchair, shakes Emmeline's hand. His clean brown hair is tied back neatly in a pony tail, and his eyebrows are practically long enough to do the same. He is wearing an earring, a small gold hoop, in one ear, and in spite of the eyebrows – or perhaps because of them, for he uses them as a sexual appendage, raising and lowering them in a subtle teasing manner – he is not unattractive. Emmeline guesses correctly that he is in his early forties.

'I'm vaguely in charge of you,' Clem continues. 'I shall show you around, make you feel at home, that sort of thing.' He furrows his eyebrows charmingly at Emmeline.

It is a week after her arrival in Kent and they are at the university where Emmeline will be working. She is here as a JYA (Junior Year Abroad) co-ordinator, invited to look after the third-year students from her own university in Atlanta, acting *in loco parentis* for them, ironing out problems, dealing with everything from administrative hang-ups and cultural disorientation to homesickness. When the opportunity arose she had hesitated, the old objections rising like dead fish in a stagnant pond.

'You have this amazing chance to be with us on the farm, which you loved all those years ago, for a whole academic year,' Daisy said on the phone, 'and still you're procrastinating?'

'I know, I know.'

'You have to face the past someday, Em. It might as well be now.'

After all, there was nothing to keep her in Atlanta. She could rent out her house easily for the year; for though small, it was in a salubrious area with a wide drive and leafy old trees. When she mentioned, somewhat tentatively, her coming plans to her neighbour, Sally, a couple of phone calls were quickly made and Sally said triumphantly, 'I have a tenant for your house – a musician friend from New York, who is coming here to do a year's residency at one of the colleges. He was going to stay with me until he found a decent place to rent, and this is the ideal solution.'

Sally was a flute-player with the city orchestra, and her house seemed always to be filled with intinerant musicians. Emmeline sighed and said, 'Now look here, Sally. I haven't even made up my mind one hundred per cent yet.'

'So now you have.'

'Goddamn it, are you trying to get rid of me or something?'

'You need to go. You've gotten yourself in a rut here.'

'Oh baloney.'

'How long have you been at that university? Years and years!'

'I guess that must mean I'm happy there, huh?'

'Don't be dumb. There's happiness and there's ruts. I know the difference. You've become a fixture there: respected, admired – fossilised.'

'What about Chester? What am I supposed to do with him if I go?'

'Hah,' Sally snorted. 'He'll be there when you get back, I guess. If you want him, that is,' she went on ominously, the implication being that Emmeline would be a fool if she did.

'Don't go on. Chester and I are okay. He may be a man, but as they go he's okay.'

Sally picked up her flute and blew a few notes of Mozart. When she stopped she said casually, 'Okay, so I guess I imagined those odd Mondays when you came around here either in tears or raving loony mad after a weekend with your sweet Chester.'

'We've all got relationship problems, honey. You as well, with your procession of hapless fiddlers and the odd eccentric pianist. Look, you're a good neighbour, a good friend, and I appreciate your concern. I tell you what, do you want to look after Chester when I'm away?'

'I wouldn't touch him with a barge-pole, Em, believe me. Not that he's not a male beauty and all that, but he's just a bit too macho for my tastes.'

'Afraid of a real man, are you?' Emmeline teased.

'A man, no. Attila the Hun, yes.'

Emmeline laughed and changed the subject, but later the conversation preyed on her. Perhaps it *was* a good thing she'd be gone for a year.

And now she and Clem Todd are in the Senior Common Room, having coffee after a walk around the campus which is placid and still, the students not yet returned for the autumn term. The sun is warm for September: it is a perfect day – and a perfect week, Emmeline thinks contentedly as she listens to Clem expound on a new production of *Lysistrata* he saw at the National Theatre last week. She has spent the past few days wandering around the farm, getting to know the area again. It is odd how at home she feels, after such a brief stay so very long ago.

She is suddenly aware that Clem has stopped talking.

Usually a good listener, she is annoyed with herself for drifting away from his monologue. Clem speaks intelligently and interestingly, but there is something in the way that he knows this that irritates Emmeline. During their whole morning together, then lunch at one of the college dining halls where they sat at a table overlooking the Cathedral spires, he has not asked her anything about herself, and though she tries to believe that this is English politeness, it strikes her as merely rude.

'Where did you say you are staying?' he is asking her, probably for the second time as he looks rather cross.

A question, Emmeline thinks sardonically. *What fun.* Silently berating herself for her unspoken sarcasm she answers sensibly, 'At a friend's farm, a few miles outside Canterbury. Daisy and Leo Dillard. Perhaps you know them?'

'I've met them, yes. One of their sons, Julian, wrote a play I directed once. I believe he's in London now, still struggling, writing plays which may or may not be produced. He's talented, he could just strike lucky.'

'They're all talented,' Emmeline says proudly, feeling like a doting aunt. She knows Daisy's children are subsitutes for the ones she has never had, the ones she once dreamed of having with Hal. She brags about them inordinately.

'There's one left after Julian, isn't there?' Clen recalls. 'A girl.'

'Yes. Gemma.'

'That one's a drop-out,' he says contemptuously. 'I've seen her around; she looks just like Julian, but there the resemblance ends. She runs about with bells on her toes busking for a living with another no-hoper.'

Emmeline looks at him with sudden hatred. 'Where were you in the sixties?' she asks curtly. 'You must have got something out of it, at least the tail end of it. Can't you remember being young, wanting something different, something better?'

The vehemence in her voice surprises him, makes him look at her more closely. Her face looks good with emotion colouring it, even if it is anger against him. For the first time he realizes that she is attractive, and worth a bit more attention than he has been giving her.

'Hey, relax,' he says kindly. 'I didn't mean to insult the girl. I just thought it a pity, that's all. The other Dillard children are all so together, it seems, and know where they are going.'

'I think Gemma does too. It's just not the same place everyone thinks she should go.'

'Marching to a different drum, eh?'

'Don't be patronising.'

Clem sighs, puts his arm lightly around Emmeline's shoulder. 'I'm sorry,' he says, creasing his eyebrows with genuine regret. He will have to work hard now to regain this woman's good will, but he is not averse to a challenge. 'The world's a different place now – harder. If you buck the system these days, you usually lose out.'

Before Emmeline can comment he says quickly, 'Look, I'd like to show you around Canterbury, let you see some of my favourite spots. Can I start by taking you out for dinner? There's the best French restaurant outside of France not far from the Cathedral. Is Friday night any good – a week today?'

His eyebrows rise in such innocent anticipation that Emmeline is appeased, as well as slightly flattered. She knows what he is up to, but can't help flirting back a bit, feeling the buzz that a bit of male admiration gives her.

'Sure,' she says lazily, looking directly under those incredible eyebrows into the candid brown eyes. 'Friday's fine. And I love French food.'

'It's a date, as you Americans say.'

Emmeline nods, and they talk easily for the next few minutes, some kind of a rapport, an understanding, having been established. Emmeline knows it is based on sand – a slight sexual attraction, a mutual light flirtation – and will blow way with the first sea breeze that gusts in from the coast, but for the moment she doesn't care. She is in England at last, and just now, that seems like a good place to be.

A few minutes later, Emmeline is driving from the university to the outskirts of the city where she parks her car, a small second-hand Renault that Leo found for her and which she will sell when she goes home after her year abroad. Before heading into the centre she decides to walk through the Westgate Gardens by the river, admiring the late marigolds and chrysanthemums and roses. She feels so buoyant after her meeting with Clem Todd that she is even able to diffuse the familiar ache of memory the gardens evoke with a healthy stream of enthusiasm for the coming year.

Until she reaches the little bridge, that is. Until she is standing on it, looking out over the narrow river. Suddenly nothing has changed, nothing has altered. She can even hear, in the slight breeze that has come up, the whisper of her name, over and over again . . .

'*Emmeline . . . Shall we throw a penny in the water, make a wish? I'm sure this is a wishing bridge, it's small and elfish enough. There it goes – see it, Em? A little penny but a big wish. Marry me, Emmeline. That's my wish: marry me.*'

Oh God. She stands there for a long time, wondering how such an old, naive passion can affect her so strongly all these years later. Fleeing the Westgate Gardens she walks briskly into town, to buy postcards for the folk back home and to do some errands for Daisy. The main street, closed to traffic, is buzzing with people, some dawdling and sightseeing, others determinedly shopping. Emmeline is one of the dawdlers, revelling in the sights, the smells, the wonderful feel of this old English city she once loved so passionately. She takes it all in, feeling the years slipping away. So many changes here, yet so much that has remained the same. The old fifteenth-century Weavers House with the ducking-stool for suspected witches has not changed, nor the old Pilgrims Hospital. And the Cathedral itself, rising from the heart of the city like a great piercing stake, indomitable, unshakeable.

'Should we marry here, Emmeline? Strew flowers up the aisles until we are ankle-deep in them? Sing Peace and Love to the whole city, ring the Cathedral bells all night, command everyone to be as loving and happy as we are?'

Such extravagance, she thinks as she stands at the massive, elaborately carved door leading to the Cathedral Close, feeling a sad tenderness and a wry amusement for herself at eighteen; for Hal. Going inside the Cathedral she wanders around slowly with groups of French, American and Japanese tourists, looking once again at the Martyrdom, where Becket was murdered, and at the Tomb of the Black Prince. In the Crypt she walks around meditatively, lost in thought, in memories both old and new, and as she emerges into the busy streets she thinks, Well, I have not had too bad a life since I left here. She thinks of her students, her colleagues, her work. Her personal life she does not contemplate. She does not dare.

As she walks down Burgate and into one of the cobbled side streets, a strange sound edges into her consciousness like some primeval memory. It is a cavernous sound, deep as darkness, mournful yet not unpleasant. A foghorn going slightly out of control perhaps, a foghorn trying to sing, achieving at last some kind of a melody out of the darkness and out of the mist and spirits. Emmeline listens, mesmerised, then walks around the corner to see where the sound is coming from.

'Aunt Emmy! Or can I scrap the "Aunt" now? It seems so childish somehow.'

'Please do.'

'Come and listen to Baz! Isn't he wonderful?'

Gemma, dressed in another long crocheted skirt, except that this one looks like a dewy spider's web painted with iridescent blues and greens and rusty browns, pulls her along where she can see Baz, squatting like an American Indian on the ground and blowing into a pipe of some four or five feet long. It is carved out of hardwood and decorated with painted symbols: the moon and stars, tiny eerie trees, exquisite flowers. Several people are standing around, watching and listening, apparently fascinated, and more are stopping in their tracks as they walk by. Emmeline has to admit that Baz, whom she met at the farm, is not the usual type of busker to be found on the streets of Kent.

When the music ends, a few of the listeners throw coins into the floppy red velvet hat turned upside-down for this purpose, and Baz puts down his didgeridoo, for of course that's what it is, and grins up at Emmeline. 'What do you think of the didge, then?'

'I like it. Mournful yet not despairing. Haunting.'

'It's ever so difficult to play,' Gemma says. 'You have to make sure that no air gets around the mouthpiece.'

'It may be the oldest musical instrument in the world,'

Baz adds. 'Aboriginal legends say that the didgeridoo was given to the people by one of the Creation ancestors in the earliest days of human existence.'

'What a link to the past,' Gemma says dreamily. 'See why Baz loves to make didge music?' Emmeline, smiling to herself, thinks how young she is for eighteen, and again sees herself in Daisy's fey daughter.

Emmeline is offered the didgeridoo to hold, to feel the smooth wood. She learns from Baz how he makes the didges, carving them from fallen timber. Some he leaves with just the rough bark finish, others he smooths fine. The special ones, like the one he has been playing, Gemma paints or decorates. They are both so enthusiastic, so intense, about what they are doing that Emmeline, from her long distance away in years and in time, feels her heart go out to them, and a protectiveness towards them which startles her with its sudden, sharp ferocity.

'Look, I was just about to have a cup of tea somewhere. Do you want to join me? I'm hungry, too. Where can we find a nice English tea with lots of gooey cakes and things?'

'What a sound idea,' Gemma says. 'We were just about to pack up here anyway. We'll take you to our favourite place, a couple of streets down.'

Gemma and Baz put away their gear and the three walk into a café aptly named the Primrose Café, for it is decorated in various shades of yellow, with primrose-coloured curtains at the windows, oilskin tablecloths festooned with the flower and, for a subtle change perhaps, a huge print of Van Gogh's *Sunflowers* on the wall. They find a table in the corner near a window and Baz goes up to the counter to order cakes and tea, talking animatedly with the young man and woman who are obviously in charge.

'Blue and Flack, friends of ours,' Gemma says.

'Ah. Which is which?'

'Blue is the girl.' She nods to a young woman in a mini-skirt and vest covered with silk fringes like something out of an old John Wayne film. Cords with crosses and crystals at the end of them hang around her neck and a thin delicate hoop pierces the side of her nostril. She waves her hand in greeting and then runs it through her short, spiky hair, which has been dyed silver and streaked with blue. Emmeline smiles to herself, wondering what came first, the name or the hair.

'And Flack is her bloke.'

'Flack? Is that an English name?'

'It's his surname, actually. Suits him much better than Jonathan.' Gemma catches Flack's eye and he waves and blows a kiss at her. He has tiny round wireframed glasses and beautiful auburn hair pulled tightly back from his face in a long thick plait.

'It's a vegetarian café, with wonderful food,' Gemma explains. 'They've only been open since summer and it's been a struggle, though there are always people here.'

'I can understand that,' Emmeline says, admiring the homemade carrot cake and fresh scones that Baz is setting down on the table.

'All right?' he asks. 'What kind of tea would you like? Indian, Lapsang, herbal?' They choose, and Baz goes off to order it. Gemma watches him fondly. He looks so skinny, undernourished in his baggy trousers, elasticised at the waist and ankles and patterned in rich stripes of black and deep red and dark, dark blues. Over these he is wearing a handknit cotton jumper of an even deeper red which somehow suits his olive skin, his erratic long black hair which stands thick and wild and wavy, like the sea at night. Like the sea, too, it looks untamed, uncontrollable, and is a strange contrast with his peaceful, tranquil face.

The cake and scones are delicious, the tea strong and tasty, and Emmeline spends a pleasant hour in the Primrose Café. When the customers begin to thin, Blue joins them at their table.

'How's it going?' Baz asks.

'The day-to-day stuff is ace. It's all the other shit. We just heard today our rent is going up.'

'It was high enough as it was,' Flack continues, joining them. 'I don't know if we can cope with this one.'

'Your prices seems very reasonable,' Emmeline says, looking at the handwritten menu for lunch and evening meals. 'Perhaps you could afford to raise them?'

Blue and Flack exchange looks. Flack says, 'We decided to go into this because there wasn't a decent, cheap, vegetarian restaurant around, one that did vegan meals as well.'

'If we raise our prices,' Blue goes on, 'we lose customers like Gemma and Baz, and lots of our other friends who can't afford to eat in posh places. There's no point in running a restaurant if you can't cater for the people you like.'

Gemma and Baz agree, and Emmeline refrains from saying, cynically, that idealism is a tough thing to hold on to in the running of a business. Nonetheless, she finds these young people refreshing; certainly she has spent a most enjoyable afternoon with them. Suddenly realising how late it is, she offers to drive Gemma home but she refuses. 'Tell Mum I'm staying over at Baz's tonight, okay? There's a gig out near Maidstone we're all going to. I'll be back sometime tomorrow.'

It is a short drive back to the farm. After a mile or so

Emmeline turns at the sign *Woodland Farm* and drives the three-quarters of a mile up the lane alongside the woods, to the house on top of the hill. It is gleaming in the early evening sunlight, its old red-tiled roof looking rich and opulent, and the dark beams and timbers of the house stand out like black mascara against the pale creamy paint of the walls. Emmeline parks and rushes into the kitchen, eager to tell Daisy about her day.

'Am I late? I meant to get here early and help you with dinner, but I ran into Gemma and Baz, and they took me to such a cute café where I met their friends, Flack and Blue. Odd names but such sweet people, don't you think?'

'Hm.'

'Do you remember, back in the sixties, the crazy names people used to give themselves, like "Moon" or "Sunset"? I was thinking in the car just now, it was such an affectation, but the names of these kids seem to have evolved naturally, stemming from their surnames, or what they look like, act like. Much healthier, don't you think?'

'Yes. I suppose so.'

'Daisy, what's wrong?' Emmeline looks closely at Daisy, whose mouth has set like granite in her soft worried face. 'What is it?'

'Nothing, nothing. Where's Gemma, then? I thought she'd be back for dinner.'

'Oh, she's stayed over with Baz as they're going out tonight. She'll be back tomorrow.'

'Again? She's never at home these days.'

'But . . . she has been around a lot this past week.'

'Only because you are here. She's always out with Baz and that bloody didgeridoo; they think they're going to make a living out of those things — that plus the candles and their bloody stupid knife-sharpening scheme. Have you ever heard of anything so daft?'

'Well . . . it's kind of sweet, don't you think?'

'Sweet? It's imbecilic.'

Emmeline pauses for a moment, confused by the sheer force of the anger she feels coming from the other woman. Then, tentatively, 'They don't seem that different from how we were, Daisy.'

'Oh Em, grow up, stop being so soppishly sentimental. Things were a doddle then; we knew it was all really a game and that we could stop any time, grow up, get a job, join the real world again.'

'Did we?' Emmeline feels oddly hurt, betrayed. 'We didn't see it as a game then, I'm sure we didn't. We were every bit as sincere and intense as Gemma and Baz and their friends are.'

Daisy looks at her with a mixture of irritation and exasperation. 'But we had a safety net. The times were easy, affluent. Everything was open to us – education, the job market – and we opted out because we chose to. It's different for the kids now. They opt out because they have no choice, or if they are one of the lucky ones, like Gemma, who have a choice and blow it, it's going to be bloody hard if not impossible for them to get back in again.'

Emmeline doesn't know what to say. Daisy seems so blatantly angry, so vehement, and it is so unlike her. 'Do you really think it's that bad?' she says quietly.

'Yes, I do.' Daisy's voice is harsh. 'It's all right for you, Em, breezing in here and seeing only one side of it, seeing the bloody romantic side, gypsy caravan and all that nonsense. They're not us, Em, they're not living in our times. They're living in shitty awful times and they need to be prepared for it.'

'You mean accept it. That's what you're saying. Maybe they're doing something else, something better. Maybe they're trying to change things.'

'But they can't!' Daisy's voice is strident. 'Don't you see that? They know they can't, too, which makes it all so terrible, such a waste, so sad. They're just dropping out into their own little world and turning their backs on the real one.' Daisy moves away and begins throwing knives and forks down on the table.

'Is the real world so great?' Emmeline murmurs to her back.

'It's all we have, Em,' Daisy says quietly, her anger gone. 'Bloody as it is, it's all we have.'

She turns and looks at Emmeline, and as their eyes meet Em is filled with confusion and distress. Is this Daisy talking? she thinks. Daisy, her rock, her anchor in an unstable world that she herself is finding increasingly difficult to come to terms with?

'You've changed,' she says inadequately.

'Perhaps so,' Daisy answers spiritedly. 'And why not? You've changed, so have Marsha and Sojo — why not me? Why should I be the one everyone expects to remain the same? I'm not a bloody stagnant pool, for God's sake!'

Her hand pounds on the table, sharp and loud, jangling the cutlery and plates. In the silence that follows the two women stare at each other, shocked.

'Anything wrong?' The door has opened and Leo is suddenly there, looking at them warily.

'No,' says Daisy, turning to the cooker and removing something hot and steamy from the oven.

Leo glances at Emmeline, who avoids his eye. Uneasily, he takes his place at the table, picking up the local paper and covering his thoughts with it as at night he covers his body with the duvet, blanketing out the world around him. Within moments he has forgotten Daisy and Emmeline, obliterated the strangely acrimonious atmosphere into which he stumbled a few moments ago.

Daisy, knowing this, knowing he has blotted out confusion and conflict the same as he has done for years, feels uncharacteristically a flash of pure white-hot anger that would surely sizzle the unsuspecting Leo had he known about it. But he goes on reading, checking tomorrow's weather forecast with the fresh vital innocence of an early spring lamb. He goes on reading while his world shifts, quivers, then steadies itself precariously.

He never notices. One day he will have to, but not today, not now. Smiling at Daisy, he accepts with gratitude the hot steaming plate of food she sets before him.

Chapter Three

L eaving Daisy and Emmeline after dinner to check on
a sow which is about to farrow, Leo walks up and
down his clean, well-ordered farrowing shed, notes the
health and well-being of all its occupants, and feels tremors
of dissatisfaction vibrating through him like a small but deadly
earthquake. Because it is not yet dark, he decides to check
on his modest but superb flock of sheep, the pride of his
secret, hidden heart. The sheep are in a field next to the
woods which is now tinged with yellow and rusty red and
which in a month or so will be bold and brazen with autumn
colour. Leo doesn't look at the woodland; he deliberately
avoids walking in it these days, for guilty reasons he has
not yet disclosed to anyone else, not even Daisy. But then,
though he feels close to Daisy and loves her dearly, more
even than he did at the beginning, that does not mean he
tells her what is in his soul, that does not mean he verbalises
the deep and sometimes murky thoughts that swim heavily
in the depths of his active mind.

His ewes, strong and well-fed and healthy, stamp out the
seeds of discontent which have been planting themselves over
the last few months into his bloodstream. Leo is not used to

being discontented; he is used to getting on with things, and if they are not to his liking, he is used to either making them better, or ignoring them.

Walking around the sheep, on the steep side of the hill with the sea at Whitstable visible in the distance, Leo knows that some of his unrest has to do with Gemma, but not all of it. Of course he was disappointed, more deeply than he would ever admit to Daisy, that his daughter would not now be working with him on the farm, taking it over one day as everyone had hoped. Had she done as they had all expected, he would have got on with his work, built up a fine place for her to take over, and his other dreams would have drifted away like leaves on the river without another glance from him.

Slowly walking back towards the house, Leo whistles for the old yellow Labrador, Blossom, now almost fifteen and unable to walk up the hill, she is so arthritic and wheezy. She has stayed waiting for him at the top; half-blind, half-deaf, it is faith alone that tells her Leo has not abandoned her.

Leo feels as old as Blossom this evening. He is in his fifties and feels a hundred. Slowly he makes his way back to the house, the dog huffing and panting beside him.

Daisy and Emmeline, still in the kitchen, do not talk any further about Gemma and Baz, for when Leo leaves them alone to go and check on his animals, Daisy has no inclination to bring up the subject again and Emmeline, for her part, does not quite know what to say. She is surprised, even shocked, at Daisy's vehement objection to Gemma's new life; she never, ever would have predicted it, from knowing Daisy as a lucent, reckless nineteen-year-old. And so for the rest of the evening the three of them, though engaging in desultory conversation, are preoccupied, thoughtful, deciding unanimously on an early night. Emmeline, relieved, goes upstairs, troubled at the discord she is beginning to find around her.

The next day there is no time for any kind of serious conversation because suddenly the house is filled with people, crowded in every space like migratory birds at their ritual watering place. It is Saturday, and the assorted Dillard children have all returned home for the weekend for a spontaneous get-together, something Emmeline learns they do often. Paul, the oldest, is there with his fiancée; both are musicians and teach at a music college in London. Simon and Melanie are still at university – perpetual students, Leo says with a wry grin, getting yet another qualification to top off their degrees in Psychology and English Literature respectively. Julian, the embryonic playwright, is very like Daisy, electric with untapped energy and flying from one topic to another like a restless squirrel jumping from tree to tree.

The children, as Daisy still calls them, are high-spirited and lively, and seem to get on well with each other. Gemma. is home for the weekend, and with her, Baz; and Blue and Flack seem to be around constantly when the café is closed and they are not working. Baz has found a second-hand woodburning stove which will double as a cooker for the caravan, and they hope to put it in this weekend and move into the caravan next week. Emmeline notices that the other Dillard progeny are neither sceptical nor patronising of Baz and Gemma's plans; on the contrary, they seem both intrigued and helpful.

The weekend is merry and raucous, with the house suddenly filled with music, Paul attacking the piano like a man demented with his flamboyant interpretations of Scott Joplin, and Melanie, who plays the violin, occasionally joining him in a wild duet. Gemma, blessed with a strong contralto voice, warbles away like a blackbird as she goes to and fro from the barn to the house with Baz, their arms often entwined around each other as they grin at private jokes or just from sheer happiness.

The caravan, freshly painted red and gleaming like a sunset, looks beautiful, a work of art. When the stove is inserted and is finally pumping out heat, everyone comes out to admire. Inside everything glows and sparkles, the magnificent chandelier on the ceiling, the glass-fronted cabinets which hold the plates and teacups, the many tiny mirrors which reflect the intricate carving on the old mahogany wood.

'We can move in today!' Gemma shouts, euphoric and high on excitement.

'Why not?' Baz says. He is sharing a large house in town with seven other people and his absence will not be noticed if it is a few days earlier.

'We'll have to move it to the orchard. Can we move it now, then? Oh please, let's move it! We can hitch up Bones, make the move proper.' Bones is the horse who came with the caravan. He is being over-wintered in the stable next to the pig units, and his Romany owner, Jonnie, comes occasionally to visit when his health is good, stopping for hours in the stable and talking to the horse in a low whisper about times past.

With great ceremony the caravan is pulled into the orchard, a small snug area behind the barn where Gemma and Baz will be sheltered from much of the Kentish winds which will blow coldly in the winter months ahead. All the Dillards and their assorted friends follow the caravan as it slowly makes its way down the bumpy track and into the orchard. Melanie has her fiddle and plays a ceremonial polka as the procession proceeds, and Emmeline, watching them all as they dance around the caravan, feels as if she has suddenly been thrown into the midst of a jolly, insouciant circus. Only Daisy and Leo have hung back from the noisy and colourful parade; she notices them trailing along behind, their faces strained as they try to smile and join in the festivities, while their hearts are full of concern for their lovely, feckless daughter.

By late Sunday afternoon the farm is quiet, even the pigs dozy and still in the waning sunlight. Everyone has gone home, including Gemma, the last of Daisy's babies, who has packed her bags and moved out to the orchard with her Baz.

'We're home!' Gemma says, flopping down on the red velvet sofa, the bells around her ankles tinkling. 'My very first home of my own.'

'*Our* very first home,' Baz corrects with a grin.

'That's what I meant. Oh, I know we'll be so happy here! It's snug and beautiful and just right for us.'

'You won't feel too cramped, after that rambling farm-house you grew up in?'

Gemma smiles, hugs herself, throws her feet up in the air in a joyous, abandoned gesture. 'I'll feel *free*, Baz. Free, myself, *me*. Oh, life is so good, so bloody good! And you and I have a place of our own at last. We'll be alone together at last.' She lies back on the sofa, crossing and uncrossing her ankles up in the air, the little bells ringing merrily, like the celebratory peals of church bells.

'I'm glad you're here,' Daisy says to Emmeline, her voice

suddenly thick with unshed tears. 'For the first time in nearly thirty years, Leo and I are alone.'

'That's how you *started*, Daisy,' Em says gently. 'Just the two of you, all those years ago.'

Daisy finds a tissue in the pocket of her baggy cardigan and blows her nose. They are in the chicken run, and Emmeline watches as Daisy throws the hens some feed, then disappears into the henhouse to emerge with a dozen large brown eggs.

'Anyway,' Emmeline goes on, trying to cheer Daisy, 'Gemma's not really left, not properly. She might not be in the house but she's only yards away, in the orchard. Think of it like camping out!'

'I worry about her, Em. She's so headstrong.'

'So were you, Daisy. Remember how your parents didn't speak to you for years after you ran off with Leo?'

'Leo at least had a farm, some stability—'

'Bullshit,' Em interrupts. 'You'd have run off with him if he were a tinker living in a tent. In fact, you'd have preferred it.'

Daisy doesn't bother to answer this, and Emmeline takes the basket of eggs from her while she shuts the gate to the chicken run. For a few moments they walk arm in arm and in silence, until they get to a small field behind the farrowing shed where several sows in their early days of pregnancy are rooting about in the long grass and snorting contentedly as they forage. One of them, friendlier than the others, trots amiably up to Daisy and lets her scratch her hoary head. 'Meet Bella the Beautiful,' Daisy says with a giggle.

'Oh no,' Emmeline shrieks. 'Don't tell me she's still alive?'

'What a city girl you are! Of course the original Bella is

not alive; she died peacefully in the orchard at a ripe old age. No, this is one of her progeny, one of her — I forget how many greats — granddaughters.'

'Well, well.'

As they slowly head back to the house they pass Baz, carrying a couple of buckets of water. 'We'll use the tap outside the barn in future,' he explains to Daisy, 'but I wanted some hot in a hurry, if that's all right with you. The loo needs a good scrub.' Luckily there is, at the end of a small shed at the side of the orchard, an old unused lavatory, plumbed in and ready to go. This is what Gemma and Baz will use, and Daisy shudders as she thinks of her daughter struggling through frost and snow in the cold winter nights ahead to get to it.

'I can't believe you two are really going through with this,' Daisy says plaintively. 'Staying out there, with winter coming on . . .' She trails off but the intimations are there; of debilitating cold, hardship, deprivation.

Baz's face hardens, the eager smile slowly disappearing. 'It's dry and snug and warm,' he says defensively. 'It's going to be our only home when we're out on the road, so we need to get used to it, get to know it.'

Daisy says nothing, but the look on her face tells Baz exactly what she is thinking. Abruptly he turns, lifts his hand in a cursory goodbye, and walks quickly away.

When he goes Daisy is stiff, tense. Emmeline, trying to distract her, suggests they walk down to the woodland. Daisy agrees with a terse nod of her head and they walk slowly across the field and in amongst the trees.

'Hm, they are so tranquil, these woods,' Emmeline says, taking deep breaths of the tangy September air. 'I always used to think this was a tiny bit of England tucked away on your farm, all the old trees, the wild flowers, the little furry things invisibly scurrying around.'

'It's quite an ancient woodland,' Daisy responds, making an effort to stop brooding on Gemma and Baz. 'This small patch is all that's left from Henry VIII's time.'

They walk slowly, aimlessly, Emmeline taking it all in: the strange fungi growing on the ground, looking like orange peel; the clusters of wild redcurrants. A yellow and black butterfly floats past them as they amble, and above their heads a magpie chuckles.

Daisy suddenly stops and turns to Emmeline. 'Em, please talk to Gemma. She's always admired you, and you two have become close through letters and phone calls. Tell her to at least give the farm a chance; ask her to at least postpone this ridiculous venture with Baz. Let him go alone, if he wants. Their relationship should survive a year's separation, and if it doesn't, it's best they find out now anyway.'

Emmeline looks at Daisy uneasily. 'I can't tell her that. All their plans are made—'

'Look, I'm merely asking you to mention it, all right? I'm Gemma's mother, for God's sake! I know what she needs and what she doesn't need.'

She looks at Emmeline with such pleading in her eyes that Em says helplessly, 'I'll see what I can do. I'll talk to her, anyway. That's all I can promise.'

'Are you married?'

'How abrupt. Are you Americans always so abrupt? One could almost call it rude.'

Emmeline sips her black coffee and the brandy Clem has urged upon her. They are lingering over the remains of a splendid meal, mussels and lamb and vegetables in exquisite sauces. 'Hardly abrupt,' she says with a smile. 'We've talked about everything else under the sun. And we've established that *I'm* not married.'

Clem smiles back at her, his eyes under the long, thick eyebrows flickering malignantly in the candlelight. 'Does it matter?' he asks lightly. 'This marriage thing?'

It is a trick question and Emmeline knows it. Whichever way she answers she is at a disadvantage, forced to make a statement either about her interest in Clem or about how she ranks the tricky issue of dating married men. As a matter of fact she stays well clear of married men, a fact she communicates to him wordlessly by a slight raising of the eyebrows, a curt tightening of the lips.

They sit in silence for a few moments. The waiter comes, asks if they want anything else. Clem has a second brandy but Emmeline declines. Finally, after the brandy has arrived, Clem says, 'It's very complicated, this marriage business. Am I married, you ask. So difficult to say, actually. How do you define marriage? What is it? If you define it as a union of souls as well as of bodies, then no, I am not married.'

Emmeline sighs, though not audibly. She knows what *that* means. She is disappointed, for she would have enjoyed a flirtation, perhaps even a brief affair if her interest and libido were sufficiently aroused. Though her relationship with Chester has been monogamous these four or five years, he has hinted that her leaving him for nine or ten months, possibly more, will cancel out any unspoken promises between them. She wonders why this does not trouble her.

Staring at her now-empty glass, she hopes she is not going to be subject to a monologue about Clem's wife not understanding him. But Clem too is silent. He is definitely not going to be any more precise about his married state, assuming correctly that someone will eventually inform Emmeline of the existence of both his wife and his seventeen-year-old daughter, both of whom still very much live with him.

Clem is, as a matter of fact, disappointed in Emmeline. He is attracted to her, to her disciplined body, her very delectable legs, her wide open American face. He likes the way her hair is sleek and brown like a seal's, the shiny fringe covering her eyebrows and emphasising her dark, intelligent brown eyes. Usually he mistrusts intelligence in a woman, especially one with such amazing legs, and wearing such a subtly sexy dress which is creamy white and almost translucent, outlining those legs when she stands against the light.

But nonetheless, he is disappointed. He has visited America, been to bed with American women, and he likes their candidness, their intensity. He likes it especially because there is an ocean between them; eventually, one or the other has to go home, ending the liaison in a civilised manner with a poignant farewell scene at the airport. How tedious that this compelling woman should already be asking about his married state, for that meant one of two things: either that she was looking for someone to marry herself, or that she was one of those prudish types who object to sleeping with a married man. Either way it was a pity.

Clem abandons the idea of asking her to come home with him (he lives in the town, not far from Westgate Gardens, in a large Victorian house on a pleasant, tranquil street) and thinks what a pity it is, for his wife is visiting her mother in Somerset for the weekend and has conveniently taken their daughter with her. Instead, he walks Emmeline politely to her car, parked not very far away, and declines a ride home, saying it is not far and it is a beautiful evening for a walk. As he kisses her chastely good night, first on one cheek and then the other (Clem has spent time in France), some impulse makes him also kiss the palm of her hand. As he does so he wonders if he has perhaps made an error of judgement in dismissing her so soon, for he detects a regretful look in her eyes. But the look bodes well for the future, he thinks with satisfaction. She is here for the whole academic year; there is plenty of time. He waves enthusiastically as she slowly drives past him.

Emmeline waves too, and makes her way back to Woodland Farm. She feels the evening was a success, despite the fact that she now has lost all interest in Clem, knowing for certain that he is married. But she enjoyed being the object of all that charm, not in the least minding that it was purely sexual. Emmeline likes being attractive to men, likes knowing they want to get into bed with her. She knows in the logic of her head that this does not rest easily with her strong feminist sympathies, but knowing has not eradicated the need.

Yes, Clem is a charmer all right, and she did enjoy tonight, for he was bright and witty and clever and spoke a great deal about the theatre, which always fascinates her. She knew the evening would not be repeated, but accepted it for what it was: a pleasant night out with a presentable man who found her more than just passingly attractive. Yet, as he was saying goodnight, with that romantic little gesture of kissing the palm of her hand, she had grown slightly sad, thinking of all the other romantic encounters of her life which had begun that way: a candlelit dinner, a sharing of interest, sexual attraction. Some had evanesced with hardly a trace left in the memory; others had developed, grown, become a full-blown passion, but in the end had, like the others, faded away. Where are they all now, she thinks poignantly. And why are they all so unimportant? All except one, of course. All except Hal.

And then there is Chester. She thinks of him ruefully as she drives up the lane through the woods, the headlights of the car picking out the trees which are already beginning to burnish with an autumnal glow. Emmeline recalls the magnificent falls at home, especially up in the mountains where she owns a tiny summer cabin to which she retreats when the strain and hassle of city life become too stressful for her.

Chester was with her when she took possession of the cabin, buying it ridiculously cheap from a friend who was moving abroad. It is nearly five years ago, she thinks now, when she met Chester at a party, and they have been together, a couple, on and off since. He is a lawyer with political ambitions, divorced (unfortunately for his ambitions in an America still paying lip-service to family values and traditions), and an ex-football star for one of the top universities. Even Emmeline, who is not a football fan, recognised his name when she was introduced, though it was a good twenty years since those golden days of his idolatry.

He still looked like an Amerian football player: tall, big, rugged. One eye was slightly blackened when Emmeline met him, which rather piquantly added to his image, though he admitted ruefully that it had occurred when one of the young lads he coached on Saturday mornings poked his elbow in Chester's face while Chester was trying to show him how to properly pass the ball. Emmeline was drawn to him at once; that he was typical of the men who had attracted her since her return from England perhaps should have warned her off, for none of her subsequent relationships, after Hal, had been enduring. But she still, despite reason, craved men like

Chester, macho men who knew what they wanted, especially when what they wanted was her.

Chester certainly wanted her. They met on the Friday night, but didn't go home together because he was with someone else, an old friend and ex-lover he saw occasionally and with whom he remained friends. He was far too courteous to abandon her and rush off with Emmeline, though he would have liked to. That night she was wearing a striking and sexy coffee-coloured silk dress that plunged low in the front, and she looked him directly in the eyes as if sizing him up, as if wondering whether he would do.

'Tomorrow night?' he said to her as they were both leaving — separately, unfortunately.

'Sorry, this whole weekend is off. I've just bought a tiny place up in the mountains and I'm going up there for the first time tomorrow.'

'Who are you going with? Another man?' Chester asked bluntly.

Emmeline, an American through and through, was not daunted by such plain speaking. 'There is not a man in my life at this moment,' she said blithely. 'I am going, quite happily, on my own.'

This was a little game and they both knew it. Before very long Chester had been included in this adventure, and they left the next morning around ten. It took two and a half hours to get to the cottage, a tiny, compact frame house of one cosy living room and a modern, immaculate kitchen downstairs, and one attic bedroom with a double bed upstairs. They looked at the bed without saying a word and instead admired the view. One side of the house, the one facing the lake, was all windows, and the view was spectacular. There was a tiny wooden pier at the lake's edge and that was all; the rest was nothing but grassy meadows and a splendid profusion of trees, the leaves refulgent with colour, for it was the middle of autumn.

The day was long and though delightful, it passed slowly for both of them, for all they wanted to do was to get into bed with each other. They lingered not for any reasons of decorum or modesty, but because each wanted to savour the anticipation. They lunched on goodies they had bought along the way, stopping at a general store and trying to make conversation with the laconic owner. They bought bacon and lettuce and tomatoes and fresh bread and butter, and made bacon sandwiches, finishing with apples they had purchased from a farmer's stand along the empty road. Then they took a long walk in the woods, their feet crunching the bright yellow leaves underneath them and their eyes dazzled by the unusual sight of the ground being so much brighter and lighter than even the sky, which itself was intensely blue and perfect.

They lit a fire in the tiny grate, for by late afternoon it had grown quite chilly, and sat on immense cushions in front of it, talking. Emmeline was beginning to feel that old familiar dread coursing through her like an injection of a nasty drug, panicking that Chester did not want her, did not desire her, for he had not even held her hand or put his arm around her as they meandered through the day together. As if reading her mind, he suddenly rolled towards her on the cushion, pulled her down to him and began kissing her with an open, welcoming mouth as he quickly, deftly, began undoing the buttons down the front of her soft wool blouse and running his fingers under the flimsy lace beneath. Emmeline, relieved and grateful, responded with an alacrity that somewhat bemused Chester with its sudden intensity, but he wasn't averse to using it to full advantage. When, hours later, they were finally replete, each congratulated themselves silently on having at last met their match, and both looked forward to many successful repetitions of this first delightful coupling.

It's quite late after her date with Clem when Emmeline lets herself back into the Dillards' farm house: she and Clem had spent hours at the restaurant. It's quiet, hushed. Emmeline walks straight through the kitchen into the living room, which is huge, long, and dominated by a massive fireplace on one end and a magnificent leaded window at the other. The windowsill here is hundreds of years old, the trunk of an ancient oak now pitted and scarred by time and centuries. There are still embers from the evening's fire, for though the house is now centrally heated, Daisy insists on her log fire, much to Leo's exasperation.

A door opens upstairs and Daisy shouts, 'I'll be right down. I'm just getting out of the bath.' Emmeline plops down on one of the old, plain, no-nonsense easy chairs around the fire and carries on thinking about Chester. She is wondering why she is not missing him; they are supposed to be in love, whatever that means. Certainly, she has been with him longer than she has been with any other man, and she enjoys doing certain things with him, like having sex and going out for meals. They visit the theatre occasionally, though Chester is not that keen and prefers it when Emmeline goes with her colleagues. But both adore the cinema in spite of the fact that their tastes differ considerably, Chester leaning towards tough, action-packed movies which Emmeline finds tedious. Still, they compromise, they get on. Emmeline supposes this is love, though she has nothing to compare it to, except her youthful infatuation for Hal, when she knew with the ineluctable certainty of eighteen exactly what she was feeling.

What she feels for Chester is nothing at all like that, thank God. She certainly couldn't live such passion now.

'You're deep in thought,' Daisy says, appearing suddenly and flopping down in the chair next to Emmeline's. She is wearing a yellow striped towelling robe and her hair is wet, newly washed. She dries it vigorously with a towel, saying as she does so, 'What is it then? Dreaming about the attractive Clem Todd? Julian said all the female students lusted for him like mad when he directed that play of his.'

'Oddly enough I'm thinking about Chester.'

'Missing him already?'

'No, not at all. Does that mean I am heartless and cold?'

Daisy laughs and says nothing. Emmeline goes on, 'My neighbour, Sally, calls him Attilla the Hun.' Still Daisy does not speak. She has not met Chester, but she has met some of the other men in Emmeline's life after Hal and sees no reason to suppose that Chester is any different.

'Sally thinks he's too aggressive, but then she prefers boy-like men still searching for a surrogate mom. Sally accuses me of becoming a type when I'm with Chester, sort of eyelash fluttering and female and adoring. It's odd, because I certainly don't adore him, though I love going to bed with him. But I haven't adored anyone since Hal, and you know where that led to.'

'I don't think it's just Chester you act that way with,' Daisy says slowly. 'I've seen you when there have been new men in your life; you go all vampish on them. In a very subtle way, of course. You were never like that with Hal.'

Emmeline is shocked. 'Daisy, no! Surely I'm not that bad? I know I like to flirt a bit, like to play the game . . .' Her voice trails away in confusion. Gazing at the dying fire, she tries to assimilate what Daisy has just said, applying it to her relationship with Chester. True, Chester always made it plain that he liked a woman to be feminine, liked the division between the sexes to be sharp and uncontested. Emmeline cooked him meals when he was staying at her house, which she quite liked to do anyway, and he reciprocated by finding exotic gourmet restaurants he could take her to when she spent a night or a weekend with him. He did not expect her to share his interest in football and every other sport according to the season; he was quite happy to attend these things with his select male friends, most of them still carried over from his football-playing days. He did, however, expect her to be always dressed and scented and subtly sexy as he liked women to be, but this did not bother her. On the contrary, both her femininity and her sexuality gave her a heady feeling of power that she had never felt in her academic or professional life, though paradoxically, she needed male reassurances for the former in a way she never felt in the latter.

That Chester was, at times, bullish, Emmeline had to admit. Though he professed to admire her work (he was astute enough to understand that the feminist angle was important these days in politics), Emmeline sometimes felt that he would be far more contented with a docile homebody living merely to wash his socks by day and only come to life beneath him at night. Though he had hinted at times that it would be nice to get married, even live together, he did not press too often when Emmeline resisted. Chester had married young: he had three children, grown now. His marriage had been stifling and cloying and he was, quite frankly, enjoying living alone during the week and sharing his weekends with a delectable woman like Emmeline.

Emmeline wasn't sure why she had resisted moving in with Chester after all these years. She admitted to loneliness at times, but somehow knew in her heart that her loneliness would not be assuaged by him. She had tried, very briefly, living with a man soon after she had got her degree and began work, but it ended disastrously. He littered her apartment with beer cans, strew clothes around the two tiny rooms like confetti at a wedding, and expected her to be on call in the bedroom twenty-four hours a day. The latter, though flattering at first and one of the reasons she fell for him, soon became rather tiring; she missed simple things, like reading, and eventually got rid of him.

'Oh Daisy,' Emmeline says now with a sigh. 'I am such a mess still, after all these years. I do envy you, you know. You are so happy with Leo.'

Is there a pause, just the tiniest beat of a pause before Daisy answers, 'Yes, I've been very lucky, I know that.' Emmeline hopes not. Oh, how she hopes not! She looks questioningly at her oldest, dearest friend but Daisy has closed her eyes momentarily, not wanting yet to confide in Emmeline the thing that is tearing her apart: that she has never felt so lonely in her entire life as she does now.

When she opens her eyes again she is under control, and with a bright smile asks Em if she would like a cup of camomile tea before bed. Em, nodding her head, knows that the subject is closed, but she is not regretful. She cannot bear it if there is anything wrong with Daisy and Leo's relationship. Throughout the years it has shone like a beacon for her, steadfastly beaming on her need to believe that not everything changes, tarnishes, rusts or disintegrates. She would lose her own way if that light began to flicker. She cannot bear even thinking about it.

The next few weeks are busy for Emmeline. The students

are on campus, the term begun. Emmeline presents a staff seminar on American Theatre which is well-attended and highly successful. Her own students, slightly dazed at suddenly finding themselves in foreign parts, require an inordinate amount of pastoral care, which is her reason for being there.

As the weeks progress she begins to find her way around the campus. She cannot recognise the place from the stark new university it was when Daisy moved to Canterbury. It looks old, established now, its newness gone and plastered over with lawns and trees and shrubs.

'Everything going all right?' Clem asks as they meet in their shared office, a small unpretentious room with a couple of desks and a window looking out over the city in the distance.

'Sure thing. My students seem to have settled in now; they're really enjoying themselves.'

'I'm just off to town, need to go to the bank, and I rather fancy a leisurely lunch off campus. It's Friday and I'm frankly knackered. Want to come or do you have pressing things to do?'

'Nothing that can't wait until Monday. Lunch in town sounds great. My treat this time.'

She says this to establish the fact that this is strictly a lunch between colleagues, nothing more. He looks at her curiously, then nods his head. They drive in his car down to the town. 'What about the Primrose Café?' Emmeline suggests. 'They do great food. Do you mind not having meat? It's vegetarian.'

'I know a wonderful little wine bar—'

'I'd like to support the café. I've met the kids who run it, they're—'

'I know, I know. Friends of the Dillards; I've seen that wild child go in and out with her hippie friends.'

'Clem,' Emmeline begins warningly.

'Their food is good, I'll grant you that. And it's clean. We'll go there if you insist,' he gives in ungraciously.

But when they get to the Primrose Café there is a CLOSED sign on the door. Inside, the chairs are all on top of the tables and Flack is busy scrubbing the floor. He sees Emmeline and opens a window. 'What's up?' she asks.

'We've shut for a few days, trying to get our heads sorted out. We really can't afford the rise in rent unless we nearly double our prices.'

'So do it,' Clem says. 'You're dirt cheap.'

'We've put them up a bit.'

'Put them up more. There are plenty of people who can afford it around here.'

'I don't know if I want that kind of place. We don't want to be trendy, we just want to serve good food everyone can afford.'

Clem rolls his eyes. 'C'mon, Em. I'm starved. We'll go to the wine bar.'

'Where's Blue?' Emmeline asks.

'At a job interview. Nothing special, just some hours at a nursing home. I'm looking too. Maybe we can work part-time, keep this place open just at certain times.' He looks doubtful, and suddenly very young.

They say goodbye and Clem takes Emmeline to a crowded, cluttered wine bar with an excellent choice of salads and wine. Em is disturbed after her meeting with Flack, and decides to have a Campari and soda before their food arrives. She begins to relax, and to enjoy Clem's company, for he is being particularly charming now that he has got his way over where they are to eat. He orders wine with the food, and Emmeline compliments him on his choice. Things are going well, he thinks.

At one point during their long soporific lunch Clem lets his hand rest on Em's for a few moments, noting the flush on her cheek, her obvious confusion. This is the way to play it, he thinks with some satisfaction: nothing too overt, keep it slow, sensuous. There is plenty of time.

Emmeline is confused when Clem's broad stubby hand is placed on top of her own more delicate one and remains there for a full few minutes. She wants him to remove it but she hates to embarrass people, especially men, for she knows how fragile their egos are, how delicate their vanities. Surely Clem cannot think that there can be a 'thing' between them? Since their dinner together, she has been scrupulous in making sure that he is getting no messages from her indicating any interest other than a friendly, professional one.

Thankfully, before she has to take action, Clem removes his hand. Relaxed with the wine and the ambience of their lazy lunch, they leave the wine bar and wander down the main street again to pick up a book Clem has ordered. As they approach the bookshop, a soft, haunting sound, low and deep as if coming from the bowels of the earth itself, rolls like a wave to meet them.

'Christ, it's that bloody awful didgeridoo again,' Clem says, crossing the road to avoid the upside-down hat on the footpath.

'I think it's kind of nice. Sort of ghost-like, like a ship's horn on a foggy night.' Emmeline does not follow Clem but instead stops to listen to the didgeridoo. 'That was great, Baz,' she says when the young man finishes his song. She begins to put some money in his hat but he stops her.

'Gemma says you're practically one of the family, and I don't busk for family. Didge music should be free anyway, like sunshine, like air, like water. How depressing it is that everything has to be paid for these days, that commodity is all, that money is our god. What a sad society we live in.'

'Hm,' Emmeline says, slightly taken aback. 'Er, where's Gemma?'

'Gone down to the Primrose Café to bring us back some falafels.'

Clem, who is standing impatiently on the other side of the street, calls to Emmeline, 'I'll just go and pick up my book. Meet you here in a few minutes, all right?'

'Right.' She turns again to Baz. 'I'm glad you and Gemma are living on the farm,' she says impulsively. 'I love seeing you and your friends wandering around, looking like multi-coloured birds in some exotic tropical paradise. It lifts me somehow. Perhaps it is because I find myself there, or rather the person that used to be me, the one I have lost.'

She is babbling and blames the wine, but Baz does not think her at all strange. 'I wish you would tell Daisy that,' he says fiercely. 'She thinks I am a demon spirit come to whisk her precious daughter away.'

'She's worried, Baz. Gemma's her last little chick.'

'Jesus, I am not carrying her into the underworld. Believe it or not, I love Gemma too and wouldn't involve her in anything that would hurt her.'

'No one thinks you would.'

'Daisy does,' he says truculently. 'She can barely speak to me, you know. I doubt if I can stick it out on the farm until spring, with Gemma's parents acting like I was the devil personified.'

Emmeline says helplessly, 'I wish I could do something. It all seems like such a terrible misunderstanding.'

'You could talk to Daisy,' Baz says. 'You could tell her she'll lose her daughter for good if she tries to hold on too tightly. Gemma is already champing at the bit. She needs space, and her mother's attitude is only making her more determined to get it, even if it means leaving the farm earlier than we had intended.'

There is a shout and a wave from down the street: it is Gemma, returning with a paper bag full of what must be their lunch. 'Talk to Daisy,' Baz says urgently. 'Convince her that Gemma knows what she is doing and so do I.' He squeezes Em's hand briefly before turning away and walking to meet Gemma.

Do you? Emmeline says to herself as she watches Baz and Gemma amble hand-in-hand towards her. Do either of you really know what you are doing? Did I, at that age? Did Daisy, did Hal?

But what did it matter, in the end. Does knowing what we are doing make it easier, or better? Do we make fewer mistakes that way? Perhaps, she thinks sombrely, but at what price? What about the things we lose, the experiences we must surely miss?

Clem has returned from his foray into the bookshop to come and claim her, and after a few obligatory words to Gemma and Baz, whisks Emmeline away back to the university. He tries to charm her into the light flirtatious mood that he finds so satisfying but she is silent and distracted.

Bugger! he thinks explosively. What a waste of a good lunch. He is so annoyed that he deliberately turns off his charm for a moment, barely granting goodbye to Em as he drops her near the office then goes off to try and park in the ridiculously overcrowded parking facilities on campus.

Emmeline doesn't even notice. She is withdrawn, troubled by the turbulence she has found both in herself and in those around her. She wonders, sadly, if indeed it was a good idea to return to England.

Chapter Four

'*B*onjour, Emmeline! Ça va?'
  'Marsha, is that you?'
'None other, my friend, *ma copine*.'
'Where are you?'
'France, of course. I'm telephoning to welcome you back to Europe. When are you coming over to see me?'
'I'm supposed to be working here. We can't all swan around playing at being French ladies while a gorgeous Frenchman supports us.'
As a matter of fact, Marsha's husband Jean-Luc is pot-bellied, round and hairless, but he has a certain something about him, rather like a stolid old leafless oak, that is enduringly compelling. Marsha adores him, and he her.
'You haven't been over to see us for ages. The children are all grown now. Bring Daisy, the two of you come. Brittany is not so far away from Canterbury.'
'Closer than it is from Atlanta.'
'Exactly. So promise?'
'Promise. In the spring, okay? Maybe Easter holidays.'
'*Formidable. C'est superbe.*'

When Emmeline gets off the phone Daisy says, 'You really must go over there, now you are so close.'

'I told her we might both visit at Easter. Just you and me.'

'I'd love that. I wish we could go to Italy as well, see Sojo.'

'I can't remember when I last saw her. I know she and Marsha get together often. Isn't it amazing what good friends they have become over the years? They are so different.'

'Complete contrasts. Especially at the beginning.' They grin at each other, remembering. The nostalgia sparks off other memories and soon they are pleasantly reminiscing, Emmeline encouraged to recall the good moments, the happy ones, instead of the distressful time that ocurred later.

*

'Look at Marsha, she's fast asleep! Hush, don't wake her. It's all this night-life — she can't cope with it.'

Emmeline and Daisy were whispering across the prostrate bodies of Hal and Leo. The four were lying on deckchairs, filling every exposed pore of their bodies with sun. It was the fourth day out at sea and the passengers of the *Castel Felice* had settled into a satisfying routine of dancing and partying all night, sleeping through most of the morning, and collapsing after a late lunch outside on the decks where they read and snoozed and enjoyed the warm balmy weather.

Emmeline turned back to Hal, with whom she had been reading a scene from an Edward Albee play, *Who's Afraid of Virginia Wolf?* Hal said, 'It would be fun to act in it together one day, in a real theatre in front of a real audience.'

'We'll have to be lots older,' Emmeline objected. 'We

can't play Martha and George at our age. We'd get stuck playing the young couple.'

Hal hunched his shoulders slightly, creased his face with a worried frown, added a gravelly depth to his voice, and suddenly he seemed twenty years older. 'I say, Leo, old fruit,' he called in an entirely different voice, turning towards the other couple stiffly, like an older man, 'would you believe in me as one of your father's contemporaries?'

Leo didn't hear him. He and Daisy, in the deckchairs next to Emmeline and Hal, were surreptitiously groping each other under a towel, hoping nobody would notice. Soon they would casually get up, wander away from the others and make a mad dash for either her cabin or his, depending on which was empty. The afternoons were their only chance, for during the night either Sojo or Marsha monopolised the all-female cabin, and Leo was unfortunate enough to have a cabin-mate who did not like to party, preferring an early night and then morning calisthenics on the top deck.

'Sorry,' Hal said with a grin to Leo's oblivious back. 'Didn't mean to intrude. What about you, Marsha? Think Emmeline and I could play an older couple with any conviction?'

Marsha, awake now, but lost in her own thoughts, didn't seem to hear either, so Hal gave up and began reading the script again with Em. Marsha did indeed have her mind on other things. She had, after the first day on board, tried to get into a routine of early nights and a sensible rising time, but certain events of the previous night had both scandalised and troubled her. She had been woken from a deep and virtuous sleep by things going bump in the night in the bunk above her, but before she could cry out in sheer terror and panic she recognised the muffled whisper of

Sojo, and knew at once that it was not the spirit world which had awakened her. Thinking Sojo was merely talking in her sleep, Marsha relaxed, until she heard the timbre of a masculine voice mingled with Sojo's mutterings. *'Ohhh,'* the voice went. *'Ahhh, arghh.'*

A week ago Marsha would not have believed it, but after several days on this extraordinary boat she'd believe anything. Closing her eyes she pulled the blanket over her head and wondered what it was exactly that Sojo and the unknown male were doing. She knew, of course, that they were copulating, as the books put it; or 'engaged in endangering their souls in mortal sin', as the nuns would say: but what exactly happened, other than the basic biological act of penetration and ejaculation, to cause those moans, those groans, those melodies of sheer delight, of joy? She wondered dismally if she'd ever know.

Now, the next day, she was sitting on a deckchair next to Emmeline clandestinely reading one of Daisy's books, something wickedly entitled *Sex and the Single Girl*. She had St Augustine's *Confessions* tucked away in her handbag and wondered perhaps if he was not on to a good thing: all that profligacy and naughtiness in his youth and turning to chastity only when he was burned out and exhausted.

She shocked herself by these thoughts. Sojo, coming up to them with an Italian sailor in tow, said, 'Everyone, this is Giorgio, isn't he beautiful?'

'What happened to Nöjd?' Daisy muttered.

'The tempestuous passions of the sunny South, honey, blew away all traces of that Northern iceberg,' she said with a mischievous grin. She squeezed Giorgio's arm, thinking about last night. 'This man is the sexiest beast I've ever met.' Looking at Daisy and Emmeline's faces she added quickly, 'Don't worry, sweetpeas, he can't understand a fuckin' word of English.'

Giorgio smiled widely. He was several inches shorter than Sojo and probably a stone lighter. Marsha, too intrigued, embarrassed and confused to admonish Sojo on her language, looked at Giorgio surreptitiously. Were they *his*, those sensual animal groans in the night, those sighings of ecstasy?

Giorgio caught her eye and she straightened her spectacles obliquely. Wisps of hair had come out of her tightly coiffed bun and she tried to tuck them back, but to no avail. She felt as if she were crumbling like an overbaked cookie: the top button of her blouse was undone in the heat of the lazy afternoon, her hair was awry, her legs were immodestly bare with her longish skirt pulled up to the top of her thighs to indulge them with a feel of the sensuous sunrays fingering the boat. Giorgio was looking at her legs and she fought the impulse to pull down her skirt. Instead, she closed her eyes and heard once again in her head, *'Ohhh, ahhh, argh!'*

'Are you all right, Marsha?' Emmeline was staring concernedly at her. 'You look rather flushed. Perhaps you've had too much sun. Here, put on some of my suntan oil.'

Marsha obeyed weakly. Then she determinedly shut her book, pulled out St Augustine, and avidly began to read.

'Should we go for a wander, Em?' Hal suggested. 'I'd like a cold drink.'

He took her hand and they walked across the deck, but before they could get very far they were drawn to the sea and stopped to admire the calm of it, the deep azure colour. 'Look at it, the vastness, the power,' Hal said. 'I can't get enough of it, can't stop coming out here on deck to just stare at it. I wonder if we came from the sea?'

Emmeline said nothing, not knowing what to say.

'Sometimes I want to drown in it.' Hal's voice had changed, become sombre. 'Sometimes I want to lose myself in it for ever.'

He worried her when he talked like that, when his mood changed from flamboyant high spirits to an almost gloomy contemplation. They were young, they were living in the best of all possible times: why should he want even to think about drowning? Occasionally when he held her hand, when he looked at her with those dreamy blue eyes, he grew morose, troubled. Perhaps he didn't love her as she loved him? Yet sometimes he clung to her as if he were indeed drowning and she was his lifeline. It frightened her, but she didn't mind it. She didn't mind anything he did.

They never made it to the bar. Instead, they stood for ages at the ship's railing, watching the sea, then walking around and around the decks, passing groups of people playing cards, or lying in the sun, or strumming guitars and singing Dylan songs. Hal never let go of her hand until they finally found a solitary, isolated deckchair tucked away in an almost inaccessible part of one of the lower decks. They stopped here, snuggling together in the chair, Hal's arms around her, his face next to hers. He kissed her, again and again, and she felt stirred, aroused. But then he slowly stopped, seemingly contented, and they lay there, their arms wrapped around each other, and watched the sun beginning to sink slowly into the deep accepting bosom of the darkening sea.

That night, as every night, they congregated for a disco in the crowded front bar of the ship. A jukebox played constantly; the smooth wooden dance-floor was so packed that people were jiving all over the place, in the aisles, the doorways, even on top of the bar once, until the two culprits were removed by the stewards. Hal had recovered his high spirits, was almost manic, grooving with Daisy, trying to get Leo to have a drag of his joint. 'God, man, I get high enough just *breathing* on this boat,' Leo laughed, and Hal laughed too and bought him a beer instead.

'*I can't get no satisfaction*,' the music blared. The Rolling Stones song was a favourite amongst them, and it played again and again, compelling everyone with its catching, intense beat out on to the dance-floor. The beer, mostly a Dutch brew called Oranjeboom, flowed copiously, joints were passed around, the music pulsed and vibrated as the ship ploughed steadily across the Atlantic. '*I can't get no . . . satisfaction*,' Mick Jagger cried and a thousand voices cried with him, sweating and rocking and rolling to the pounding beat and swaying of the ship in the night sea. The smell of Oranjeboom and the aroma of marijuana mingled with the salt of clean young sweat and the salt of the ever-present ocean. They danced and they danced, Sojo with Nöjd (for Giorgio was on duty and anyway theoretically not allowed to socialise with the passengers), Daisy and her Leo who was stomping and throwing his body about in what he said was an ancient Aboriginal war dance; and Hal and Emmeline, Em's body throbbing and soaring like her heart, like her spirit: lost in the dance, in the night, in the sea, in Hal.

Marsha was dancing too. She was too frightened to retire to the cabin because of what she might again encounter in the depth of the night. What troubled her was not the act itself, nor even Sojo invading the privacy of the cabin with that Italian sailor. No, what shocked and appalled her was her own prurient curiosity about the act that had occurred right there above her in the deep, unknown dark. So she decided that she would venture into the light, go dancing with the others, and there she was, hair loosened from its prim clips, glasses askew, sensible shoes kicked off somewhere and lost under a table, face bright red and eyes shining as she bopped with a wild-looking Spaniard with a dozen strands of black beads bouncing on his chest.

'Dig Marsha,' Daisy called to Emmeline as she rocked past.

'She's way out, look at her go!'

'Sat — is — fac — tion!' Marsha was shouting with the others. 'I — cain't get no . . .'

'Can you believe it is the same person?'

They laughed and they shouted; they sang and they threw confetti that someone had produced. They danced until three or four in the morning and then went off, mostly in pairs, to the cabins, or the bars, or to roam the decks until the sun came up.

'Emmeline?' Hal said, taking a last joint that was offered by Sojo and offering it to Em, who, much wiser now than she was a week ago, knew exactly what it was and inhaled deeply before passing it back. She had never smoked dope until this boat, this *Castel Felice* or happy castle, happy home; she, like Marsha, had attended a small, provincial high school where such things, even in the mid-sixties, were unheard of. Moreover, the school was in the deep South, North Carolina, at that time years behind the rest of the country, much to the satisfaction of its more reactionary residents.

'Emmeline, should we go up on deck and wait for the sun to rise? Perhaps today we'll be lucky.'

They had tried before, but the mornings had always been cloudy. Tonight, or rather in these early hours of the morning, the sky was clear, starry, and a ripening moon shone eerily over the dark sea.

Hal ran down to his cabin, grabbed a blanket and wrapped

it around them as they went outside and snuggled together in the isolated deckchair they had found earlier. They talked sleepily; they always seemed to have things to say to each other. Gradually, their voices hushed, their light embrace deepened, and they began to kiss, to touch gently, to caress softly.

Suddenly Hal said, 'Look, Emmeline, it's getting light. I think today we'll see the sunrise. Come on, let's go to the back of the boat, there'll be a view from all sides.'

He took her hand and they ran down the deck and towards the back, where there were other couples, arm in arm, waiting for the sun, as well as the odd solitary contemplative and a small cluster of rainbow-clad youngsters clearly stoned and waiting for enlightenment.

The sunrise was faultless, pink and orange and golden across the sea, and the talking, the giggling and fidgeting stopped as everyone stared, bewitched and silenced by the awesome scene. And then someone whispered, 'Look. Dolphins.' And sure enough there they were, seven or eight of them, perhaps more, following the boat, playing with it, leaping gracefully through the waves, glinting red-gold in the rising sun.

'Magic,' Hal whispered.

'Magic,' echoed Em, looking from the shining iridescent sea to the dolphins to Hal's golden hair, sparkling in the sunrise.

He caught her looking at him, registered the love, and said, without thinking, 'I love you, Emmeline.' The sudden radiance in her face prompted him to say it again, the words gathering strength and surety the second time. 'I love you.'

Emmeline could not answer at first, and Hal could not make out if the drops on her face were the spray from the sea or tears. But she didn't need to speak. He knew how she felt, and was humbly grateful for it.

'Marry me?' Leo said to Daisy on either the fifth or the sixth day at sea. He had told her he loved her on the second night.

'We don't have to get married,' Daisy said audaciously. She felt very daring saying this, very liberated and modern, as she had been feeling since the first time she and Leo had made love. It had been the first time ever for her, though she had come marginally close over the past year with a young American lad she had met while travelling. She was fond of him, but the very real threat of babies, combined with the residues of fear (she was not, in her most secret heart, quite sure she could handle full-blown Sex with a Capital S yet) put her off going all the way with him. During a visit to New York, however, she was persuaded by some friends to go on the Pill, and the whole clandestine nature of it (for she was, of course, not married), made her feel mature and wise and daring. But after she had been on it for several weeks her ardour cooled for the boy in question, and she took off for the West with her new friends. She stayed on the Pill – having gone through all that trouble, she felt it would be a waste to stop – and when Leo appeared, it all seemed fated.

'We could just live together,' Daisy went on now, scandalising herself for even suggesting it. She was relieved when Leo replied, 'But I want to marry you. I want to marry you and live with you and have babies with you, if you want them.'

'What about university?'

'I'll wait. If we're engaged.'

They both thought about this. Three years seemed a dreadfully long time. 'Or you can re-apply to begin next year at the university in Kent. It's only two or three miles from the farm. We can get married and rent a place between the two, and both do what we want to do. I can commute every day to the farm, and you can get your education, become a solicitor as you had intended.'

'Well, more like my parents intended, to be honest. But why not? It'll keep them from totally disowning me, when they find out I'm not taking up my place at Manchester this year.'

This solution seemed immensely satisfactory at the time. But when Daisy eventually moved into the farmhouse, she was so enamoured of it all, the house and the landscape, the pigs and the sheep, the orchard and woodland and fields and meadows, that she could not bring herself to leave, to plod about a stark new ugly university campus and sit at stuffy old lectures in which she had no interest whatsoever. She belonged at Woodland, on the farm and on the land, and there was where she firmly decided to stay.

'Marry me?' Giorgio said to Sojo in the middle of coitus one night in the cabin. Unfortunately Sojo didn't understand him because he spoke in Italian. He asked her every night after that, but it wasn't until they reached Italy that she finally realised what he was saying.

Sojo hadn't wanted to tie up with a sailor. What she had in mind was a bit more sophisticated, an English gentleman perhaps, or a French count. She was an addict of romantic novels and knew that girls from the wrong side of the tracks usually got their man if they went about it the right way. True, none of the heroines in the books she read were black, but that didn't spoil her blind faith in the tales. These were the times of the Civil Rights movement: she knew her moment would come. Perhaps one day she would write the definitive black romantic novel. She knew she had it in her.

But Giorgio was something else. He was, quite simply, mind-blowingly sexy, and if she, Sojourner Truth Wilson, knew anything about anything, it was about sex, or so she had always believed. But Giorgio was quite another story. To begin with, he felt it was his duty to pleasure her thoroughly before even thinking about his own pleasure, something Sojo had never encountered in her many years of experience.

'Uh, Giorgio, what are you *doing* down there?' she had asked with some trepidation the first night he took her to bed. Or she took him, to be precise.

'*Cicciona. Bellezza.*' Sojo didn't understand the words but she gathered, correctly, that Giorgio was muttering endearments.

Then the talking stopped and something incredible was going on, something she had never experienced before.

'Wow, Giorgio. Do you think you should—? Oboy, Giorgio, oh fuckin' hell, man . . . no, don't stop, ohhhh!'

This is what woke Marsha in the small hours of the night, what made her avoid the cabin like the plague for the rest of the voyage and prowl the decks and the disco like some newly-awakened nocturnal creature. Surprisingly, this did not turn out to be such a burden as she had expected. On the contrary, to her shock she discovered that she took to the night-life like a sleek city cat newly awakened after a long day's snooze in the sun.

'Just imagine, all these years I've lived, twenty-two, and I never thought I was a night person,' she expanded to Emmeline and Daisy and Sojo early one evening as they all happened to be in the cabin at the same time, dressing to go in for dinner. 'I used to think it was virtuous to go to bed early and get up early.'

'It is,' Sojo said, pulling on a pair of dazzling blue hot pants. 'That's why I avoid it.'

'I can't help occasionally feeling wicked, though,' Marsha went on. 'All that Catholic guilt, I guess.'

'What, just because you're dancing and having a few drinks every night?

'It's okay, I'm shedding it fast,' Marsha grinned. 'This boat does wonders for the eradication of guilt.' She looked at her plump happy face in the mirror and decided that sin and dissipation were good for her, for her skin glowed, her eyes shone. She looked distastefully at her brown A-line skirt, her pristine beige blouse, and said, 'Can anyone lend me something to wear tonight? I'm bored with my clothes.'

Emmeline found her a pale orange dress, made of a thin flimsy cotton, with a high waist just under the bosom and long sleeves. The low square neck was trimmed decorously with lace, as were the sleeves. Sojo lent her some soft yellow Italian shoes with a high heel that she found awkward at first but soon got used to.

'Doesn't this show too much, uh, you know?' Marsha said, blushing to see cleavage as she looked in the mirror.

'Flaunt it, honey,' Sojo advised. 'You look great.'

'You do, honest,' Daisy said.

'Maybe I should wear a sweater? I have a nice brown cardigan . . .'

They all hooted. 'No sweater, Marsha.' Daisy was too tiny to lend her any clothes, but she did dab some kind of exotic musky perfume behind her ears, and Sojo gave her a couple of silver chains with amber-type stones hanging from them.

These nestled beguilingly in her cleavage. Marsha looked longingly at her cardigan.

'I'll do her hair,' Sojo said. 'Come on, you guys, get out the combs and brushes and hairspray. I've been dying to do this since we got on this goddamn boat.'

Giorgio, on his way to the sailors' mess, spotted the four of them heading towards the dining room, giggling like adolescents. His darling Sojo looked as eye-catching as usual, in soft knee-high boots with those wonderful blue shorts and her accommodating breasts swinging gently under a thin cheesecloth top. But it was that other one, that funny American Marsha who amazed him. She looked like a peach in that orange dress, and her hair — well, he never knew she had so much. Usually it was wrapped and strapped to her head like a plain brown parcel. Now it was all over the place, teased and wild but slightly tamed by a headband of orange and black. She looked good, he thought. She wasn't his type — Sojo was that — but she looked damn good.

Marsha, myopic without her glasses which Sojo insisted would ruin the hairdo, saw Giorgio's handsome face in a pleasant blur and stared wantonly deep into his eyes. She didn't realise she was doing this, of course, because without her glasses she couldn't quite focus. But Giorgio was startled, startled and flattered. He might be marrying Sojo but, by God, he had seen his *Zorba the Greek*; he knew that when a woman asked, it was a man's duty to accommodate.

They celebrated Marsha's metamorphosis by ordering fizzy white wine and Marsha drank three glasses, which was excessive for her. Instead of the disco there was some kind of a fancy dress dance and party in the ballroom that night, and though none of them had dressed up, they were happy to participate in the fun. On their way to the dance

they met Giorgio again with some of his mates. He kissed Sojo
surreptitiously behind the other sailors' backs, having to stand
on tiptoe to do so. Marsha watched; she was close enough to
see his lips more or less clearly, see how they opened as they
closed over Sojo's. What were those lips doing to Sojo that
night in the cabin, making her cry out the way she did? Once
again he caught her looking at him and this time he stared
back, sensuously insolent, but unfortunately she missed it,
for by then the crowd had pulled her back and all she could
see was an unsatisfying blur.

'Marsha, you look terrific.'

The American Marsha had met on the first night out was
dancing with her, holding her remarkably close for a graduate
of Bible college. He too looked not quite as clean-cut as he
had when she met him; he was excited and dishevelled, like
a schoolboy after seeing his first naughty pictures. He pulled
her tightly to him as the Italian singer with the band was
crooning a Roy Orbison song – *'It's ooooo – ver . . .'* and she
could feel something hard between his legs pushing against
the soft fabric of her dress. The nuns had warned her about
this, and she wondered why she had no sense of evil; why,
instead, her body flowed nicely against his hardness, her
soft breasts against his chest, her soft belly against his . . .
whatever.

'Should we go out on deck?' he breathed heavily in her
ear. She contemplated it, but decided not. Though she was
tempted, there was something awkward and lumpish about
him that instinct warned her would get lumpier and clumpier
the minute they were alone together.

'I think I'd like to go to the Ladies Room,' she said
demurely, leaving him on the dance-floor. But before she

could get to the edge of the floor the music changed to a catchy Beatles tune — '*Love me do,*' and the wild Spaniard she had danced with the other night caught her around the waist and began whirling her around the floor.

'You is too much sexy tonight, big woman,' he gasped between exertions. 'Your body, it is so white. I love this body.'

She forgave him these boldnesses, assuming his command of English was at fault. But she did receive a major jolt when the dance ended and he buried his head in her bosom, right there on the dance-floor, and ran his tongue down her cleavage.

She leaped back as if he had bitten her; indeed, she thought he was about to. She was not unmoved — the sensation itself had not been unpleasant — but he smelled strongly of Oranjeboom and cannabis and she was wise enough to know that he was quite a bit more than she could handle. So she said again, 'Excuse me, but I think I need the Ladies Room,' and fled away out into the night.

She wandered on to the deck, feeling she needed some fresh air as her body felt most peculiar, warm and moist, both inside and out. The ship was pitching slightly; clouds were gathering, the ice-smooth surface of the sea broken. Marsha stood there for a long time, feeling her skin cool with the fresh breeze, but her insides remained disturbingly hot, agitated. All around her couples were snogging, giving up the pretence of looking out at the water and intent only on touching, feeling. A tiny shudder went through her and she decided this was no good for her chest, all this sea air on her exposed bosom; she would be no good to the nice French Catholic family if she arrived suffering from bronchitis or pneumonia. Feeling sensible and therefore more stable, she walked determinedly off the deck, along the corridors of the ship and down several sets of stairs until she got to her cabin. She would put on her cardigan and then she would feel much better. Her mother had advised her to make sure and wear it at all times on the voyage. Everyone knew how treacherous sea breezes could be.

The cabin was, to her surprise, unlocked. They had probably forgotten to lock it in their rush to get to dinner; this had happened once or twice before. She knew the others weren't there; she had passed the dance-floor and seen Sojo dancing with Nöjd, and anyway Giorgio was working tonight. Emmeline and Hal had also been dreamily dancing, and Leo and Daisy were one of the couples smooching up on deck. She went in, the door slamming shut behind her. Before she could switch on the light an arm flew out and grabbed her around the waist and the sound of soft, mellifluous Italian was wafting in her ear like a strange but compelling melody.

'Giorgio! What are you doing here? Sojo isn't expecting you for hours.'

He didn't understand what she said, but automatically began to explain what he was doing lurking in the cabin – not that Marsha understood him, either. He had unexpectedly got an hour or two off and thought that he would pop in on the off-chance to see if Sojo had perhaps made a fleeting visit to repair her make-up or some such thing. To tell the truth, he didn't quite trust her with that sculpted blond Scandanavian, and a slight suspicion made him wonder if perhaps he would find her in bed with what she called 'the iceberg'. In this he needn't have worried; what he did to Sojo in bed made her completely faithful, at least for the time.

When the door had opened and it wasn't Sojo, it was surely the next best thing, that American with the pure white bosom who had given him the eye so wantonly just a few hours ago. Feeling manly and Zorba-ish, he swept her into his arms and ran those same lips which Marsha had observed earlier over the part of her breasts which were exposed.

'Giorgio, what are you doing? Giorgio . . .?'

Marsha knew she should tell him to stop; she had learned this from the nuns, but unfortunately — or fortunately as the case may be, for to this day Marsha holds the memory of that night in her heart like a shrine — she had learned it in the mind, in the cells of logic, and not in her emotions. Whatever it was he was doing to her breasts, now to her nipples which had somehow slipped out of her bra and thence out of the dress, was not something which happened every day, and she wanted to know how long it would continue before she simply died of it.

'Giorgio?' she murmured, holding for dear life on to his thick black hair while his gentle hands took over the job on her breasts that his lips had started. 'Do you think you should . . . that we should . . .?'

Giorgio had learned some English and he used it to full advantage now. 'Is okay. Okay okay okay. Yes? Okay?'

And now his hands were kneading, rolling over her breasts just as the ship was doing, rolling over the waves, and she couldn't answer him because at the same time his tongue was doing things in her mouth that she had no idea tongues could do. She thought fleetingly that it didn't seem very American and hygienic but Europe was much older and presumably wiser and Giorgio certainly seemed to know exactly what he was doing . . .

When she could breathe again, she found that instead of saying, 'No, no, no, no!' like any good Catholic girl would have done, she too was muttering, 'Okay, okay, okay, okay.

Ohhh, yes,' for by then Giorgio's hands were where no other hands had been before, not even her own, for goodness sake, and though she jumped at first, his fingers were so soft, so light, so compelling that she thought she'd wait a bit before saying no: it felt so amazingly, excruciatingly, fantastically wonderful.

Though it all went on for quite a long time, Marsha never did get around to saying no. She had only one qualm, when Giorgio adroitly pulled on something that she knew would prevent her from having a baby. She had heard Father Jerome expounding on the evils of birth control enough times to know what was going on, but as Giorgio began slowly, gently, inserting himself inside her, the qualm disappeared and all she could feel was profound gratitude that he had had the foresight to think of these things.

'Okay?' Giorgio said tenderly after it was all over.

'Okay,' she replied truthfully. She had heard him moan, 'Ohh, ahhh, argh,' and knew why, knew the secret, for she too had groaned the same thing, more than once. She felt replete and contented. She knew it would never happen a second time, not with Giorgio, for she did not love him and he had his beautiful Sojo, but she knew what it was now, knew that when it was time for this miracle to touch her life again, she'd be more than ready.

He kissed her gently, helped her straighten her clothes, her dress which somehow had never got taken off but had rolled down off her shoulders and up from her hips so that it was wrapped around her waist like one of those plastic tubes that children wear in the water.

'Thank you, Giorgio,' she said simply as they eased themselves out of the cabin.

'Thank *you*,' Giorgio said gallantly. He really was very proud of his English.

They parted at the top of the stairs, Giorgio to return to work, Marsha to stand at the railing of the boat, hugging herself for she still didn't have her cardigan, and to muse about the wondrous thing that had just happened. In her rational mind she knew she had sinned, according to the rules she had been brought up with; in her heart she felt utterly at peace. Instead of guilt, she felt contentment: more than that, she felt overwhelmed, humble but proud at the same time. This, then, was what life was all about. This, then, was what being a woman was all about. Had it not been Giorgio, Marsha would have shouted it to the world, especially to Em and Daisy and Sojo, but she knew this was a secret she would have to keep always. Holding these awesome, dazzling things to her heart, she watched the sea swelling under the stars for a long, long time, until she finally got cold and had to go inside.

'Hey, look at Marsha, she's really crumbled!' Daisy said to Leo. It was a little joke between them all, how Marsha, after a few days on the boat, had crumbled like a biscuit, her prim neat edges going first, then the rest of her.

'Lord, she looks dishevelled,' Leo observed. 'If it wasn't Marsha I'd think—'

'Don't think it. Not Marsha. She might look as wild as the night is turning out to be right now, but inside she's as pure as the driven snow.'

'I don't know, did you see all the wine she drank tonight?'

'It'll take more than a few glasses of wine to really set Marsha loose,' Daisy said.

Marsha, inside now and dancing with the American, saw

them looking (she had retrieved her glasses) and waved at them. Then she abandoned herself to the primal beat of the music, moving her legs and her body, so that she didn't know which was the beating of the drums and which was the drumming of her heart. She danced as she had never danced before, as she would never dance again. It was her day, her night, her time, and unlike many, she recognised it at the moment of its occurrence. For that, she was grateful, and she promised herself that other moments too she would savour, moments of grace, of joy. She would acknowledge them always, she vowed, not let them pass over her like the flight of a bird, barely seen, barely experienced. In one enchanted night she had altered irrevocably both physically and emotionally, and she knew beyond any doubts that she had been waiting for this day for a long, long time.

The boat rolled on, and so did the night, each gathering motion, momentum. There was a storm at sea which later they discovered to be the tail-end of a hurricane. Those who were seasick returned early to the cabins, but most of them were too young and sure of their immortality to be affected by the pitching and groaning and swaying of the *Castel Felice*. Leo and Daisy found an empty cabin and made love, and Emmeline and Hal, expelled from the decks which were closed during the storm, sat in the near-empty lounge bar and dozed together on a cushioned settee, too tired even to talk but not wanting to separate and go to their different cabins.

The sea was rough for another twenty-four hours or so, and then one morning they came out on deck to find the sun blazing like summer, the ocean blue and clean and unthreatening once again. And there, in a haze in the distance, was land, appearing like Brigadoon out of a time warp, magic and mystical. England, and home for some, for others a Mecca.

Emmeline, standing with Hal amongst the crowd of people at the railing, wept. As she was to weep nearly thirty years later when she returned.

Chapter Five

The autumn is clean and perfect this year, the air crisp and cool, the colours gloriously bright and clear. In the orchard Baz makes love to his Gemma in their first home together, sometimes not even waiting until they have turned the faded velvet sofa into its hidden bed but lying with her on the soft red cushions which are as luxurious as clouds and, in their love-intoxicated state, as heavenly. Around them the trees glisten and gleam with colour and in the mornings the grass is crunchy with frost which seems to tinkle under their feet when they emerge from their hideaway.

'Oh Baz, we can't leave here, not yet!' Gemma cries one moonlit night with the ground white and the air luminescent with promise.

'I don't want to leave yet,' Baz replies. 'It's not the right time.'

'It's all right if we don't go near the house. Mum drives me crazy with her little caustic remarks and Dad is just as bad, pretending we don't exist, like he's pretended all his life when things are not to his liking.'

Baz wraps his gloved fingers in hers. The caravan gleams red and glowing in the moonlight, and a sudden spasm of love for it, and Gemma, and the night, makes his breath catch. He is wearing a blue woolly hat pulled tightly down over his irrepressible hair and no fewer than three jumpers, as is Gemma, who has now exchanged her bare feet for sturdy army boots. Though it is only late October, it is quite cold, but there is no wind and the cold is energizing.

'The trouble with not going near the house,' Baz says reflectively, 'is that it makes your mother cross. She already accuses me of keeping you away from the family.'

'Oh, sod the family!' Gemma cries. 'The sooner we are away from here the better, if that's the way they are going to behave.'

This makes Baz rather sad, for in truth he has always loved Gemma's huge rambling close-knit family, coming as he does from a rather scattered unit of incompatible step-siblings and step-parents, all of whom have long ago gone their separate ways. He likes, enormously, Gemma's three brothers and her sister, Melanie. Given the chance, he could have liked, even loved, Daisy and Leo also, but his feelings towards them are now understandably tainted by their animosity towards him, and he finds himself surly, even mean, in his chance encounters with them around the farm.

'Be patient, love,' Baz says to Gemma. 'In six or seven months we'll be ready to go. We can stick it here until then.'

Gemma nods, and buries her face in Baz's woollies. She can stick anything for ever, she thinks passionately, as long as they are together.

The moon, full and beaming, looks down on them with what looks suspiciously like an amused, cynical smile on its old, scarred face.

*   *   *

Flack appears one day, early, on his way to Whitstable where he has a job interview. He is dressed neatly in old but clean green cords and a sombre black jumper. The job is for assisting part-time in a video shop. Blue and Flack have re-opened the café but know they cannot carry on without earning some extra cash elsewhere.

'The pay is shit,' Flack says, 'but it'll help.'

'Where's Blue?'

'At the café. We'll need to get used to carrying on with just one when the other's working. Not that I have high hopes of getting this,' he says darkly.

Baz and Gemma are silent, remembering the last job Blue applied for, as a cleaner in a nursing home. 'Twenty-seven people applied, poor buggers, for that bloody job of Blue's,' Flack says now, reading their minds. 'Twenty-seven people for a shit job paying bugger all – Blue didn't have a chance. They decided on a "mature" woman, they said, some poor sod of thirty with three little kids who was practically blubbing with gratitude for the peanuts they were going to give her.'

'I know,' Gemma says. 'I tried all summer to find something. I couldn't compete with all the students, fighting like crazy for whatever's going. Thank God I've got my candles.'

'How're they doing?'

'Ace, now with Christmas just over two months away. People love candles this time of year, goes back to pagan times I'm sure.'

'Look,' Baz says to Flack, 'Gemma and I have helped out in the café before, when you started out, so if you get this job, tell Blue we'll come whenever we can.'

'Except for Baz's didge workshops, we're pretty flexible,' Gemma says. 'Just give us a shout.'

Flack nods, knowing that they mean this. He leaves for his interview with a lighter heart, the encouragement of his friends giving him hope. Perhaps he'll get this job; perhaps the pay will be decent; perhaps Blue, with the help of Baz and Gemma, will be able to cope all right on her own, and they can keep Primrose Café which has become very dear, very special to him.

The autumn day looks promising. Flack grins at Baz, hugs Gemma, and goes off, suddenly brimming with confidence.

Daisy, going about her chores during these shortening October days, feels loneliness gripping her like a mangle. All her old bounce and ebullience seems to have been pounded and pummelled and wrung out of her like a thin bleached cotton sheet. The hens' silly cackling irritates her as she feeds them, cleans their nest boxes, collects the eggs; the sows in the farrowing stall seem grumpy and bad-tempered as she checks the piglets, notes any sign of encroaching illness to report back to Leo; and the sheep seem haplessly dull and uninteresting as she makes her daily round of the flock. But this is nothing compared to the overwhelming inertia she feels when doing the pig records. For years she has noted down numbers of sows and piglets, dates of births and weanings, data which tells Leo when the sow must be put to the boar, which sows have proved most productive, fertile. When the children were growing up Daisy faced this task with pleasure and alacrity, happy to be helping Leo, happy to be busy. Now, with all the time in the world, the job has become hopelessly tedious, as have all her farm chores which for some reason have suddenly struck her as meaningless and trite.

Once, long ago, she would have tried to tell these things to Leo, but she has learned that to do so would only frustrate both herself and him, for Leo does not talk about the dark night of his or anyone else's soul but can discuss only the daylight things: the children's schooling, a slight slump in the pig market, the results of a local by-election. Leo can hold a dialogue with the land, with his animals, with his own hidden spaces, but he cannot communicate with the thing he loves above all these things: his own wife, his own dear Daisy.

At first, it did not much matter. 'What a weekend!' Daisy would sigh on many a Sunday night, after the house had partially emptied of friends from London. 'Don't you wish you were in London sometimes, more part of it all?'

She didn't really want to be in London, but she needed to talk about it, share with Leo the exciting things happening in the city, talk to him about the music, the politics, the places that all her friends raved about. 'It's the *last* place I'd like to be,' Leo would say.

'Oh, I know that. I'd really rather be here too, but just think of all they are doing, seeing, *experiencing*.'

'Hm,' Leo would mutter, and then, 'I'm exhausted, love. Can we turn off the lights?'

Mostly, in those early days, these divisions did not much matter. Until the day when Daisy came home from hospital having been quite ill after her appendix burst on the operating table, and Leo, filling their bedroom with flowers, brought her a cup of tea, kissed her distractedly, and said, 'I'm going out on the farm for a bit, Daisy, if you're all right.'

Daisy wasn't all right. She was feeling weepy and fragile and had come the closest she had ever been to death and she wanted to talk about it. 'You said you did the chores before picking me up at hosptal,' she said rather tearfully. 'You said there's not much to do on the farm.'

Leo sighed, and stayed at Daisy's side, but he was so

wooden, so distant, that she soon gave up trying to talk to him and told him to go. She understood that he had been shaken to the core by her illness, by the fact that he could have lost her, and that he had hidden these feelings deeply because that was the way he coped with such enormities. And yet she needed him to talk about these things, share them with her. The first slight quivers of loneliness ran through her that day, like almost imperceptible earth tremors, doing no structural damage but causing a slight unease, a small uncertainty, and who knew what unseen internal damage. Daisy, not giving to brooding – not then, at any rate – got on with her life: her children, her many friends, her orphan lambs and sickly piglets, her many and varied farm chores. It was enough, and all she ever wanted. She had no regrets, as she so assuredly told Emmeline; none at all.

But then, suddenly, it was all over. Daisy knows in the logic of her brain that it did not really happen abruptly, this erosion of the very substance of her life, but gradually, first with the children growing up and leaving home, then with the slow and inevitable mechanisation of the farm, leaving her with fewer and fewer chores to do. To Daisy, however, it was sudden. One minute she was the busy, competent farmer's wife with five young children; the next she was totally alone and often unoccupied, wandering around the big empty house staring at mirrors that once reflected bustle and activity but seem now to her to reflect nothing: her own nothingness, perhaps.

If only she could talk to Leo. She tried once, when Gemma first told them she was not staying on the farm. 'That Baz has bewitched her,' Daisy stormed and ranted. 'Not only is she leaving the farm, she wants to live like a gypsy in that horse-drawn antique.'

Leo didn't answer. He was too deeply buried in the quicksand of his own disappointment to let Daisy be dragged down there with him, not understanding that she *needed* to be with him so that together they could pull themselves up. 'If that's what she wants,' he began, then trailed off.

'But what about you, you've been counting on her coming on the farm. How do *you* feel?'

'What does it matter?' Leo countered. 'She's made up her mind and that's that.'

And so they each brooded alone, Leo refusing to talk about it again, and Daisy poisoning herself day after day in the empty house with bitter regrets for the past which was irrevocably over, and the future which for her now seems as bleak and chilling as a desolate coastline on a freezing winter's day.

Leo may not talk much to Daisy, but he talks to himself in his head. As he walks around the fields checking on his beloved flock of sheep, of which he is inordinately proud, or mends fences, or spreads dung on the barley stubble, he holds long silent conversations with himself: about Daisy, whom he loves so much he has been afraid to tell her so for years, fearing that the very mention of something so profound would cause it to turn into ashes before his very eyes; about Gemma, with whom he is bitterly disappointed; about the emptiness that he sometimes spots out of the corner of his eye, lying in wait for the passing of time to jump, to snarl, to attack.

It never occurs to Leo to share these thoughts with Daisy. As a boy his mother discouraged any discussions of feelings, and emotions were things that were bad enough to have, let alone talk about. His father, though perhaps more sympathetic, was as constrained as most men of his generation, especially those working on the land; he was far too busy, and too taciturn as well, to spend time idly with the spoken word. And so Leo talks to himself during the long days, driving his tractor across his grasslands or his barley stubble, and when evening comes he is all talked out and wants only to sit in the big scruffy armchair by the fire, Daisy at his side, watching the news or a bit of sport on the telly.

These days, however, such idyllic evenings do not bring peace to Leo. He is brooding on something else these gentle October days, not just on Gemma and her abandonment of the farm, but something perhaps even nearer and dearer to his heart than that.

Daisy, wrapped in her own loneliness like a moth in a cocoon, shivers in the autumn evening. Leo, lost in thought, does not notice.

'Emmeline, this is Tony Pembury. He's our bat man.'

'Excuse me?'

'Tony, this is Emmeline Lake, our American friend.'

'Nice to meet you, Emmeline. What a lyrical name, it sounds as if it should be in lights somewhere.'

Emmeline looks at him strangely, an odd feeling of *déjà vu* going through her. Leo has just introduced her to this man who has driven up to the farmhouse in an ageing yellow van and has now got out, standing with them in the pouring rain.

'Come on inside,' Leo says. 'We're getting soaked. Daisy'll be delighted to see you, Tony. You haven't been around for ages.'

'I've had some work on this past six weeks. Everyone is suddenly remembering the gales of last year and wanting their roofs done before winter.'

Emmeline has just come from the orchard, where she has been visiting Gemma and Baz. It is Saturday morning and she was properly invited, for morning coffee.

'You're honoured,' Daisy had said petulantly as Em was putting on her jacket and getting ready to go. 'I never get invited.'

'Oh Daisy, you know you are welcome any time.'

'Hardly. They never even come up much to the house any more, except when Gemma needs the kitchen space to make her candles. I think she's even doing that in the caravan now, over that tiny stove. They just don't want to see us, that's all.'

Emmeline, exasperated, said, 'Well, can you blame them?'

'What's that supposed to mean?'

'Daisy, for God's sake, you've got to stop being so pigheaded. You've got to accept Gemma and Baz for what they are, and stop trying to mould them both to your own expectations.'

'I only want what's best for Gemma, you know that.'

'Do you? I think it's more than that. I think you should be honest with yourself. You're scared shitless of being alone, of being without a single one of your brood. That's okay, but goddamn it, you've got to admit it to yourself, accept it. With Gemma here, working on the farm indefinitely, you wouldn't have had to face whatever it is you can't face inside yourself. Stop using her as an excuse, okay?'

With that Emmeline had gone out the door, not even looking back to see how Daisy was reacting to her little speech. It had been something she'd wanted to say for weeks, but now she was afraid she had gone too far, upset Daisy irrevocably. And so it was in an irritable mood that she arrived at the caravan, which was warm and cosy despite the cold rain lashing the apple trees outside. When Baz went out to get some more water for the kettle, Emmeline turned to Gemma and said impulsively, 'Gemma, are you sure you want to do this? Perhaps you should at least give the farm a year's try. If it didn't work, I'm sure your parents would be happier, knowing that at least you made an attempt.'

Gemma looked shocked, betrayed. 'Mum set you up to this, I know.'

'She asked me to talk to you, that's all. Some time ago, but I hesitated. To be quite honest, I actually do think you know your own mind, maybe even need to go away. But there is such a thing as compromise, you know. Maybe a year to think it over wouldn't be such a bad idea.'

Gemma put down her cup and started to get up, then sat down again restlessly. The many gleaming mirrors in the caravan reflected two sombre women, one neatly dressed in chino trousers, a long red ribbed jumper knitted out of silk; the other wearing clumpy laced-up boots, a long patchwork skirt, and a fuzzy old angora cardigan of bright multi-colours. 'Mum thinks that all I need is a year away from Baz and I'll capitulate,' Gemma said sadly. 'She's so wrong, you know. I can't stay. I need to get away, to travel, to do my own thing. I'm never going to be the girl I was at eleven, twelve, so infatuated with the farm, the animals. I started to change way before Baz, but they won't ever believe that.'

Emmeline put her arm reassuringly around Gemma's shoulders. 'They'll have to, honey,' she said with a great rush of affection. 'In the end, they'll just have to.'

Now, in the kitchen with Daisy and Leo and Tony, Emmeline looks at Daisy to see if there is any coolness there, any animosity over her blunt speaking earlier that morning. But Daisy seems her usual friendly self, though perhaps slightly paler, slightly tremulous. As she pours Emmeline a coffee, their eyes meet, and Daisy nods, smiles slightly.

Reassured, Emmeline turns her attention to Tony. He is filling Daisy and Leo in on the job he has been doing for the last few weeks, and Emmeline listens, liking the sound of his rich, mellifluous voice. It is quite entrancing, that voice, deep and hypnotic. The rest of him is quite ordinary: medium height, a pleasant face, longish dark hair streaked liberally with silver. Because of the dark colour of his hair, or the olive tone to his skin — or perhaps it is something within him, something imperceptible — there is a sense of singularity about him; something foreign, separate.

His voice, however, is certainly English. The talk now has turned to bats, and when there is a pause in the conversation Emmeline says, 'I'm sorry, but I don't quite understand what Tony does. Why did you call him a bat man, Leo? It makes me feel he should be wearing a mask and a blue cape.'

Leo explains. 'Tony works for an organisation that helps and advises on bats. They're a protected species in this country. One isn't allowed to destroy them or disturb them in any way.'

'So what do you do, exactly?' Emmeline asks Tony.

'All sorts of things. Go out and identify bats, record where they are. See people who have discovered bats in their attics or barns and don't know what to do about them. Give talks, often at schools. Today I was out with a farmer; some of his effluent was poisoning a woodland, killing not only the habitat of the bats but of other wildlife as well. I had to make sure he was doing something to rectify the situation.'

'Tony came out here last summer and identified some

bats we discovered in the attic,' Daisy says enthusiastically.

'A lovely colony of brown long-ears,' Tony murmurs.

'We think they're still there,' Leo carries on. 'Some of
them haven't left yet for the winter like most bats do. We
have to do some re-wiring up there so we asked Tony to have
a look, make sure that what we plan won't disturb them.'

Emmeline, beguiled, is amused that bats are such a Good
Thing here, her acquaintance with them being limited to
grotesque paper effigies on Hallowe'en. As they talk on,
mostly about the vagaries and idiosyncrasies of brown
long-ears, she wonders wryly what Chester would make
of all this, or even Sally. Bats are certainly not a topic of
conversation in the circles she frequents in Atlanta.

At first she listens with a slight trace of condescension,
not really hearing what they are saying but entranced by
the timbre and melodiousness of Tony's voice. Gradually,
however, she realises she is being drawn in by the subject.
Tony has the ability to explain things clearly, intelligently,
and he has a natural love and enthusiasm for his subject which
is contagious. His voice is strong and assured, contrasting
sharply with his gentle, somewhat sensitive face. He speaks
of the bats as parents do of their babies: tenderly, proudly.

'They're blind, aren't they?' Emmeline asks at one stage,
pleased with herself for knowing something about these
strange, rather distasteful creatures.

'On the contrary, they have well-developed eyes. But they
also "see" with sound, something called "echo-locate". That's
how they find food at night, in the dark. People assume
they are blind because they use sound rather than sight to
find food.'

He goes on to explain what bats eat, and at one point,

in answer to a question from Emmeline, says, 'I don't know exactly why or when I became so fascinated by bats. I've always been something of a naturalist anyway, and I think bats interest me because they are so old, so ancient. Their ancestors were flying around fifty million years ago, you know. I like that kind of continuity, makes me feel secure, somehow. It would be tragic if we wiped them out now, either through modern technology, or carelessness, or whatever.'

They finish their coffee and Leo says, 'Come on, let's go up to the attic and have a look.'

'Can I come?' Emmeline asks Tony. 'I'd love to see some bats.'

'All you'll see are bat droppings now. They'll be roosting. I'm just going to have a look at what Leo needs to do up there, see if he can go ahead without disturbing them.'

'I'm disappointed,' Emmeline says lightly, almost flirtatiously.

'Are you?' He looks at her thoughtfully. 'I'm giving a talk on bats next Friday night, for Greenpeace. I'll have some bats there. Come along if you like.'

'Tony's talks are fascinating, Em,' Leo says encouragingly. 'We'd go with you, but we have something else on that night.'

'I'll collect you, if you like,' Tony says. 'I live only a mile or so from here, and I go right past the farm lane on my way into town.'

Emmeline feels slightly trapped. Listening to a talk on bats over a cup of hot coffee in a cosy English kitchen amongst friends is a bit different from sitting on some hard chairs in a cold village hall with a bunch of bat fanatics and Green obsessives.

Tony is watching her, half-smiling, half-serious. He knows her dilemma, doesn't really expect her to come. He only asked her because it slightly annoyed him, her flip, playful remark about wanting to see some bats. She is so American, he thinks: so slick and assured and smiley. And yet . . . there was something wistful about that smile, when he complimented her on her lovely lyrical name. He had a great-aunt in Ireland whose name was Emmeline; his mother took him to visit her there once when he was a boy. He hasn't heard the name since. Suddenly, he hopes she will accept his rather teasing invitation.

Emmeline knows it is a challenge, so she accepts gracefully. 'I'll be happy to go with you,' she says, and as his sardonic half-smile broadens into a genuine grin, she realises this is quite true. At least it will be a change from Clem Todd and his persistent monologues, interesting though they are, on stage design or the post-modern British theatre. It's not so much his lecturing her that she is beginning to find irritating – though it would be nice to express *her* opinion occasionally – it is more the fact that he puntuates his sentences with the odd pressure on her arm, the random silent innuendo. Any more of it and she will accuse him of sexual harassment, she thinks sourly. Sexual games, like other games, only give you a buzz if the two players are similarly interested. She certainly is not interested, and he should have picked up on that by now.

What she has not taken into consideration is Clem's remarkable vanity. It simply never occurs to him that Emmeline does not, deep down in her sterile American heart, fancy him.

It isn't a village hall after all, but rather a cosy meeting house in Blackfriars, near the heart of Canterbury. It certainly isn't cold; there is actually a fireplace with a warm, glowing coal fire, and though the chairs are only wooden folding ones, the room is carpeted and pleasant, with huge posters of seals and whales and dolphins all over the walls.

'Emmy!' Emmeline looks around to see who is calling her, and finds herself being hugged and kissed by Gemma, who is wearing a short wispy skirt with her leggings and army boots and a Greenpeace T-shirt. 'I didn't know you were coming here tonight.'

Tony is in the front of the room, setting up his projector and screen, carefully placing his square box with the three bats in a warm place in the corner. 'I'm so glad you've met Tony,' Gemma enthuses. 'He's marvellous, you know. Does so many things. He's the lead guitarist for a really good local band; we've been to one or two of his gigs and they're great. They do all sorts of things, rock and folk, some old stuff and a lot of their own music which is ace.'

Another surprise, Emmeline thinks. She looks at Tony with renewed interest, trying to see the rock musician in the mild-looking man fussing with his bats up in front of the room.

'We've heard him do his bat talk before, in front of some conservation group,' Gemma is saying. 'Blue is on the Greenpeace committee and suggested that they should get him for the evening. He goes all over Kent educating people about bats. It's amazing how many people still consider them a pest, try to kill them off when they find them in their attic or something.'

Emmeline sees Baz, who comes over to her and gives her a warm hug. Blue greets her, and then Flack, whose long hair is not bound by a plait tonight but flows copiously and luxuriously down his back. 'Sorry you didn't get that job you were after, Flack,' Em says.

'Same old thing,' Blue says with shrug. 'Too many people after it.'

'Mainly students again,' Flack says. 'What with grants down to practically nothing, there's a dozen applicants for every part-time job.'

'Anyway, we're still plodding along,' Blue says cheerfully. 'The café's been doing great business lately, maybe it'll be enough.' She smiles reassuringly at Flack who is looking despondent. He lightens up at her smile and looks at her fondly. She is wearing silver iridescent tights with a steel grey mini-skirt, and all sorts of flowing things, scarves and shawls and kerchiefs, which waft and wave like banners as she rushes around the room greeting people, arranging seats, checking that everything is ready for the coffee and tea which will be served later.

Emmeline takes a seat and looks around her. The audience, which already seems to number around forty or fifty with still another few minutes to go, is a variegated crowd: a sprinkling of Gemma's friends, a handful of elderly county matrons in beautifully tailored wool suits, old men in tweeds, young family groups with children milling about shouting and excited. There is a great deal of conversation and laughter: she is surprised to see how much fun everyone seems to be having. She somehow thought that the members of an environmental pressure group like Greenpeace would be sombre, serious, dull.

The evening starts with an introduction by a boyish-looking man of about forty who is the chairman of this branch. He obviously knows Tony well for he praises him highly, much to Tony's obvious embarrassment. Then the talk begins, and from the very first moment the audience is spellbound. Tony is an electric speaker, surprisingly passionate yet funny and completely natural. As he talks he shows slides of bats in all their splendour: flying, roosting, feeding, and by the end of the talk Emmeline is as eager as the rest of the audience to see one of these amazing little creatures for herself.

'I have three pipistrelles in here,' he says when the slide show is over. 'Pipistrelles are the smallest of the fourteen species we have in Britain, only about five grams in weight and with a wingspan of about eight inches. If I had a completely sealed-off room I'd let them out so you could see them in flight, but they would lose themselves in seconds here – they can get into the tiniest hole or space, as you can imagine. But what I'll do is this: the cage has glass sides and a wired top, and you can come up here a few at a time, the children first, and watch them feed. I've got their evening meal with me: tiny little worms which I have to buy specially.'

The children run up, fascinated. Tony is patient, unhurried with them. 'You're not allowed to keep bats as pets,' he explains in answer to a young girl's questions, 'but you are allowed to look after injured or abandoned bats. All three of these were injured, and though they are fine now, I can't let them go because they would die. They have no territory, you see, and bats are very territorial.'

It takes a long time for everyone to look at the bats. The committee members are selling homemade cake and biscuits with the coffee and tea, and a stall has been set up selling recycled paper products, T-shirts and books. No one seems in a hurry to go; the atmosphere is rather like an impromtu party. Several people come up and talk to Emmeline, including the man who introduced Tony.

'I'm Barnaby Brackenbury,' he says, shaking Emmeline's hand.

'Barnaby Brackenbury,' Emmeline repeats, loving the alliteration. 'I'm Emmeline Lake.'

'Tony said he was bringing you tonight. Wasn't it a fascinating talk? I always feel like rushing out and saving the bats of the world after listening to Tony; there is something very evangelical about his talks. I've asked him to bring you out to the pub after we lock up and he said it's up to you. Will you join us? Here is my wife, Marjorie.'

Marjorie is a tall, large-boned woman with a voice like a boomerang, circling the entire room with its depth and resonance. 'Do come,' she shouts. She is always shouting, partly because she herself is slightly deaf in one ear, and partly because she was raised as the youngest in a family of six children, and so had to learn to shout when she was quite young to make herself heard. She is about the same age as her husband, with unusually thick curly hair and a rather haughty turned-up nose, giving her an insolent air which belies the easygoing wife and mother of their obstreperous young daughters.

'Do join us,' Marjorie repeats. 'For once the children are at home with a babysitter. They've heard Tony's bat talk a hundred times already, I should imagine, and only show off when they come now.'

'I'd love to join you,' Emmeline shouts back unthinkingly, then looks around embarrassedly but no one seems to have noticed.

'Jolly good,' Marjorie shrieks, to Emmeline's great delight. She has been in England for well over a month now and this is the first time she's heard someone say 'jolly good'.

'It's all arranged then, right?' Barnaby says happily. He is as bald as his wife is hirsute: where her hair curls dense as a hedgerow on her broad skull, Barnaby has nothing but a soft fuzz, rather like a baby's. Because his face is so cherubic, and has such an appealing boyish look about it, the naked scalp is rather an asset, making him seem oddly young and innocent. Emmeline warms to him at once, and looks forward to her first evening for years at an English pub.

'Bloody marvellous talk, eh?' Marjorie Brackenbury is shouting over the pub's hum an hour or so later.

'Not bad, not bad,' Barnaby says with a grin.

'I say, don't be so condescending, Barnaby. Tony gave us a jolly good show and you know it.'

Emmeline smiles obliquely. Marjorie's conversation is punctuated by these wonderful archaic expressions, derived from watching too many old British war films with her surly Army officer father, who had married late and was as old as the hills when Marjorie was growing up. In spite of the shouting and the jollies, Emmeline finds herself enjoying Marjorie's company, for she is sparky and genuinely kind-hearted.

Barnaby Brackenbury is, of necessity, quieter than his wife. He is rumpled and slightly harassed in a friendly way, like a bemused English sheepdog, albeit a bald one. Marjorie is always, in a very un-English manner, touching him, running her fingers through his fuzz, slapping her arm around his shoulder in extravagant, matey gestures.

'I say, how splendid that you are here for almost a year,' she is shouting now at Emmeline. 'You must dine with us. Leo and Daisy too; I haven't seen them for eons. Tony, you must bring her. Tony is a frequent visitor to our house.'

'The children love his bats,' Barnaby says obscurely.

'They're always trying to poke sticks at them,' Tony says sardonically.

'True nature lovers!' Marjorie hollers.

The pub is crowded, but no one turns to look. Marjorie and Barnaby go here regularly; it is just around the corner from their house. The pub is old, dark and slightly seedy, in a wholesome comforting way, like an ageing dressing gown with ancient stains from years of bedtime cocoa.

One person, however, does turn to look. One person surreptitiously twists around to stare at the lively foursome hogging up the best table by the fireplace. It is Clem Todd, there by sufferance with his wife Celia, a pinched, pallid woman with baby blonde hair and invisible eyebrows and eyelashes. Celia, fed up with the machinations of their adolescent daughter, has dragged Clem out of the house 'to discuss their child', which has resulted so far in a half hour of each blaming the other for the girl's misdemeanours.

'God, it's that loud-mouthed neighbour of ours,' Celia says irritably. 'Don't look up, I don't want to talk to her.' Clem tries to look away into his beer but it is too late; Emmeline has glanced up, seen Clem. She lifts her hand, smiles fulsomely. He grimaces in a semblance of a smile. Celia is watching him closely.

'Who is that woman?' she asks bluntly.

'One of my colleagues at the university.'

'What's her name?'

'Emmeline Lake.'

'Oh God. Not another actress.'

'I told you, she's a colleague.'

'You've never mentioned her.'

Clem is silent. Celia interprets this rightly: Clem intends to sleep with Emmeline Lake. He never discusses the women he intends to seduce; he has a strict moral code about this. Oh well, Celia thinks, at least the woman seems his own age. At least he's never gone for students. She is surprised to find how little she cares, how little she is interested in Emmeline Lake.

Clem, however, is interested in Emmeline's companion, that builder chap, Tony something or other. He was doing a job on Clem's roof once but there was a spot of trouble and Clem had to call in another builder. What the hell is Emmeline doing with him? It annoys Clem, seeing her there so obviously enjoying herself, not even glancing his way again. He watches her smile at something the builder says, then lean towards that obtrusive neighbour of his, that loud woman, and say something to her.

'Her?' Marjorie's voice peals loud and strident through the buzz and hum of the normal pub conversation as she glances back at Celia and Clem. 'That's his wife! Didn't you know he had one?'

Emmeline nods. Clem's face burns. Celia's blanches. 'No, I bet she bloody well didn't know,' Celia murmurs, and for the rest of the evening Clem has a great deal of explaining to do.

As Tony drives Emmeline back to the farm he says, 'Of course, Clem Todd would be a colleague of yours. I forgot that he's in your department.'

Emmeline says nothing. Tony drives on in silence, wanting to say more but knowing it is none of his business. He was aware of Clem unable to keep his eyes off Emmeline this evening at the pub, aware of how distasteful this seemed to him. He doesn't like Clem Todd much. He rather hopes Emmeline doesn't either.

*   *   *

Daisy is waiting up for Emmeline. She has not spoken to her, not alone and in private, since Emmeline confronted her the morning she was going to visit the caravan. For a week now Daisy has been brooding on Emmeline's words, recognising the inherent truth in them but unable to admit to herself even now that she is using Gemma as a lid for her own desolate emotions which are seething like worms inside her. The inertia she has been feeling has intensified, making ordinary tasks like feeding the chickens something impossibly heavy and exhausting. The house sighs and moans around her in the autumn gales which have been whipping the leaves off the trees all week, and Daisy is sure she hears it crying during the long wet afternoons, grieving for its lost children just as Daisy grieves.

Leo has long been in bed, but Daisy cannot bear to join him. For ages now she has had trouble sleeping, lying awake for hours listening to Leo's heavy breathing beside her. The house keeps her awake; it weeps heavily, it sighs, it despairs. Sometimes Daisy knows she is slowly going mad but the thought no longer distresses her. She no longer cares about anything, not even Gemma, she sometimes thinks.

She is waiting up for Emmeline because she does not want to lie awake alone in the big bed upstairs, Leo next to her but as far away as if he were in some inaccessible desert or mountain range. Gratefully she at last hears the door open, and Emmeline enters the chilly living room.

'Daisy, what are you doing up? Aren't you cold? The heating must have gone off ages ago and the fire's nearly out. You must be freezing.'

'I'm fine. Don't fuss, Em.'

'Are you all right?'

'Yes, of course I am. Anyway I don't want to talk about

me tonight, okay? I want to hear all about your evening out. Tell me what you think of Tony.'

Emmeline would rather talk about Daisy, for she has been worried about her, sensing her restlessness, her increasing isolation. But Daisy is smiling reassuringly at her, and Em knows that if Daisy doesn't want to discuss what is bothering her, there is no one on earth who can make her.

'We had a good evening. Met some friends of yours, Marjorie and Barnaby. I liked them.'

'We've known them for years. I like them too. Barnaby owns the best bookshop in town. It's tiny and cramped and chaotic, but it's full of wonderful books, lots of art books especially, and poetry collections you just can't find anywhere else.'

'We went to a pub afterwards. Would you believe Clem Todd was there? With his wife.'

They giggle conspiratorially, and it is almost like old times. Daisy asks questions about the evening until finally Emmeline says, 'Tell me about Tony. I've been dying to ask you about him all week, but there hasn't seemed to be much chance to talk.'

'Tony? Well, he's a bit of a strange sort of bloke, very self-contained, with so many different interests. Did you hear about his band?'

'Yes, someone mentioned it.'

'He's around our age, I would imagine, and rather a sixties misfit, I sometimes think – like us.'

'Us?' Emmeline asks quizzically, raising her eyebrows.

'Well, maybe not like us, at least not on the surface. I suppose we're all pretty Establishment now, aren't we. Leo's a hard-working farmer – but then he always was, wasn't he, in spite of that ten-day aberration on the boat.

But I've become a nice respectable sensible farmer's wife, working along with her husband with no outside interests at all except the land and the animals, and you are now a pillar-of-the-community academic with a good solid job, credentials . . . Perhaps we're not misfits after all. Strange that I feel like it sometimes, and I sense you do too.'

Emmeline wants to pursue this last remark but Daisy rushes on. 'Tony's lived around here for years, but we've only known him for about two or three. He's got a university degree in botany or zoology or something like that but he's never made a proper career of it. Somewhere along the way he picked up the building trade and does odd jobs when he needs the money. He loves his bats and his guitar, goes off on long walks all by himself with not even a dog to keep him company, and that's about all, as far as I know.' Daisy smiles thoughtfully. 'I don't know why I called him a misfit just now,' she continues musingly. 'He seems happier and more assured than most people I know.'

'What about women – does he have one? Has he ever been married? He's not married now, is he?'

'Ah ha, so this is what you've been dying to ask me! I'm surprised you just didn't ask *him*, in the blunt manner you used when you asked Clem Todd.'

Emmeline laughs. 'It didn't seem revelant, somehow. He never asked if *I* were.'

'Well, unlike our Clem Todd, Tony has never married. As far as I know, there isn't a woman on the scene.'

'Ah. Gay.'

'No, he was living with a woman when we first met him, but something happened, I don't know what. They went off somewhere on holiday together, and Tony came back alone. We never saw her since. It was a shame, for she seemed quite pleasant, though we didn't see that much of them. It was only when Tony was on his own that we got to know him.'

Emmeline nods and looks thoughtfully into the fire. 'You're not interested in him, are you, Em?' Daisy asks curiously. 'He's not at all your type.'

'What is my type?'

'Well, from the ones I met after Hal, they all seem to be oozing with a kind of male ripeness, rather like a spiky passion fruit ready to burst its skin with an over-abundance of macho virility.'

'You make them sound hideous.'

'None of them were my type, Em. You know that. Actually, I'd have thought Clem Todd was much more your sort than Tony. He's a simmering sexpot of sorts.'

'Well, he's married.'

'Thank God. But you can tell he likes women within about two seconds of being with him.'

'Or lusts for them, you mean.'

'Hm. Yes. Not the same thing, is it?'

'No. Not at all.'

They stare at the embers of the fire, which Daisy had stoked up again when Emmeline came in. The silence is cosy, companionable. Then Emmeline says softly, 'Am I imagining it, or is there something in Tony very like Hal?'

Daisy turns to her, startled. 'I never noticed.'

'I did. From that first day, in the kitchen. It's the compelling way he talks, I think, about something he feels passionately about. Like the bats. Hal used to talk that way about the theatre.'

'I remember. He had even me getting excited about the playwright Arnold Wesker once and I hadn't even heard of

121

him. To this day I remember all about him, all about the plays he wrote then.'

'And the way Tony listens, as well. Hal used to do that too, sit so quietly when someone else was talking, as if by the slightest movement he would miss their words, their meaning. I've never met anyone since who listened like that, so attentive and still.'

'Yes, you're right. I can see it now. He has Hal's gentleness, too. And sensitivity.'

'Well then,' Emmeline says lightly, getting up to go upstairs to bed, 'you are absolutely right. He isn't my type, is he? Not if he's anything else like Hal.'

'Emmy,' Daisy begins, troubled, but Emmeline interrupts, 'Hal was an aberration, a grave mistake. If there's anything I've learned, it's not to make mistakes more than once.'

'But Tony's not Hal! Not even remotely like him in the way you're thinking.'

'He's like him in too many other ways.' She shivers, suddenly cold. 'Come on, Daisy, let's go to bed. I'm exhausted, aren't you? It's so late.'

The stars are large and compelling coming in Emmeline's bedroom window and she stands looking out at them, unwilling to draw the curtains. There is a frost on the lawn and it is only the beginning of November. She reminisces about pumpkins, the way the frost looks on a field of them in the first hours of the morning, and thinks of home. She remembers, as if in a dream, her old life of work and pleasure: her research and teaching, her energetic social life, her longstanding relationship with Chester. Her friend and neighbour Sally would be starting her new season with the orchestra now, and there would be concerts to go to, and dinners in smart trendy restaurants with Chester, and thought-provoking lectures to attend with her colleagues at the university.

Bats? she thinks wearily as she gets into bed. Where do they fit in?

Nowhere, she concludes. Nowhere at all.

But she cannot sleep. She remembers the way Tony said to her, as they drove up the wooded lane and approached the farmhouse, 'Watch out for Clem Todd, all right? It's none of my business, and I wasn't going to say anything, but—'

He broke off helplessly, stopping the car and turning off the engine.

'I'm a big girl,' Emmeline said lightly.

'I feel a fool. I know you can take care of yourself. But I know Clem.'

'I'm beginning to do so also. Please don't worry about me.'

He shut off the car lights but before opening the door he looked at her, her face white in the outdoor light that Daisy had left on for her. 'All right, all right,' he answered brusquely. 'You can handle it, I shouldn't have interfered.' But his face belied his words, for there was a gentle concern there, a comradely tenderness. He touched her softly on the shoulder and then opened the door, watching her until she had gone into the house.

Tenderness, Emmeline thinks now with the incandescent stars inside the bedroom, shining on her face as she tries to sleep. *Softness.* She cannot abide that in a man, not since Hal. To her it is unbecoming, or worse, a deception.

She sleeps fitfully. Her bed becomes a boat, rocking unsteadily in waves of moonlight. She dreams, as she sometimes does, of men who look like the young Peter O'Toole, all blond and lanky in a desert sunset. They ride away from her, on camels or on trains and planes, but she remembers how their arms felt around her, how gentle their blue eyes looked before they pushed her away, ran off across the sand or down the platform, across the runway.

She wakes before dawn, her face sodden with tears shed during her dreaming. *Not again*, she swears silently to herself as she brushes them away. *Never again*. With this promise she drifts into a restless sleep until morning.

Chapter Six

'*A*lan! Here, boy. Alan Lamb, come here! I've got some barley for you.'

A great fat lumbering ram, sleek with health and well-being, races up to Gemma and Emmeline and allows Gemma to scratch his head while he greedily feeds from her hand. 'Julian and I raised Alan practically from birth, bottle-fed him day and night. Such a pathetic little orphan lamb he was, half-dead when Dad brought him in. The boys named him after one of England's cricketers. We won't let Dad get rid of him even though he's quite old now.'

Emmeline scratches the sheep tentatively on his fat neck and feels the lanolin greasing her fingers. She and Gemma have met behind the chicken run, Gemma on her way to the barn and Emmeline having gone out to collect the eggs. Emmeline has come home earlier than usual from the university and is enjoying the last hour or two of the day's sun. The weather has suddenly turned unseasonably mild, but no one expects it to last more than a day or so.

'Come with me to see Baz in the barn,' Gemma says. 'He's set up a workshop there, to make his didgeridoos. He wasn't going to, with Mum and Dad so grumbly about us living in the caravan, but Dad said he could use a corner of the barn and it's so convenient.'

Baz has, in the last couple of weeks, actually got a couple of orders for his didges. He has been diligently taking them to various craft fairs and festivals, and recently his photo was in the local newspaper, along with an article on didgeridoos. Emmeline and Gemma find him in the barn, sitting cross-legged on a bale of straw, blowing into a finished instrument. 'Try it,' he says to Em. She does, and cannot even get a sound out of it.

'It's really hard,' Gemma says. 'All I get are squeaks and grunts.'

'What on earth made you decide to try your hand at didgeridoos?' Emmeline asks. 'I never even heard of them until I came here. They're a whole new world for me. Like bats.'

Baz smiles. Emmeline thinks how endearing his smile makes him. And so very young. 'There's been a fantastic increase in didges over the last ten years,' he says. 'It's really exciting, because it parallels a rebirth, a spiritual awakening which seems to be happening everywhere. It's so primal, comes right from the earth. We're living in a new world of ecology, of things of the spirit, of our new awareness of Mother Earth.'

Emmeline, living in the old world of consumerism, materialism, and the breakdown of anything even remotely spiritual, says nothing but is rather touched by Baz's ingenuousness.

'The Aboriginals believed strongly in the power of song,' Gemma takes over. 'Their ancestors believed that the land and all the creatures on it were dreamt into existence by the Wandjina, or creation ancestors, and that these must be remembered on the exact place where the dreams occurred, by songs or stories. "Songlines", these places are called, and the didgeridoo has a big place in them.'

'It's just the thing for the New Age,' Baz says, his face eager, intense. 'The very sound of Creation itself. Who knows, maybe the didge is given to us by the gods, to bring wisdom and understanding to the people, to help us heal the earth, heal ourselves.'

He speaks with such energy, such fervour, that Emmeline can't help smiling. Who is she to be cynical, she says to herself, remembering how in London she, along with dozens of others, halted all the traffic going into the city one day by stopping each car, handing each driver a flower, and wishing them peace and love before letting them drive on again. She remembers how the sixties were also to be a New Age, the Age of Aquarius, of freedom, of joy and the end of war, racial strife, poverty.

And look where we are now, she muses. *Can't you see?* she wants to say to Gemma and Baz. Can't you see the condition the world is in? The sixties and all it stood for has been soundly rejected, don't you understand? The world is leaning precariously to the right: you will not be tolerated here, as at least we were tolerated. There were more of us, too, many more, and we lived in a world that was beginning to look hopeful. There were jobs then, and at least we weren't homeless, and people spoke of the community as if it were something to be proud of. We even managed to stop a war in the end, with our marches and our protests and our campaigning.

But of course she says nothing like this. She watches Gemma trying to blow into the didgeridoo, making it squeak, and Baz tickling her and making her laugh, and she feels incredibly sad about it all, sad for them and for herself and for this poor cracked and bleeding earth that no amount of didge music will ever heal, in spite of what the Aboriginals believe, or what Gemma and Baz would like to believe.

'C'mon,' Gemma says to Emmeline a few minutes later, 'let's leave Baz to his work. I can see the signs, he wants to get on.'

They leave the barn and walk along the orchard, pausing to acknowledge Alan Lamb who comes bounding up to them in the hope of more barley. Then they wander down to the sheep pens where Leo, busy amongst his sheep, waves absentmindedly at them.

'I'd better get these eggs over to your mother,' Emmeline says after they have wandered around a little longer, reluctant to go in on this unusually mild late afternoon. 'I think she's planning omelettes for tonight. An early dinner, then I have to work on an article I've been asked to write on regional theatres.'

'You spend a lot of time writing papers or researching or preparing things, don't you?'

'Do I? I hadn't noticed.'

'Mum always said you were a brilliant actress; you won the scholarship to the drama school and all that. She said you were dead ambitious when she met you on that boat. Have you ever regretted giving it all up?'

Emmeline takes a few moments to think about this. 'I never thought of it as giving anything up,' she finally answers. 'When I left England and returned to the States, I found that all my longings to act had somehow died.'

With Hal, she thinks, without any bitterness.

'I just didn't have the heart for it any more,' she goes on to Gemma. 'I'm sure Daisy has told you all about my reasons for quitting the drama school. I was in a state: confused, unhappy, grieving. When I was able to think clearly again I had no idea of what I wanted to do. I went back to college mainly because I didn't know what else to do, but by the time I had got my degree in drama and the theatre, my old love for it was rekindled. Only by then I had changed: I wanted to study it, write about it, teach it, rather than act in it.'

'I've read your book,' Gemma says. 'Or rather tried to. The one on Chekhov and the Russian theatre. Some of it I enjoyed, the rest was a bit too deep.'

Emmeline smiles. 'It was sweet of you to try.'

They are walking around the orchard now, feeling the last of the sun on their bodies. The apples have all been harvested; the orchard looks bare and autumnal. 'Oh, hell,' Gemma suddenly cries. 'It's so unfair. You changed direction, and Mum totally did. From planning to be a solicitor, she ended up a farmer's wife with no job of her own, no further education – and completely contented, as has been obvious for years. And yet look at all the fuss being made about me!'

Emmeline has no answer to this. The two women stand silently together, looking out from the top of the orchard to the sea a few miles away. It is beginning to get dark now, but it is still not cold. 'I can't wait to get out there,' Gemma whispers fiercely. She waves her arm randomly at the fields, the sea, the world. 'I just really cannot wait.'

*

'Oh, I can't wait, Hal! Are we really here? Is that England I'm looking at?'

Hal and Emmeline were standing on the deck, watching the bustle on the pier, waiting impatiently for their turn to be called in to see the customs men who had set up an office in the ship's main ballroom. It was taking hours, for the officials were interviewing each passenger personally. More than one were not permitted even to touch England's hallowed shores, but Emmeline had all her documents of acceptance to the drama school and had no fears of not getting a visa. Sojo was furious, because her passport had been stamped with only a three-week tourist visa. When the official had asked her what she intended to do in the country, she had said, 'Work, of course. Find a job.' Overcome by the shock and horror of this, the customs officer gave her a severe lecture on work permits and the evils of taking on employment without one. 'Do you think I want to stay in your goddamn country long?' Sojo told him, becoming cross with his overbearing manner. 'I'll be in Italy soon, so just cool down, buddy.'

Marsha was staying on the boat until it arrived at its next and last stop, Le Havre. 'I'll miss you,' she cried to the others, tears rolling down her face. 'Visit me in France.'

Giorgio, watching this tender display, thought it really was his duty to comfort the poor girl that evening, which he did in the very best way he knew how.

'Oh Giorgio,' Marsha murmured, going back to her cabin after a sad dinner in a near-empty dining room. Most of the passengers had disembarked at Southhampton; only a handful were travelling on to France. There was a melancholy feel to the boat that evening, echoes of partings and endings. It made her feel terribly weepy, so that when she entered what she thought was an empty cabin and felt Giorgio's Italian arms around her, fingers already meandering under her sweater on to the skin beneath, she felt only relief and a sudden rush of contentment.

'Hm, again?' she muttered when her lips were free. She

thought fleetingly of Sojo, whom she had hugged and kissed goodbye only a few hours ago with tears in her eyes, and waited for a tint of guilt to stain the pure white bliss of lust but no remorse came, perhaps because she had watched Sojo inveigle the still-adoring Nöjd into helping her carry her bags off the ship and accompanying her on the train to London.

'Oh, Giorgio,' Marsha said again as she found they were both lying down on one of the bottom bunks and that not only her sweater but also her slip and her bra had somehow disappeared.

'Is okay, okay.'

And somehow it was. Marsha, having thought she would never ever make love with Giorgio a second time, found herself being pleasured all over again. It seemed a fitting ending for the voyage, and for the beginning of her new life in France.

Daisy was also beginning her new life that day. Instead of catching the train to Manchester as she had planned, she found herself in a car driving to Kent with Leo and a rather formidable woman with a bosom like a ship's mast and a pink suit more suitable to a royal garden party than standing about Southhampton docks waiting for her son to disembark.

The man driving the car, Leo's father, was small, sturdy and laconic, speaking only when he was spoken to. But his eyes were warm as well as sharp, and Daisy took to him at once. Unfortunately, he was to die only a fortnight later of a sudden massive heart attack, leaving Alma, his wife, to soldier on valiantly and grumbling for at least the next thirty years.

'What does your father do, dear?' Alma asked, not very pleasantly in spite of the endearment and a fixed smile on her face. She had not been pleased when Leo, returning home to his rightful place on the farm after five years abroad, insisted that this tiny dolly-bird with a too-short skirt accompany them.

'He's a solicitor,' Daisy replied.

'That's nice, dear.'

'So is my mother.'

This, unfortunately, was not so nice. Though impressed, Alma nonetheless disapproved. She prided herself on never having worked a day outside the home and wouldn't even help her husband on the farm, believing firmly that a woman's place was inside. She wasn't indolent: she cleaned and tidied and baked; she joined the WI and became president; she worked at one of the charity shops two afternoons a week. 'I just don't know where the day goes,' she sighed to the other women at the coffee morning every Tuesday. 'There just doesn't seem to be enough time.'

Alma looked at Daisy again, obliquely in the driving mirror. The girl looked like a tart in that short dress with the funny high waist, and all that straight lank hair falling into her eyes. Alma really was dreadfully disappointed. First Leo went off without so much as a by-your-leave instead of staying home on the farm, helping his father, joining the Young Farmers and Young Conservatives and settling down with one of the local landowner's daughters. Then, instead of arriving home chastened and repentant, here he was with some little floozy with a cheeky smile and bare knees.

'Should we stop for a drink?' Leo's father said, driving into the car park of a large, rather imposing pub.

At the pub Daisy found a public telephone, where she surreptitiously rang her parents to tell them she had arrived safely but would be a few days late getting home to

Manchester. Of her changed plans, she kept silent. She had no doubt at all what their reaction would be.

Hal and Emmeline, on the train to London, were also silent, each wondering what the city would bring to them. Success in the theatre, any kind of success, was what Hal was longing for. Hal, was what Emmeline wanted. How politically incorrect that was, Emmeline was not to realise until many years later – not that she would have cared at that moment if she had.

The train came in at Paddington and they took the underground to Charing Cross. 'Trafalgar Square!' Emmeline shouted as they stood amongst the pigeons, amongst the tourists, and stared up at the immense lions. 'I've seen it so often in pictures, and here it is, here I am! Oh God, I've never seen so many pigeons in my life!'

Hal laughed and leapt down the steps two at a time, dragging Em with him. 'I'll show you Trafalgar Square when there isn't a pigeon in sight.'

'I don't believe it.'

'True. I promise you.'

'It's a deal!' They kissed on it, and then hand-in-hand walked down to the Embankment, still carrying their bags, and down to Waterloo Bridge and over it to the other side, and then around across to Charing Cross bridge and back where they started. 'Oh London, London, I love you!' Emmeline cried to the lions as they sat on the steps and ate the fish and chips they had bought, still wrapped in newspaper much to the delight of Emmeline.

Hal, watching her, was moved by her clear, uncomplicated joy. He felt cleansed, purged by it, and was grateful. Em made him feel buoyant, hopeful; she diluted the black despair that sometimes came over him with her lightness, her shining optimism. He wanted to hold on to her for ever, shield her from hurt, just as she shielded him from his own bleak moments. 'Oh Em, I do love you,' he murmured, and as he said it, felt it to be true. He was filled by such a calm, sweet happiness that he grabbed Emmeline, hugged her so tightly and for so long that she looked at him questioningly, wondering if something was wrong.

Suddenly exuberant, Hal kissed her soundly, whirled her around, and then, to her astonishment, rushed away from her, back towards the Underground station. He returned almost at once with four or five bouquets of flowers, chrysanthemums, all colours and sizes, which he unwrapped one by one and threw gallantly at her, much to the delight of some French schoolchildren clustered nearby.

They stayed for a week or so with Hal's father in Shepherd's Bush. He was a teacher at one of London's minor public schools, and slightly embittered by it all, the world and his place in it. He felt cheated for being fifty-five in what was beginning to be Swinging London, though it had not been named as such yet. He had married late, to a colleague who taught games, and who had left him when the boy was five years old. Hal shunted between the two of them for the next twelve or thirteen years until his acting skills, and a good Drama A-Level created the opportunity to go to the States with the rep company.

Hal's father mostly ignored Hal and Emmeline when they arrived, which was fine with them both. His mother, living in Dundee now, was no problem; a phone call and a vague promise to visit her sometime seemed to satisfy her. Emmeline occupied the hard narrow bed in Hal's old room while Hal bedded down on the sofa; this clearly was unsatisfactory, and Em made plans to move to her own place.

With Hal's help she finally found a reasonable bed-sitting room in a clean, rambling house in Earl's Court, not far from the Underground station.

'This is so neat, just what I want,' Emmeline enthused on the day she moved in. She and Hal had just been to Woolworths to buy a couple of cheap saucepans, some plates and cutlery, tea towels and other basics, and Em was happily putting them away in the tiny cupboard above the Baby Belling cooker. It was the first time she had lived away from home other than the past three summers doing summer stock, or rep theatre as she supposed they called it here, in the hills of North Carolina. She felt very grown-up and wise.

Hal was making a curry, breaking off now and then to whirl Emmeline around the tiny room as his old radio, which he had given to Em, blared out Sonny and Cher's hit '*I got you, Babe*'. The pungent smell of spices pervaded the tiny room with its one easy chair, a single bed against the wall which doubled as a sofa during the day, a tiny sink and cooker. They had had a crazy, idyllic day, for the weather was unseasonably hot for late September in London, and they had spent it first doing their domestic bit, moving Emmeline's few possessions into the bed-sit and doing their necessary shopping, and then wandering to Carnaby Street where the tiny boutiques with names like Domino Male jostled each other for space, spilling out pop music from their open doors. They browsed through a shop selling 1920s dresses and Victorian shawls, another displaying outlandish art nouveau cufflinks and earrings under huge photographs of Mick Jagger and the other Rolling Stones. Finding a tiny coffee shop with one empty table in the corner, they grabbed it and ordered two espressos. Hal picked up a newspaper someone had left on the table while Emmeline watched, with fascination, the people around her. Music from a radio somewhere filled the tiny coffee bar with sound, the Byrds' hit version of a Dylan song: '*Hey, Mr Tambourine Man*'. Em hummed along, tapped her feet, swayed with the rhythm.

'Che Guevera's left Cuba but no one knows quite where he is,' Hal said, not looking up from the paper. 'Sounds bloody fishy to me. Oh God, not again, yet another group of old-timers protesting against the Beatles' MBE. Listen to this . . .'

Hal read her bits and pieces — a snippet of a speech by the Prime Minister, Harold Wilson; a short item about a New York University graduate arrested for burning his draft card; part of an article on Malcolm X who had been assassinated earlier in the year. But Emmeline couldn't concentrate. On this heady day her own life was far too exciting for her to focus on world news. She stared, entranced, at the people around her: two young women wearing such sheer blouses that they might as well be completely topless; young men with hair that seemed to be getting longer and longer wearing what looked liked all-in-one flared trousers and waistcoats; skirts that made her own modest minis seem dreary and long; and everywhere a profusion of colour, music, babble.

Later, not wanting to be indoors on such a perfect day, they wandered around Hyde Park, ending up lying on the grass, talking about starting drama school the following week.

'I'd love my own theatre company eventually,' Hal said. 'I don't just want to act, I want to direct, produce, be involved with the set design, everything. I'd like to have a core of dedicated people to work with, so that I can listen to their ideas, learn from them. And I want to do plays I believe in.

136

There're so many playwrights I'd like to direct – Osborne, Joe Orton. And Pinter, God, how I'd like to stage a Pinter play.' Hal and Emmeline had just been to see *The Homecoming* at the Aldwych Theatre, and were still talking about it.

'I can't wait to start next week,' Em said. 'We can work together, won't it be fun?'

Hal agreed. 'We can do scenes together, help each other. Next week drama school; next year, the world!'

'Those theatre programmes, right? *Henry Allen and Emmeline Lake.*'

'Right!' Hal lay back on the grass, eyes half-closed against the sun. Emmeline looked at his dear sweet face and said, suddenly troubled, 'I'll get so much from you, Hal. You're so much more experienced than me, you've done so much professional theatre already. But what will you get from me?'

Hal sat up and ran his fingers through her hair which looked the same colour as the sunlight streaming through it and said lovingly, 'I get so much from you, Emmeline. You'll never know just how much I get from you.' He put his arms around her and held her like a lifeline, and did not let her go for a long, long time.

When they finally got back to Earl's Court and ate a rather late curry, the weather had completely changed. It had begun to rain, lightly at first but by eleven o'clock that night it was thundering down. They were cosy enough in the tiny basement room; they had switched on the small one-bar electric fire even though it wasn't cold, only damp. Hal had bought Emmeline a Buffy St Marie album for a 'bed-sit warming' present, and with it an old second-hand record player he had found in Carnaby Street. Buffy crooned about love in her wonderful American-Indian voice as they half-sat, half-reclined together on the bed-settee, sharing another bottle of rather lukewarm white wine.

Hal took Emmeline's hand and kissed it, then kissed her lips, gently, sweetly. She kissed him back with more eagerness than she had intended; the wine was making her soft, pliant.

He pulled slightly away and stroked her hair again. After a moment he said, 'I promised to show you Trafalgar Square without pigeons, right? Well come on, let's go!'

'What, now? You're crazy!'

'Yup. Come on, right now, before we have a chance to think about it. Better grab a raincoat or something.'

The rain was torrential and they ran for the Underground, but they did not have much time to dry off before they reached Charing Cross. By then it was almost midnight and if anything, raining even harder as they rushed into Trafalgar Square and stood there under the lions, giggling and clinging to each other.

'Look, Emmeline — no pigeons! I told you I'd take you here when there were no pigeons and no tourists. Isn't it worth getting drenched?'

Emmeline laughed and reached out to touch his wet face and he kissed her hand and grinned. 'God, I can hardly see you. It's like standing in a waterfall, but it's a warm rain, isn't it? It's a warm night.'

'It's the most beautiful night there has ever been!' Emmeline exulted, the water pouring through her long hair and running like a river over her breasts.

'And what a day it was before the rain began! Wasn't it a perfect day, Em? Have you ever had such a perfect day?'

When they got back to Earl's Court they were soaked down to their underwear, which they stripped off in separate corners of the bed-sit, their backs demurely turned to each other. Emmeline felt slightly awkward, exposed, yet strangely excited, and wondered if Hal was feeling the same, wondered if tonight would be the night when they would make love for the first time. She mostly wanted it, but she was frightened, also. Like Marsha, she had been brought up in a strict, religious family where sex was a punishable offence outside the sanctity of marriage. She didn't believe in that now, didn't go to church any more either, but vestiges of purity remained or, if not purity, the fear of being slightly sullied, slightly worn. She no longer believed in Hell and damnation, but some core in her refused to disperse entirely the belief that a woman should remain pure and virginal until her wedding night.

And she was, after all, still very young, for in those days, eighteen was young, perhaps more so in America, in those adolescent days of cheerleaders, and bobby sox, and pom poms, and earnestness. The sixties, those decadent, faraway times, were virtually unheard-of in the small southern town where Emmeline was brought up. Though not quite as sheltered as Marsha, having been to a co-educational high school, and having had a few summers away from home with a theatre company, she was still in many ways very much a product of her upbringing.

And so when Hal, unlike Leo with Daisy, and Giorgio with Sojo (and Marsha, though Emmeline was never to know of this), did not try to whisk her immediately off to bed with him, she was at first relieved, for, though she would have gone more than willingly, she thought that on the whole it was better they didn't. There was all that messy business about contraception, for one thing, though naturally Sojo had told them all about the Pill one evening in their cabin when they were getting ready to go out to the disco. Daisy had admitted that she was on it too, which slightly shocked Emmeline. But Daisy was so obviously in love, and so wallowing in her newly-discovered sexuality, that she was a shining example of the new liberation that the Pill was expected to bring to women.

'You really must get on it,' Daisy had told Em one night on one of her fleeting visits to London.

'Hal and I . . . well, we're not exactly sleeping together. Not yet.'

Daisy, sensual and blooming, was rather surprised by this, but understanding. 'Taking it slowly? I suppose that's not a bad thing.' She looked somewhat doubtful.

'I'm not against sex before marriage,' Emmeline said hastily. 'It's just that . . . well, like you said, we're not rushing things.'

Daisy nodded wisely, feeling much more than a year older than Emmeline. 'I think you ought to go on the Pill, you know. Now. I know a birth-control clinic, the Marie Stopes Clinic, that prescribes the Pill to single girls. You and Hal are bound to take the plunge eventually and it's better to be prepared.'

Emmeline listened, but did not take the advice. What she could not bring herself to tell Daisy (because she did not want to appear to be criticising her and Leo's relationship) was that she was relieved that Hal was not pressing her to sleep with him because she wanted to marry him, and live happily ever after with him, and felt that he, like her, was content to wait until that happened. Before Hal, marriage had never entered her mind: she wanted an acting career, nothing else. But meeting Hal had changed everything. Simply, she was no longer listening to the sixties injunction of doing whatever

it was you wanted to do (as long as you hurt no one else)
— but rather the old Biblical cry of whither thou goest I will
go: full stop. And though Hal hadn't mentioned marriage
yet, his actions, his words, implied that they would certainly
be together for a long time, which, Emmeline knew in her
heart, would eventually lead to the inevitable: marriage,
children, the lot.

And so, in short, she felt she had plenty of time.
Inexperienced herself, except for a few encounters with
spotty and awkward youths who groped her inexpertly in
the back of their father's car, she intuited correctly that Hal
was too, and she rather relished having weeks, months, even
years to get to know each other slowly, their bodies as well
as their minds and their souls.

The fact that Hal was not like the one or two post-
pubescent gropers she had come across, and treated her
gently, tenderly, did not strike her as strange. They had
their fair share of kissing, and cuddling, and the fact that
Hal never took these proceedings any further was, to her, a
mark of his respect for her. Emmeline had grown up hearing
that word often: it was something a decent Christian boy
was always supposed to have for decent Christian girls. The
books and magazines Emmeline read when she was thirteen,
fourteen, fifteen, upheld this idea: a boy treated a girl like a
lady, like a chaste princess, like a madonna.

Whether Emmeline, whose incredulous eyes had been
widely opened on the *Castel Felice*, still really believed
this, was hard to say, but because Hal apparently did,
she chose to as well. It was not as if she condemned
Daisy and Leo, or Sojo and Giorgio, but rather that she
felt, in a slightly smug manner (and of course she could
never tell Daisy this), that she and Hal were somehow

different, somehow special, for taking their time, waiting, letting their love grow and expand, letting it breathe for a time in a cerebral space before jumping into carnality and pure animal passions.

And so when Emmeline suddenly found herself naked in a tiny bed-sit frantically trying to dry herself with a small inadequate towel, with Hal doing the same in the opposite corner, she was suddenly plunged into a profound embarrassment. But she needn't have worried, for sneaking a surreptitious look at Hal, she had a glimpse of a bony, elongated back and neat white buttocks, both of which were turned firmly to her. She dressed quickly in a long baggy shirt and dry underpants, and any awkwardness was soon dispelled by the sight of Hal in her old flowery dressing gown, for he had nothing else to wear.

'Well, I suppose you have me for the night,' Hal said as they both laughed. 'I daren't venture out in the streets of London in this, and my clothes are saturated.'

'Plenty of room,' Emmeline replied, and they both looked around them at the cramped little space and laughed again.

They slept together in the narrow bed that night, sharing one pillow, holding each other and listening to Buffy crooning on the record player about making spaces for each other in their separate lives. They kissed a bit, caressed, talked and murmured silly, endearing things to each other, and still Buffy sang on fatalistically about staying on only until it was time to go for good. Hal drifted off into a deep but fitful sleep while Emmeline felt the warmth of his body, heard his erratic sighs and kept awake and vigilant the whole night. They hadn't had sex, but to Emmeline they had made love, for what else could you call it, this intimacy, this sharing a bed, this touching and holding? She felt strangely contented and in command, as if in the act of denying themselves, they were building up to a longer, more secure future together.

Sojo showed up in Earl's Court one day, carrying an old battered suitcase and wearing long white plastic boots with her ubiquitous hot pants. Emmeline came home from her class one afternoon, glanced through the open door of the bed-sit opposite and found Sojo chatting to the Australian occupant. She was sitting on his bed and sharing his tea and sausage rolls as if she had known him for months.

'Sojo, I haven't seen you in weeks!' Emmeline shouted. 'I tried to write to you at that place you and Nöjd stayed at in Finsbury Court.'

'What a dump. Yuk. I never got your letter.'

'How did you find me here, then?'

'Hal's father. I thought you were still there so I phoned.'

'Where's Nöjd?'

'At Finsbury Court. I couldn't bear it any more.'

'Your bed-sit was pretty grimy, I remember.'

'No, dopey, not the bed-sit. I couldn't bear Nöjd. All that posing in front of mirrors. The only fire in his loins, sugar, burned strictly for himself. Yuk.'

The Australian, who was listening to all this with salacious pleasure, said, 'Cor, how 'bout trying me, Sheila?'

'Very funny,' Sojo said witheringly then, more benignly, 'Thanks for the tea, buddy. Em, which is your room?'

They talked all night, and in the morning Emmeline left Sojo sound asleep in her bed while she went off to her classes. 'We'll have to find her a place to stay,' Hal said when she told him about Sojo during their first break. 'You can't both live in your tiny room. She can always stay with me at my Dad's place for a few days; at least it's bigger than yours.'

But when Emmeline returned to Earl's Court that evening Sojo had already solved her housing problem. 'Here I am, Emmy baby,' she called as Em began unlocking her room. She was standing at the door of the other basement room, the Australian's, and he was behind her unwrapping something out of a paper bag and throwing it into a saucepan. 'Les here has said I could move in with him for a while, till I can sort something out. He's got lots more room than you, sugar, and is happy to share.' Les grinned dazedly and offered them a beer. 'Let me do that, sweetie pie,' she said to him, taking away his rather grotty spatula. 'Now, do you have any spices here? Paprika, that sort of thing?'

A few weeks later, when Marsha showed up from France, Sojo was still living in Les' bed-sit. 'Are they lovers, or what?' Marsha demanded, Europe and Experience having made her exceptionally outspoken.

'I don't ask, Marsha. There's only one bed, a double one.'

'Well, of course they're lovers then. You don't sleep in one bed and not have sex, for goodness sake.'

Emmeline started to protest but Marsha interrupted. 'I thought Sojo wanted to go to Italy. Has she heard anything from Giorgio?'

'Yes, she had a letter last week. He's at sea again. Sojo's still trying to get there. Anyway, never mind her for now, tell me about you! You know you're welcome to stay with me until you can find a place, but we'll have to take turns sleeping on cushions on the floor. I'm sure you can stay at Hal's dad's place. We were going to put Sojo there before she found Les.'

'Thanks, Em. I need to find some work, waitressing or anything, so that I can get back to France next spring. I miss it already and I've only just left.'

'So why did you leave?'

Marsha sighed, settling herself back in the easy chair. She had had her hair cut very short, all wonderful angles, and it suited her. She was wearing a flattering black trouser suit; the trousers were flared, the jacket was hip-length and collarless, very simple and very becoming. Emmeline had seen something very similar on Jean Shrimpton in a glossy magazine, and though Marsha was quite a bit plumper than the model, she now carried her weight with much more self-confidence.

'Why did I leave? Well, if you must know, my dear Emmeline, I was fired. My nice respectable Catholic family fired me.'

'Goodness. Why?'

'Because I had an affair with Madame's younger brother, Jean-Luc.'

'Gosh. An affair? You?' It came out before Emmeline could stop herself.

Marsha smiled secretly to herself. How young Emmeline was, she thought; she had never really realised before. Marsha looked at her with all the sagacity and experience of her twenty-two years. 'It happens,' she said primly. 'Even to good Catholic girls such as myself.'

Emmeline listened, fascinated, while Marsha told her the story. It seemed Jean-Luc was only in his mid-twenties himself, being some twelve years younger than Madame. He was living with his sister and family at their home in Paris, studying dentistry, and so had ample opportunity to get to know Marsha, in every meaning of the word.

'But surely,' Emmeline wanted to know, 'the family couldn't have been that against it? You are both unattached; it's not as if he were married or something.'

'Jean-Luc was not exactly discreet about it towards

the end. He, uh, suggested one afternoon that we, er, have a siesta in Madame and Monsieur's big double bed with the pure goose-down eiderdown. We had our own beds, you understand, but narrow and uncomfortable, and unfortunately in separate rooms. And then there was the cold spell—'

'The cold spell?'

'Yes, a freak snowstorm, freezing temperatures, and it only being late November. Haven't you had it here?'

'Well, yes, it has been bitter. I've spent a fortune on this electric heater.'

'So you can start to understand. You know what the Europeans are like for central heating, they seem not to really believe in it. I mean, it's freezing in here now, can't you feel it?'

'Now that you mention it . . .'

'Anyway, neither Jean-Luc nor I had a lick of heating in our rooms. And there was Madame and Monsieur's big double bed with the goose eiderdown, and a big fireplace with a decent supply of coal, and Madame and Monsieur out for the whole day.'

'And the children?'

'Simone and Pierre were visiting friends, and not due back until the evening.'

'I see,' Emmeline murmured faintly. She moved the electric fire closer to Marsha.

Marsha, smugly, was sure she didn't, but let it pass. 'It was a lovely afternoon,' she mused. 'There was still frost on the grass outside, but Jean-Luc and I were snug and warm under that quilt—'

'Weren't you nervous?' Emmeline interrupted, still unable to believe this was Marsha telling her all this.

'No, why? We had the house to ourselves, hours to fool about in . . .' she trailed off and looked lubriciously into space.

'Well, uh, what happened? I mean, did Jean-Luc's sister and her husband come home and catch you?'

'Oh, much worse. It was the children.'

'Oh no! They caught you in bed?'

'Not exactly. Their young friend had become ill, and the father brought Simone and Pierre home early. Jean-Luc and I suddenly heard footsteps running upstairs and the dulcet voices of those awful children calling, '*Maman, Papa?* Where are you?'

'Oh Marsha, I'd have died,' Emmeline cried.

'Yes, well, I nearly did. Especially as they had interrupted during a particularly pleasant moment.' Her eyes glazed over at the thought of it.

They were both silent for a moment, Emmeline suddenly stung by an unexpected envy; Marsha overcome by pleasurable nostalgia.

'So go on,' Emmeline said, breaking the silence.

'We did the obvious, dived under the covers. The little horrors ran in the bedroom thinking it was their mother and father playing games, hiding from them like they sometimes do on a Sunday morning before church. They bounced on the bed and started prattling on about their day, with Jean-Luc and I bare-fanny naked under the covers.'

'Oh dear.'

'In the end Jean-Luc, pretending to be his brother-in-law – he can imitate anyone's voice, and it was muffled under the sheets – somehow got the kids out. We got dressed *tout de suite*, came down discreetly – and from different directions – and said their parents had suddenly remembered an appointment and gone out for a bit.'

'How clever you are, Marsha. I'd never have thought of anything like that.'

Marsha sighed. 'The trouble was, it didn't work. When the parents came back that evening and were kissing their little darlings good night, the revolting creatures started to beg them to play that game again, "the one we played this afternoon, *Maman, Papa,* up in bed with you, when you hid under the eiderdown". It didn't take long for Madame and Monsieur to figure things out. I was immediately dismissed, for corrupting minors. I must say I was surprised; I thought the French were much more liberal than that. Father Jerome, who found me the place, did say that it was a strict decent Catholic family I was going to. Goodness, to think I was actually overjoyed when he told me that. How foolish one is when one is young,' she finished rather pompously.

'Oh Marsha, I'm so sorry.'

Marsha rubbed her hands in front of the electric fire. 'I'm not,' she said cheerfully. 'I hated the job. I only regret leaving Jean-Luc. That's why I've got to get back there in the spring; he'll be finished with his dental college by then and hopefully will have a job, and help me find one.'

As Emmeline made up her bed for Marsha, and one for herself on the floor, she found it difficult to equate the shy, diffident young woman she had met on the boat with this outspoken, extremely sophisticated person who somehow managed to make her feel like a slightly backward child. 'Marsha,' she said as they got into their beds, 'how did it feel to . . . you know, to lose your virginity. I mean, you had a religious upbringing just like me. Did you feel guilty?'

As Emmeline shut off the light Marsha smiled to herself,

thinking of Giorgio. 'No, honey, not in the slightest. Why, did you feel guilty with Hal?'

Em wondered crossly why everyone assumed she and Hal were having sex. 'We're not lovers,' she said curtly.

Marsha sat up in bed and peered down at Em, studying her face in the pale light of the streetlamp coming through the thinly curtained window. 'Hey, okay, don't be so defensive. That's the great thing about these times, you can do your own thing. If you don't want to sleep with him—'

'But I do!' Emmeline suddenly cried, realising as she said it that it was true. 'I love him so much!'

'Well then, it'll happen. Stay cool, Em. When you feel it's right, it'll happen.'

Before Emmeline could reply there was an imperious banging on the door. 'Let me in, it's me, Sojo. I just got in and got your note. Open the goddamn door!' Emmeline opened the door and Marsha and Sojo threw themselves into each other's arms, shrieking and exclaiming and greeting each other like two old comrades-in-arms. After a moment they broke apart, drew Emmeline in, and hugged and laughed all over again.

'All we need is Daisy,' Sojo said. 'What a reunion it would be then.'

'She's with Leo, on the farm. Should we surprise them with a visit?'

'We could easily get a train down to Kent.'

'It's Saturday tomorrow; you don't have classes on Saturday, do you, Emmeline? Let's go in the morning.'

They all agreed that this was a splendid idea and began throwing things in overnight bags then and there, to be ready to catch the earliest train available. After just a few hours' sleep – for they couldn't stop talking, there was so much to catch up on — they were at Charing Cross British Rail station, waiting for the train to Canterbury, to find Daisy and to pick up where they had left off on the now, to them, legendary boat where it had all begun, so fortuitously and so well. They had every certainty that it would go on as it had started, joyful and sanguine and sublime everlastingly, just as they themselves would be enduringly hopeful, forever young.

Forever young. Waiting for the train, excited by the heavy flurry of snow that had suddenly, miraculously, begun, Emmeline knew with ineffable certainty that the future, always so tantalisingly out of reach, was here rushing to meet her, to take her by the hand and run with her. Confident, assured and serene, she boarded the train for the next journey.

Chapter Seven

I t is snowing in Canterbury now, the first time it has snowed this early in the year (it is only mid-November) since the 1960s. Emmeline found the farm lane covered with an inch or two of white when she left for the university this morning, and it is still coming down now, fat fuzzy flakes which attack her windshield like lacy spiders. She is as excited as a child, as she was all those years ago when she and Sojo and Marsha arrived at the Westgate Station to find Canterbury white and gleaming in that other freak, unexpected snowfall. Having lived in the Southern States for most of her life, where snowfall is rare, she finds it an unexpected treat.

She is not alone in this. Her students, a few of whom she sees running about the campus romping in the snow like puppies, are red-cheeked and high on the buzz the snow has given them. She wonders wryly what their attendance will be at their seminar today. She herself has a staff seminar, but that's not until the afternoon. This morning she will be in her office, working on a paper, and just being around in case any of her students need to see her with any problems or whatever. She looks forward to having the whole morning to herself; she doubts whether any students will tear themselves away from the festive white campus outside to seek pastoral care today.

First, she goes into the Senior Common Room for coffee and one of the apple doughnuts to which she has become partial. She nods to a couple of lecturers she vaguely knows and settles in comfortably in the warm, plush room. Outside through one of the large windows she can see the snow still coming down; the trees and the ground are covered with it. Settling with her decaffeinated coffee and a newspaper, she begins to read the lead story on the front page when Clem Todd, carrying his coffee and a Danish pastry, says disgruntledly, 'Snow, that's just what we need. I'm giving a lecture at twelve and I'll bet the hall is half-empty, our dedicated and committed students running about making snowmen or some such thing.' He sits down next to Emmeline.

'Don't be silly, Clem, you know your lectures are always full,' she says. She went to one the first week she was here, and her students were enthralled by Clem, not so much by what he said, but by the way he said it. He had style, Emmeline had to admit. He had begun his career as a vigorous young trendy lecturer, dressing not unlike the students themselves but with more flair and subtle sophistication, and often joining them in the Junior Common Room for coffee and conversation – implying that he preferred it to the somewhat sterile atmosphere of the senior one. The students loved this, of course, and felt he was one of them. To be fair, he was genuinely concerned with them, and good with them, but this did not mean he wasn't concerned also with his image. That initial image has not altered, even though he is now forty-four and can't, technically, be classified as young, though he still of course thinks of himself as such.

Since that unfortunate night in the pub a few weeks ago, when Emmeline had seen Clem across a crowded room and come eyeball to eyeball with his wife, Clem has been circumspect in his relations with Em. Now, however, having just been adored in the drama studio by two nubile young women students, having given up some of his free time to advise them on a scene they were rehearsing for a workshop production, he has quite forgotten his wife and is in good form to try again with Emmeline.

'By the way,' he begins, after getting himself and Em another coffee, for both are loath to leave the warmth of the Common Room and cross through the snow to their office, 'I've got tickets to see *Volcano* in London this Saturday night. Have you read about the play? A brilliant production, apparently. Henry Allen is in it, and he's had rave reviews. Would you like to go?'

Emmeline feels her blood thin, become watery, ineffectual. She still has not got used to the proximity of Hal, only sixty-odd miles away in London. Daisy had asked her again if she wanted to book tickets and she had replied firmly that she did not. She knows she cannot face Hal ever again, not even from the distance of thirty years and across a proscenium arch. She doesn't want to anyway. Some things, she knows, are better left untouched, left to memory, left to time.

'Can't your wife make it to the play?' Emmeline asks, hedging.

'Celia is not much interested in theatre,' Clem says shortly. This is not entirely true, for Celia is quite catholic in her taste: she just likes to go out, anywhere, any time. Where there are crowds of people, where something is going on, whether it is a pop concert or a Shakespeare play or a night at the pub, there Celia likes to be. She is not at all selective.

'Thank you, it's kind of you, but I've been invited out to dinner that night with some friends.' Emmeline, with great relief, has suddenly remembered this.

'What a pity. You couldn't possibly . . .?'

'No, it's all arranged. I couldn't change the date now.'

Clem nods. Well, Celia will be pleased, he thinks truculently. He wonders where Emmeline is going, and with whom, and hints, 'Anything exciting?'

'Just a dinner party,' she says enigmatically. 'But it should be fun.'

'Welcome, welcome, welcome!' Marjorie Brackenbury shouts from the doorway of her big white house, and an avalanche of snow slides down from the balcony into the tiny front walled garden.

It is Saturday night and the temperature has remained at freezing all week, with intermittent snow falling every day, sometimes slight, sometimes heavy. 'I can't remember weather like this in November, not for years anyway,' Daisy says as they climb out of Leo's sturdy estate car with the four-wheel drive which has safely brought them into town. Leo has managed to keep the lane up to the farm clear but the roads are icy, treacherous. It is beginning to snow again now.

The Brackenburys live outside the West Gate in an area called St Dunstan's. Their house is one of a picturesque terrace with huge bow windows, four storeys, and a dinky wrought-iron balcony outside the first-floor window. Their basement floor is usually let to students, but they and their three children manage to fill the rest quite efficiently.

Across the road and just down a few yards, Clem and Celia Todd are leaving their house – a newer brick building, rather square and imposing – and rushing to their car which is parked outside. Clem is cross because due to a tantrum by their daughter, they are running quite late. He is also in a vile mood because the forecast is for more snow and it will be deadly driving back tonight. Being stranded in London because of the snow with Emmeline, tucked away into a comfortable but discreet hotel, would have been entirely to his liking, but the thought of it happening with Celia makes him cringe.

Celia is already in the car when Clem hears Marjorie bellowing her welcome to the entire street and, looking up, sees Emmeline's enticing legs, encased in black velvet, going into the Brackenbury's house with that Dillard couple, the people she lives with. Then, a moment later, a yellow van drives up and the driver, seeing Clem, says coldly but politely, 'Are you just leaving? I'll back up and wait for your space.'

Clem nods, infuriated. It's that yobbo builder, that bat fanatic, and Clem intuits rightly that he also is going across the street for dinner. Revving unnecessarily loudly, Clem drives off, his evening now thoroughly spoiled. He has never liked the man, and he likes less the idea of him hanging around Emmeline. Perhaps he should abandon his pursuit of her, he muses, nearly hitting a red sports car as he pulls out into the road. She is confirming all his prejudices about Americans being totally devoid of taste.

Tony parks his van, glaring distastefully at the Todds' Rover pulling away. He bangs the brass lion's head knocker on the brightly painted blue door and Marjorie hollers, 'Wonderful to see you,' kisses him boisterously, and whisks him upstairs to the first floor where the living room is.

'I'm not too early?' Tony asks.

'Not at all. Leo was concerned about the snow, which is why we decided to start so much earlier than usual. Have some mulled wine.'

The others are already seated, holding thin ceramic wine cups and sipping the contents gratefully. A small woodburning stove glows with flame and heat, and from the sofa next to it, Emmeline smiles at him. He greets the others and sits down next to her.

'And how is a Southerner like you coping with all this snow?' he asks.

'Great fun. It's like being on a permanent holiday. Nothing seems quite real.'

Barnaby, sitting opposite on another small settee, Daisy next to him, says, 'The bookshop is dripping with every cold and flu virus imaginable. I can hardly hear what the customers say to me with all the sneezing and coughing and nose-blowing going on. My books will be contaminated for months with germs secreted by browsers. I suggest you buy your Christmas presents at Waterstone's; they seem to attract a healthier clientèle than I do.'

From across the room Marjorie cries, 'Now, now, no shop talk, Barnaby. You have an entire weekend off, the first time you haven't worked on a Saturday for ages, and probably the last time, I should imagine. What's the point of having that jolly nice and efficient assistant if you can't relax and have proper days off?'

Barnaby smiles vaguely at his wife's admonishments and then is distracted by his three daughters, who suddenly appear, their television programme over, to be kissed goodnight and put to bed. Barnaby says, 'I'll take them up, love. You're doing the dinner.'

'No, no, no, no. The girls and I can manage quite well

without you, can't we, darlings? You attend to our guests. There is oodles of mulled wine in the kitchen; go and refill everyone's cup.'

Barnaby does as he is told, but there is a wistful expression on his face as he lingers for a moment, watching Marjorie briskly and efficiently whisk away the children. When he has gone, Leo, who has been sitting in a dark blue armchair in the corner, says, 'The rewiring is almost finished now, Tony. Thanks for all your help with the bats.'

Tony has been at Woodland Farm three or four times since his first visit to inspect the attic; he usually comes in the evening, to check that the work done by the electricians has been carried out to plan and has not disturbed the bats who seem to be roosting there for the winter.

'It's not usual for bats to roost in buildings like that; usually they leave by autumn and find somewhere underground to winter – disused mine-shafts, that sort of thing,' Tony says. 'Sometimes, though, some of the brown long-eared stay behind, like at your place.'

'Is that what Clem Todd had in his house that time?' Daisy asks.

'No, they were pipistrelles. They're so small they can get into the tiniest gaps imaginable. A colony of pregnant females had gathered in the walls behind some outside hanging tiles.'

'So that's how you know Clem,' Emmeline says. 'Did he call you in to advise him what to do about them?'

Tony grins. 'As a matter of fact, he had called me in as a builder. I was supposed to tear down the old tiles and replace them with new, along with part of the wall. As soon as I got up there to look around I found the bats.'

'Clem had a fit,' Daisy says. 'Tony suggested he wait until

autumn when the bats were gone to do the job but Clem wouldn't hear of it.'

'What a dilemma,' Emmeline murmurs.

'Not at all,' Tony replies. 'There was no way I was going to do the job then. The whole maternity roost would have been destroyed. So Clem fired me and hired another builder immediately.'

'Oh no! So the bats were killed?'

'No, luckily. I called in the Nature Conservation Organisation and the work was stopped before the new builder had even set up his scaffolding.'

Emmeline looks at Tony inquisitively. 'So that's why you dislike Clem so much.'

Tony shrugs. 'He was totally unreasonable about the bats. It only meant a delay of several months, but he wouldn't even listen when I tried to explain.' He grimaces. 'I could have used that job, too. I had just come back from six months backpacking in South America and was pretty skint.'

'Goodness. On your own?' As soon as Emmeline says this she remembers what Daisy had told her about that trip, that Tony had split up with the woman he was living with during the journey.

'Yes,' Tony says after a slight hesitation. 'I did most of the trip by myself.'

He hadn't started travelling alone. He had begun with Carrie, the woman he lived with, and with another couple, friends of hers. Malcolm and Irene were teachers of Spanish who were taking a year off to practise their language, come to grips with South America.

Within a couple of weeks, before they had even left Lima, Carrie and Malcolm were continuing an affair they had begun a month or two earlier, except that this time they were less discreet, and a distraught Irene confronted Carrie with her suspicions. Carrie, breaking down with either guilt or, more likely, a calculated hope that Irene would return home with Tony and so leave her and Malcolm on their own, confessed all, but unfortunately for her, things backfired. Malcolm, horrified at the disclosure, felt his infatuation for Carrie disappear without a trace like a stone in quicksand, and without a backward glance at his ex-lover whisked Irene off on the next plane to Mexico, determined that a fresh start in a new place would be what he and Irene needed to put this unfortunate and — as he saw it now with opened eyes — insignificant episode behind him.

Tony, unfortunately for Carrie, was in no way interested in a fresh start and instead resolutely left her crying in the hotel in Lima as he packed his rucksack and set off for Lake Titicaca, determined to complete the trip as intended. When he returned from Peru Carrie met him at the door of his house, contrite and loving, not having bothered to move out because she was sure she could get around him. She did really love him, she had decided, and saw no reason why their easy and amicable living arrangement needed to be changed. But South America had changed *him*, sanded and polished him like a desert stone, and he greeted her stone-heartedly. That he could not forgive her was the excuse he gave her, but in reality, had he still loved her, of course he would have, for he was basically kind and hopeful and understanding of human foibles. More important, perhaps, he was not cursed with any excess of male vanity, and so it was not his ego that Carrie had damaged, but something softer, truer, more vital.

Carrie greeted him effusively, with affection and warmth and a refrigerator full of delicacies, but something had happened to Tony in South America. He had fallen in love with Peru, with its mountains and deserts, its people and its culture. From Lima he travelled eighteen hours in a bus to Ariquepa, staring at the towns growing rice and bananas in the middle of the desert, and slowly he found his feelings for Carrie overcome by the vastness around him, the villages, the people. At Ariquepa he bargained for wool at the market and bought alpaca wall hangings; at Puno on Lake Titicaca he saw the floating islands and in their mysterious splendour he realised how unimportant Carrie had suddenly become in his life. On New Year's Eve he was back in Lima, waiting to go home, and when all the people of the city, as was their custom, threw paper out of the window — old bank statements, accounts, all the clutter of the past year — Tony, approving, threw out Carrie's photograph that he still had in his wallet and determined to begin his life back home alone and with no regrets.

By his journey's end, Tony had fallen in love with the country in such a fiery way that his old love for Carrie seemed pale and watery beside it. Though he realised this was partly because he had made himself thrust her out of his heart and his thoughts, for she had hurt him too much to let her linger there, it was also because he knew that he wanted, now, trust and continuity in a relationship, something he realised he would never have with Carrie. And so, patiently, calmly, he tried to explain this to her when he arrived home, longing for his empty house, for some peace in which to contemplate his journey and learn from it. Finally, after two days of stubborn persistence, Carrie finally accepted that he really did not want to live with her any more. Sulkily, she left, and Tony was, at last, blissfully alone.

He has lived alone since then — happily, he tells himself, and indeed he is. Tony has the blessed gift of selfcontainment. He is comfortable with himself, and solitude does not depress nor frighten him. He works when he needs the money, and by now his dependability and skill as a builder ensure that he always has jobs in spite of the recession. His wildlife work is his passion and keeps him intrigued, alert, and occupied for days on end. In spite of his reputation for being something of a loner, he quite likes people, and the gigs he performs with the band satisfy any need for socialisation. On days that he is not working he takes long walks in various woodlands to check on bat boxes, or to just to enjoy the countryside; and during the long dark winter evenings when there is no gig he plays his guitar at the kitchen table, or listens to music on the stereo, or watches wildlife programmes on television.

'And how did you like South America?' Emmeline is asking him now as Barnaby brings in a basket of hot bread rolls. 'I've never been there, but I'm fascinated by what I've read. I love the writers, Marquez and now Isabel Allende — all that magic realism, that life and colour.'

Marjorie is serving watercress soup, which they eat on little trays around the wood-burner because it is, according to Barnaby, far too cold in the dining room tonight.

'It's snowing again,' Leo says as Barnaby passes around the rolls and butter.

'Come away from the window, Leo, and eat your soup,' Marjorie shouts. 'We all know it's frightfully cold outside; we don't need you to remind us.'

The food is delicious; the soup is followed by spicy chicken and rice, with a mixture of vegetables. Afterwards there is a hot pudding in deference to the weather, with a special dessert wine that Barnaby urges them to try.

During cheese the talk becomes less general, with Tony chatting to Emmeline, telling her about his trip to Peru (leaving out Carrie and the others), and Marjorie going upstairs to answer a call from one of her daughters. Leo, restless, says he is going outside for a few moments to see how bad the snow is. Barnaby, on the floor now in front of Daisy, adding more wood to the fire, says, 'I saw Gemma and Baz yesterday, not far from the bookshop. They were busking, and she was singing to Baz's didge. I must say it was extraordinary: who would ever think you could sing to one of those? I didn't know the song; it was terribly melancholy, but oddly touching. I was quite moved.'

'She has a good voice,' Daisy says. 'She could have studied music like Paul. She could have done so many things.'

Her eyes suddenly and unexpectedly fill up with tears. Barnaby, resting his hand lightly and comfortingly on her arm, moves up to sit beside her and says, 'It's been that bad, Daisy?'

The warm room, the awareness of the strange snowy world outside, Barnaby's genuine concern, penetrate Daisy's normally intact defence mechanisms and she says without thinking, 'I've been so lonely. She's only moved across the farmyard and into the orchard, but the house is suddenly empty, a shell – nothing.' A tear slides down her face but she brushes it away before anybody but Barnaby notices.

'What about Leo, have you talked to him? Perhaps you two should go away together for a time; when did you last have a holiday? Leo could get someone in for the farm, and Emmeline is there to look after the dog and the hens.'

'Oh Barnaby! If Leo and I were to go away for six months

on our own we would still not talk. Not about the things that really, truly matter. I can't remember when Leo last told me how he was feeling. Oh, I don't mean whether his back was aching or he felt tired or he was concerned about one of his sows being ill – I mean the other things, like whether he's happy, you know?'

'Have you asked him?'

'Oh God, if I do, he just smiles and says distractedly, "Why shouldn't I be happy? I've got a thriving farm, a loving wife, great kids—"'

'Well,' Barnaby says as Daisy pauses. 'Perhaps that's all true. Perhaps there is nothing more to say.'

But the expression on his face is doubtful, and so Daisy responds, 'There's got to be more, in him and in all of us. How does he feel about growing old, about his life so far, about the future? What does he think about the kids all gone? God knows I've tried to tell him how *I* feel, but he clams up and says things like, "That's life, Daisy. Kids grow up and leave home." Every time I try to talk to him I get a variation on that. I've given up; there's no point.'

Barnaby has no time to reply for Leo and Marjorie are back in the room, and Leo is saying that they really must go home now because the snow, which has been falling heavily all evening, is quite thick on the road outside. 'Come and look out of the window,' he tells them, and everyone except Daisy and Barnaby obediently cluster around the long high window looking out over the street.

Barnaby, putting his arm briefly around Daisy's shoulder in a warm, loving gesture which threatens to bring tears to her eyes again, says, 'It's a hard time you're going through, love. And I can understand your loneliness. Sometimes when

Marjorie and the girls present a united front against me I feel lonely too.'

They look at each other and smile ruefully. 'Thanks, Barnaby,' Daisy whispers. 'Thanks.' She presses his hand as she joins the others at the window.

'I think we'd better go,' Leo says. 'I know it's early, but it looks as if the snow has been coming down heavily for a couple of hours. I'm afraid we won't get up our drive.'

'Spend the night here,' Marjorie bellows. 'We have masses of room, though you might have to share a duvet. But we're all chums, aren't we?' She stands in front of them formidably, as if she were physically going to stop their departure.

'I can't leave the stock, Marjorie,' Leo says. 'I'm afraid we really must go.'

'I must go too,' Tony says. 'My road will be impassable as well if this keeps up.'

But when they get to the cars, having been waved off by a tireless Marjorie who roars down the whole street: 'Super evening, what? Smashing company, thank you so much for coming. We must do it again soon, yes? Do drive carefully!' they discover that Tony's van has a flat tyre.

'Don't bother with it now,' Leo says. 'That van is dreadful on a slippery road anyway. Jump in here with us and you can spend the night at our place; we can collect your van tomorrow.'

The roads are far worse than they have anticipated. Leo drives at a crawling pace and even then he skids more than once. When they get to their lane he drives several yards before the car skids one last time and becomes firmly entrenched in a snowdrift. 'We're going to have to abandon the car and walk up to the house,' he says after unsuccessfully trying to manoeuvre it out. 'It'll be worse further up. Does everyone have boots? The snow is quite deep.'

Everyone has, for they came prepared. With much noise and laughter, for everyone except Leo has had a fair bit to drink, they spill out from the car and begin to walk.

'Poor bloody sheep,' Leo says passionately, taking Daisy's arm and striding out in front with her at a brisk pace, as brisk as the snow on the ground will allow.

'What about poor bloody us?' Daisy asks, stomping in step with Leo over the snow.

It is a good three-quarters of a mile up the lane to the house, but Emmeline doesn't mind the walk. The snow has stopped and an almost full moon is appearing from behind the clouds, glistening on the white trees, on the white path ahead of them. She and Tony spontaneously link arms and follow the other two, albeit at a slower pace, and are soon left behind by the other couple.

Tony is quiet, enjoying the night, enjoying the walk up this eerie moonlit path with this intriguing woman, who gratifies him by remaining silent too, not chattering away and breaking the stillness, the peace of the night. They walk for five or ten minutes without speaking, until suddenly Tony whispers, 'Look, ahead of us. Right on the path. A barn owl.'

Sure enough, facing them, its eyes bright in the moonlight, sits the owl. Tony wonders if it is wounded and they approach it cautiously so as not to frighten it, but it suddenly takes off, white and beautiful and silent as it flies into the ghost-like trees.

'What magic,' Emmeline whispers. She shivers slightly and Tony, without thinking, puts his arms around her, draws her to him, and says, 'You're cold.' She looks at him, startled, and he thinks he has offended her with his sudden embrace and pulls back slightly to look at her face. He sees that her eyes are sad in the pale light, her expression troubled.

'What is it?' he asks gently. 'What's wrong?'

'Nothing,' she starts to say, but the night and the intimacy of the snow stops her from dissembling. 'An eerie feeling of *déjà vu* again, that's all,' she tells him. 'It seems to happen frequently these days.'

'The owl?'

'No, but everything else. The snow, this walk through the woods.' *You,* she nearly says, but doesn't. *Especially you.*

*

'Emmeline, can you hear me? This is a rotten line, all crackly. I'm catching a train in a few minutes to Canterbury, while they're still running. It's snowing hard here. College has been cancelled for the beginning of next week — all the teachers have this flu bug or something that's going around.'

They were snowed in by then; Leo had only just made it up the lane after picking up Emmeline, Marsha and Daisy that same morning. The Whitstable Road was still open, though treacherous, and Hal managed to catch the last bus which dropped him off at the bottom of the farm lane.

Emmeline was there waiting for him. It was six o'clock and dark, and the others had wanted to go with her, but she wanted to meet him alone. The snow had temporarily stopped, and there was such a bright full moon reflecting the whiteness of the snow that she didn't need to use her torch at all.

'Emmeline, you're here! I wasn't quite sure where to get off, but the driver knew Woodland Farm and where to stop. What an amazing night, and what a beautiful wood! Come here, you look cold. Let me warm you. Come under my coat, love. God, you look beautiful in the snow and moonlight, like an ice queen, like someone who should be riding a unicorn.'

*

Tony and Emmeline stand in their awkward midnight embrace for several moments. Emmeline clings to him like ivy on an oak, and Tony, though not understanding, nonetheless does not want to let her go. He realises with something of a shock that he is beginning to fall in love with her. This is why he has been hanging around the farm lately, ostensibly to check out the bats; this is why he was humming when he dressed for dinner that night in his clean jeans, his best thick plaid shirt. He feels a moment of pure joy, then the logistics of it plunge him into despair. He has less than a year, and then she will be gone.

They walk the rest of the way in silence, but their arms are around each other. Emmeline's thoughts are a jumble, leaping backward and forward across thirty years in time. She thinks she can still feel Hal's heartbeat under his coat in the silence of the snowy woods, and then she senses Tony beside her and remembers how comforting his embrace felt, and yet how disturbing.

Leo and Daisy have got a fire going and a bottle of brandy out. They are feeling too festive to go to bed just yet, and Leo wants to relax now that he has driven them safely home. Well, almost home, he thinks with a smile. He enjoyed the walk, it reminded him of that terrible November and December in the 1960s when he first took over the farm, when the farm lane was cut off for ages, and he and Daisy used to drive the tractor down to the bottom of the track to pick up food and supplies for the animals.

They talk for over an hour, even Leo expansively loquacious when Emmeline asks him questions about the farm, until he decides he'd better have one last look around the sheep before bed. Daisy, alone with Emmeline (for Tony has gone with Leo), impulsively goes to her, embraces her warmly, and says, 'It's so good having you here, Em. I know I've been a bit of a grump, and I'm sorry.'

'It was me, trying to tell you what to do. I should just keep my big mouth shut.'

'No, some of the things you said were very perceptive. I've actually thought about them a lot.'

'Ah, Daisy! If only I could apply some of that perception to myself.'

They are silent for a moment, arms around each other, each thinking their solitary thoughts. Emmeline is relieved that Daisy seems more herself tonight, and that she harbours no resentment for the things Emmeline has said about her, about Gemma.

Daisy is thinking about Barnaby. For the first time in months, she feels calmer, less desolate. It was just talking to someone about Leo and me, she says to herself: someone sympathetic, understanding. Emmeline would have been all those things too, of course, but something always stopped her when she began confiding in Em. Daisy thinks it is perhaps because Emmeline needs so much to believe in Leo and Daisy's marriage, to believe they are still as happy in each other as they were on the boat. Daisy hates to disillusion her, for she feels that that is all Emmeline has left as far as relationships go – her belief that at least others have managed where she herself has failed. Emmeline's own relationships have certainly been disastrous.

They break apart and smile at each other. 'Ah Em, I'm

so glad you're here, so glad we have a whole year together. Our other meetings through the years were so short.'

'I know. I can't tell you how good it is to be here, how settled I feel, how at home.'

'You had hoped it would be, once. You planned to settle here.'

'I know. That was before.'

They are silent for a moment. Then Emmeline says, 'Do you know that it rained every day for the entire month before I went back? Every morning, I would wake up in that poky little room in Earl's Court, usually in tears, and hear that goddamn rain on the sidewalk outside the basement window.'

'You were a mess then, I do remember that. Leo and I tried to get you to spend more time at the farm, but you wouldn't come.'

'I couldn't. Too many memories. But you trudged all the way out to London to see me whenever you could. Have I ever thanked you for that, by the way?'

The two women laugh. Daisy says, 'Well, now that you mention it—' They laugh again.

Leo and Tony come in and soon the Dillards go up to bed. Tony and Emmeline linger by the fire. 'I was just telling Daisy how I love it here,' Emmeline says. 'It's as though I've never been away.'

Tony feels strangely elated when she says such things. 'Daisy said you haven't been back since you were here in the sixties. That's a long time.'

It isn't exactly a question but it feels like one. Emmeline hesitates, then says, 'I avoided coming back. My time here was so good, and then it ended so badly.'

He waits for her to go on, but she doesn't, except to say,

'I don't know which is worse, coming back to a place where you have been excruciatingly happy, or where you have been unbearably hurt. Either way you are risking pain.'

'Even now, even all these years later?'

'Something remains, even if it's only a breath, a wisp. There's always a lingering trace of the joy you felt then, and equally of the pain. With the one, you are bereft because it is gone; with the other, you run the danger of opening old wounds.' She stops and is quiet for so long that Tony wants to go to her, hold her, but before he can she turns to him and smiles, lightening the mood. 'I'm just wallowing in nostalgia tonight, I'm sorry. It must be the snow. Let's talk of something else.'

'Fine with me. Tell me more about Atlanta, your life there.'

And so Emmeline talks. She tells him about her university, about her students. She describes the State of Georgia; the city in which she lives and works, the mountains outside where her summer cabin is located. Then, because he is a good listener, she tells him a little bit about Chester.

'We're supposed to be a couple,' she says with her usual frankness. 'But we've only spoken on the phone once since I've been here, and neither of us are good letter-writers. I'm afraid this year is going to put a big strain on our relationship.'

'Do you mind?'

She thinks carefully about this. 'If I were in Georgia, I'd probably say yes. Here, I don't seem to be missing him at all.'

'Is he that hard to resist in the flesh?' Tony asks teasingly, but there is a tight constriction in his chest that he recognises is jealousy.

Emmeline laughs. 'He's attractive, yes, if you like the all-American hero type. I did, over there. I also liked not being alone, having someone to go to concerts with, the theatre, parties. I guess I use him, in a way. But he certainly uses me too.'

The fire is dying now, there is not much left but embers. A wind has come up and the large room has suddenly become cold. Emmeline and Tony stare at the last bit of moribund flame, each brooding on their own thoughts. Tony wonders why the hell he has let himself fall for a city foreigner with an unhappy past and an on-going relationship with an all-American hero, while Emmeline contemplates the messiness of her personal life.

'Shall we go to bed?' she says suddenly, and for one wild euphoric moment Tony thinks she means together. 'I'll go first and use the bathroom, if that's all right,' she adds. 'Goodnight, then. It's been a wonderful evening. See you in the morning.'

'Yes, fine. And, uh, yes, it *has* been a lovely evening.'

Tony would at least like to kiss her goodnight, really kiss her, but all this talk of Chester has totally deflated him. Besides, he's not about to risk his heart again to a feckless woman; he's had quite enough of them in the past. And so with a brotherly pat on the arm he kisses her lightly on the cheek and says good night, watching her go up the stairs with more than a little regret.

Emmeline, who expected to be kissed properly, is stunned. She does not want to go to bed with Tony (he is definitely not her kind of man), but she wants him to want to go to bed with her. After all, he is unmarried, unattached, heterosexual, and available: what is wrong with her that he seems so totally disinterested in her as a woman?

She now feels deflated, her confidence as eroded as a rocky coastline pitted by the sea. Crawling into bed she lies there as miserably as an adolescent, feeling as humiliated and rejected as a seventeen-year-old with no date for the Senior Prom.

And so in their adjoining rooms Tony and Emmeline lie awake, listening to the wind howling through the poplars outside on the hill, seeing the snow blazing around their uncurtained windows. They are only physically a few metres away from each other, but miles apart in every other way. Finally they sleep, fitfully. Emmeline dreams her dreams of blue-eyed boys and loss and pain, and Tony dreams of Peru, strengthening himself in his sleep against the love for a woman by remembering the steadfastness of a love for a country. In his dreams he is alone, canoeing up the Amazon or walking in solitude across the mountains.

Emmeline too is alone in her dreams, but it is not through choice. And there, of course, lies the difference.

Chapter Eight

*I*n the next couple of weeks the snow melts, leaving the
city sloppy and slushy, the countryside wet and forlorn.
It is December and a heavy fog envelops the area for days,
depressing everyone except Gemma and her friends who
continue to weave in and out of the orchard like bright
exotic threads on a dull grey tapestry. Between Gemma
and her mother there is a polite rapport, unsatisfactory to
either of them, but Daisy is too preoccupied these days to
do anything about it. Baz keeps out of the way, busy with
his didgeridoos, his workshop, his busking, while Gemma is
making hundreds of candles to sell for Christmas. Leo just
gets on with the farm, though increasingly he is tormented
by a decision he will soon be having to make. He knows
that whatever he does, there will be repercussions. He is
not quite sure how to handle it, so he loses himself in the
fog, spending more hours than necessary walking around the
sheep, checking for illness, for foot rot, for ewes caught in
brambles or wire at the far edges of the field.

On Friday afternoon Emmeline comes home from the
university late and exhausted. 'Oh, what a day!' she moans,
drinking a smoky tea Daisy has set in front of her. 'Nothing

but problems with my students. One kid has lost his passport and he's flying back home for Christmas in a couple of weeks; another is missing seminars like mad and I had to go all heavy on her today . . . I could go on and on.'

'At least you're busy,' Daisy says moodily, pouring herself a cup of tea and sitting opposite Emmeline. 'At least you have a job.'

Em looks at her sharply. 'Is that what's troubling you? Would you like to leave the farm, go out to work?'

'No, not really. I'd just exchange one kind of meaningless slog for another. Not that I'd get a job anywhere, at my age. Jobs are scarce for the young and well-qualified: I wouldn't have a hope.'

'Well, what about going back to college? You've got several places of higher education right at your doorstep. It's not too late for you to still be a lawyer, you know. The newspapers are full of stories about sagacious seventy-year-olds getting degrees.'

'Heavens, no. I wasn't all that interested years ago in becoming a solicitor; I'd loathe it now. I don't want to go back to education just for the sake of it, Em.'

'Then just what is it you *do* want?' Emmeline asks kindly.

Daisy thinks for a moment before answering. 'To be passionate about something again. To care. About something that is important, or at least that I think is important. I want to be intense again as we were all those years ago – you and Hal about the theatre, Leo about farming and me about first the animals, then the children. And about the other things too, the mega things: Vietnam, Civil Rights, nuclear disarmament.'

'Daisy, there's plenty to get passionate about today, you know. You said yourself the world's in a mess.'

Daisy sighs and peers distractedly in her empty cup. 'I know, I know. I must sound so puerile, talking in circles, contradicting myself. I suppose what I'm saying is that I just want to *feel* again. Something other than this great sense of loss.'

Gemma's arrival interrupts this conversation. 'Mum, I hate to ask, I really do, but our old van won't start. Can we use yours? I'd never ask only it's terribly important.'

'What's up?' Daisy asks.

'We're supposed to be going into town, meeting Blue and Flack at the shelter before they open the café for the evening.'

'Shelter?'

'Haven't you read about it in the local newspaper? Some charity groups have started a temporary shelter for the homeless, down in the old warehouse at the edge of town. They began it during last week's severe weather and hope to carry on through Christmas. The trouble is, they're terribly short on volunteers, so we're going down tonight to give a hand. Please, please, *please* can we borrow your car? We're late as it is.'

She is in such a rush that Daisy knows there's no point in saying anything else and gives her the car keys. 'When will you be back?'

'I'm not sure. We're meeting with the organisers first; we'll find out then when they need us. Thanks for the car, I really appreciate it.'

She is out of the room before Daisy can answer.

'Passion,' Emmeline grins. 'Intensity. A cause. There you are, Daisy.'

Daisy grins in return. 'I suppose you have to be young,' she murmurs, suddenly serious. 'How odd. All this time

I've been longing for the emotions and feelings of an eighteen-year-old, never realising that they died long ago, along with my unmarked body and my crystal-clear mind.'

Emmeline tries to protest but is hushed by Daisy. 'Look, hadn't you better get ready to go out? Isn't tonight the evening you're supposed to be at Tony's for a meal?'

Emmeline has not forgotten, but she had no idea how late it is. 'I'd better get ready. Is there enough hot water for a bath?'

'Plenty. Go on up now, before Leo comes in and decides he wants one before dinner.'

Emmeline runs upstairs, thinking of Tony. She has only seen him once since that night of the snowfall, for he has been avoiding the farm. Like most sensible people, Tony tries to avoid situations in which he'll be hurt, and he knows, quite simply, that Emmeline will hurt him if he persists in allowing himself to love her. She would not do it deliberately, of course, but given her past history of relationships, her on-going if unsatisfactory liaison with the all-American hero, combined with the fact that whatever happens, she will be going back to the States in spring or summer . . . none of these are ingredients for a lasting relationship, or even a temporary one of any satisfaction. Tony, unfortunately for him, he sometimes thinks, is a man who cannot enjoy a fleeting, sexual relationship with a woman. The problem is, he falls in love; and it follows then that his cosy, harmonious life, which had contented him previously, suddenly seems to him sterile, lonely, unfulfilling, and the nesting instinct courses through his veins in all its biological and hormonal glory.

Tony knows this: it has happened before, and threatens to happen again with Emmeline. He knows with clear certainty that the relationship, if it ever developed, would end in a final parting at the airport or some such impersonal place, leaving him behind and alone and bereft. Tony has had enough of partings, of endings. They leave him feeling old and ill and tired, and often also in some considerable pain.

And so it isn't Tony who has instigated this evening's dinner at his place. He had gone over to the farm to deliver some special pig feed Leo had asked him to pick up, and of course had stopped to have a chat with Daisy. Emmeline had come in then, seemingly genuinely pleased to see him; indeed even, he could swear, flirting with him, saying how she would love to see his house, see his bats flying around (he lets them out for a short time in the evenings when he is home), look at some of the wall-hangings he brought back from South America. When Leo walked in on this scene and said, innocently, 'You really should see Tony's house; it's the lodge-house from an old, very grand estate, and Tony's done it up beautifully,' Tony had no choice but to offer the invitation. 'And have him do you one of his Lancashire hotpots,' Leo said with a mischievous grin. 'It's what we have every time we're invited over.'

'I haven't a wide repertoire of culinary skills,' Tony admitted.

'Except for the hotpot. It's quite an experience, Em. Make sure you eat nothing for twenty-four hours ahead of time.'

And so it is that Emmeline finds herself driving the short distance to Tony's house, wondering what it is about this man that intrigues and attracts her so. For attracted she is. She has finally admitted it to herself, after their last evening together when she had felt so soundly rejected by him. That rejection still stung, and when he fortuitously appeared at the farm that evening, Emmeline saw it as a second chance.

She dressed with care for the evening: a long, plain but sensuous black skirt, discreetly and stylishly slashed in three places up to the thighs; a clinging ribbed jumper.

'Goodness, Em, you're just going over for a bite to eat and to see some bats,' Daisy exclaimed. 'You'll frighten the life out of Tony.'

Which turns out to be not that far from the truth. Emmeline arrives looking glowing, expectant and, to Tony, predatory, confirming all his old fears about becoming involved with this woman.

'Tony, what a wonderful house!' Emmeline exclaims sincerely, admiring the many wall-hangings, mostly of rural South American scenes, and the lovely wooden carvings filling the many shelves and small tables.

Tony is pleased she likes it. He bought the house seven years ago when it was in a thoroughly dilapidated condition, the owners of the whole estate having come by hard times and selling bits off wherever they could. Before that, Tony had lived in a series of rented accommodations. A creature of the sixties, he did not want to be tied down with a mortgage, fettered, until he perceived that there was also freedom in owning your own place, in having somewhere to stay whatever your circumstances. Freedom, he had to admit, was much easier if you did not have to rely on others: on landlords, friends, family.

Like Emmeline and Hal, Tony was in London during the mid-sixties but, unlike Emmeline, he was still there in the early seventies. He came at first as a university student, and actually completed a degree in zoology, a sound Second which surprised him, for he was too caught up in the excitement of his generation to do much studying. It was much more important to learn to play the guitar, to go on peace marches and demonstrations, or to hang out in Hyde Park for hours in the spring, cutting lectures and seminars to discourse passionately with his fellow truants. In the winter it was Carnaby Street, sitting in warm coffee bars and instead of watching the world go by, feeling that *you* were the world, or if not, that at least you were helping to make it go around. Control, that's what we felt we had then, he would sometimes think. We felt we could shape events, rule the world *our* way, with our love and hope and unique optimism. And this is where we differed from Gemma and Baz and their friends: we dropped out because we thought the world would follow, embrace our philosophy and idealism while they, on the other hand, are running away from what they see as a corrupt world, embracing an alternative lifestyle because they are, rightly, both afraid and scornful of the things they witness around them. Unlike us, they understand that they are powerless, in the long run, to change society. We, mistakenly, were sure that we could.

After Tony got his degree he travelled, going to Eastern Europe, then Afghanistan, with a young woman he met on the ferry from Dover who was hoping to hitchhike to India but hadn't a clue how she was going to set about this. She was travelling alone except for a miniature parrot in an old brass birdcage. The parrot unfortunately (or fortunately, according to Tony) died before they had left France, though Jessica insisted on carrying the empty birdcage with her through several more countries before giving it away to some hippies in what was then Yugoslavia.

Tony was besotted by Jessica. She had wild red hair and wore long Indian kaftans, and unless it was actually snowing she never wore shoes. After their travels they lived together in a seedy flat in West Kensington, taking on odd jobs in shops and restaurants to support themselves. It never occurred to Tony to use his degree in any way; there was nothing specific he wanted to do with it, but he also felt life was too precious to waste by devoting himself to a career just for the sake of making a great deal of money. What he earned was enough to get him what he wanted; luckily, his needs and his wants were not great.

He stayed with Jessica for three or four years and parted with her with regret. Their relationship, which had begun with such exhilaration, had dwindled — or accelerated as the case may be — into acrimony and vituperation. Jessica, as the late sixties turned into the seventies, became, or so Tony saw it, more and more excessive. She didn't just smoke the occasional joint, she used dope constantly, all day long if she could afford it. When she partied, it was as if it were the only party she had ever been invited to, and would ever be asked to again; she drank, and danced on table tops, and would not come home until long after all the guests had gone and the sun was finally coming up. Jessica would still be awake, still dancing, lost and alone, finally giving in to Tony's gentle pressure to come home, where she insisted on making love for hours until they both collapsed, exhausted, into a deep, troubled sleep.

At first Tony loved the wildness inside her. At first he partied with her, and responded to her intense, erratic love-making with an equal intensity of his own. She was as crazy and bizarre in this as she was in everything she did, and they spent more time in bed than they did out of it in the first year or so. But instead of Jessica's appetite waning, instead of turning outward after the initial euphoria was over and evolving into something just as intense, perhaps, but steadier, more stable, she gradually began craving more, not just of sex but of everything. It was as if, seeing the sixties beginning to fade, she was trying to hold on to it by frantically grabbing to excess everything that had made her feel good then, instead of using it as a foundation for whatever came next.

Tony tried to steady her, calm her, soothe her. He nursed her through excruciating hangovers and emotional turbulences with tenderness and love, but each one wore him down, left his own psyche bare and shaking. Some part of him began to crave wholesomeness: clean walks in the country, good physical work outside instead of waiting on tables in the local café, proper meals instead of a couple of bottles of cheap wine and a newspaper full of chips. Trying to instil some of this into their lifestyle, he was mocked by Jessica, told he was becoming dull and boring, and as if to make up for it, she intensified her own wild day-to-day existence.

In the end it was Tony who left her. He could no longer handle her, either her manic highs or the despairing lows that inevitably followed. After several false starts, when he either threatened to leave, or did actually go but only temporarily, he left finally after a party one night in a house in Chelsea.

It was five in the morning, and winter. The last person had either passed out, gone home, or crashed out somewhere in the Chelsea house a good hour ago, and Jessica was still holding a bottle of some cheap bubbly and trying to play a Jimi Hendrix record, her hands unsteady as she scratched the needle on the turntable. 'Jess, come on, time to go now,' Tony said wearily, for the third or fourth time. They were staying only across the road that weekend, at a friend's flat, and he was tired, slightly drunk, and wanted his bed.

'Want to dance,' Jessica murmured, beginning to sway

sensuously and unsteadily to the music. Someone said, from the heap of stoned bodies draping the furniture and floor, 'Wanna dance, wanna dance,' and then passed out again.

'Home. Bed.' Tony gently took her arm and steered her across the room, but she tore away from him, shouting, 'Let me go, stop trying to spoil my fun. You're like a great black raincloud. Stop it!'

Tony took no notice; it was the time of morning when she often was belligerent. 'Come on, love. I'll take you home to bed,' he said automatically, for he had done it countless times before. Suddenly, he didn't want to do it again. Suddenly, it seemed infinitely wearisome to have to sit at her bedside with cold compresses, later bringing her endless cups of coffee, and spending the whole day coping with her tears and her recriminations. And then, at night, the love-making. It didn't matter how tired they were, or if Tony had to be up early the next morning for work, Jessica would insist on hours of intensive, often bizarre, passion. He had never thought sex could be tedious, but with Jessica it was becoming that way.

Before he could get her to the door she broke away, grabbed the wine bottle which he had taken from her, and took a long swallow, then poured the rest over her face and her hair. 'Make love to me now, Tony. Fuck me, right here, right now.' She dropped soundlessly to the floor and reached up for him, but he avoided her hands and said, 'Come with me now, Jessica. Or it's all over. I mean it, this time.'

Something in her face darkened, but then she turned and began unbuttoning the tiny pearl buttons in her embroidered waistcoat, exposing her bare breasts. She did it in such a way that he knew she was not that drunk or stoned, for she touched her nipples as she unbuttoned in a sly, calculating way, the way she knew always excited him.

'I'm telling you again, Jessica, I'm going now. Come on, it's just across the road, and we can go to bed, make love there if you want.'

'No. Here. Now.' She lay there caressing her breasts, smiling, expectant, sure of herself and of him. 'Goodbye, Jessica,' he said softly and walked out of the house.

He never saw her again. He half-expected her to follow him, but she never did, and later that morning, just before noon, he went back to their flat and packed his bags, and never saw her again because after staying a couple of weeks on the other side of London with friends, he went to Ludlow for a long overdue visit to his parents, who had been complaining that they never saw him these days. He spent the next three or four months in Shropshire, aimlessly working at odd jobs, taking long walks in the countryside of his childhood, and worrying his parents to death with his obvious melancholy and seeming lack of ambition.

When he returned to London Jessica was gone, and no one knew where. No one ever heard from her again. Tony stayed in the city for a few more years, playing with a band, picking up the pieces of his life after Jessica, but gradually the place began to suffocate him. As a child he had grown up in the fields and meadows and forests of the Wales-Shropshire borders, fascinated by its alternative natural life of plants and animals and insects which was far more interesting to him at the time than the lives of the people around him. Had it not been the sixties, had not the wild, exuberant spirit of the times appealed to something deep and feral in him, he'd not have stayed as long as he did in London, for it was not his natural habitat.

A job doing research at his old university for one of his professors rekindled his love of wildlife, and eventually he moved to Kent, taking on a poorly paid and part-time job with a wildlife trust. Because it wasn't enough to live on, he also did odd jobs as a builder's assistant, and so gradually learned the trade until he was able to branch out on his own. The life suited him: he was his own boss, he could work when he chose and so have time left for his other interests, and most of all it was outside, where he preferred to work.

And so the years had gone. Between Jessica and Carrie there were other women, and one he had very nearly married, but luckily both of them had realised in time that it would never work, for in their short period of living together they disagreed over everything, from what type of bread to buy, to what they wanted from life. Though they parted amicably, Tony was nonetheless bereaved, and the sense of loss and isolation he felt for months afterwards clouded the relief of being in command of his own life again.

And so Tony listens now to Emmeline complimenting him on his house, and his hotpot, and his choice of music (a Brahms piano concerto), and is more than a little wary. She looks so good, with her seal-like hair sleek against her head, her smile warm and wide and accommodating. They are sitting now on the worn black leather sofa that used to belong to Tony's parents, drinking some very old Scotch whisky that Tony has had for months but has never bothered opening. Emmeline is having only a little one for she is driving, though she hopes Tony will ask her to spend the night. She senses his interest and is feeling good about herself: confident, assured, unlike the last time. She is waiting patiently for him to make the first move. She is sure that this time it will be more than just a brotherly kiss on the cheek.

Tony is indeed more than ready to make this first move. His prior rational admonishments to himself, accelerating into flashing red warning lights when Emmeline appeared dressed for seduction rather than for an evening spent getting to know about bats, have eked away as surely as the whisky in his glass. He is just about to take her in his arms when the phone rings, shrilly and imperiously.

'Oh, hell. I'd better get it.'

It is Daisy. 'Sorry to bother you, but I've just had a phone call from the States, from Emmeline's friend Chester. He needs to talk to her tonight, apparently, so could you please ask her to phone him as soon as she gets home? It doesn't matter what time; as you know they are hours behind over there.'

'What's up?' Emmeline asks, getting on the phone. 'Is something wrong? Did Chester tell you what the hurry is?'

'Yes – something about needing to know right away when you are coming home for Christmas.'

'But I'm not!'

'Well, your Chester doesn't seem to know that. He's just had an invitation to some congressman's house for a pre-Christmas dinner party. It must be fairly important; Chester was positively inflated by it all. The bloke is apparently someone very influential, and Chester wanted to make sure you are back in time for the event.'

'Oh, great,' Emmeline says sardonically. 'How nice to know I am so missed. I suppose I should be flattered that he wants me on his arm to enhance his position as a discerning heterosexual male.'

Daisy ignores this and says apologetically, 'Look, I'd have

left a note, but your man was rather in a flap. He needs to confirm all this tonight, and I suddenly thought, what if you didn't come back to the farm, spent the night there?'

'What a suspicious mind you have,' Emmeline grins, glancing around to make sure Tony hasn't returned from the kitchen where he has tactfully disappeared.

'Well, I saw the way you were tarted up tonight. Anyway, for goodness sake, if you're not coming home, ring Chester from there, tell him you're staying at the farm for Christmas. I don't want to have to explain if he rings again tomorrow morning.'

They hang up, and Emmeline ponders what to do. She decides to leave it for a bit, for Tony has returned and she doesn't want to talk to him about Chester right now. Tony smiles at her politely and says, 'You haven't seen the bats yet. I thought that's why you came.'

Emmeline had forgotten all about the bats. 'Why, sure,' she says insouciantly, his rather cryptic remark throwing her off-balance. 'Of course. Where are they? I had sort of thought they'd be flying around all over the place, like in Gothic horror films.'

This annoys Tony. It strengthens the resolution he made in the kitchen not to get involved with this woman, who is obviously using him as a diversion to make her time in England more amusing, and to give her entertaining anecdotes with which to beguile her all-American hero.

'No, I'm afraid I don't live with bats flying through the house by the hundreds. Nor do I wear a long black cape and have fangs. The three bats I have rescued live, as you know, in a large wire cage, and sometimes when I give them their evening meal I let them out in the spare room upstairs, for ten minutes or so, to give them a bit of freedom.'

'I'd like to see them,' Emmeline says meekly, upset at the coldness in his voice.

They go upstairs to the spare room which is carpeted but unfurnished. Very gently Tony lifts out the bats, one by one, from their cage and opens his hands. Slowly they stretch out their wings, one at a time, and begin to soar and swoop joyfully around the room. 'Oh, how marvellous!' Emmeline exclaims spontaneously. Like Tony, she is sitting on the floor. As she watches, the three pipistrelles seem to dance in mid-air, stopping occasionally to alight on the top of the curtain rail or, once, on Tony's shoulder. For the first time, she can understand everyone's urge to protect these creatures. They are both ancient and very much alive; they are a link between past and present. To destroy that link, Emmeline decides, would in some way, however small, diminish us as civilised *homo sapiens*.

Gratefully she thanks Tony, and when the bats are put away again they walk slowly downstairs. Tony, thawed by her genuine interest, has relented in his suspicions of her, but not enough ever to contemplate a relationship with her. He feels that Chester's imperative phone call to Emmeline, whatever that was all about, was a warning, and he'd be a fool to ignore it.

'Would you like a coffee before you go?' he asks Emmeline politely when they reach the living room again.

'That would be nice,' Emmeline says. 'But only if you have decaffeinated.'

'No, I'm afraid I don't. You could have tea. Or hot chocolate, or a Bovril drink. I use Bovril in my Lancashire hotpot.' They look at each other and laugh. The evening which had begun so voluptuously, so seductively, with slit skirts and Brahms and old mellowed Scotch has turned into a cosy matey affair with a lecture on wildlife and a hot drink. The irony is not lost on either of them.

'I'd love a hot chocolate,' Emmeline says.

As Tony goes into the kitchen to make the drinks, Em relaxes on the sofa. She likes this room, with its colourful depictions of South American scenes, with its profusion of overlarge plants, with its old, even shabby, but extremely comfortable furniture. She stands up and investigates the bookcase. There are, of course, numerous books on plant and animal life, as well as a fair number of volumes on space, astronomy, human genetics, the evolving of the universe. Not a single book on the theatre, she thinks with a smile.

They drink their chocolate like two old comrades, totally at ease with each other. Emmeline is sitting cross-legged on the sofa, her ankles tucked up carelessly underneath her long silk skirt and wearing a jumper of Tony's, for she became chilled sitting so long in the spare bedroom, watching the bats. Her glossy lipstick has long since worn off and her sleek hair has been ruffled out of place when she put on the pullover. She looks plain, ordinary, and to Tony, much more endearing than she did when she arrived.

Emmeline, relaxed and happy, has enjoyed talking to Tony for the past hour. He makes her feel calm, at ease; he makes her feel herself. When at last she stands up, ready to go, she would like to reach out to him, touch him, hold him, but cannot. Once, years ago, she reached out to someone very like Tony and was rejected cruelly. She cannot face it again, not even now, not even after all this time.

And so, foolishly and awkwardly, she holds out her hand for Tony to shake as they say goodbye at the door of her car. Tony takes it but instead of shaking it, holds it lightly and kisses her gently on the lips. Though it is certainly purely a kiss of friendship, it is done with such warmth and affection that Emmeline does not, cannot, feel in any way humiliated or rejected, the way she did with him the other night.

As she drives home she feels strangely satisfied, though the evening has not at all turned out the way she had expected. Perhaps for the first time in her life she can have a close male friend, she thinks wonderingly. Perhaps for the first time she can just enjoy a man's company, without all that will we or won't we go to bed stuff.

The thought fills her with such an intense relief that she feels almost lightheaded. When she gets back to the farm she is still so full of an easy peace and contentment that she can't even be bothered to enter into a verbal conflict with Chester, who is furious, over long-distance, with her decision to spend Christmas in Kent.

'I'll have to find someone else to take,' he says belligerently, implying that the someone else will not only accompany him to the dinner but to his bed as well.

Emmeline doesn't even care. She wishes Chester an early Merry Christmas, hangs up swiftly, and goes to her own bed in the most tranquil state she has been in since her arrival in England.

'Flack, look at this. There's an evening job going at an off-licence.'

Flack grabs the newspaper from Baz and looks at the advert. 'No good, it's during prime time at the café. Blue couldn't handle it on her own.'

'Of course I could. Our customers are generally pretty good; if they have to wait a bit longer to get served they won't mind.'

'I'll help,' Gemma says eagerly.

They are inside the caravan, lounging about and relaxing after a busy day. Baz has been frantically making didgeridoos; he has had two more orders. Gemma spent the day helping out at the shelter for the homeless, joined by both Blue and Flack for an hour or so in the early morning before they had to open the café. It is late, long after midnight, but no one seems tired. Baz and Gemma are curled up on the faded red velvet sofa and the other two are on cushions on the floor. The wood-burning stove is pumping out more than enough heat to keep them warm and comfortable, and the light of a couple of small oil lamps reflects in the tiny mirrors and in the glass of the chandelier.

Flack, rolling a cigarette, says to Gemma, 'You're supposed to be making a hundred candles for that new craftshop, and you're working longer than any of us at the shelter. You won't have time to help at the café.'

'I can spare three evenings a week, which is when they want someone at the off-licence. Go for it, Flack.'

Flack grunts. He has lost track of how many jobs he and Blue have applied for: waiting on tables, ushering at the cinema, shop assistant at a bakery, care assistant at an old people's home. It was always the same story: too many applicants for too few jobs.

'We need the money, Flack,' Blue says gently. 'Why don't I go for the job?'

'I'll do it. It really doesn't matter which one of us brings in the cash, and I can do most of the preparations beforehand. Then you, and Gemma if she really doesn't mind, can do the dishing out and last-minute stuff.'

Blue nods. They really do need to make some money soon, if they are to keep on with the café. The extra rent has nearly wiped them out, and Flack refuses to raise the prices any more, or to cut down on the portions they serve. She totally agrees with him on this, but she knows too that it would devastate him if they lost Primrose Café. Flack loves to cook, and loves people: it is the perfect set-up for him.

'Have you thought about changing your supplier, Flack?' Baz says now. 'You're paying Simon more than you would anywhere else, you know.'

'His stuff is good,' Blue says. 'His veg are all organic, fresh, and his flour and pulses and seeds are quality stuff too.'

'There's no point in serving rubbish,' Flack says. 'I love good food. I'm not serving anything else.' He sets his lips stubbornly, re-lights his cigarette.

'Okay, okay, I don't blame you,' Baz says. 'I'm just trying to find a way out, that's all.'

They are silent for a few moments. There *is* no way out, Blue is thinking. Already we have moved up above the café, given up our small but adequate flat to live in one cold squalid room with no loo but the one downstairs in the restaurant. Aloud, she says, 'Well, we'll give it a try, anyway. This off-licence job — if Flack doesn't get it, I'll try for the next one. With Christmas coming, there will be more around from now on.'

Flack nods, reaches for the beer he was drinking, and knocks over an old hardback book which had been placed on the tiny table next to him. 'Oh, sorry,' he says, picking it up. As he does so, a photograph falls out.

'Look at this,' Gemma says.

'What is it?'

'An old photo I found in this book of Mum's.' She passes it around. 'I got the book from the house: it's a collection of poetry that has been sitting in our bookshelves for years. I felt in the mood to read some poetry and Mum said to take it.'

'She's mellowing out a bit, is she?'

'I don't know. Perhaps she is. She seems very distracted lately, a bit vague. But not quite so awful and negative about everything I do, which makes a nice change.'

'What a great photo,' Blue says. 'Who is it?'

'Don't you recognise her? It's Emmeline.'

Blue and Flack look again at the black and white photograph. A young girl in a long dark skirt and a soft ruffled blouse is reclining on a bale of hay. 'That's the barn here,' Flack says.

But neither of them recognises Emmeline. This girl has long pale hair with ribbons in it, and a wide, trusting smile that Blue has never seen on Emmeline.

'I'd never have known her,' Flack says. 'Except maybe for the eyes.'

'I wonder who took the photo? It's very good, very artistic. I wonder if it was that old boyfriend of hers, the one Mum told me about . . .?'

*

'Em, now look this way. Great, great. Now another smile, but just a bit of one; fine, fine. One more, but can you look serious now, and not at the camera, but a bit over my shoulder? Oh, marvellous!'

'Who do you think you are since you got that camera – David Bailey?' Emmeline laughed, coming down off the haystack and brushing bits off her soft, deep-blue velvet skirt.

'You just look so terrific in that outfit,' Hal said, helping her down and picking the hay out of her hair.

'You look pretty good yourself,' Emmeline murmured. Hal was wearing tight brown corduroy trousers and a white frilly Beau Brummell shirt he had picked up at a second-hand shop near college. They were all going through their *Tom Jones* phase now, having seen the film a second time around and deciding what a lark it would be to dress like that. The look particularly suited Hal. His thick blond hair had grown longer, touching the shoulders of the collarless shirt, and his eyes seemed bluer, larger, deeper. Just the sight of him made Emmeline feel desperate, with what she was not sure. She assumed it was love.

It was the Sunday after everyone had arrived at the farm from London, the weekend of the snow when first Sojo and Marsha and Emmeline turned up, and then later Hal. The snow had stopped, leaving the fields and woodlands icy and gleaming. The trains and buses were running again, albeit precariously, and several others from London had joined them, including Les, Sojo's Australian roommate. During the day they had helped Leo distribute hay to the sheep and feed the pigs, then spent hours romping in the clean, crisp air, making angels by lying flat on their backs and moving their arms up and down in the snow to make wings.

They built a snow person — it had to be androgynous because they couldn't decide whether it was to be male or female — and dressed it in an old tartan kilt, a mangy fox stole that Daisy had found in a cupboard, and a green woolly vest. They put a turban on its head and a marijuana pipe in its mouth and formed a circle and danced around it, whooping and chanting and laughing so hard they ended up first falling about in the snow and then pelting each other in an irrepressible snowball fight. That done, they tumbled into the house in high spirits, deciding to continue the party atmosphere by dressing for dinner in whatever bizarre or elegant or amusing clothes they could find. They spent a pleasurable and giggly hour going through dozens of articles of clothing abandoned and left behind by Leo's mother and sister, which had remained untouched in old wardrobes and chests of drawers.

Emmeline loved the old velvet skirt she had found, which had obviously belonged to Alma in her youth. The antique ruffled blouse was her own, found on a dusty junk stall in the market. When Hal had finally finished taking the photographs of her, they walked back hand-in-hand from the barn to the house, both snuggled under Hal's big black coat. Before they went inside Hal said contentedly, 'Oh, how good it is to be here, after London. I love this place, the rambling old farmhouse, the barn, all the animals. Look at that oak tree out in the field in front of the house – do you know Leo said it must be almost a thousand years old?'

Emmeline looked at the tree, now skeletal with the winter ice. Its trunk was immense and hoary, its limbs short and stubby but prolific. As they gazed across the field, something great and pink suddenly appeared in the snow, leaping and frolicking about like a Walt Disney creation.

'Good God, what's that?' Hal asked.

'It's Seamus, Leo's boar,' giggled Emmeline, who had been to the farm once before, on her own, for a couple of days to visit Daisy. 'He's always getting out apparently, loves to play and leap about. It drives Leo crazy, but Daisy loves him. I think she sometimes deliberately lets him out so that he can enjoy himself. You stay here and try to head him off. I'll call Leo.'

It took ages to entice Seamus back to his warm clean pen, for he was having such a delightful romp in the snow. Leo was beginning to lose his temper, resorting to chucking stones at the boar's massive ribcage to prevent him from charging down the lane. 'I'll run down to the field behind him and chase him back,' Hal shouted, though he was panting and out of breath after a good half hour of running after the boar.

'You're knackered. I'll go and get some of the others,' Leo shouted back.

'Seamus will be in Canterbury by the time they get their boots on and come out here. I'm fine.'

Leo, puffing too, grunted and ran after Hal. Every time they got Seamus near his pen, the boar wickedly and victoriously bolted, almost as if he were playing a game, leading them on. Leo fumed and swore, Hal ran and sweated and ignored Leo's curses and lashings of temper, until finally, Seamus seemed to suddenly tire of the game and walked meekly back into his pen.

'Bloody fucking boar,' Leo swore as they slowly made their way back to the house. 'Daisy spoils him, treats him like a lap dog. He's a bloody farm animal, not a house pet.'

Hal knew better than to laugh or even smile. 'It's because she loves this place so much. The farm, the animals—'

'I know, I know,' Leo said, softening. 'I'll never change her.'

Hal clasped him on the shoulder. 'You wouldn't want to, Leo.'

Leo stopped walking and looked at Hal. Hal's face, in spite of the frost, was beaded with sweat, but he was grinning. Leo, grudgingly, began to smile, then to chuckle. 'No,' he said in a rare flash of intimacy. 'No, I wouldn't change her for the world.'

They walked in a companionable silence until they got to the farmhouse door. 'Thanks for helping me,' Leo said, realising that Hal had stuck it out for over an hour, running after that bloody animal when he could have been inside by the fire with the others. 'It's a sodden job, getting them in when they've no mind to co-operate. And it's hell, doing it alone.'

'That's okay. The exercise did me good. Better than my fencing class any day.'

Leo shook his head. Hal lived in a different world, a world he'd never understand, but he liked the lad despite their differences. 'Tell you what,' he said with a grin. 'A month or so of farming and you'd be in such good shape you'd be able to play Hamlet for two matinées and an evening performance without losing a breath.'

When they got inside Leo stacked up the fire in the beamed living room and brought out some of his homebrew beer. There were several gallons of it; it was pronounced not only drinkable but splendid and was all consumed before the last ember had finally died. Les had brought his guitar and was bellowing out a lusty version of '*The House of the Rising Sun*', in his element with such an appreciative audience. Now and again someone lit a joint, passed it around, and Leo found himself wondering what his mother in Leeds would think of all this. It was like the boat, only cosier, more intimate somehow, and he felt a kind of pride that all this peaceful merrymaking was going on in his own home. He liked to think that although Alma would surely look upon the innocent revels with horror, his father would have approved. Leo felt the dead man's presence hovering around benignly, and was content.

Leo's father had unfortunately died only a week or so after his son's arrival home. When Alma moved out, in an almost indecent hurry, Daisy moved in. This scandalised the farming neighbours, who though not close, were vociferous; it scandalised also the entire little village clustered not far from the farm lane. Co-habitation was not the norm then: only marriage, in the villages and small towns of England. Leo and Daisy, in deference to the memory of Leo's father, had decided to postpone their nuptial festivities until after Christmas.

Leo wasn't sure how he felt about living with Daisy and not being married to her, especially in the family home and in the big four-poster bed in which he had been born. He would have preferred to be married, but he knew also that he could not live in close proximity to her and not take her to his bed as he had since their second day together on the ship. How confusing the times were, he thought that night, refusing the joint but pouring himself another homebrew, listening to the singing and laughter. He had just returned from a country which still appeared to be living in the early fifties, and here he was suddenly bowled into these bewildering sixties. He liked it – thought it exciting, stimulating – but once outside with his animals, in his fields, it all passed him by like high racing clouds in a strong wind. Simply, he was, for most of the time, too busy even to notice.

Leo, his arm around Daisy, looked around him and thought that perhaps this old room wasn't that different in Henry VIII's day, with the music, the singing, the wine, the high spirits. And then he nearly laughed out loud, for Les, as if reading his thoughts, had switched from a Joan Baez song to 'Greensleeves'.

Still smiling, he caught Emmeline's eye. She was sitting by the fire in her lovely long skirt, with ribbons of the same rich and opulent material threading through her hair like tame velvet snakes. Her hand was resting on Hal's shoulder as on a jewelled cask, and indeed Hal looked like some rare precious stone, his face clear and luminous, his hair shining, those remarkable eyes relecting the firelight like exquisite blue glass.

As Leo watched, Emmeline turned her gaze on Hal, but he didn't notice. He was staring into the middle of the room at the candles, oblivious to Em, to the love she was emanating like the radiation from a star. He was in some place of his own, deeply there, and somehow Leo knew, and was troubled by the knowledge, that it was a place where Emmeline would never be able to follow him.

Chapter Nine

D aisy walks through the crowded streets of Canterbury feeling sick at heart. For the first time ever, Christmas has defeated her. She thinks of the numerous presents to buy and to wrap, the gargantuan amount of food to prepare, and feels so exhausted she wants to sleep until spring.

Ordinarily, the thought of all her absent children returning home for the holiday, which they do every year, spurs her into a tornado of energy, and she actually enjoys the preparations. This year should be even more fun, with Emmeline here, with Paul bringing his fiancée, with Baz and Gemma, their attention now focused on the shelter for the homeless, far less feisty and touchy than they have been of late. But she just cannot get herself together, and as she walks aimlessly down the main street which is closed to traffic but almost impassable through hordes of rushing bodies, she wonders what on earth she is doing coming into town on a Saturday afternoon. The decorations, the noise, the glitter of tinsel, seem meretricious to her this year. Street vendors clog the road, prolifically selling hot dogs, toy rats which run about on a string, cheap Christmas wrapping paper. There are musicians everywhere: men in full Scottish regalia playing bagpipes, a group of South

Americans in garish ponchos dancing as well as playing tiny guitars and pipes, singers with guitars, fiddles, even miniature bands complete with keyboards. Baz is nowhere to be seen; the doleful earthy sounds of his didgeridoo would be lost in this cacophany of sound, for every store has its music also, mindless taped music, blaring out both Christmas carols and rock'n'roll indiscriminately from the open doors into the streets.

Daisy is unsettled by all these bustling people who seem frantic, irritable, unsoothed by the chimera of Christmas Spirit stalking the streets. People push and don't apologise, or just don't notice. A cold wind has come up, making everyone restless and bad-tempered, as teachers say children become when there is a fierce wind outside the classroom. She rounds a corner and sees a woman huddled in the doorway of a solicitor's office which is shut for the day. The woman, not very old, is sitting on the ground, several torn knapsacks with odds and ends of clothing strewn about her like confetti, hunched up against the wind. Daisy hesitates, and meets the woman's eye, but there is nothing there. No begging, no pleading. No contact. Nothing. Daisy goes on.

She does not feel like Christmas shopping any more, but neither does she feel like going home. Wandering down a side street not far from the Cathedral, she finds herself in front of Brackenbury's Bookshop, and impulsively she goes inside.

The place is busy, jammed with people. The shop is part of a very old building with rickety wooden staircases, narrow elongated rooms, low ceilings haphazardly strewn with the odd heavy oak beam. There are two more floors apart from the ground one, and the walls along the stairs are lined with books so that the congestion there is sometimes impossible. No one seems to mind; the shop, in spite of its peculiarities or perhaps because of them, is busy and popular.

There is another assistant there besides Jim, Barnaby's main helper: a young girl who works Saturdays and the odd weekday afternoon. Daisy nods hello to Jim whom she has seen before and goes upstairs, telling herself she wants to browse in the poetry section. Barnaby's cluttered office is next to the poetry, the door open to reveal a jumble of books, papers, invoices, letters, and one moribund houseplant. Barnaby, sitting at his desk, looks up, takes off his glasses, and says delightedly, 'Daisy, what a breath of fresh air on a hectic Saturday! Is there life outside this musty bookshop? Come inside, have some coffee and tell me about the world out there.'

Daisy gratefully joins him. Barnaby moves a carton of books, an unopened bottle of milk, a photograph of Marjorie and the girls, from a wooden armchair and motions Daisy to be seated. The kettle, on the floor, is already coming to a boil, and Barnaby finds another mug, wipes it with a tissue, and puts a heaped teaspoon of instant coffee in it.

'The shop is packed. You must be doing well,' she remarks.

'Yes, we are. It's gratifying that people are still spending money on books.'

'I really like to come in here. It's so conducive to browsing. It's a wonder anyone buys anything: one could just lounge about and read entire novels without ever leaving the place.'

Barnaby pours boiling water into the mugs and opens the carton of milk. 'I hope you don't take sugar. I don't think there is any.'

'No, no, that's fine.' Daisy suddenly feels awkward. She has stopped often, throughout the few years she has known the Brackenburys, in the shop, and chatted with Barnaby, but this is the first time she has drunk coffee with him in his office.

'I'm not intruding, am I? I mean, you are usually so busy. I hate to bother you.'

'I've been on the upstairs till all morning and things are actually slowing down now; I've just closed it. The Christmas-present type books are mostly downstairs anyway. Jim and Fran can cope for a bit longer down there while we have our coffee.'

They drink for a moment in silence. The coffee is vile but Daisy hardly notices. She says, hesitantly, 'Barnaby, thanks so much for the other night.'

'Oh, don't thank me. It was Marjorie who organised it all, did the cooking. I'm sorry you had to leave so early because of the snow.'

'It wasn't just the dinner, though that was delicious, as it always is. I did phone Marjorie to thank her. I just – I wanted to thank you, too.'

The extraordinary thing about Barnaby, Daisy thinks, is that he understands. She does not have to say another word, does not have to explain how very much his sympathetic listening the other evening meant to her. He just nods his head, smiles kindly, and says, 'It was my pleasure, Daisy. My pleasure.'

They can now relax and talk of other things, though Daisy is very much aware of taking Barnaby from his work and makes several attempts to go. 'Have another cup of coffee,' he says, stopping her. She accepts happily, in spite of the acrid unpalatable drink he places in her hand. 'It's a nice change for me,' he continues, 'talking in sentences, rather than the cursory words. Marjorie and I communicate in loud monosyllables over the children's steady hum of noise. When at last they are in bed, we seem to fall asleep in front of the television.'

He talks for a bit about his daughters, on whom he dotes.

When Daisy comments on this he says ruefully, 'I'm terribly soppy about them, and I seem not to see them much. Marjorie is so efficient, has such a strict routine, there's hardly room for me. It's dinner at six, as soon as I get home – all of us together, which is nice, of course – then Marjorie and I do the washing up while the girls are allowed half an hour to watch their carefully selected video cartoons.' He rolls his eyes wryly.

'Then it's their bath-time. Marjorie supervises that, naturally, and then it's story-time and bed. I do occasionally get to read them a bedtime story, but I'm told that I get them too excited and take too long.' He pauses, looking preoccupied. 'She's an excellent mother,' he continues, as if wanting to make things very clear. 'I can't fault her in any way.'

'I've always admired her,' Daisy murmurs. The conversation seems to have dispersed into a sudden, uneasy silence, and she stands up to go. This time Barnaby does not stop her. 'I'd like the two of you to come to us for a meal before Christmas,' she says. 'What night can you make it?'

'It may be awkward,' Barnaby says slowly. 'I've rather got myself tied up in the evenings. Didn't Gemma tell you?'

'No, I haven't really seen Gemma and Baz much lately, not to talk to. They are both so busy with that shelter for the homeless.'

'So am I, you see.'

'You?'

'Don't sound so incredulous, Daisy. They're desperate for help, you know. Your Gemma and her friends are the mainstay of that place; the whole thing would probably have closed without them. But they can't be there all the time. Baz was in here last week, telling me all about it, and I found myself volunteering to do three evenings a week running the soup kitchen they've set up.'

'Well, well,' Daisy says.

'I wish you wouldn't sound so surprised. Am I that much of a selfish uncaring oaf?'

'Oh goodness, of course not, Barnaby. You've always cared about things. Look at all your work for Greenpeace. I suppose I'm just – I don't know.'

Barnaby is struck by the sudden look of pain on her face. 'What is it?' he asks gently.

'I'm merely jealous, that's all,' she says lightly. 'Of your energy and commitment. I thought it was just Gemma and Baz and Blue and Flack, all those bright young people, who had it, but of course you do too. I can't blame my apathy, my lack of passion, on getting older now. You can't be more than a few years younger than me.'

'If that,' Barnaby smiles. 'And besides, my father in the West Country has just become a proselytising and vociferous member of the Green Party. No, you can't blame a lack of passion on getting older, Daisy. You'll have to do better than that.'

His words, which on the surface seem harsh, are strangely comforting, soothing. He is looking at Daisy thoughtfully, and before she can answer him, says, 'I'm on my own at the shelter, those three nights a week. One person is not really enough to dish out food and clear up. Why don't you join me?'

Daisy, standing and about to leave, stares at Barnaby. Shaking her head she is about to say no, when suddenly into her mind comes the image of the woman resting in the solicitor's doorway in town. Barnaby's eyes, warm and intelligent and full of compassion, meet hers, but she sees only those other eyes: blank, empty, not blind but unseeing. Not wanting to see, perhaps – and who could blame her?

Wearily she nods her head. The old exhaustion has crept

back into her bones, her blood. She says, apathetically, 'Of course I'll help, Barnaby. How can I refuse? What evening do you want me to begin?'

'I'm rather desperate for help tonight, actually.'

'Tonight?'

Barnaby nods. 'I'm going there just before seven, but you can come whenever you can get away.'

'All right,' Daisy says reluctantly. 'I'll be there.'

Barnaby starts to go to her, to give her a brief embrace, thank her, but she quickly turns and walks out of his office and down the stairs before he can make a move. He stares after her, then determinedly puts both Daisy and the shelter out of his mind as he goes downstairs to help with the till.

'You're what?' Leo says at dinner that evening. Daisy has called him in early, explaining what she was doing.

'The shelter?' Emmeline adds. 'You?'

'Thanks,' Daisy says sardonically. 'Am I such a selfish uncaring oaf, that this is such a surprise?' Echoing Barnaby's words, she grins, the first time she has felt like smiling since she left the bookshop. In truth, she is terrified. The dead empty look in the woman's eyes on the street haunts her. She doesn't know if she can face other eyes like that. They fill her both with terror and with guilt.

When she goes, Leo and Emmeline wash up amicably together, then Leo goes off to check a small hitch in his automatic feeder. Emmeline, who has not long been home from the university, changes into a dark green linen skirt with a jacket to match and ponders what blouse to wear with it. She is about to go back to the university to meet Clem Todd at the theatre there. Though she sometimes enjoys Clem's company, when he is not being smugly arrogant or meaningfully sexy, she wishes she were joining Tony and his band at the pub where they are booked for a gig this evening. Tony asked her if she wanted to come along, and she regretfully had to say no.

Emmeline has seen Tony a couple of times since that night at his house. He came once to see Leo and ended up staying for a vegetable curry. Another time Emmeline ran into him in the Primrose Café, where they shared a pot of mango tea and a fat thick wedge of chocolate fudge cake. Emmeline feels unpressured, comfortable, with Tony now, and she understands it is her own attitude which has changed. Accepting the fact that a friendship is all that is on offer, she is not diminished in her own eyes because Tony does not attempt, or even seem to want, any kind of a physical, sexual relationship with her. On the contrary, the knowledge seems to have freed her in some way, so that she is able to enjoy him as a person, not a sexual being. Because the feeling is so new to her, she finds herself musing on the reasons why she has never been able to have such easy relationships with men before. Hal, her experience with him, began the trouble, of course; indeed, she understands that most of the damage was done then. But she was also too young, too inexperienced, to repair that damage as it might have been mended. Instead, in her miserable and self-blaming state, she became involved with a series of men who made the damage worse.

Joel was the first one, and she couldn't have chosen a more unsuitable, destructive encounter after her aborted relationship with Hal. She was in her third year of college by then, having spent the first two in a fragile, wounded state, still unable to stop grieving over the loss of Hal, the loss of England, the loss of all her dreams and plans and ambitions. She had been accepted at a university in Washington, DC, which was reputed to have an excellent Drama Department. Emmeline dutifully studied, attended lectures, made notes, and was praised highly by her teachers. She did not audition for any of the university productions – she no longer wanted to act – but if any of the production team needed assistance on props, lighting, costumes, whatever, Emmeline helped, skilfully and willingly. Though she performed most of these jobs by rote, mechanically, by her third year something of her old love of the theatre began to return.

With it came a tentative interest in the opposite sex. She became slightly infatuated with a fellow student called Joel, who was later to become a moderately successful playwright and actor. Joel was everything Hal wasn't: brash, sexually arrogant, sure of his effect on women. The first time they went out together was to a party, at a bleak, high-rise apartment building where another student, Myra, lived. The party was to celebrate Myra's approaching wedding to an older man she didn't love, purely to get out of what she called the rat-race of student-theatre life, to which they were all, at the time, committed. Myra, proud of her escape to affluent suburbia, threw the party to introduce everyone to her soon-to-be husband, and to gloat a bit over the other students.

The other students, unfortunately for Myra, actually thought she was pathetic, and pitied her for selling out. But that did not make them averse to showing up in droves, bringing friends and drinking, as if it were water, the vodka and gin that Myra's fiancé had provided. It was not the usual student beverage of beer and more beer, with the occasional bottle of cheap plonk: this was the real stuff, and plentiful. And so the party was unusually hot and sizzling quite early on in the evening.

Emmeline was excited. For the first time since her return

from London, she felt like joining the world again. And for the first time since Hal, she felt attracted to someone, felt the first stirrings of desire. She and Joel had just finished working together on a production of Shaw's *Heartbreak House*; Joel had been stage manager, and Em his assistant. She found him seductively charming, and was thrilled when he asked her to go with him to the party.

Joel had asked Emmeline because he felt slightly sorry for her, this quiet, rather meek and serious girl who had done a competent job as his assistant stage manager. He felt that he owed her a favour after all her uncomplaining toil, for he knew he was not the easiest of people to work for. Luckily he was free at the moment, between women, and he knew that he would feel good, virtuous, if he asked Em on a date. She obviously had a crush on him, which was fine with him, because after all she was quite attractive. It was when the plain ones became infatuated that he grew annoyed: the pretty girls he could take.

Emmeline surprised him that evening at the party by being not just pretty but quite stunning. She was wearing a short, pale pink dress, knitted in some kind of light clingy wool; it was sleeveless and cut into a low V-neckline which exposed parts of Emmeline he had never seen before. After a few vodkas, he was positively lusting after her, and kept kissing her white neck which was long and exposed and utterly bewitching.

Myra, the hostess and bride-to-be, had had too much to drink and was vacillating between manic laughter and incipient tears. Her wedding dress, a ridiculous frock of frills and net and ornate tucks and laces and trains, lay spread out decorously on the big double bed in the bedroom for everyone to look at, like a virgin about to be sacrificed. Into this room couples came and went, ostensibly to admire the dress but in reality to indulge in a bit of groping and fondling, for the door locked, and it was the only empty room in the apartment.

Emmeline, unfortunately, had begun drinking on an empty stomach, and was far more intoxicated than she realised. She remembered Joel kissing her on the neck; she remembered liking it, wanting more. She had not kissed a man since she left Hal, and her response did not go unnoticed by Joel. He poured her another gin and tonic, made her drink it, saying it was mostly tonic and she mustn't get dehydrated. 'Coming into the other room?' he said softly, for his eye had been on the bedroom for some time. He waited until another couple came out and then with alacrity pulled Emmeline towards the open door.

Emmeline remembered going in willingly, though unsteadily. She remembered seeing the stark white wedding dress staked out on the bed before Joel closed the door gently, locked it, and turned out the harsh overhead light. Then before she understood what was happening, he pulled her down with him onto the floor.

She didn't remember what happened next. The contact with the floor must have done her in; she must have passed out for a few minutes, probably longer, for the next thing she remembered was Joel lying on top of her, removing something wet and slimy from between her legs, and saying, 'Come on, get up now, I'm finished.' He somehow managed to pull up her underpants, pull her dress down, and get her out of the room, and put her to sleep on an empty sofa where she didn't wake up until the next morning.

Half the party had spent the night there, but Joel wasn't amongst them. Emmeline, waking up ill and nauseous, made her way alone back to the tiny flat she shared with her roommate. There were small patches of blood on her underpants and she understood from that, and her hazy recollections of Joel on top of her, exactly what it was that had happened.

It wasn't until months, possibly years, later that the horror of it, the unutterable knowledge that she had lost her virginity through a rape, hit her. At the time she was too ill to comprehend, too confused and shocked. When her head began to clear she tried to tell herself that it was a good thing: it was about time anyway, and after all, she was in love with Joel. She gullibly assumed, by his act that night, that he loved her too, that this was to be the beginning of her first real love affair. For a few days she waited patiently for him to phone or come over. Of course this was illusion, but the reality of what had really happened was too ugly and nasty even to contemplate. So she told herself, with a kind of sick, perverse pride, that at last she was a real woman: a man actually wanted her, and not just any man, but one as handsome, as sought-after, as Joel.

He never phoned, he never tried to see her. She found out a week or so later from her roommate that Joel had left town, for it was summer and college was over. When she next saw him, at the start of the fall term, he was courteous but distant, the only indication of what had passed between them a slight worried frown creasing his forehead. When Emmeline also acted as if nothing had happened, the lines in his face cleared, and for a few moments he was almost friendly, offering to buy her a coffee in the canteen before her next class.

And so it was not until Emmeline had graduated and begun work at a small college in Maryland that she had her first full sexual relationship. He was a colleague called Daniel, a year or two older than her and not unlike Clem Todd, except that he was unmarried. When Emmeline noticed in herself, once again, the first stirrings of physical attraction, she was determined not to blow it, as perhaps she had done, she sometimes thought, with both Hal and Joel. Her confidence after those two experiences was at an all-time low, but was beginning to rise slightly with Daniel's salacious attention. Determined to do this one right, she began to perfect the feminine wiles that were so distasteful to Daisy: the flirtatious manner, the seductive clothes, the clever make-up and repertoire of sexy small talk. She hardly realised she was doing it. She had never been that way before, but secretly she couldn't help feeling that if her former naive self was responsible for the two destructive experiences she had had with Hal and then Joel, then it was time she changed. Now, desperate for some kind of love, some kind of a normal man-woman relationship, all the 'How To Get Your Man' tips so prolific in women's magazines when she was growing up reasserted themselves in some long-forgotten memory bank and urged themselves into her consciousness.

Surprisingly, it worked. Or – and this is the difference which Emmeline is only now beginning to understand – it worked with some men. Whether these men were attracted to her because of all the subliminal messages she was pumping out, or whether she chose them unconsciously because of their difference to Hal, was a chicken and egg problem. Whatever . . . Daniel was the first to succumb, and he succumbed for two years, until finally Emmeline got bored with the effort of constantly trying to divert his roving eye with even more audacious attempts at sex appeal, and ditched him.

This set the pattern for all Emmeline's future relationships. The men she attracted, or the ones she was attracted to, were the ones who played hard games, ran around in packs, were knowing and tough, macho, into sex rather than love. Some were obvious about it, but most were subtle, covering their secret dislike of women with a cloak of smooth velvet charm. And so the years passed, and though emotionally they were never fulfilling, she became more and more engrossed in her career and fortunately found the satisfaction there which she never attained in her personal life.

Emmeline drives to the theatre thoughtfully, contemplatively. Thinking about the past has made her sad, but lately she is feeling more optimistic about the future and so refuses to brood. She turns her thoughts to the event ahead. She is not looking forward to this evening with Clem; there are too many hidden agendas, too many little games that must be played out. Tony has taught her how to relax with a man, how a male-female friendship can exist without tension and wariness, without competition and the chalking-up of imaginary points. She has had a difficult week at the university and does not feel up to Clem. She wishes once again that she were meeting Tony.

Clem Todd is not like Tony. Clem may be charming, but he is not easy to be with. He actually doesn't like women much, thinking their minds infinitely inferior to his own. He does like to fuck them, and thinks about this often, but that is something else entirely.

Clem Todd is also not naturally sensitive, though he believes he is, as do many of his students, for he is quick to detect problems, unerring in pointing out both the fallacies and the occasional brilliances of their work, and supportive in all their endeavours. Clem is a good tutor, and much of this is because he thrives on the adulation a good tutor receives. But that is neither here nor there. He likes – he craves – being thought sensitive and caring, and brilliant and charismatic, so he works at all these things, and succeeds.

Unfortunately, Clem Todd has been grossly insensitive to the feelings of his American colleague, Emmeline Lake. Noting Em's new demeanour, a lightness of being, an easiness about her that was not there before, Clem wrongly attributes this to himself, and in spite of the fact that Emmeline has given him no encouragement, he believes an embryonic passion is germinating within her. For him, of course.

The change in Emmeline comes from her new self-awareness, her new confidence in herself as a total woman in body and mind, rather than a sex symbol on the one hand, and an intellectual academic on the other. She is learning reams about herself, and profiting from it. Her new relaxed aura makes her even more attractive, and Clem, lunching with her quite often now in either the college dining hall, or sometimes in the town, is becoming quite besotted in his little way. Emmeline, full of her new friendship with Tony, is determined to make a friend also of Clem, who can really be quite nice when he chooses. And so it was that when he asked if she were going to the production at the university on Saturday night, and could they meet, she accepted.

The play is a new one by a playwright Emmeline had never heard of before, performed by a well-known touring company. It is interesting, well-acted, and both Clem and she enjoy it. At the interval they go to the bar for a drink, Clem's hand on Emmeline's elbow, much to the interest of a cluster of Em's students nearby. One of the more impressionable female students has a crush on Clem, but Emmeline is relieved to see that Clem treats her no differently from the others, and indeed seems unaware of the infatuation. As a matter of fact Clem is very much aware of it, but it happens so often he is quite used to it. He doesn't at all fancy students, finding them uninteresting as potential bed partners, not enough of a challenge. Also, just lately he has found that the female students remind him too much of his own daughter, Eliza, and the thought is intensely disagreeable. He has had too many confrontations with Eliza not to detest thoroughly that whole age group.

'I say, Emmeline! Yahoo there!'

Emmeline and Clem both look up, startled, to see who is shouting at them. It is Marjorie Brackenbury, plunging through the sea of bodies crowded around the bar like a great seal after a fish. 'Got you!' she bellows, clutching Em's arm. She nods cursorily to Clem. 'Jolly good play, don't you think? I'm here with the other playgroup leaders; we treat ourselves to an outing once a month. Poor Barnaby forgot it was my night out and promised to help at that new shelter, so I had a dreadful time trying to find a babysitter at the last minute.'

She says this fondly, not at all cross with Barnaby. 'Is he enjoying the work?' Emmeline asks.

'I'm not sure enjoying is the right word. He's only been there a few times, and he's been appalled and shocked. He's determined to carry on, though, and it's a jolly good thing: someone has to do it.'

The play is shortly to start again and Emmeline excuses herself to go to the Ladies, leaving Marjorie extolling her husband's virtues to a disgruntled Clem. As she washes her hands at the sink she sees in the mirror that the woman next to her, a woman of around her age, is having a wash. While all around them well-dressed theatregoers tidy up their hair, put on fresh lipstick, this woman is washing under her arms with a wet, soapy paper towel, reaching beneath a voluminous man's shirt to do so. The woman is calm, unrushed, oblivious to the oblique glances she is attracting. As Emmeline watches she finishes her washing, dries herself with another paper towel, and puts on the layers of clothing she has taken off for her wash: a torn black jumper, an old cardigan, then a second, larger jumper, then a short cape, an ugly blue plaid, reminiscent of jumble sales in unstylish suburbs. When she is finished she looks up and catches Emmeline's eye and acknowledges her with a mixture of sadness and amusement and, most predominantly, with a look of complete and utter resignation. There is no bitterness in the look, and no accusation. Emmeline, desperately wanting to say something but knowing that nothing would be adequate, watches as the women puts on a brown woolly hat, a shabby man's overcoat, and picks up her assorted carrier bags and walks out slowly, with great dignity.

Emmeline thinks of the woman throughout the second act, and when the play ends she would like to tell someone about her. But not Clem. For the third time that evening, she wishes she were with Tony.

Clem notices the wistful look on her face and mistakenly thinks it is for him; he curses the fact that his wife is at home and not doing something sensible like visiting her mother in Somerset. An intimate coffee and brandy at his house would be just the thing right now. He is irritated with Emmeline for not having a place of her own, for living in that remote farmhouse with God knows how many people in and out the whole time. 'Would you like a nightcap somewhere?' he says hopefully.

'No, thanks. I'm exhausted, Clem. End of term and all that.'

He nods. There is time, he thinks. There is plenty of time. He has discerned a definite softening in her towards himself, and he is confident enough of his own charm to know he can make the most of this. As he kisses her chastely good night he allows his hand to linger on her waist, but not so long as to put her on her guard. He drives away satisfied, knowing that it is only a question of time.

'A colleague, eh? Work? You wouldn't take *me* to the bloody play, oh no.'

Celia, not taking her eyes off the telly, attacks Clem verbally as he walks in the door.

'What're you on about? Of course I was with a colleague.'

'Why do they always have to be women? And is it really, truly, necessary to kiss them every time?'

Clem groans, slumps into a chair. Celia, sensing her advantage, turns the sound down on the televison. 'I've been so bored here on my own. And you off making a fool of yourself, feeling up so-called colleagues in the theatre car park.'

Clem groans again. It is barely twenty minutes since he parted with Emmeline, and already one of Celia's spies has telephoned. He thought he recognised one of her bosom pals in that group Marjorie was with.

'I was with someone from my department, and I wasn't feeling her up, for God's sake. It was an innocent good-night kiss.'

As he says it, he knows he has made a mistake. Celia loves him on the defensive, and though she no longer really cares what he is up to, and with whom, she likes making him squirm.

Perhaps this isn't going to be such a boring evening after all, she thinks maliciously, and turns off the telly with a vengeance as she prepares to do battle.

*   *   *

Daisy is also kissed as she opens her car door and says good night to Barnaby, but affectionately on the cheek, followed by an impulsive embrace. 'Oh Daisy, I'm so pleased you came! You were great with them, just great.'

'I only talked to them. Had a bit of a giggle when we were dishing out.'

'That's just what they need. I'm so useless at it. I come over all heavy, seem to lose my sense of humour. All I can think of is the sheer awfulness of their plight, of being homeless.'

'I know.' Daisy lingers at her car, parked next to Barnaby's behind the shelter. 'They are all so normal,' she says at last. 'The homeless are so like us. There was a young man Julian's age, a nice open lad. He left his hometown in the Midlands, ran into some bad luck, and since winter he's been sleeping in empty barns, or down by the railway tracks.'

'Thank God they started the shelter. I'd hate to be outside tonight. It looks like a freezing fog – will you be all right driving home?'

'Oh, fine, fine.' Daisy lingers, not wanting to go. Her mind and heart are so full of the things she has seen tonight that she wants to talk and talk about it for hours. She could tell Leo, of course. Indeed, she will try. He will listen, offer the odd comment, but what can he know, how can he share this? The trouble with Leo cutting her off all these years, not sharing his soul with her, is that now that something has touched *her* soul, deeply and importantly, she is not so sure that she wants to share it with *him*.

Barnaby, noticing her hesitation, says, 'Should we go for a drink somewhere? It's not late.'

'What about Marjorie?'

'She'll be sound asleep in front of the television. What about Leo?'

'He'll be wide awake in front of the telly.'

'Well, they don't need us then, do they! Shall we go?'

They look at each other and laugh. Arm in arm they leave the cars and walk into the town, to find a nice quiet pub where they can talk to their hearts' content. It is very late when they return to their respective homes and not only is Marjorie asleep in front of the television, but so is Leo. Daisy, coming in, wakes him gently.

'Oh, you're back,' he mutters sleepily. 'Is it that late?'

'Late enough.'

'What was your evening like?'

'Interesting,' Daisy says vaguely.

Leo nods. Though the television is still on, he has not really been watching it, not tonight. His mind has been racing with plans, with ideas. He knows they are far-fetched, crazy even, but he knows also that this is his last chance. He has at last almost come to a decision.

'Are you all right?' Daisy asks, noting his preoccupation.

'Yes, of course.' He frowns slightly. 'Why shouldn't I be?'

Daisy is silent. She waits for him to ask where she has been, what she has been doing so late, but he only says, 'I'm bushed. Let's go to bed.'

And so she doesn't tell him. For the first time ever, she has a secret from Leo.

Chapter Ten

'*Y*ou won't believe this,' Baz says, coming home to the caravan the next day at seven in the morning.

Gemma, waking, says, 'Oh, Baz! How was it? Were there many people there? Did you have any trouble? Did you get a chance to get any sleep? Who else was on with you? I don't see why I can't do a night-shift, just because I am a woman.'

'Because they are all men there, Daisy. And sometimes there is violence. You know as well as I do that some of the transients are addicts, alcoholics. There was actually a nasty punch-up tonight between two of the men.'

'I worried about you. I didn't fall asleep until the early hours.'

'That was daft. I was on with one of the organisers, Miles, a community worker. He's good – tough when he needs to be, sympathetic and kind the rest of the time.'

Gemma reaches up and wraps her arms around Baz. 'It was your first night-shift; I didn't know what to expect.'

'Nor did I, I must confess. Except for this one incident, it was a fairly quiet night. Full, too. All eleven beds. We put a couple of mattresses in the lounge but we still turned a few away. Miles said we couldn't put down any more mattresses, because of fire regulations.'

'And what about the women? What about the poor bloody women? Why can't they use the shelter?'

Baz shakes his head helplessly. 'Miles says you can't have a mixed shelter; there's too much potential for trouble. He's trying to get a separate one started, though.'

'Oh fine, great. In the meantime, where do the women go? Back out in the streets?'

'There aren't many homeless women around here, Gemma.'

'That's what they say. I saw a couple at the soup kitchen the other evening.'

'I know, I know.' Baz gets up, puts the dark green enamel kettle on top of the wood-burning stove. 'We just have to keep fighting for a women's shelter, that's all.'

'Always something to fight for,' Gemma murmurs.

'Oh hell, I almost forgot what I raced home to tell you! It's about your mother.'

'Mum?'

'You won't believe this.'

'That's what you said when you came in.'

'She was there.'

'What? Has Dad thrown her out?'

'Don't be silly, not as a resident – as a volunteer.'

'Good God! Mum?'

'Do you want some tea? I'll have a cup and then crash out. Are you staying in bed or coming out?'

'Tell me about Mum.'

'She was just leaving when I arrived. She's doing the soup kitchen three nights a week, with Barnaby.'

'You're right – I *don't* believe it.'

Baz takes the boiling kettle off the stove, pours it out into a fat brown teapot. 'Well, why not? She hasn't got a job, doesn't do anything—'

'Oh, come off it, Baz. She's always busy, cleaning the house or the hens, mucking around on the farm . . .'

'Maybe so, but most of the time she doesn't need to. I've never seen such a fucking clean henhouse in all my life.'

Gemma laughs, then looks thoughtful. 'I can't imagine her doing the soup kitchen. I would have thought it was far too rough, somehow. Mum has had such a sheltered life, really. Apart from her year roaming America, and that crazy boat-trip when she met Dad, it's just been the farm and us kids.'

'Well, she won't last. I'll give her a week and she'll be running home to Woodland Farm.'

'Hm. Maybe.'

Baz yawns. 'My turn in bed now. I'm shattered.'

Gemma rolls over and pulls him towards her. 'I think I'll stay in bed with you,' she says languidly. 'I think a day in bed is just what I need.'

'I'm going to go right to sleep,' Baz warns.

'We'll see about that,' she murmurs. 'We'll just see about that.'

Blue, serving a mushroom Stroganoff and courgette pancakes to some customers, notices across the restaurant that Flack, putting down the telephone, looks both startled and pre-occupied. Taking him into the kitchen she says, 'What's up, Flack?'

'That job. At the off-licence.'

'The one you didn't get?'

'The bloke wants me. The other guy suddenly quit, just didn't turn up.'

Blue stirs a large saucepan of carrot and parsnip soup and says, 'Did you say yes?'

'Do we have a choice? The pay's shit, but he wants me for several nights a week.'

'It would help with our rent.'

'I know.' Flack shakes his head. The kitchen smells rich and succulent, and the customers in the other room look contented. Flack too is contented when he is slicing, peeling, chopping, adding a bit of garlic to this, an experimental sauce to that. Before he and Blue got Primrose Café, Flack used to cook for his friends, spending all his dole money on the ingredients. When his father died and left him a bit of cash, there was no question of what he wanted to do with it. Primrose Café had, after a precarious start, begun to pay its way, until the rent suddenly escalated.

Blue, preparing some garlic bread, smiles reassuringly at Flack. 'I'll be fine on my own, with Gemma to help. At least you're not working weekends.'

A bell in the other room tinkles as new customers come in. 'We'll be all right, Flack, you'll see,' Blue says as she leaves the kitchen.

Flack is not so sure.

Before Christmas, Emmeline sees Tony's band perform for the first time. They are giving a charity performance in one of the large halls in the city, to get funds for the shelter which now has an official name: the Northgate Hostel. More bedding is urgently needed, and more equipment for the soup kitchen, not to mention clothes, furniture for the lounge, and some amenities like a television, perhaps a pool table, for the residents. These will all be bought second-hand, of course, but it would be comforting to have furniture without missing legs, mattresses which are not quite so revoltingly malodorous, saucepans which have not been burned and scoured so many times that there is a permanent charred smell about them.

It is a Friday night and the hall has been festively decorated with balloons, miniature Christmas trees, holly and mistletoe. When Emmeline drives in with Leo and Daisy, not only are Tony and the band already there, setting up, but also Baz and Gemma, finishing off the decorations. 'Blue and Flack will be here later, when the café closes,' Gemma tells Emmeline. 'Everyone is taking turns running the bar.'

Leo has found a small table for them against the wall. 'They must not be expecting many people,' Emmeline says worriedly. 'There are only a few tables set up on the sides.'

'Obviously you've never been to a gig before,' Baz says with a smile. 'The floor's cleared for dancing.'

'It's so huge. It's going to be empty. Look, it's eight o'clock and there are only twenty people here.'

'Em, you're such a worrier!' Daisy exclaims.

'Chill out, Auntie Emmy.' Gemma pats her hand affectionately like she would an ancient maiden aunt. Which I probably am to her, Emmeline thinks ruefully. But she does so much want this evening to be a success. She's seen the tremendous effort put into it.

Tony joins them, for the band members, having set up, are not yet playing but are wandering around seemingly aimlessly, chatting to friends, getting a drink at the bar. Tony is wearing a long-sleeved copper silk shirt, jeans, and his black hair with the silver flecks is tied back in a headband.

'Hey,' Daisy grins, 'your shirt's the same colour as my hair. Well, as my hair used to be, when I was young.'

'I can't wait to hear you play, Tony,' Emmeline says.

'I hope you like it. There's going to be a mixture of people here, so we hope to do something for everybody. Some sixties and seventies music for the likes of us, some of our own new numbers, and hopefully everything in between.'

Eventually, as the hall begins to look less empty, the band starts to warm up, then Tony introduces everyone. Besides himself on the guitar, there are three others, as well as a drummer, a wild-looking young man with a manic grin, and a woman with fluffy auburn hair who is the lead singer. By this time not only are the tables filled but the dance-floor is crowded with people standing, watching the band, swaying to the music. Emmeline is fascinated by the cross-segment of the population represented in the festive hall. There are, of course, Gemma and Baz and their friends, rainbow-like and patchworked and layered and beaded; and there are many other young people as well, the boys in jeans and T-shirts, the girls in a great deal of black, wearing skirts ranging from minis to ankle-length. Every age and social group seems to be represented, for Emmeline spots people of her age standing around with drinks in their hands next to the clusters of young people. There are couples in their thirties dressed casually but with style, others the same age more formally attired with the men in suits, the women in party frocks and high, high heels. Sixty-year-olds wearing jeans and jumpers tap their feet to the music, and several plump grey-haired matrons in woollen skirts and court shoes seem to be selling raffle tickets.

'Why isn't anyone dancing?' Emmeline asks Marjorie Brackenbury.

'Wait, there's plenty of time!' Marjorie shouts. 'You Americans are so impatient.'

But one person *is* dancing – on her own, oblivious to the

crowd now scattered around the hall. She is dressed in an old-fashioned tweed skirt, coming just below her knees, and her feet are clad in sensible brown walking shoes. She wears a fussy white nylon blouse with a ludicrous bow in front, and her short fair hair is frizzed in an unbecoming perm, tight as lambs' wool. Emmeline can't tell if she is twenty or fifty; probably somewhere in the middle, she thinks. The woman dances and dances, in some luminescent world of her own, her odd pug face transported, sublime.

'Who is that?' Emmeline asks the others.

'Her name is Glenda; she goes to all Tony's concerts. She lives in the home for the mentally disabled, at the top of town. Someone brought her down and will collect her when the evening ends.'

Emmeline watches, fascinated. Glenda, still alone on the dance-floor, rocks back and forth in the same rhythmless step she has been doing for some time. Tony and the band are playing one of their own numbers, a fast raucous piece that Emmeline, to her surprise, rather likes. It has been a long time since she listened to rock music; she put that away with Hal, with the sixties, with the person she had been then and no longer wanted to be.

The hall is full now, yet still no one dances, no one but Glenda in her solitary rhythm, her contemplative movements. No one stares at her, though, and no one laughs, or points, or seems to be taking any notice of her at all as she twists and turns and twirls in a totally natural, uninhibited way. Only Emmeline watches, entranced. She watches Tony too, for it is the first time she has seen him in the band. She realises that he is quite a fine guitar player; and he is having such fun with it all, with the music, the crowd, the ambience, that she can't help but smile as she watches him. Already his brown headband has either fallen off or been taken off, and his hair, silvery in the lights, flops over his face every time he looks down at his guitar. He is exuberant, wild, crazy, and for a daft moment she feels she could love him like she loved Hal: the spirit in him, the energy, the creative charge.

The moment passes, as it must. Emmeline suddenly notices that about eighteen or twenty newcomers have entered the hall, and her heart sinks. 'Oh my God,' she exclaims to Leo, who is sitting next to her. 'There's going to be trouble now.'

The young men and women who have entered seem ominous, filtering into the hall, after first stoking up at the bar, like something from out of the underworld with their black leather clothes, their heavy boots and thick belts. Two of the men hover in front of Emmeline's table, put their drinks down on it. Emmeline feels a tremor of unease – worse, of fear – shoot through her as they stand talking, watching the band, staring at Glenda who is still gyrating to the music of her soul. The men are big, both of them. One is at least six foot six inches tall and he wears a black leather sleeveless vest, his bare white arms, the size of bolsters, covered in tattoos. His hair is ebony, waist-length and tangled, as is his beard. The other man is not much shorter, and he too has hair tumbling uncontrollably down his back, and a dark sinister leather jacket covered with metal studs.

'Bikers,' Daisy says, in answer to Emmeline's whispered query. Daisy doesn't look at all worried, which surprises Emmeline, for even *she* knows that bikers and the New Age types that are hovering around Gemma and Baz's table are not exactly kindred spirits.

Suddenly a small, fussy-looking woman who surely must be in her late seventies, with a blue-rinsed perm, a soft pink jumper and pearls, assertively approaches the taller of the bikers.

'Heavens, she's not the bouncer, is she?' Emmeline asks with trepidation.

The others at the table laugh. 'As Gemma says, chill out, Em,' Daisy shouts over the music. 'She's only selling them a raffle ticket.'

This turns out to be true, and Emmeline watches, amazed, as the bikers buy a sheaf of tickets. At this moment Baz walks by, dressed in what looks like an Afghan poncho and cotton drawstring trousers in sea-blue covered with whirls of red patterns. A small crystal dangles from his left ear.

'Hey, you,' one of the bikers bellows at him as he passes them by.

Emmeline stiffens and cravenly looks towards the exit, wondering what the hell she is doing here. In Atlanta she goes to smart concerts with Chester or Sally: chamber music or symphonies; she goes to the theatre and to the cinema. At the parties she attends with Chester, the hosts play music by k.d. lang or, if nostalgia is called for, old Ella Fitzgerald albums. Nobody listens to Dylan any more – Tony and the band have launched into a spirited rendition of '*Maggie's Farm*' – and nobody, *nobody*, hangs out with bikers. She is feeling terribly out of her depth, and frightened to boot.

'Hey!' The other biker is now also shouting at Baz, who has walked past without acknowledging them. Probably scared witless, Emmeline thinks.

'Oh God, do something!' she hisses to the men, to Barnaby and Leo who are sitting there complacently. As she watches she suddenly screams, for the taller biker has grabbed Baz by the shoulder, no doubt as a preliminary to flattening him.

'Watch out!' Em screams, then cowers as a half a dozen leather-clad tattooed men stare at her.

'Watcha problem, lady?' The biker holding on to Baz turns to Emmeline but doesn't loosen his grip.

Emmeline feebly mumbles, 'Let go of him,' wondering why in the hell no one else is coming to the rescue.

Baz by this time has turned around to look at his assailant, and to Em's amazement, clasps the biker's shoulder in a comradely manner and shouts, 'Mike! How're things? Speak up, I can't hear over the music!'

'How's the bike?' the tall man yells.

'Sold it. Needed four wheels, so I sold the motorbike.'

The two men nod. 'Good bike, that. Old, but sound.'

They talk for a bit, then Baz ambles away. Leo, watching Emmeline's face, says, 'Mike owns the motorbike shop in town. Baz inherited an ancient bike from an older brother, and Mike sold him parts, helped him get it MOT'd.'

Emmeline, feeling a fool, slumps down in her seat. But she hasn't time to stay there long, for suddenly, as if a signal has been given, everyone is on the dance-floor, moving and jiving and rocking and twisting, and the music goes wild, and so do the dancers, and the evening has begun, really begun. Emmeline, dragged reluctantly on to the dance-floor by Barnaby, who is a mean dancer, suddenly, after the first few tentative steps, remembers what it is like to dance to a live band, to loud relentless music. She begins to let go, to move, to live the music, as Glenda did, as all the people around her are doing.

'Does it never stop?' Emmeline asks Tony, hours later, as he comes over to talk to her during one of the band's infrequent breaks.

'Not till about one or so,' he smiles at her.

'It's wonderful, Tony. I haven't danced like this since my college days. And I love your music. I really do.'

'I hoped you would.'

'It's funny, I felt real strange here at first. Kind of silly, you know? Like what was I doing here, at some teenage party or something. But your music cuts through all that. I was just me, dancing. I haven't felt so free and terrific in ages.'

They grin at each other, then Tony is off and playing again, and Emmeline is dancing, dancing, dancing, like Glenda in a world of her own, a world made up of nothing but sound and rhythm and movement and joy. Tony, on stage watching her, has a moment of regret, wishing for things he cannot have. He attacks his guitar savagely, and the moment passes. But in his head will always be the memory of Emmeline, arms thrown over her head in a gesture of abandon to the music, *his* music, eyes closed, ecstatic, radiant.

The next evening Emmeline, seated rather formally at a stylish restaurant with some of her colleagues from the university, cannot help comparing tonight's occasion to the gig last night. The food is exquisite, the décor elegant, the clientèle genteel. Em, thinking of the bikers, the cheese rolls on sale for fifty pence, the beer-soaked dance-floor, smiles enigmatically in the middle of a discourse by Clem Todd on post-modernism. It is an intelligent, thought-provoking discourse, but Emmeline's head is still too full of Tony's music to pay it more than cursory attention.

'Well, it's better than the usual turkey and etcetera staff Christmas dinner,' Clem says as he and Em walk out of the restaurant together.

'I quite enjoyed the meal,' Emmeline says politely.

'I feel full and bloated. It suddenly seems miles away to my house.'

'Do you want a ride home?'

This offer is exactly what Clem has been waiting for. 'I'd love one,' he says. 'You've never seen my place, have you? Why don't you come around now, have another coffee before you make your way back to the farm.'

'I'd never sleep,' Emmeline says. 'I can't drink coffee at night.'

Somewhat flattened, Clem retorts, 'I've got decaffein-ated.' Bloody Americans, he thinks, and wonders if it is all worth it.

Emmeline, feeling full and drowsy, yet at the same time rather exhilarated by end-of-term relief and having seen all her students safely off to the airport for their Christmas vacations at home, does not feel quite ready to go back to the farm yet so she accepts. She assumes, without actually thinking about it, that Clem's wife will be there. And so Clem gets into the car with Emmeline and they drive to the other side of town where they stop and park on a street which seems vaguely familiar to her.

'Why, that's where the Brackenburys live,' Emmeline exclaims.

'I live opposite.'

They get out of the car and walk towards the house. At that same moment, Barnaby Brackenbury and Daisy Dillard are walking towards Barnaby's house, having left the shelter together. The two couples spot each other and wave awkwardly, tentatively, not quite understanding what the other is doing there.

'Emmeline!' Daisy cries across the quiet street. 'I thought you were at a dinner.'

'It's just finished. I'm having coffee with Clem and his wife.'

Wife? Barnaby thinks. Celia left a note on their door only this afternoon before leaving with her daughter for Somerset, asking Marjorie to feed the cat because Clem always forgot.

'What about you?' Emmeline cries. 'Weren't you at the shelter tonight?'

'Yes, I'm just on my way home, stopping first for a hot chocolate with Barnaby and Marjorie.' *Marjorie?* Clem thinks. He knows that Marjorie has taken the children to see a pantomime at the Marlowe Theatre, for he met her coming out of the house. He also knows they won't be back until late, for there is a little party for the children afterwards on stage. Marjorie told him (and the entire street) all this, fretting in her booming voice that the children would be dreadfully late getting to bed.

'Do you have a ride home?' Daisy asks.

'I have my car, what about you?'

'Actually, I could come home with you. Leo needed the car to see some farmer about buying more sheep, so he dropped me in town. Barnaby was going to take me home.'

By this time the two couples have met in the middle of the road. Luckily there is no traffic, for they are all standing there indecisively, all for various reasons disgruntled and frustrated. No one makes a move to go in for their respective coffees and hot chocolates, for it seems rude not to invite the others, yet neither Clem nor Barnaby intend to socialise with each other. Clem is florid with both brandy and fury, for he had intended offering Emmeline some precious Calvados he had been saving for a special occasion, and then offering her a bed for the night so that she didn't have to drive home.

Emmeline feels discomfited because Daisy and Barnaby are looking at her somewhat oddly, as if she shouldn't be having coffee this time of night with Clem. This irritates her, for she is a grown woman, he is a colleague; it is perfectly natural that they should have a coffee together after a staff dinner.

Barnaby does not know why he is feeling cross and frustrated. He had genuinely forgotten that Marjorie was out, but when he remembered, a sudden, unbidden, forbidden, thrill went through him. He wanted Daisy all to himself, he realised, for just a bit longer. They have already done three nights together at the Northgate Hostel, and the experience has bound them in an intimate way as all their years of friendship never did. Barnaby finds this deeply satisfying, something he wants to enjoy and cherish.

And Daisy? Walking back with Barnaby through the empty but still-lit streets of the city, past the Cathedral, stopping to look at the river by the West Gate, she felt a new surge of energy, expectation, hope, such as she has not experienced for years. She doesn't know if it is Barnaby, or the shelter, or what, but it is as heady as alcohol, as potent as a drug. Whatever it is, she is not going to let it go easily. She feels alive for the first time in months.

'Maybe we should go back to the farm now?' Emmeline suggests, starting to feel cold and rather silly standing out here in the middle of the street.

'Good idea,' Daisy agrees, suddenly not wanting to see Marjorie, for she does not know Barnaby's wife is not at home. It would somehow not be right, the spell of this evening broken by Marjorie's kind, but exceedingly loud voice. 'We can have a coffee at home.'

With relief the two women wave the men goodbye, jump in Emmeline's car, and take off rather too quickly up the road.

'Well,' Daisy says mischievously, 'and whatever were you up to with Clem Todd?'

'And you?' Emmeline counters. 'What were you doing meandering dreamily up the sidewalk with Barnaby Brackenbury?'

They laugh lightheartedly. They are not serious, they are teasing, having a bit of fun, pretending they are young girls again, young women with the world dangling like a pomegranate before them.

Still standing in the road, watching the car drive away, Clem and Barnaby finally turn, nod curtly and disagreeably to each other, and stomp in to their respective houses.

'What do you think?'

Baz, standing back, admires the Christmas tree he has just inserted in a blue plastic bucket filled with sand.

'Nice one,' Flack enthuses. 'Where did you get it?'

'Donated by a local bloke. Not at all straggly, is it?'

'No, it's sound. What about the decorations?'

Pulling up a stepladder, Blue says, 'One of the newsagents gave them to us. I'm getting quite all right at begging. Ancient stock, by the look of it, but never mind.' She wavers precariously on the ladder trying to put up a silver angel which immediately topples off. 'I'm useless at this,' she moans.

By this time several of the residents have come into the lounge to watch. One of them, a man of about fifty, hands Blue the angel. 'Thanks, Clifton,' Blue smiles. 'Want to come up and give a hand? There's room on my ladder for two!'

Clifton blushes, shuffles his feet. He is dressed neatly and primly in a worn but clean shirt, and baggy old cord trousers. His short grey hair is combed straight back from his forehead, exposing an habitual worried frown that is a permanent fixture on his face. A year ago he was disabled by a stroke which left the fingers in his right hand paralysed, and he lost his job — he was a clerk in a large building society in London — and his confidence. Having lived for years alone and solitary, he could no longer face his bleak bed-sitter when he returned from hospital, and an inexplicable terror of facing his empty room every day, of trying to cope with opening tins and in general fending for himself with a crippling disability, drove him to a kind of breakdown. Within six months he had lost his home and his dignity as well as his health and his job, and had spent the last year sleeping in the parks and streets and Undergrounds of the city until he drifted into Kent after the terrors of London became too much for him.

Blue has fixed the angel to the top of the tree, to the applause of the men standing around. 'Cor, to hell with the angel, *you* should be on top of that tree,' one of the men, Arnold, shouts. Arnold is the oldest man at the hostel; he is seventy-three, an ex-Navy man and for years a chef at a seaside hotel. He lost his job and his digs when the hotel closed and he was too old to find more work; he has been homeless for eight years now. He will die homeless, he knows, but the rum staves off that knowledge and he is usually cheerful, gregarious, and slightly drunk. An odd but close friendship has developed between Clifton and Arnold since the shelter opened. Arnold, as large and grizzled and hoary as Clifton is small and slim and smooth, regales the other man with wild — but true — tales of his life in the Navy. He has a medal for distinguished service and proudly displays it often. Both staff and residents are fond of Arnold.

The lounge is starting to look vaguely festive now, in spite of its old brown linoleum floor, its sad furniture. Baz has brought holly from the woods at the farm, and the tree is beginning to look quite acceptable. Suddenly the door opens and Gemma, breathless, runs in, toting a heavy carrier bag. 'Look, I've got these,' she says, opening the carrier and unwrapping a dozen fat, tall candles. 'This will make the place look a bit cheerier tonight.' It is Christmas Eve.

Clifton and Arnold help set the candles around the room, which is beginning to get dark as it is already three in the afternoon and pouring with rain outside. 'Can we light them now, just for a few minutes?' Flack asks. 'Blue and I have to be back at the café soon.'

The candles are lit and the men, who have been laughing and boisterous, suddenly become quiet. 'It's the fuckingest prettiest thing I've seen in years,' Arnold says, so over-whelmed that he slips the small bottle of rum out of his back pocket and takes a surreptitious swallow when no one is looking. 'Aside from those legs over there,' he chuckles raucously, pointing at mini-skirted Blue.

A young man has walked in and is standing behind them, staring. He is no more than twenty-one and his clothes, old denim jacket and jeans, are soaked with the rain. He looks at the tree, the holly, the candles, and to his horror his eyes fill with tears. Racing out of the room he rushes into the dormitory, sees with relief that it is empty, and throws himself down on his bed where he cries as if his heart is breaking.

It is Christmas Day and still wet. Heavy, torrential rain thunders on the old tiled roof of Woodland Farm, beats against the lead-paned windows. Inside, however, it is dry

and warm, luxurious even, with the largest fire Emmeline has
ever seen blazing in the fireplace. Daisy looks at all her adult
children and feels humbled with gratitude, the more so as her
thoughts keep turning to the shelter, to the people who will
be spending Christmas on borrowed beds, or, worse, outside
in doorways.

Daisy also, on this Christmas Day, is filled with guilt: for
her past lethargy, her whinging self-pity. How could she have
ever felt her life to be empty, with the richness of her family,
with her children so healthy and full of promise? She has never
been struck so forcibly by her good luck before and it has made
her tremulous, frightened even, knowing that luck can change
without reason or warning. But this fear spurs her, makes her
determine she will no longer sit back and let life take control
of her. She wants to be part of it now, wants to help steer
the ship, wherever it is going.

The evening before, Daisy and Barnaby did their last soup
kitchen for a few days, for none of them are needed during
the holiday. The Northgate Hostel has had more volunteers
than they can use, mostly from people who themselves have
no families and who are too far away from friends to share
Christmas with them. They are happy to be in company other
than their own: by being thrown in with people far worse off,
their own loneliness is assuaged.

The soup kitchen was full, last night. There was a vegetable
stew, thick and nourishing, and masses of fresh bread. 'Hey,
this stuff is not bad, not bad at all,' praised a woman known
only as Josy. She was the exact same age as Daisy and carried
all her belongings around with her in an assortment of carrier
bags. Miles, the organiser, had offered to put down a mattress
for her in one of the utility rooms, despite the fact that the
shelter was for men, but Josy refused, even on the nights it

was snowing. 'I got me own places to shelter,' she had told Miles. 'I'm best on me own, mate.'

The boy who reminded Daisy so much of Julian was eating his stew in isolation in the corner of the room. When he came to collect his meal, Daisy noticed his swollen, red-rimmed eyes, and realised with horror that he had been crying. When she had served the last resident she went up to him and said, 'Mind if I sit down?' The young man, whose name was Kelvin, shook his head without looking up.

'How's the stew, then?' Daisy asked, unperturbed by the lad's lack of response. Her maternal instincts had risen to the fore like hackles on an angry dog and all she could see was one of her own children sitting there where Kelvin sat. 'Nice tree,' she went on as the boy ate silently. 'And how pretty, with all the candles around the place, all lit up.'

Still there was no response. This is Christmas Eve, Daisy thought passionately. It is Christmas Eve and this young lad the same age as my son is sitting in a shelter for the homeless, surrounded by strangers. A tumble of words cascaded from her mouth before she could stop them or even think of what she was saying. 'For God's sake, Kelvin, why aren't you at home with your family? Do you have a family? Do you have a home somewhere? You must have done, once. Where is it now, what's happened to it?'

Kelvin at last looked at her. The paleness of his thin face emphasised the redness of his eyes and the dark circles beneath them. 'Tell me about it, love,' she said softly. 'Tell me about it.'

She had expected a tale of separated parents, a single mother perhaps, or possibly a drunken stepfather. All the stereotypes of a young man in trouble came to mind: problems with drugs, school expulsions, alcohol abuse, petty crime, all stemming from an unloving, uncaring, probably violent poverty-struck home.

So it surprised Daisy to hear Kelvin say, 'Me mum and dad don't know I'm here. They think this place is some kinda youth hostel place.'

'Why don't you tell them?'

'They'd be that upset, like.' He passed his freckled hand over his eyes for a moment.

'Kelvin, can't you go back? Or don't they want you?'

He looked at Daisy with something like surprise. 'Me mum hated me to go. Dad too in his way. It was just the work, see. I always had jobs, ever since leaving school. Two years in an old people's hospital, a porter, like, and then the place closed. Weren't nothing else nowhere, so me and a mate hitched down here.' Once again the hand, trembling slightly, passing over the eyes.

'Where's the mate now?' Daisy asked quietly. 'Gone back?'

'Up in London somewhere. Missed being in a city, but I don't know . . . I kinda like it where it's quieter, no one bothers you. We didn't want to be split, but . . .' He shrugged. 'I tried it for a few days. London. Couldn't hack it. Didn't feel safe, like.' He was silent for a moment. 'It was all right in the summer. Jobs on farms, pickin' things.'

'Why didn't you go back home, when the work stopped? Before winter set in?'

Kelvin shuffled a bit, looked down at his empty plate. 'Me mum, she was right proud of me. I wrote her that I had a job, see. With trainin' an' all. And now she's got an address for me, she's that chuffed — thinks I'm settled and all.' Kelvin suddenly looked up at Daisy and frowned. 'You won't let on? That I lied?'

'Of course not,' Daisy sighed. Kelvin still looked worried so she said, reassuringly, 'Maybe it won't be lies for ever. I know Miles has been talking about finding some kind of community training for you.'

'He's a good bloke, is Miles.'

They were quiet for a few moments, watching the candles flickering, the tree-lights sparkling and reflecting in the tinsel decorations. Impulsively, Daisy said, 'Would you like to come out to my place tomorrow, for Christmas Day?'

Kelvin looked embarrassed. 'Gemma already asked me, earlier on, but I said no. If I can't be home . . .' his voice trailed off.

'We'd all be very pleased to have you,' Daisy said gently.

'Like I said to Gemma, this here's home now. For a bit. I reckon I shouldn't desert the others, like. Ole Clifton, and Arnold. And Josy said she wouldn't miss the meal they're laying on for us for nuthin' . . .'

Once again his voice trailed away. Daisy, understanding, patted his hand and Kelvin looked at her gratefully. 'It's better'n what it was, you know? It's better'n outside.'

When Daisy arrived back at the farm that evening, she went straight to the caravan – without being asked, without hesitating – and found Gemma and Baz cooking their evening meal, something creamy with butter beans and peanuts, over the tiny stove. 'You asked Kelvin to come to us for Christmas Day,' Daisy said without preliminary.

Gemma looked puzzled. 'Why, yes. He's not coming, though.'

'I know. I asked him too.'

'He wouldn't have felt at home, Mum. However we want to help, there're some barriers that can't be broken.'

239

'I know,' Daisy said again. 'The thing is, it could have been Julian. Or you.'

'Or Baz.'

'Yes.'

Gemma motioned her mother to sit down. 'Is that why you've been so afraid of my leaving the farm? Is that why you've been giving us such a hard time?'

Daisy nodded. 'At first it was. Sheer terror for you: I was sick with it. Then I became angry, told myself you were just copping out, unable to face life.'

Baz, who was still standing at the cooker, said, 'Maybe I should go, let you talk alone?'

Daisy turned to him. 'No, no, not at all. You're part of this.' She closed her eyes for a moment, uncertain as to how to go on. 'You see, I was terribly wrong. How can someone who has done so much for people like Kelvin and the others, be opting out? Miles has told me how the shelter never would have survived its early days without you and your friends.'

'It's no big deal,' Baz said. 'Someone had to do it.'

'But you're the only ones who did. Oh, the rest of us came in later, but it could have been too late then.'

'It doesn't matter when you join in, Mum,' Gemma said kindly. 'There's no hassle.'

'You see,' Daisy went on slowly, 'I thought you were copping out, escaping from life, so to speak – unlike *us* all those years ago, sure we were going to change things in a big, big way.'

'No one can do that,' Gemma said.

'No one can do anything except their little bit,' Baz added. 'What else, in the end, is there?'

What indeed? Daisy, looking at her daughter with the mass of beaded plaits, her bells, her serious face reflected in the glittering mirrors of the caravan, wanted to say many things, things like how proud she was of her and Baz, and how much she loved them. She would have liked to tell them also how much she had learned about herself through them, or, perhaps more precisely, how she had found something she thought she had lost irrevocably. But the myriad reflections in the shining glass around her were blurring as tears filled her eyes and she said, simply, 'I'm sorry, love. Truly sorry.' Embracing them both quickly, she walked out of the caravan, letting the tears spill over as she made for the farmhouse, feeling them as something warm and healing. Consoling.

And now, looking at her friends and family crammed into the long living room, several large tables pulled together to make room for everyone to sit at Christmas dinner, Daisy dishes out turkey and vegetables with great contentment, missing perhaps only Barnaby, who is of course home with his own family. But it is lovely to have Emmeline here, she thinks, watching her chatting with Tony at the far end of the table. Tony arrived earlier with a case of wine and a sack of Kent cobnuts. 'From my tree,' he said. 'I buried them ages ago in the garden, and they've kept just fine. We'll roast them in front of the fire after dinner.'

Not only are all the younger Dillards there, but also a number of their assorted partners and friends who have chosen to celebrate the day at Woodland Farm. The room looks not unlike a medieval castle, with its blackened beams, the ancient oak windowsill, the roaring fire, the holly and ivy picked from the woods and garlanded around the walls and ceiling. To Emmeline it seems out of time, unreal, and once again that familiar feeling, that tightening of the heart, that strange sensation that she is living in an old lost dream

241

returns to haunt her, remind her of loss, of time fleeting and ephemeral.

Daisy, opposite her, catches her eye and Emmeline knows that they both are sharing the same thoughts, of that first Christmas at Woodland Farm, when she and Hal and all the London crowd came to stay with Daisy and Leo. Daisy raises her glass to Emmeline and says, quietly, 'To the past. It gave us some good memories.'

Emmeline raises her glass and drinks. It moulded us too, she thinks, made us what we are now, like it or not.

At the other end of the table Leo's mother, Alma, who is down from Leeds for the holidays, says, 'Do you remember, Emmeline, that first Christmas Leo and Daisy were married? And you came up from London to visit?'

Leo and Daisy weren't married yet, but Alma refuses to acknowledge that a member of her family ever lived in sin. 'I recall it very well,' Emmeline replies.

'That was certainly a strange Christmas.' Alma, sitting at the top of the table near Leo, purses her lips, to make sure everyone understands it was not *her* kind of Christmas.

Though Alma is eighty now, the years haven't mellowed her, though they have been kind to her physically. She looks healthy and hearty, wearing a bright red wool dress and matching red high-heeled shoes, and a red brooch on her bosom which has grown more ample and assertive over the years. She travels everywhere with her terrier dog, Winston, a rather nasty animal who is this minute sitting on Alma's lap trying to nick bits of turkey from her plate, much to the annoyance of everyone sitting around her. The old farm Labrador, Blossom, has retreated in terror from the snappy and bad-tempered Winston, and is hiding dolefully under the kitchen table.

'Thank you, dear,' Alma says to Emmeline as she takes the gravy. She approves of Emmeline, feels she brings some respectability to the motley crew at the farmhouse, what with Leo dressed in his old (albeit clean) farm jeans and Daisy running about with those perpetual things on her legs which aren't even trousers but look like footless tights, even today on Christmas Day. Alma, though for years a farmer's wife, prides herself on never having let herself go, never lowering her standards in any way. Sitting like the Queen Mother next to Leo, she feels smug and satisfied, knowing that if none of the others look dressed for the occasion (except perhaps Emmeline in a long wool skirt and an attractive blue blouse) at least she is.

'More turkey, Grandma?' Gemma asks. Alma frowns first at Gemma, who has at least a dozen thin plaits in her hair today like some kind of native Aboriginal, and then scowls at the plate of turkey. Daisy never cooks it properly, she thinks, helping herself to a huge slice.

'No, no, not any of that nut thing, whatever it is.'

'It's vegetarian, Grandma,' Paul grins. Alma looks at him and shudders. Although he is her oldest grandchild, he has as little sense as the others, spoiling his handsome face with that unshaven look and wearing that ridiculous collarless shirt like the workmen wore years ago.

'I'm afraid I can't get on with this vegetarian nonsense at Christmas. It's not Christian,' Alma states piously.

Her grandchildren are alert now, sensing fun. Her jibes and criticisms never rile them, only make them laugh. Daisy wishes she were as tolerant.

'Baz and I don't eat meat,' Gemma says.

'It shows,' Alma says enigmatically. 'It's not natural.' She helps herself to more turkey.

Gemma shakes her head and the tiny bells she has put at the end of her plaits tinkle as she does so. 'Nor are bells in the head natural either,' Alma continues. 'It gives me a headache every time you nod your head, young lady.'

Baz laughs and says, 'Think of it as jingle bells, sleigh bells ringing, all that stuff, Grandma.'

Alma winces. This ruffian with the wild hair sticking straight up out of his head, like the mane of a black lion, calling her 'Grandma'? She drinks her wine, which is far too dry for her liking, and glares at Leo, whose fault all this is, for marrying Daisy and not a decent Kentish landowner's wife.

'Having a good Christmas?' Gemma murmurs to Baz later, when it has turned dark and Leo and Daisy have lit the candles on the Christmas tree.

'I love Christmas. It's so pagan,' Baz replies, fingering the crystal Gemma gave him which is hanging from his neck on a cord.

'Hey Baz, know any Christmas carols on your didge?' Paul asks.

'No, but I can make you sounds like waves on the sea, like things growing in the earth.'

'Right on. You make those vibrations in the background and I'll get a melody on the piano. Melanie, you join me with your fiddle. Simon, what happened to your flute, do you still play? You should do, Mum and Dad spent a fortune giving you lessons.'

Bantering, organising, Paul, the oldest Dillard child, gets everyone together before they can fall asleep in front of the fire. They begin to make music, tentatively, then gathering harmony. Tony gets his guitar from the car and joins them, and Flack, who is also there with Blue, produces a harmonica which he plays beautifully. Alma, watching, cannot believe she is listening to Christmas carols played by a young man with a long plait down his back. She is sure the vicar would not approve: it must surely be sacrilegious.

But she soon decides not to worry, because whatever music they are playing, it is certainly no Christmas carol *she* has ever heard before. It is eerie, rather celebratory yet sad at the same time, and she definitely does not approve of it, especially when Gemma begins to sing a song that sounds like seabirds on a lonely island.

'Christmas was different in my generation,' Alma mutters to herself with an indignant sniff. '*Silent Night*' and '*God Rest Ye, Merry Gentlemen*' and no nonsense.

Alma forgets. She forgets Daisy's first Christmas at the farm, a generation ago, when Daisy was the same age as Gemma and Leo's hair still looked like a smooth brown berry instead of crinkled all over with a thick coating of grey and white.

Emmeline doesn't forget. The strange, haunting music invades her, and the look of all these young people, dressed in their vivid colourful clothes, their hair beaded or braided or just growing wild, brings back to her memories so poignant, so sharp, that she feels cut in two with their strength and potency. Behind each person there seems to be a spirit lurking, filling the room with ghosts. In the dark corner by the old oak windowsill Emmeline puts her head down and weeps for these ghosts, for all of those crazy hopeful boys and girls, including herself, who are gone now, leaving nothing but shadows, memories, old dreams.

Tony, in the middle of a song, is the only one who notices. Quietly putting down his guitar without stopping the others, who carry on playing and singing, he unobtrusively goes over to Emmeline's corner and whispers, 'What is it? What is it, Em?'

She tells him. For the next half hour, there in that dark private corner, the music playing around them, Emmeline tells Tony why she has never returned to England.

Chapter Eleven

'*Leo, good heavens! What on earth are you wearing?*'

Leo, carving the Christmas turkey, looked rather sheepishly at his mother. 'It's, uh, my Christmas present from Daisy.'

'But what is it?'

'It's just a jacket.'

Accepting a large portion of turkey from her son, Alma objected, 'But it has no collar, dear. How can you have a jacket without a collar? And that rounded neckline – it looks dreadful.'

'It's a Beatles jacket,' Daisy said between clenched teeth, spooning vegetable curry on her own plate. 'You've heard of the Beatles?'

'Who hasn't? Shocking. The *Telegraph* was quite right when it wrote of the moral corruption of a country whose young people swoon and become hysterical over something as low and vulgar as pop music.'

'Mrs Dillard, your generation swooned over Frank Sinatra,' Sojourner Truth said with a grin.

Alma looked at her uncomfortably. She had nothing against coloureds, of course, but it felt strange sitting with one at the family dining table which had once belonged to her dead husband's mother. She was rather glad the young woman with the funny name she could never remember was seated at the other end, for she hadn't any idea of what to say to her. Not only was she a different colour, but she was an American as well, for goodness sake. But perhaps, Alma mused, that was why her hair was red? Perhaps the coloureds in America had red hair? And were they always as large as this one, who though not fat was exceedingly tall and big, almost like an Amazon? And those breasts . . . Alma did not like to think about it, but she could swear that the girl was not wearing a brassière under that black flimsy, almost see-through, blouse.

'That's right, what about Frank Sinatra?' Daisy echoed. 'Didn't he cause a few riots now and again?'

Alma was on safe ground now, talking about Frank Sinatra. 'That was different,' she said firmly, putting them all in their place.

Marsha, sitting opposite Alma, said, 'Would you like some vegetable curry, Mrs Dillard?'

'A curry at Christmas? I'm not a heathen, you know.'

'Poppadoms?'

'Brussel sprouts, please.'

Marsha handed her the sprouts with a merry smile playing around her lips. She was in a gay and mischievous mood, having just spoken for a half hour to Jean-Luc in France, who assured her of his undying love and promised her marriage and the prospect of keeping her own white teeth for the rest of her life.

'I will be finished with the dental college in spring, *ma chérie*,' he told her. 'Then I will send for you quickly.'

'Before my teeth all fall out?' Marsha quipped.

'You joke, but I have noticed that some gumwork may be necessary on your upper palate.'

Alma took the sprouts and looked around to see if there were any roast potatoes about. There seemed to be none, only that funny yellow rice with bits floating about in it.

'Do you see any potatoes, dear?' she asked Marsha, resigning herself to having to talk to Americans, as there seemed to be at least three of them at the Christmas table.

She appraised Marsha over the dreadful dry wine Leo had given her (you'd have thought by now that he would remember she liked sweet). The girl seemed normal enough except for a peculiar haircut, all angles like a geometry lesson. The others had all raved about it, saying it was the latest thing from London. Well, Alma thought, if that was the rage in London, she was glad she lived in Leeds. But at least Marsha was dressed normally enough (if you overlooked that short skirt) − not like Daisy in some white lacy all-in-one thing she called a jumpsuit, which fanned out like the trousers of a common sailor at the ankles.

Daisy was common, Alma told herself sadly, no matter what Leo said about her solicitor parents, and her university place which she never bothered to take up. Anyone who could meet her at the station wearing a white PVC raincoat could only be common. She looked forward to getting Leo alone, to warn him.

Emmeline, at the other end of the table with Hal, asked Alma if she wanted some salad. 'A salad? With a roast dinner? No, thank you,' she said severely.

A strange lot, the Americans. That one who had just offered her salad had pinned mistletoe and holly all through her long, rather straggly blonde hair, and yesterday she wore bits and pieces of winter flowers, diehard roses and chrysanthemums, woven in and out of it, with long feathers dangling from her earlobes. It made her look like an unkempt hedgerow, Alma thought. Shame, because she was a pretty girl.

Daisy and Leo, finally finished serving, sat down and began to eat, but before they did, Leo clinked his wine glass with Daisy's and kissed her there and then, without any sense of propriety. Alma closed her eyes and wished that her dead husband, James, had forbidden Leo ever to leave England, to spend his susceptible years roaming through barbarian countries.

Still with her eyes closed, she briefly wished James were here. But only briefly, for though, in her way, she had loved him, she was most relieved not to be a farmer's wife at long last, and to be living in Leeds amongst civilised company. She also had a rather sneaking suspicion that James, instead of being rightly disapproving of Leo's new choice of friends and fiancée, would have enjoyed the company, for he liked sparkle and fun far more than was good for him.

After dinner, when it was dark, Daisy lit a dozen candles on a huge fir tree in front of the window. 'What happened to the fairy lights?' Alma exclaimed.

'We thought real candles would be nicer,' Daisy said. 'Don't you like them?'

'A bit of a fire-trap,' was Alma's only comment, though to herself she admitted that they were rather festive, rather like a child's Victorian Christmas.

It all got slightly better after that because everyone, and rightly so, tried to jolly her up a bit after letting her miss the Queen's speech, serving up dinner at that peculiar hour and not reminding her of the time. 'Why don't you play the piano for us, Mother?' Leo asked, and the others, benevolently, cried, 'Oh yes, please do.'

She played for almost an hour, all the old carols, and they sang. She was surprised they knew the words, those Americans, especially the coloured one. They applauded her with great enthusiasm when she had finished, and the blond boy, Hal, who would have been quite good-looking if his hair weren't so long, actually thanked her and sat her in the most comfortable chair by the fire.

The evening should have ended there, Alma thought later, but then they insisted on making music themselves. Although Alma knew Leo was perfectly able to play all the Christmas songs on the piano, for she had taught him herself, he played songs she had never heard of, and that Soho or whatever her name was plunked away at a guitar, of all things. Whoever heard of a guitar at Christmas?

Alma watched and listened, relaxing in spite of herself, not even bothering to remonstrate with Emmeline as she snuggled on to Hal's lap in a most undignified manner, tickling his cheek with the bits of holly in her hair. Daisy was singing some song that everyone seemed to know, for they all joined in on the refrain: '*Where have all the flowers gone?*'

'How like Joan Baez she sounds,' Hal said.

'*Who?*' Alma asked, but didn't bother to listen to Hal's reply, because the wine, the fire, the music, were sending her off to sleep. The last thing she heard before she dozed off was Emmeline, saying softly to Hal, 'What a wonderful Christmas. Life is so good, so sweet!'

'You make it that way, Em.'

'Do you think I'm naive? You're not laughing at me?'

'Oh Em, how can you think that? You give me back my *own* innocence, my *own* hope. You make me believe things can change, that *people* can change, become what they want to be.' He stroked her hair gently, pulling out a bit of

251

mistletoe that was hanging precariously over her ear. He looked intense, serious. 'You've made me believe people can escape themselves, Em. When I'm with you, I'm the person I want to be, rather than the person I'm sometimes afraid I really am.'

It was lucky that Alma was asleep, because she wouldn't have approved of the way Hal kissed Emmeline when she looked perplexed over his words.

'Oh Hal, I want this to last for ever. I *know* this will last for ever!' Em cried as Daisy sang and the candles on the tree flickered.

*

'And did it?' Tony asks gently. 'Did it last for ever?'

'Does it ever?' Emmeline replies. 'Will it for Gemma and all the rest of Leo and Daisy's children? Will it for Baz and Blue and Flack? Did it for you?'

There are no answers, of course. 'How could I return to England?' Emmeline goes on. 'How could I come back, confront my own innocence, idealism? Better to forget, to get on with the present.'

'Or to remember it, Em. If we don't remember, we become far too cynical.'

Emmeline smiles at him. 'Go back and play your guitar,' she whispers gently. 'That reminds me of the good things, gives me hope again.'

He touches her hand, lightly and warmly. As he picks up his guitar again Em is aware of a continuity that belies all the changes that have occurred since her one and only other Christmas at Woodland Farm. Since Hal, she has been frightened of change. She feels oddly contented that some things, like the candles on the tree, the music, even Alma's astringent remarks, have remained constant all these many long years.

*

'Emmeline, stop worrying. Why is it that whenever things are going well, you are terrified they will change, come to an end?'

'I don't know, Hal. I guess it's because nothing has ever been this good for me before. I keep panicking that I'm going to get hit by a bus or that you are going to suddenly disappear and all this will be over.'

Emmeline and Hal were standing on the bridge over the river in the Westgate Gardens, a few days after Christmas. They had been roaming aimlessly around the town, supposed to be on some errand for the farm, but that took only a few moments and the rest of the afternoon was spent ambling around the city, stopping at various coffee bars for cappuccinos, wandering around the river at Blackfriars, walking in the crypt of the Cathedral.

'Don't you think I feel the same? Don't you know that I panic sometimes, wondering if I've dreamt you, wondering if I'll wake up one day and you'll be gone?' And I'll be alone again, he thinks but doesn't say, facing once again my terrors, my dark secrets: the blackness.

They leaned on the railing of the bridge, watching the parent swans gliding down the river with their nearly full-grown young. Hal put his arm around her waist, holding her tightly, almost desperately, murmuring her name like a mantra, like an incantation that would protect him, guard him against evil. 'Shall we throw a penny in the water, make a wish?' he said suddenly. 'I'm sure this is a wishing bridge; it's small and elfish enough.'

They delved into their pockets to find a coin, and Hal threw it into the water, the swans rushing towards it hoping to find bread, some kind of a titbit. 'There it goes, see it, Em? A little penny but a big wish. Marry me, Emmeline. That's my wish: marry me.'

And so, impetuously, each as surprised as the other, they became engaged. They ran hand-in-hand into the town to all the second-hand shops so that Hal could do it properly, buy her a ring, ceremoniously put it on her finger. At the third shop Hal found just what he was looking for, a delicate gold band with a single pearl embedded plainly in the centre. It fitted Emmeline perfectly, but he wouldn't let her put it on, not yet. Taking it from the shopkeeper in a plain paper bag, Hal brought the ring and Em to the Cathedral.

'I want to put the ring on your finger here,' he said softly to her as they stood looking down the main aisle. 'Let's go around to one of the side altars; they're less forbidding.'

In the end they stopped at the Martyrdom, the place where Thomas à Becket was murdered, because, Hal said, there was a feeling of awe, of grandeur and mystery there. 'And that is how I feel about you,' he said, taking her hand and slowly slipping the ring on her finger, then holding on to her as if afraid she would vanish, dissolve: evanescent as the scent of the Cathedral itself, rich and musty with the ancient smell of piety, of worship.

Later, she wondered at Hal's choice of venue. At the time it did seem right, fitting, the drama of it, the romance of it. But later she wondered if Hal had subconsciously chosen the site as the scene of his own martyrdom, had embraced it, even welcomed it.

Back at the farm their friends were delighted, and the evening turned into a festive party for the engagement. Alma had, fortunately, returned to Leeds, for there was not only the subversive Beatles music but also the more dangerous albums of the Rolling Stones which they played all night in nostalgic celebration of the jukebox on the *Castel Felice*.

'When are you getting married?' Daisy shouted above the music. 'You're not going to beat us to it, are you?' Their wedding was planned for late January, not that it needed much planning. All they wanted was a registry office and their friends from London as witnesses.

'Hey, don't rush us,' Hal laughed. 'I'm enjoying the engagement.'

'There's no hurry,' Emmeline said softly, but in her heart of hearts she did not mean it. She wanted to marry Hal today, this minute, wanted to live with him, go to bed with him, make love to him. But she made herself be patient. They had a whole lifetime together, so why rush things, why not savour each step at a time. She had such simple faith in Hal, such trust. She was never to have this for anyone else again, and though she knew that was as it should be – for putting one's faith in anything mortal was puerile, a folly – its loss left her staggered for a long, long time.

After Christmas the rain stops and it turns cold and windy again. The beds in the shelter are always filled, the soup kitchen used constantly. Some of the residents are transients, coming in to shelter for one or two nights and then moving on, while others, like Kelvin and Clifton and Arnold, linger indefinitely. Miles has great plans for the Northgate Hostel, hoping to make it into a permanent hostel and rehabilitation unit as well as a temporary shelter, which gives Daisy hope for Kelvin and those like him.

Josy is still around, though she never sleeps in. Another woman, Irene, much younger than Josy, comes and goes like a pale spirit, carrying two old torn knapsacks and speaking to no one, her eyes as lifeless and spiritless as the rest of her. Sometimes Irene accepts a mattress on the floor in one of the empty rooms, but often she disappears for days at a time. No one will ever know Irene's story, and indeed, she has herself forgotten it. It was never anything she wanted to remember, and oblivion is much more conducive to her survival than a head full of memories.

Others come and go. There is another young man, Kelvin's age, who was a student, but his grant was merely a pittance and he couldn't survive on it. Unable to find enough work to supplement his grant, he soon gave up the struggle, dropping out completely. His parents, having left England some time ago to live in Spain, neither know nor care about his plight.

'Is everything all right?' Barnaby asks Daisy one evening after she has been talking to the ex-student.

'Yes.' She looks pensive.

'What is it?'

'Oh, just that young lad. Middle-class parents, educated – another of my preconceptions of the homeless gone out the window.'

Gemma pops her head in the hostel kitchen, looking for Baz. She's wearing a long plum-coloured cardigan, obviously hand-knitted, which comes down to her knees nearly covering a short faded print skirt. 'I like your jumper,' Daisy says.

'Jumble sale. Sound, isn't it? And look at these earrings I found, real peacock feathers. Genuine sixties stuff, I love it.' She smiles at Daisy and impetuously embraces her before rushing out again.

Daisy, watching Gemma go, looks a bit misty, and Barnaby wants suddenly to hold her, as she held Gemma. He settles for putting an arm around her shoulder.

'She has the knack of making do with so little,' Daisy says musingly, still thinking of her daughter. 'You know, they're so skint all the time, but they never ask me or Leo for money. They struggle on with their candles and busking and the odd jobs they find, and they seem so content with it all.'

'They're young.'

'Yes. I keep forgetting what it was like. I'm such a fool sometimes.' There is a sadness as she says this that makes Barnaby feel quite odd, protective somehow, and full of tenderness.

'Aren't we all?' He looks at her kindly, more than kindly, and something lurches somewhere inside Daisy. 'Fools, that is,' he finishes.

'More than what is good for us,' she says lightly, knowing that this sudden euphoria rushing to her head is as daft as anything she has experienced.

'But fun sometimes. A bit of crazy foolishness can be fun, you know.'

They are no longer, of course, talking about Gemma or Baz or the past. They have somehow switched on to themselves, acknowledging with their insouciant words and careless flirtation that there is an attraction growing between them, but like the mature adults that they are, they can handle it. It is merely a bit of fun, a bit of frivolity; it will go no further than this, and it will cheer them both up during the long hard winter.

Feeling both wise and cherished — a heady combination — Barnaby and Daisy finish clearing away the plates and innocently leave the shelter together, as usual calling in for a quiet drink to unwind before heading home to their respective spouses.

'Barnaby is so much more relaxed since he began work at the shelter,' Marjorie Brackenbury says to Tony one Saturday morning when he pops in to return a book he has borrowed from Barnaby. She has kindly insisted he stop for a coffee, and plies him with homemade chocolate chip cookies and slices of fresh apple tart.

'I thought it would make him even more stressed, that on top of the bookshop, but it's been good for him. For Daisy, too, I think. Had you noticed how lethargic she was becoming?'

Tony nods circumspectly and eats his third cookie. They really are delicious; Marjorie is an excellent cook.

'I do miss the old boy in the evenings, you know. Never thought I would; I'm so fagged I usually fall asleep.' Marjorie looks thoughtful, then, noticing Tony eyeing the cookies, says heartily, 'Have some more. I love to see people enjoying their food. I say, you must stay for lunch!'

Tony refuses, for he is rehearsing some new music with the band shortly. As he leaves the house he notices, opposite, Clem and Celia Todd walking to their car, arguing vociferously.

'Sulking all morning, just because you have to take *me* to lunch for a change,' Celia says loudly.

'Shut up, will you? I'm not sulking.'

'Oh no, not much! What do you call not speaking to me all morning, then?'

'Peace,' Clem mutters. 'Bliss.'

This sends Celia over the top. 'Bloody bastard,' she screeches. 'You never take me out, and all I asked for was one measly pub lunch out in the country somewhere—'

Tony, opposite, gets into his van and loudly shuts the door, starts the engine and drives away.

'Jesus, you loud-mouthed fishwife,' Clem hisses, pushing Celia into the car. 'That bloody builder must have heard every word.'

'So who gives a shit,' Celia shrugs. 'As if everyone doesn't know of your affairs anyway. I heard all about your last lunch with that American, sharing a bottle of Rully. *And* you paid for it.' Clem's lavishness with the wine has been distressing her all morning, since she first heard of it.

Clem swears. Celia's spies are getting sharper, he thinks angrily; they certainly got the details right. 'Was it white or red?' he asks sarcastically.

Celia smiles malignantly. She knows, all right, but isn't going to answer, not now. She'll wait until they are at lunch, wait until she sees what kind of wine he orders for *her*. She puts on her seatbelt, settles down into the seat, and decides to order the most expensive lunch on the menu.

Daisy begins calling in at Brackenbury's Books at odd times, when she is out shopping in Canterbury. Whatever Barnaby is doing, he always stops it immediately and whisks Daisy upstairs to his mangy office and urges foul coffee upon her which she accepts with joy and alacrity as if it were the proverbial manna from heaven. Though by now Daisy has realised she is thoroughly infatuated with Barnaby, she refuses to be disconcerted by it. By nature faithful and loyal, she does not want to hurt Leo, even though he has hurt her more than once by his silences, his withdrawals. She tells herself, foolishly perhaps, that she can keep everything under control. But she is magnetically drawn to Barnaby, who, away from Marjorie's booming commands, is as expansive as Leo is incommunicative. Daisy opens like the flower she is named after in the sun of his affectionate interest.

These days Barnaby shuts the office door when Daisy visits, not liking the knowing, rather perky looks of his assistants, Jim and Fran, when he closets himself in with Daisy. He is, in truth, somewhat besotted by Daisy, and he is enjoying every minute of it. He has had these mild infatuations before: Marjorie, in many ways, is a forbidding woman, and though he adores her, he is slightly in awe of her. And so whenever, in the past, he has relaxed with a woman, he has found himself falling slightly in love with her. None of these attractions have ever been serious; indeed, none of the women involved even knew about his silent adoration. Barnaby is not into adultery, but a little bit of honest attraction, of harmless flirtation, is always, he feels, more than welcome.

'Here you are,' he says to Daisy one opaque February afternoon, handing her a cup of murky brew in a cracked mug.

'Oh, how nice, coffee and a bit of quiet! The town is packed out, I don't know why. Lots of tourists already; summer will be impossible.'

'Very foggy out, or so Jim tells me. I've not been out of the shop all day.'

They exhaust the topic of weather and sip their coffee happily. Barnaby, looking at Daisy, thinks she looks exceptionally lovely today, and notices how her rich copper hair shines damply with drops of mist. If he were more observant, he would notice that the flecks of grey that permeated the copper locks are no longer in evidence, but being a man, and being in love, he never actually noticed them in the first place. She looks so damp and dewy sitting there that he finds her almost overwhelmingly endearing. He suddenly wants to kiss her, which certainly wasn't on the agenda. Standing up awkwardly he makes his way to her side, tripping over a pile of newly arrived GCSE guides, and takes her in his arms.

'Barnaby, we mustn't,' Daisy gasps after about five minutes, having thoroughly reciprocated his kiss.

'No, you're right. We mustn't,' Barnaby murmurs, letting her go so that he can catch his breath.

He is just about to grab her again when there is a swift knock on the door. 'Yes, what is it?' Barnaby snarls.

A tall elderly man in a pale, pristine raincoat opens the door and says, 'Excuse me, but do you have any of Auden's poetry?'

Barnaby glares at him and says, very unprofessionally, 'Have you asked the assistants downstairs?'

The man, unfazed, glares back. 'Yes, they sent me upstairs.'

Barnaby stomps out to the poetry section while Daisy pulls herself together. She feels wild, exhilarated. When Barnaby returns he hands her a slim paperback book: it is *The Love Poems of John Donne*. 'I know you like poetry,' he says, 'from our conversation last night at the pub.'

Daisy picks up the book and opens it, reads the first poem: '*I wonder, by my troth, what thou and I/ Did, till we loved? . . .*'

And suddenly, crazily, she wonders too. All her years with Leo, all the intimacies and childbearing and pleasures and pains of her long marriage are forgotten in this *coup de foudre*, this bolt from the blue, which she recognises as love.

'I want you to have it,' Barnaby says, indicating the book. 'I want you to have it because—' He is interrupted by the immaculate light-tan raincoat, looming once again in the doorway.

'I think, actually, I'd prefer Stephen Spender. You have some in an anthology. Is there not a collection? Other anthologies?'

Barnaby looks despairing and goes off again. When he returns he has forgotten what he was saying, and Daisy, frustrated, knows she will never hear the words that hovered so sweetly on the tip of his tongue. 'Thank you,' she stammers, in the silence now between them. 'Thank you for the book.'

'Ah yes. The book. You see—'

'Excuse me.' A large woman in a blue track-suit is standing in the doorway. 'So sorry to bother you.' This is dripping sarcasm, and she looks witheringly at Daisy, whom she clearly accuses of keeping Leo from his customers. She continues aggressively, 'I've been all through your drama section and I don't see any plays by Thomas Hardy.'

'No, I'm afraid not. You see, I don't believe Thomas Hardy wrote plays. We have his novels, of course, and a complete collection of his poetry.'

'Nonsense. Of course he wrote plays.' She and Barnaby glower at each other, sudden adversaries. Daisy opens John Donne and hides her face in love poetry.

'If you'll kindly come this way, Madam, I'll show you exactly what we have by Hardy,' Barnaby murmurs, ostentatiously unctuous.

Daisy leafs through the poems while Barnaby is gone. 'These are beautiful,' she says softly when he returns, having anchored the woman with Thomas Hardy.

'And you, my dear,' Barnaby says even more softly. 'I want to say . . . I need to say . . .'

'Useless! A well-known playwright like Thomas Hardy and not one of his plays in your shop. I'm afraid I shall have to go elsewhere.'

262

'By all means, Madam,' Barnaby says through clenched teeth. 'Try Waterstones, or W. H. Smith's. There is a small Dillons on the top floor of Athena, and we have several other very good booksellers. Do let me know if you are successful. I would be most interested if you find a collection of Thomas Hardy's plays.'

'I say,' calls the raincoat, from the depth of the poetry section. 'Are you sure this is all the Stephen Spender you have? What about Christopher Isherwood? Have you anything at all by Isherwood?'

'Good Lord, who was that wraith that just stalked out the door?' Tony, who has just come up the stairs, rolls his eyes in mock terror at Barnaby and Daisy. 'She ran right into me, nearly bowled me over, and then practically ordered me not to go in. She says you don't even stock Thomas Hardy.'

'Oh, for—'

Knowing that she will never now hear what Barnaby wanted to say to her, Daisy gets up to leave. 'Coming out for lunch on Sunday?' she asks Tony. 'Marjorie and Barnaby are invited, and Emmeline is home. Are you busy that day?'

'No, nothing planned. Yes, I'd like to. Thank you.'

Daisy leaves, too self-conscious to give Barnaby the light goodbye kiss she gives to all her friends, unaware that her sudden discomfiture is as revealing as any kiss could be. 'Thanks for the book,' she smiles shyly at him. Their eyes meet, lock, then she waves awkwardly and is gone.

Tony has seen the John Donne, noticed the title. He has seen, also, the smile, the look. He is not surprised, for he has been observing Barnaby and Daisy together over the past weeks and is troubled by what he sees. Leo is a friend. So is Barnaby. So are both their wives. He has known the four of them for years.

'Barnaby,' he says, refusing a cup of coffee, 'it's not on, you know.'

Surprised at this bluntness, Barnaby says, 'It's not what you think.'

'But it will be.'

Barnaby starts to protest, because, like Daisy, he is convinced of the innocence of it all. He loves Marjorie, is devoted to his daughters, would do nothing to damage that. All the same, he is thoroughly enjoying his infatuation with Daisy. It makes him curiously happy, this little secret. He adores Daisy, he cherishes her. He is also half-crazy with lust for her, but this only adds to the fun. He certainly never intends to do anything about it. The little bit of kissing in the office just now was an aberration, some harmless titillation, which will certainly go no further. Like Daisy, he foolishly believes he is in control.

'Don't worry about it, Tony. Nothing will come of it, I promise you. I don't want it to, and I'm sure Daisy doesn't either. It's something that has just happened, is just there, but we don't do anything about it, don't even speak of it.' Barnaby has forgotten that he almost did, right there in the bookshop, when he gave Daisy the love poems. He has not forgotten the kiss, but he is not about to mention that to anyone.

Tony is not convinced. Troubled, he listens to Barnaby changing the subject, talking about the latest escapade of his oldest daughter. 'And what about you, Tony?' Barnaby asks when he has finished his anecdote. 'What about you and Emmeline? You're suddenly so blunt and inquisitive about *my* love life — what about yours?'

Tony laughs. 'I don't have one, thank God. Too much of a hassle. I haven't any time anyway these days.'

'And Em?' Barnaby persists. 'What about Em?'

'Barnaby, be serious. Would you get involved with an

ambitious American career woman with a past strewn with disastrous relationships? Not to mention an ex-football hero waiting back home to claim her when she returns, as she inevitably will?'

Barnaby chuckles. 'Well, putting it like that, maybe not. But then I'm married.'

'That hasn't stopped you playing a dangerous game with Daisy.'

Barnaby looks cross. 'I told you it's not dangerous; we can handle it. Anyway, we're talking about you.'

'There's nothing to say. Emmeline will be out of the country soon. She finishes work here in the spring.'

When Tony leaves the bookshop these words prey on his mind, in his heart. Although the cold penetrative fog has lulled him into thinking winter will last for ever, he cannot escape the fact that Emmeline will be gone in just a few months' time. He will miss her, he knows. Keeping her at arms' length, keeping her as a friend and not a lover, has not exactly worked, has not exactly lessened his feelings for her. He knows he will be as bereft when she is gone as he would have been, had they had a full-blown love affair.

Taking a deep breath, he plunges through the fog, then remembers he has forgotten to order a new book on fungi that he wanted. Irritated with himself, with Barnaby, worried about Leo and Daisy and their marriage, concerned about Marjorie and the girls, Tony is not cheered by a slight hint of spring in the air, which he is suddenly sure he can detect through the bitter fog. The sight of daffodils in the shops, though they have been there for weeks, also daunts him, as do the crocuses he spots poking their blatant heads through the seedy winter grass.

Spring, he thinks despairingly. *It will soon be spring*. For some reason neither the thought of all the wildlife suddenly coming awake again, nor the countryside in bloom, nor any of the other delightful perks of spring, can cheer him. He wishes gloomily that winter would go on for ever.

Chapter Twelve

'*E*mmeline, Marsha, guess what! Oh, guess, guess!*'
Em, perched on Marsha's bed sharing a rum baba with
her, looked up as Sojo burst into the room. The window of
Marsha's bed-sitter was wide open, letting in the first whiff
of spring. Marsha had fortunately found accommodation just
down the road, also in Earl's Court, and the three of them
were in and out of each other's rooms often.

Sojo, grabbing a bite of rum baba, said with her mouth full,
'Giorgio's home from sea! He just phoned. He's staying with
his brother, in Tuscany or is it Umbria? He wants me to come
at once to visit, and the rest of you as well.'

Marsha began to hop around excitedly. 'Oh, how fab!
Italy, romantic Italy. I'd love to go, does he really want
us all? It would be the next best thing to France, I guess.
Jean-Luc is studying for his exams and there's no hope of my
getting there until they're all over. He says I'm too much of
a distraction.'

'What about Easter? It's early this year. Easter in Italy!'

They all began talking excitedly, making plans. Marsha ran
out to the bakery down the road to buy more rum babas,
to celebrate. She felt quite wealthy, for she had a job now,

cash in hand, no questions asked. She worked for a somewhat dubious school of journalism where foreigners from emerging newly-rich nations spent a fortune thinking they were getting an education. Not knowing a thing about journalism, Marsha had given herself a crash course with musty, old-fashioned library books, and managed to bluff her way through lay-out and editing. For this she received fifteen quid a week cash, and the head of the school, a naturalised Burmese with jowls the size of soup bowls, gave her a letter saying she was a student, and so she now possessed a year's visa on her passport.

Sojourner hadn't a visa, but it didn't trouble her, since her heart was in Italy, even though her body was still in the Australian's bed. She also had a job, for cash as well, in the bakery that sold rum babas. Today was her day off.

Hal came in, looking for a script Emmeline had borrowed from him. 'Hey, bambino, wanna go to Italy for Easter?' Sojo asked him, pinching his bottom.

'Mama mia, Italia?' He grabbed Sojo and waltzed around the room, chanting in a broad Italian accent, 'Eee-ta-lee, a-mor-eee, whoppee!'

'We've been invited to visit Giorgio,' Sojo shrieked.

'Fabulous. Count me in.'

'You'll have to watch Em,' Marsha teased. 'All those Italians lusting after that blonde hair—'

Hal jumped on the bed, drew an imaginary sword. 'I vill keeeel zem,' he said, chasing Marsha with sweeping fencing gestures.

They hollered and laughed and horsed around until Hal had to go; he was meeting someone from drama school to work on a scene. Kissing Emmeline, he said, 'See you tomorrow, love.'

Em nodded, fingering her ring, her beautiful pearl engagement ring. She still loved it, though someone at college had cruelly told her that pearls meant tears, and didn't she know that? For some reason it made her uneasy, apprehensive, though she knew it was just a stupid superstition.

Hal left, and Sojo said, 'Doesn't he ever stay the night?'

'Sometimes,' Emmeline said defensively.

'Oboy, if it were me and Giorgio . . .'

'We can't all be like you, Sojo.'

'Why doesn't he move in with you?' Marsha asked daringly. Since Emmeline and Hal had got engaged, Marsha assumed that they were sleeping together, and for some reason Emmeline never got around to correcting her. She felt that Marsha, with her new European sophistication, would think they were simpy or something, would not understand. 'Your mom wouldn't have to know, being so far away,' Marsha went on. 'No one from home would ever know, and no one here would ever mind.'

'Hal feels he ought to stay for a time with his father,' Emmeline improvised, for the truth was, the question of their living together had never been raised. One didn't do that sort of thing, not without scandalising one's entire family. 'The old man's kind of lonely. Anyway, there's plenty of time when we're married.'

When we're married. The words sang in Emmeline's head, and she chanted them over and over to herself like a mantra. Hal wanted to marry her, Hal was going to marry her. She couldn't believe her luck, couldn't believe that the fairy-tale was coming true. She looked with pity on Marsha and Sojourner: they did not have Hal, would never have Hal. With all her heart she pitied them, and thanked various deities and saints she no longer believed in, that it was she who had Hal, and not them.

*   *   *

Italy. Giorgio's brother and wife and assorted children lived in Umbria, in a little village on the shores of Lake Trasimeno. The brother, Marsilio, owned the village shop which also doubled as a tiny bar, where Marsilio sat at the one square wooden table all day playing chess with his friends while his wife, Lucia, gossiped with her friends and bartered at the till over their home-grown produce. The shop was in the front part of an old rambling house with a courtyard in the middle and Siena tiles on the roof which badly needed repairing. The whole house, which had belonged to Giorgio and Marsilio's father, needed work, but the brothers seemed not to notice, nor care.

Emmeline loved it, and so did the others. The house was huge and they each were assigned a room, tiny stark rooms with bare wooden floors and windows looking out to the courtyard, though Sojo never slept in hers but surreptitiously crept into Giorgio's bed every night. Not that anyone seemed to object, for Marsilio and Lucia were as laid back as the early spring flowers lazily and haphazardly growing around the scrappy courtyard.

Giorgio, in his element, was besotted all over again with Sojo, enjoying the open lust and envy on the faces of all his friends and assorted relatives. He was proud of his beloved Sojo, and proud too of the bizarre collection of foreigners, English and American, that he had picked up on the boat from New York. His friends were the talk of the village, and because they were lively and didn't put on airs, were soon accepted into the friendly community. Because the weather was hot and sunny, they spent a good deal of time outdoors, dozing about on the shores of the lake with a few bottles of red wine, or wandering around the outskirts of the village picnicking in olive groves.

One day Giorgio borrowed his brother's old van and drove them all to Florence, which was about a two-and-a-half-hour drive away. When they got there they decided to split up, for everyone wanted to see something different, and meet again for a late lunch at a restaurant Lucia had recommended.

'I'm heading for the market, all those luscious leather belts and bags,' Sojo announced in Italian to Giorgio. 'And I want to go alone, you'll only distract me. I need space when I'm shopping.'

'*Bellezza*, command me.'

'Can it, Giorgio.' He looked perplexed so she continued in Italian 'You know you just want to find a bar somewhere and have a cool alcoholic drink in some shady corner. Go on then, be off. See you in a couple of hours.'

'I'm going to the Uffizi,' Marsha announced, clutching her guidebooks.

Hal and Emmeline departed together. Hal had said he wanted most of all to see the Michaelangelos, particularly the *David*, and Emmeline had said she'd like that as well. She pretended not to notice Hal's slight hesitation, indeed convinced herself that she had imagined it. She could not conceive of his wanting to wander around this romantic city without her, any more than she could conceive of doing it without him. It was a city for lovers, a country for lovers, and something treacherous inside her began to hope that here they would at last physically become lovers. She was rather ashamed of these thoughts, however, for she knew Hal's attitude towards sex, towards sleeping together, to be far worthier than hers, far nobler. Though they never discussed it, she knew that he was protecting her, shielding her, and knew too that when they married, she would be glad they had waited. She probably hadn't lost all vestiges of her church upbringing yet, she decided ruefully; probably she would only feel guilt or misery if she and Hal embarked on a full sexual relationship before marriage.

Or so she told herself. And yet more and more, in London where the sixties were fast becoming some kind of phenomenon, some wild and exuberant party where the old values, the old standards, the old prejudices were being constantly questioned, constantly turned about and examined and often discarded — more and more Emmeline felt restless, wanting from Hal something that went against all her upbringing, all she had learned at the feet of her family. She sensed it went against Hal's sensitivities too, and this made her feel ashamed.

She blamed herself, of course, as women have done since Eve was burdened with all that guilt for the seduction of Adam. She told herself she was sinful (though rationally she scorned that word and all its horrid religious connotations); that she was too grounded in the physical, the carnal, instead of — like Hal, whom she worshipped — in the ethereal, the cerebral. She secretly thought that she was too sensual, earthy, somehow abnormal, tainted. She did not judge herself by the standards and behaviour of her friends, or by the happy-go-lucky morals of the day, but by Hal — and his attitude and behaviour only enforced what she had learned as a child. And so she mentally punished herself, chastised herself for not being as worthy as her beloved, and strived even harder to be patient, to emulate him and wait for their wedding day, in whatever far-off future that may be.

And so Emmeline, excited by Florence and all there would be to see that day, waved goodbye to the others and went off with Hal. The weather was warm but not hot and sticky;

there were some tourists about, but not impinging on anyone's delight and enjoyment.

Marsha, standing in rapture before Botticelli's *Birth of Venus*, suddenly felt quite hot and flushed, no doubt from the combination of all that coy naked flesh combined with sexual frustration after all the weeks of separation from Jean-Luc. She also had to admit to herself that seeing Giorgio, looking tanned and virile and oh so very Italian, had stirred the sediment of memory not quite in her head but in her belly (or thereabouts) and she could not help thinking of their two encounters on the *Castel Felice*. Nostalgia seemed to be making her breasts tingle, she thought as she stared at Venus.

'*E stupendo*,' a voice whispered in her ear, in a thick Italian accent. '*Come te.*' Beautiful, like you, the man was saying, and though Marsha didn't understand the words, she comprehended well enough the slight but firm pinch on her plump bottom.

Before Marsha elbowed the man, she luckily looked around, and found to her delight that it was Giorgio himself. 'What are you doing here?' she said. 'I thought you were going pubbing.'

He did not understand her but he liked her smile, was encouraged by it. Ever since the visitors from London had arrived, Giorgio, though honestly enamoured with his Sojo, had been haunted by the memory of his two illicit encounters with Marsha. He knew about Jean-Luc, of course, and was genuinely happy for her, but he did not like to think he had lost her for ever. He felt that as he had so ably and thoroughly initiated her into sex, it was only fair that he should reap some of the benefits from it.

By some lucky quirk, Marsha felt exactly the same. She loved her Jean-Luc and was delighted that Giorgio and Sojo seemed to be getting it all together, and hoped that their relationship would continue to thrive. But she felt that in some small way Giorgio was hers also, and saw no reason why he should not continue to be.

This, at any rate, was how they rationalised it to themselves; the truth was, they were both in a fraught and tangible state of lust. Marsha blamed it on Italy and the Botticelli. Giorgio was too sensible to blame anything: he just accepted it. He followed her as they made their way sensuously around the gallery, their fire inflamed by the voluptuous paintings and all those exposed bosoms of plump maidens, the firm buttocks of archangels.

'I'm rather hot, I think I need an ice cream,' Marsha panted at one point, standing in front of Titian's *Venus of Urbino* who lay nude and sensual and suggestive, her fingers resting tantalisingly on her not-so-very-private parts.

'I want you, I need you, I adore you,' Giorgio said in Italian. Neither understood much of what the other was saying, but they did remarkably well in recognising the body language.

They found the restaurant and licked mint ice cream from each other's spoons and once, daringly, from each other's lips. 'Oh my, you are a sexy devil!' Marsha exclaimed boldly, and Giorgio smiled proudly, understanding her meaning.

The morning was delightful, though all too short. He kissed the back of that wonderful exposed neck standing in the church of Santa Croce looking at a fresco by Giotto, and fondled her buttocks surreptitiously in a crowded shop selling postcards of the sculpted genitals of Michaelangelo's *David*. On the Ponte Vecchio, which was crowded, Giorgio restrained himself to staring lustfully at her while she browsed in the goldsmiths and jeweller's shops lining the fourteenth-century bridge, until Marsha felt that she would melt, dissolve, turn into something hot and bubbly under that heated fiery gaze.

'Oh, you two ran into each other?' Sojo called merrily as they approached the trattoria where they'd planned to meet for lunch. 'Hey, look at this leather belt I bought at the flea market, and you won't believe the price!'

Emmeline and Hal arrived a few minutes later. They were both somewhat quiet, Hal for some reason preoccupied.

'It's all these things, these amazing masterpieces, all here, all around us,' he had said in the Piazza della Signoria when Emmeline asked him if something was wrong. The vast statues loomed around them like ghosts, yet they were too real, too substantial, too sensuous to be spirits. Hal lingered before the *David* for a long time, moved and also troubled, and was unusually quiet for the rest of the day.

'It makes you wonder why you should bother with your own poor creative efforts, when you see something like that,' he said later to Marsha when she, like Emmeline, asked him why he was so quiet. But though this was the truth, it was only a small part of it. The rest of it he could not explain even to himself, let alone anyone else . . .

That night, sitting around the courtyard with candles and lanterns lit, lingering over a late, late meal, Hal watched Emmeline, admired the blue wild flowers she had pinned in her long sunny hair, noted the neat curve of her breasts under her thin smock-like dress, admired the lovely legs stretched out and crossed at the ankles. He admired her as he had admired the dozens of works of art he had seen that afternoon, noting both perfections and flaws, not letting the occasional discord disturb his enjoyment of a harmonious whole. His thoughts as he watched Emmeline were clear and cool as a fresh body of water. He admired her, he cherished her, he respected her, and he was deeply grateful to her for loving him.

Emmeline, feeling his gaze, looked at him, and he took her hand, kissed it gently. Quite late, when everyone decided it was time to go to bed, he walked her to her bedroom, kissed her gently again, and said, 'I do want to marry you one day, Emmeline. You do know that, don't you?'

'Oh yes. Yes, of course I do.'

'I'll make you happy. I promise I will. Do you believe me?'

'I never doubted that. You make me happy all the time. And I'll make you happy, too – oh, I know I will, I truly will!'

By this time they were in the room, sitting on the narrow bed. 'Can I stay here with you tonight?' Hal said, holding on to Emmeline as to a lifeline. 'Can I sleep in your bed?'

'Oh Hal,' Emmeline sighed, thinking, *At last, at last.*

They got into bed awkwardly. Emmeline had shyly gone to the bathroom and put on her nightdress, which was long and white and chaste, and when she returned, Hal was in the bed with the covers pulled up. He was not naked but wearing underpants and a T-shirt. The room was light with a dazzling moon and a profusion of stars shining into the courtyard and into the open window and as Emmeline got into bed next to Hal he turned to her, took her face in his hands, looked sombrely into her eyes, then began kissing her, again and again and again.

After some time, Hal moved so that he was half-lying on top of her. She felt his weight and began kissing him more intensely, caressing his back, his shoulders. She moved slightly so that he could reach her breasts, wishing she could take off her nightdress but not knowing how to without embarrassment. His hand grazed her breast for a moment and she felt it harden and grow hot and aching, but then he moved and began stroking her shoulders. Her hands, around his body, moved tentatively down towards his buttocks, still clothed in the cotton underpants, but by then he had stopped the kissing and rolled gently off her so that they were lying side by side.

Neither moved, neither of them said anything. Emmeline, moonlight on her face, waited. Something else was sure to happen; this must have been the first stage, the second was bound to be imminent. Her whole body was telling her that this couldn't be all, that Hal could not possibly stop now, that surely he must be feeling as she was, hot and liquid, odd, needing, wanting, waiting.

But Hal was no longer touching her; he was staring at the ceiling, at her side but no longer there, and wherever he was, she knew she could not follow him. She lay there and wondered what she had done wrong, why he had turned from her, why he did not want her. I am not woman enough for him, she thought in despair. I am not attractive nor sexy nor feminine enough.

As they lay there in that strange, unhappy silence, Emmeline's doubts began, grew, escalated like a minor battle turning into a major war. She had failed Hal, failed herself; though he loved her, she was physically unattractive to him. She blamed herself utterly, for Hal, her idol, could not possibly be to blame.

Hal, sensing her tears, finally took her hand and said, 'I love you, Emmeline. It's so good being here next to you, knowing you understand, knowing that we can enjoy each other without rushing things.' He held her hand tightly and she ached now with guilt for wanting things too soon, before time. She felt tarnished, sullied with her own lust, abject before Hal's goodness. And yet a seed had been planted somewhere inside her: whatever Hal said, a destructive plant had taken root, reminding her always that if she had been more womanly, or desirable, or whatever it was that men wanted, all his talk about cerebral love would have disintegrated like cobwebs at the touch of a hard and demanding flesh-and-blood hand.

He fell asleep first, turning away from her with a sigh and facing the bare whitewashed wall. She fell asleep hours later, and when she woke he was gone, but at the side of the bed was a freshly-picked gardenia which she recognised as coming from the large plant in the earthenware pot on one of the courtyard steps. The smell of it filled the room, filled her head and her heart, and her despair of the night before lifted; at least Hal still loved her. She vowed she would live up to that love, however hard it sometimes seemed. With a much lighter heart, she washed and dressed and joined the others at breakfast.

Everyone was up by the time Emmeline arrived in the shambolic kitchen which was crammed with all the leftovers from the shop: piles of tins of fruit, boxes of tissues, cheap plastic toys, cartons of soap powder. Marsilio and Lucia were already in the shop, their languid voices meandering into the kitchen like distant bells, harmonious and pleasing. Hal looked up from his coffee and smiled so lovingly at Emmeline that for a moment she knew pure bliss, joy, sublimity. What had happened – or didn't happen – last night was transformed into something so right, so perfect, by that sweet smile that Emmeline's doubts and self-flagellations remained dormant for the rest of their time in Italy.

Marsha also smiled blissfully at Emmeline that morning at the breakfast-table, but she was doing that to everyone. The night before, Sojo had gone to bed before the others, saying she had a headache from her delirious shopping jag at the market in Florence and wanted a peaceful night. In Italian, which she had picked up during her last stay in Italy with Giorgio, she told him she wanted to sleep alone that night, as she would be restless with the bad head and would only keep him awake. She kissed him fondly as she said goodnight, and effusively wished Marsha pleasant dreams, which neither Marsha nor anyone else noticed because they were too wrapped up in their own thoughts.

When she left, Giorgio waited for a decent interval – approximately two minutes – and then moved over next to Marsha who was sitting in a patch of shadow slightly away from the others. Brightly chattering away some nonsense in Italian for the benefit of Marsilio and Lucia, he managed to sit so that his fingers were pressed up against the wonderful pliable roundness of her hips and upper thighs. He felt all prickly with lust for his darling Marsha, having spent the whole afternoon, after their lunch with the others, following her around Florence to carry on the lighthearted courtship begun during their morning sightseeing. In the sweet sunlight of a hidden garden he had managed to lift up her short skirt and feel that heavenly angel silkiness of the inside of her thighs; in the Museo dell'Opera del Duomo he pressed up against her magnificent back and buttocks. 'Ohhh,' Marsha sighed, then broke away reluctantly as two Germans with guidebooks stared sternly at them.

They wandered around looking at the sculptures, which, in their glazed state, seemed to consist mostly of glistening thighs and naked torsos, and imagined themselves to be alone and naked and glistening. At Donatello's statue of Mary Magdalen, Giorgio's hot fingers probed inside Marsha's thin cotton blouse and briefly, surreptitiously, touched the nipple under her bra, on the pretext of buttoning an undone button. Marsha, eyes half-closed, felt Mary Magdalene's eyes upon her and hoped the saint remembered what it was like before she became converted.

In the dark shadows of a musty church they behaved more decorously, until Marsha bent over in a dim corner to read the inscription on an ancient tombstone, and Giorgio, unable to resist that plump rounded bottom turned so beguilingly towards him, caressed it slowly, sensuously. Bursting out into the sunshine again, they felt dazzled, stunned, and resumed their sightseeing haphazardly, brushing up against each other often, touching when they thought no one was looking. At last, coming face to face with Giambologna's powerful huge sculpture of the raping of a Sabine woman, they became nearly undone, and had to quickly find a trattoria where they could cool off with a cold drink before they simply wrestled each other to the floor and made love.

And so it seemed for ever, that evening, before Marsilio and Lucia finally went off to their beds, yawning and grumbling goodnaturedly about who was going to open up the shop in the not-too-early morning. Then Emmeline and Hal wandered off, saying a vague goodnight, too engrossed in each other to notice Giorgio's suntanned hand now well ensconced under Marsha's skirt which she had taken up another two inches just the other day. Marsha was as oblivious to them as they were to her, for Giorgio's fingers had been doing incredible things to her for quite some time now. 'Sweet dreams,' she muttered inanely to Hal and Emmeline's retreating backs.

Giorgio, suddenly cognisant of the fact that they were, at long last, alone, got up, made an audacious and theatrical charade of saying goodnight to Marsha (the windows of the bedrooms looked out into the courtyard), and abruptly left her and disappeared. In a pre-orgasmic daze, she somnabulantly, as a woman drugged, made for her bedroom, to find Giorgio waiting for her, naked and erect, hardly able to wait until the door was closed before falling upon her and peeling off her clothes, both of them trembling now with the giddy relief of being alone together at last.

'Did you have a good night?' Sojo asked with a twinkle the next morning.

'What?' Giorgio replied with a jump.

'A good sleep? Good dreams?'

He stared at her suspiciously, but she looked back at him innocently, majestic and serene in her livid patterned mini-shorts and skimpy elasticised halter top. 'My headache's fine now,' she announced cheerily. 'Back in my bed tonight, hm?' She tickled him robustly under his chin.

'I cannot wait,' Giorgio murmured, gazing dazedly at her erect nipples, which were outlined clearly beneath the halter.

Marsha, hearing but not understanding their conversation, because they spoke in Italian, said sincerely, 'I'm so glad you are better, Sojo, and back to normal.'

The two women smiled at each other, oblivious of Giorgio who did not quite understand what, if anything, was going on. Marsha, who had had a most satisfying night, was content not to repeat it — at least not for a year or two or three. Sojo, who had also had a pleasant night, enjoying a reposeful sleep in a solitary bed, thought nonetheless that she wouldn't want to repeat the experience regularly, though very occasionally would be quite acceptable. The two women smiled at each other a second time, understanding each other completely, and from that day onwards were the closest and dearest of friends in spite of the distance between them . . .

*

'Bloody weather,' Leo says to Tony who has just driven up to Woodland Farm. 'I could do with a month of sunshine.'

'You should go with your wife and Emmeline to France at Easter-time.'

'Too much work to do on the farm. I wish this fog would lift. It's been going on for days, too depressing. Anyway, go on up to the house; I'll join you as soon as I've put the tractor away. Emmeline's still at the university. She said she won't be home for dinner tonight, she has a meeting or something.'

This makes Tony feel guilty, for it is true that he tends to come to Woodland Farm when he knows Emmeline will be home. He didn't think he was quite so obvious about it, though. 'Actually, I've come to check your attic,' he says sheepishly, 'see if it's okay. It won't be long before the bats come out of hibernation and I want to make sure there is nothing that will disturb them.'

'Stay for dinner,' Leo urges. 'We're eating early. Daisy is off to the shelter; it's her evening on. You and I can collapse in front of the telly – I think there's some football on.'

Tony agrees, but somewhat uncomfortably. After his cursory talk with Barnaby in the bookshop, he feels he is hiding something from Leo, though in truth, if Barnaby can be believed, there is nothing to hide. Tony decides he has no choice: he has to believe Barnaby, for if he doesn't the complications are convoluted and enormous. And yet he could not help watching him with Daisy last Sunday, when they all gathered at Woodland Farm for a meal. Tony is used to patient observation; he has been observing wildlife for years and cannot help noting things that others miss. Daisy and Barnaby seemed to alternate between an erratic restlessness and a secretive, sensual, calm; they either studiously avoided looking at each other, or caught, and held, each other's eyes slightly more often and much longer than normally.

His uneasiness becomes more salient during the meal that evening. Daisy serves breaded fish, jacket potatoes and a fresh green salad, but she eats little of it herself. She seems jumpy but ebullient, looking particularly attractive in a fuzzy soft-blue jumper which she wears with jeans. She has changed her hairstyle so it fluffs becomingly around her face, and it makes her look younger, softer.

She leaves before Leo and Tony have finished their dinner, saying she might be late back; that if Leo is tired he mustn't wait up for her.

'She and Barnaby sometimes stop for a drink,' Leo explains when Daisy has gone. 'They need to, to unwind. I think they both get very upset, very troubled, over what they see at the shelter.'

Tony says nothing. Leo looks at him, then says slowly, 'Daisy needs this, you know, this voluntary work she's doing. Since the kids, especially Gemma, moved out, she's been like a lost sheep. But all of a sudden she's got back all her spark, her energy.'

Tony still cannot think of anything to say. He knows he should say something like, 'That's good, great,' but is it? Uneasily, he thinks not. He thinks there are other, darker reasons why Daisy has had this metamorphosis, but he cannot voice these to Leo. And so he brings the conversation around to safer subjects, to the bats. He has had a look round the attic and has found that the work done there has not made any major disturbances: when the bats come out of hibernation, they should feel at home. Tony longs to see them out and about again, flying reassuringly in barns and lofts and old buildings and attics. He finds the presence of bats comforting; their very history, their ancient lineage, makes him feel there is after all in life a continuity, a thread that cannot be severed, slashed by chaos and confusion. An order to things is what he sees when, every year, the bats emerge from their winter roosts and take their place in the bustling spring awakening.

And yet as spring approaches, Tony is aware also of something threatening, some loss, which is of course connected with Emmeline. Normally not a brooder, Tony finds a glumness settling over him as February turns to March and the signs of the coming season are too obvious to be ignored. He has become moody, distracted. He knows he is not very good company these days.

Leo is talking, and Tony has not been listening. 'I'm sorry, Leo, I've been preoccupied,' Tony admits. 'What were you saying? Something about your woods?'

Leo sighs. This is the first time he has spoken of this to anyone, and it was difficult, arduous. Now Tony is asking him to repeat it. 'I'm thinking of selling it,' he says in a rush.

Now Tony is all alert, all attention. 'Why? To whom? What for?'

'The university has approached me. The administrators, last year. You know how the campus is expanding – it already stretches to the other side of those woods – and they are eager to acquire more land. They've offered me a good price.'

'Sell the woodland for building? Leo, you can't! It's established, so beautiful! Such old trees, and the wild flowers – and what about the bats? I've got boxes there—'

Leo laughs, rather ruefully. 'I knew you'd say that. For God's sake, don't make it worse.'

'But . . . what does Daisy say? The children?'

'They don't know. You're the first person I've told.'

Tony takes a deep breath. 'Why? For God's sake why are you doing this? Your family will be devastated.'

Leo hesitates. They are sitting in the big living room but there is no fire, which makes the room somehow unwelcoming in spite of the central heating, the soft light of a couple of table lamps in opposite corners of the room. This room needs a fire, Tony thinks irrelevantly. It was built around a fireplace which was always meant to be alight, for heat and comfort and cooking, for just living. Without a fire the room seems inanimate, dead.

Leo begins to speak, and it is soon obvious how difficult it is for him to say the things he is now telling Tony. It is a story of several years of financial difficulties, of pig prices dropping at the most unfortuitous time, of Leo unable to recover losses fully. 'I gambled, and it didn't pay off,' he finishes quietly. 'At that time I had no idea which way the market would go, but I took a chance that pig prices were rising, so I expanded, bought more sows, built new farrowing pens. Unfortunately I was wrong; the bottom fell out of the market. I incurred debts that I still haven't paid off, though of course now the market is quite strong.'

'I had no idea. I knew things were somewhat dicey a year or so ago, but I thought you had weathered all that.'

Leo leans forward in his armchair, unconsciously rubbing his hands together at the cold grate, as if unaware that there is no fire to warm them there tonight. 'The money I could get from the woodland would do more than clear my debts, Tony.' He hesitates, unable even now to voice what the real problem is, the real reason for needing money. So he merely says, 'I could handle the debts, I suppose. But there are other

285

things I want to do. Buy sheep, for instance. I'd like to build up the flock, go into early lambing, make decent sheep runs like we had in New Zealand when I worked there all those years ago. I can't do that without a sizeable amount of cash.'

'But Leo, the woods?' Tony is dumbfounded. He thinks of the masses of primroses in the spring, the profusion of bluebells. He thinks of the birds, the squirrels, the foxes. He thinks of his bats. 'You can't,' he says finally. 'You can't let all that be destroyed, for building, for Christ's sake.'

Leo gets up abruptly, begins pacing up and down on the worn but still good wool carpet covering the sloping floor of the old room. 'Do you think I don't know? Do you think I haven't agonised over this for months? I'm afraid I haven't much choice, Tony. I'm fed up with being in debt and I'm fed up with not being able to do the things on the farm that I want to do.'

'I can understand that. But it's so drastic—'

Leo shakes his head truculently, stubbornly. 'Look, Tony, I know how you feel, you're a conservationist, you're into ecology, being green, all that. I thought I was too, as much as a farmer can be who is trying to make a decent living from it. I've tried to farm in a balanced way, with as little harm to the environment, the earth, as possible. But it's not just the finances, it's . . . I don't know. I'm getting tired, getting old.'

'Oh, now come on—'

'I am, Tony. I'm well over fifty, and feeling it. I had hoped one of the kids would want to stay on the farm, give a hand, begin to manage it so that I could begin to take it easier. Start doing things with Daisy – travelling, that sort of thing.'

'It's a shame none of them were interested.'

'Oh, it's all right, they've got their own lives. In the end, you see, this farm is mine, my responsibility. It's all I have. I know I've got Daisy, and she's been a tremendous help, but it's not her place like it is mine. She's not responsible for it like I am. I think in the end that I should be able to run it the way I want to.'

There is an edge to his voice, something bellicose in it, that Tony doesn't quite understand, but when he tries to extract from Leo exactly what he plans to do with the farm if the woodland is sold, he confronts a barrier. Once again Leo has retreated into himself where no one, not Daisy, nor Tony, nor anyone else, can reach him.

'You've made up your mind, then?' Tony asks finally.

'I think so, yes. I've been pondering it for months.'

Tony is stunned. He wishes he had the words to plead, cajole, reason; he wishes he had the money to buy the woodland himself; he wishes he knew how to save it without ruining Leo financially. The two men sit in a desolate silence for three or four minutes, each with thoughts scurrying wildly like rabbits blinded by a sudden strong light. How long the silence would have continued they are not to find out, for suddenly Emmeline is there. Neither had heard her come in and both are startled to hear her say, 'Hello, are you two all right? You look pretty gloomy — is anything wrong?'

They both jump up, begin speaking at once, assuring her that everything is fine. Leo, after a few moments, looks at his watch and says he is tired, has been up early, is going to bed.

When they are alone Emmeline says again, 'Are you sure everything is okay? Leo looks a bit melancholy, and you seem pensive.'

Tony shakes his head. He doesn't want to talk about the woodland yet, not even to Emmeline. Besides, though Leo

287

did not tell him to keep it secret, he feels it only right that Daisy should know about it first. It hurts him, thinking of the wood decimated, its trees ruthlessly cut down to make way for more concrete and steel. He feels unbalanced, unearthed. This seems to happen more and more lately, when he reads about great motorways cutting across ancient moorlands, or reservoirs drowning fertile valleys. He worries about his bats, worries about the world, worries about himself, how he will breathe in a concrete forest, a leaden landscape.

'Tony?' Emmeline is saying. 'What is it?'

Tony sighs. He would like to take this woman in his arms, make love to her. She is sitting on a huge floor cushion opposite him, her pale brown hair pushed back behind her ears, her eyes wide with concern for him. He looks at her so vulnerably, so tenderly, that she is moved, wants to go to him, wants to touch him. Both of them make a slight movement towards the other but they are arrested by Daisy's sudden presence.

'You startled me. I forgot you were still out,' Tony says to her unthinkingly, as Emmeline retreats into the kitchen to put the kettle on.

'Yes, er, it's late, I know, but we — that is, me and Barnaby — had so much to talk about. The shelter, you know. We had a spot of bother tonight. One of the residents came in fighting drunk and created havoc. There was a great deal of sorting out to do. We had to call the police in the end, unfortunately. And then we just couldn't go home, we needed to talk . . .' Daisy trails off miserably.

'Daisy, it's all right, you don't have to explain to me,' Tony says kindly. He has always liked Daisy, ever since the day she brought him a baby owl that Leo had found, slightly wounded and abandoned in the woods. Daisy had heard that Tony was the local naturalist, and having had bad luck herself in the past trying to rear wounded birds, thought she'd take the creature, an exquisite white barn owl, to someone who presumably knew what he was doing. Tony nursed the owl day and night, and it survived. From then on, Daisy always had a soft spot for the quiet man with the deep soothing voice, as he did for her, for she made him laugh, cheered him up with her bounce and exuberance. He was especially grateful for this when he returned from South America, his relationship in ruins. Leo and Daisy compassionately and unobtrusively took him over, inviting him for meals, introducing him to their other friends, encouraging his music and the band which he was just beginning to form, and in general introducing him to life again, for he had become very insular during his years with Carrie.

Daisy offers him coffee, tea, a nightcap, but Tony, sensing she wants to talk privately to Emmeline, declines. When he goes, Daisy joins Em in the kitchen and says, 'I'm exhausted. It was really a harrowing evening. I was quite frightened at one point.'

Emmeline looks at her astutely. 'Odd that you look so radiant.'

Daisy flushes. 'Em,' she begins warningly.

'Don't worry, I'm not going to pry. I just wish that this newfound energy and commitment and meaning you seem to have suddenly found in life had more to do with the Northgate Hostel and less with Barnaby Brackenbury.'

Daisy pulls out a kitchen chair and slumps down on it. 'I know what you're thinking,' she says slowly. 'It isn't true.' She neglects to mention how she and Barnaby clung to each other tonight at the pub car park when they were saying good night, neither wanting to leave the other. She neglects also to mention the urgency of the embrace, broken only by the fact that they were in a public place and were soon disturbed by the presence of others.

'I guess I'm not thinking of much,' Emmeline says. 'I'm not one to make moral judgements. But saying that, I can't forget about Leo.'

Daisy looks up grimly. 'Leo? Dear, wonderful, kindly Leo, whom everyone loves and admires? Leo the rock, the foundation? Leo, who can do no wrong? My dear Emmeline, let me tell you what it is like being married to Leo.'

And so she does. She tells Emmeline about the silences, the loneliness. She tells of how, especially after the children were grown, Leo retreated more and more into his work, his farm, his animals, sharing his soul with the land more than he ever did with Daisy. She tells it all honestly and fairly, not making it a criticism of Leo but simply a fact: this is the way things are and have always been.

'And it was all right, it really was,' she finishes at last, 'when I had the kids home. There was so much going on, and when they were older I had them to talk to, to share things with . . .' she trails off, shrugs.

'But when they left, you went slightly crazy. No wonder. I can comprehend much better now, your wanting to hold on to Gemma.'

'Yes. The loneliness, you understand. Terrifying.'

They are silent for several minutes. Daisy's story has so surprised and unsettled Emmeline that she doesn't know how to respond.

'So you see,' Daisy finally says, 'don't begrudge me Barnaby.'

Upstairs in the bedroom Leo is lying awake, unable to sleep. Talking to Tony as he did this evening, unleashing even such a minute part of his soul, his vision, has unstrung him. He is beginning to believe that dreams perhaps do come true. He is beginning to have hope.

Soon, he must tell Daisy.

'You'll have to talk to Leo,' Emmeline is saying downstairs in the kitchen. 'Surely you can explain how you feel, how you need to communicate?'

Daisy looks at Em kindly. 'You Americans are very big on communication. The thing is, it only works if both parties want to. Leo is quite happy the way he is and cannot see the point of endless soul-searching, as he calls it.'

'You've got to talk,' Em repeats helplessly.

Daisy says, quietly, her face in repose but her voice trembly, 'You see, it's become more complicated than that. I'm not quite sure I want to any more.'

Upstairs Leo tosses and turns, reaching an arm out for Daisy before remembering she still has not come to bed. *I'll tell her tonight*, he thinks sleepily. *As soon as she comes upstairs to bed.*

But when she does, he is sound asleep. Quietly getting into the bed beside him, Daisy does not sleep. But for the first time in years, she does not feel lonely as she lies beside her oblivious, slightly snoring, husband.

Chapter Thirteen

*T*hat same night, on the pavement right outside the Cathedral, a calm, slight figure sits on a blanket on the ground surrounded by at least fifty candles of all sizes and shapes and colours, a dozen or more of them lit. The icy fog has permeated the Cathedral Close, and the Cathedral itself looks eerie, frozen in its pool of hazy light. The people coming out of the great doors shiver: inside they were warmed by Mozart (there was a concert, a youth symphony orchestra) and their own zealous fervour (one had to be committed to come out on a night like tonight); outside they are faced with a damp cold mist that numbs noses and fingertips and the spirit too.

But there is, beyond the massive, intricately carved wooden doors of the Cathedral Close, something odd, something not quite of this world, or so it seems to the concert-goers at first glance. Gemma, opaque and dewy in the thick fog illuminated by her candles, sits wrapped in a bright blue wool blanket, her many plaits tinkling with their bells and beads whenever she even slightly moves her head. A few feet away sits another figure, Baz, his long hair stiff with the cold and mist and standing up majestically all over his head like an awesome, dignified, African chieftain. Baz is playing his didgeridoo, and the sound moans and throbs like a great tide in a dark sea, like wind on a lonely hilltop.

The audience from the concert, passing by, are at first offended by this primitive harmony jarring so appallingly with Mozart, and the pagan candlelight obliterating the memory of the reverential, sacred lighting in the magnificent crevices of the Cathedral. But one or two stop, entranced, then others, and soon there is a small crowd gathered around as a few enlightened souls see the connection, the thin fragile thread, and are moved by it.

When Baz finishes his music, his hat on the ground clinks with coins, and many more people are buying candles from Gemma. Her candles are indeed beautiful, small masterpieces, works of art. The colours are imaginative, variegated, her shapes strong and unusual. Some candles are delicate, wispy, fragile but functional; others are solid and earthy, but they all are made to burn for hours. It is not only their quality and attractiveness that compels people to buy tonight, it is something else, something primitive and magical, something pagan and Christian both. It is to do with lighting up the dark, the fog, the opaque night, to do with frightening away spirits, or sin or evil, to do with holding on to luminosity and dispelling dark and murky chimera – either without or within.

'I've sold at least two dozen, maybe more,' Gemma says delightedly when the crowd has dispersed. 'Some people bought two or three, and one woman bought five.'

'We can buy that extra oil lamp we need for the caravan. Or buy the part we need for the van. It's just about clapping out, you know, but we can't get rid of it until we're on the road.'

'Steady on. We need food, too. We're out of everything, even teabags.'

Though they are both cold, neither makes a move to pack up and go. The Cathedral Close is empty now, and only a few scurrying people go by in the street. Gemma's candles burn lower and lower, but she is loath to blow them out.

Baz looks at her, takes her hand, rubs her cold fingers between his warm palms. 'Gemma, you don't regret any of this, do you? Giving up the farm, living like this, always broke, scraping along—'

'Oh, stop it!' Gemma cries. 'How can you say that? I often think how lucky I am, to be doing what I want to do, in my own time, when I like, how I like.'

'It's still new,' Baz says seriously. 'Maybe one day you'll be sick of it. You'll want more – a proper place to live, decent clothes, some security . . .'

'All the things I'd have had if I took over the farm, you mean?'

'Yes. Something like that.'

Gemma stares thoughtfully at the candles, at the melted wax making rainbow marks on the pavement. 'Who's to know what any of us will want in the future?' she says. 'And who's to know if what we get is anything like what we'll want. Look at the blokes at the shelter – Kelvin, Clifton, the others. All Kelvin wanted was a job, to make his mum proud. All Clifton wanted was to carry on unobtrusively at his job, putting figures in columns, and coming home to his cat. Did he ever tell you about his cat? Do you know he still cries over it? He tried to keep it with him when he lost his home but the cat ran away.'

'I know, I know.'

'And the alcoholics, Baz. Did they want to end up in an old warehouse with makeshift beds, lying in their own vomit, being beaten up by one of the druggies every now and again for making too much noise?'

'Gemma—'

'Don't talk to me about *want*, Baz. We have no right to even use such a word.'

Baz puts his arms around her for she is begin to shiver now, her nose red with cold. 'Come on, love, let's get home, get something to eat.' He is filled with such a huge protecting love for her that he doesn't want to let her go, wants to keep on holding her until the candles burn right down to the ground and the pavement is nothing more than a mass of warm, brightly coloured, comforting wax.

Not very far away at the Primrose Café, in their bed-sitting room on top of the restaurant, Blue and Flack are despondently wondering what to do with their lives. At the end of the month they are closing the café, unable to make a go of it financially.

'If only I could get another job,' Flack moans. His stint at the off-licence finished at Christmas, and since then there has been nothing.

'It was no good, Flack. The café needs the two of us. Gemma was a big help while you were at work, but she and Baz will be off soon. We need to both be there.'

'So it's back on the dole.'

'For a bit, until something else comes up.' Blue is feeling far from cheerful herself, but she knows how hard it is for Flack to surface when he hits the depths of despair. She knows he has every right to despair, for the end of the café is the end of a cherished dream for him, but she also knows that they've somehow got to get over this. So she says, gently, 'You've proved what a good cook you are; everyone loved our food. Maybe when we get ourselves sorted out you can make your cakes and pies and I can sell them to wholefood shops, other cafés, maybe even go out of Canterbury and into some of the villages.'

She talks and talks, becoming animated with ideas, with new dreams. She's not sure how much of this she believes herself, but she knows it's important to keep Flack from going under.

Flack listens, first morosely, then slowly perking up. Blue knows they are over the worst when Flack tentatively, then more enthusiastically, begins to add one or two suggestions of his own. By the time they go to bed they are filled, if not exactly with hope, at least with resilience, and this, Blue knows, will at least get them through the next few weeks.

The following day Leo begins lambing, and so of course there is no time to tell Daisy of his decision to sell the woodland. In truth, though he would never admit it, he is rather frightened of doing so. He knows how important that piece of ground has been to her, and indeed to all the children, since she first walked through it that late September day when she arrived at Woodland Farm. The leaves on the trees had not yet changed colours but there was a promise, an anticipation, in the woods of rich fungi, compost, of things burying themselves deep into the soil, of berries and preparations for winter.

Barely a day goes by now that Daisy doesn't go into the woodland, if only for a fifteen-minute walk with Blossom, so that the old dog doesn't become too stiff and arthritic. Leo doesn't let himself think of this now. He throws himself wholeheartedly into his lambing, into his flock of sheep which is his pride and his joy and the source of his greatest contentment. Throwing himself into the moment, the present, he refuses to let himself dwell on anything which might be confrontational. It will have to come, he knows, but he is not going to let anyone, not even Daisy, stand between him and the realisation of his longstanding dream.

Daisy also is contented. She is working not just with Barnaby at the soup kitchen these three evenings a week, but also sometimes during the day, at Miles' request. Miles, co-ordinating his volunteers, understands that the residents respond well to Daisy, not only to her reawakened spark and energy, which seems to be oozing out of her these days like jets of water from a kinetic fountain, but also to the other side of her: the ever-patient, ever-understanding, maternal woman. Miles watches as Daisy talks to the residents, teases them, draws them out of themselves. He observes her listening, comforting. Daisy is not aware of Miles' scrutiny; she is too concerned with the men themselves, empathising with them as she does with her own children, even though some of the men are older than she is.

Miles is still negotiating for a women's hostel and hopes that one will be forthcoming before next winter. In the meantime Josy, by now one of the regulars, frequents both the soup kitchen and the makeshift lounge, often sleeping on the lumpy sofa in the afternoon before venturing out in the streets at night. Various social services have been alerted about Josy, and offers made to help, but she is suspicious of them, preferring to handle her own life in her own way. The other woman who uses the shelter, Irene, is as silent and nebulous as ever, lost in her own world and appearing in this one at odd times like a frail apparition that one can see but never touch, never communicate with.

Early one evening, as Daisy is waiting for Barnaby, Josy appears, as calmly and as placidly as ever despite intensive cuts and bruises on her face. A trickle of blood, which she has been wiping with a dirty piece of rag, has caked and hardened on her face.

'Josy, what's happened?' Daisy cries in horror.

'Sodden kids. Schoolboys, larking about.'

'But how? Where? Why? Come here, let me wash that cut for you.'

'Sitting on me bleedin' own, on a bench in Greyfriars, at the park, minding me own bleedin' business. Bored teenagers, started to take the mickey outa me. Tried to grab m'bags, so I kicked one where he'll still be feeling it. Ow, go easy!'

'We've got to get that cut clean. It's not as deep as I thought at first. Sit still.'

'Made 'em mad, that did. So the others started throwing stones at me, the buggers. Lucky ole job some old pensioners showed up, two blokes, and the boys ran off, the bleedin' cowards.'

'Did they help you, the pensioners?'

'Nah, no chance. Pretended nothing was wrong, walked past me like I was a sodden tree.'

'Why, how awful, how uncaring!' Daisy stops her ministrations and looks with indignation at Josy. 'I can't believe they didn't stop to help you. What horrid, wretched people. I'd like to—'

'Oh, stow it, Daise,' Josy says wearily. 'I don't blame the old gits. Best to keep outa trouble. I'd a done the same.'

Daisy tends Josy's wounds and says, finally, 'Nothing that requires a hospital visit, thank God. But I'll phone the police, tell them to come around at once.'

'Don't you dare! If you do I'll walk outa here, never come back.'

'But why? You were attacked, viciously and brutally. It could happen again. Those boys must be apprehended.'

'Hell, Daise, don't you understand nothing?' Josy shakes her head impatiently. 'Those lads came from decent middle-class homes, they spoke posh, I heard them; they wore smart school uniforms.'

'And so what?' Daisy says tersely.

'So what bloody policeman's going to believe me against them, eh? You just tell me.' Josy speaks truculently, but it is more because of Daisy's lack of understanding than because of any bitterness over what has occurred. It's the way life is. What is the point of ranting and raving, losing good energy which would be of more use channelled for survival, for keeping warm, finding food.

Daisy begs, pleads, swears. In the midst of this Barnbaby walks in and hears the story, and tries to reason with Josy, tries to get her to tell it to the police. Josy is implacable. By now the tissues around her right eye have swollen grotesquely, but still she refuses even to contemplate finding some justice for what has happened to her. Justice is a word she doesn't believe in anyway, so what's the point? She falls asleep as she ponders this, much to Daisy's frustration.

That night, when they finally leave the shelter, having at least persuaded Josy to sleep there on a mattress in the utility room, Barnaby takes Daisy to the pub, gives her a brandy, and listens as she cries and rants with despair and an impotent rage.

'I can't bear to just sit by and watch,' she cries with passion at one point in her monologue. 'I want so much to help, but there seems to be so little one can do.'

'You're doing something, more than most people. I know it doesn't seem enough: it never does. But you can't do more, my dear. You really can't.' Barnaby holds her hand and soothes her like an infant, though it is he who looks like the baby, with that big smooth head with thin fuzz instead of hair, those myopic grey eyes (he has taken off his glasses), those pale white fingers now twisted in Daisy's tiny child-like ones. But Daisy, grateful for his ministrations, looks at him as if he were a strong, protecting guardian angel rather than a plump-cheeked cherub.

'I think I'm falling in love with you,' Barnaby says out of the blue, disconcerted by her fulsome gaze and suddenly forgetting about Josy, the shelter, everything except Daisy's damp eyes focusing adoringly on him.

'You can't. Please don't.'

'But why? I'm not asking you to do anything about it. I'm not asking for you to love me.'

'But I do. That's why you mustn't. Love me, that is.'

They clutch each other's hands, openly and wantonly, on top of the varnished oak table smeared with puddles of beer and crisp crumbs.

'Oh ho ho ho ho!' Clem Todd mutters to Celia Todd at a small table hidden behind an ample couple on the other side of the pub. 'Is that not our neighbour, indulging in an illicit passion?'

Celia, bored, brightens up at this, and retorts spiritedly to Clem, 'You're a fine one to talk about illicit passions. You've been seen I don't know how many times wandering around town with that American woman. Nice for some, those long Friday lunch-hours. You think I don't know what else you get up to?'

Chance would be a fine thing, Clem thinks sourly, and for one of the rare times in their marriage, he tells the truth to Celia. 'I'm not having an affair with her, all right? I don't know how often I've told you that.'

Celia shrugs, losing interest, and turns again to peer at

Daisy and Barnaby, who are still clutching each other over the table. She wonders if she should slip a hint about Barnaby's machinations to Marjorie Brackenbury. That would take her down a peg or two, she contemplates. Celia, like many other people, mistakes Marjorie's booming voice for arrogance, and would quite enjoy putting her down if the chance arose.

'I should keep out of it,' Clem says, reading her thoughts. Much as he dislikes the Brackenbury's, he uncomfortably remembers the night Barnaby and Daisy had seen him with Emmeline, heading towards his empty house. He is wise enough to know that if one has nefarious leanings, one should keep in with the neighbours.

But he will, he decides, broach the subject to Emmeline, when he sees her tomorrow at work. Things are rather at a stalemate there. Although, as Celia is aware, he does occasionally lunch with her or shares a trip to the theatre, it is all strictly, and boringly, platonic. Unfortunately there has been no one else around during the long winter months to idle away the dark drab afternoons and nights, and Clem is paddling about rather querulously in the sticky waters of self-pity. Celia is, after all, so tedious in the winter, all those incessant chilblains and runny noses. Clem perks up at the thought of revealing Daisy's little foray into infidelity to Emmeline; perhaps it will even give her some ideas of her own. He watches with satisfaction as Barnaby impulsively takes Daisy's hand, kisses it in a manner that cannot by any stretch of the imagination be called mere friendship, and pulls it with his under the pitted oak table, where it remains until they finally, flushed and oblivious to everyone around them, leave the pub.

'And so then they walked out, still holding hands,' Clem says

to an implacable Emmeline the next day at work. Her face
is stony and grim. Clem interprets this as anger at Daisy,
but as usual with Emmeline he is wrong. Though dismayed
that Barnaby and Daisy are being so careless in showing their
affection in public places, she is in fact furious with Clem for
being such an avid old gossip.

'You have probably misunderstood the whole situation,'
Emmeline says coldly. 'They have been friends for years.
Friends do occasionally touch each other, physically show
their affection.'

Clem raises his hedgerow eyebrows succinctly, conveying
in that brief movement exactly how much credit he gives to
male-female friendships.

'Of course I wouldn't repeat it to another soul,' he says
with eyes closed, as if the very thought of doing something
so iniquitous quite overcomes him.

'Then why did you tell *me?*'

'Why, Emmeline!' Clem looks so hurt that Emmeline
softens for a moment, until she remembers he is an actor as
well as a lecturer in theatre studies. 'I told you merely because
Daisy is your friend; you're living in her house. I thought the
knowledge would help you to handle the situation.'

Emmeline disdains to answer and looks down at some
papers on her desk. They are in the office they share and
Emmeline has a great deal of work to do before the Easter
break in a fortnight's time. Clem is ignoring her body language
and is perched on the edge of her desk, which annoys the hell
out of her. When she looks up he waggles his smug eyebrows
eloquently.

'Clem,' Emmeline says warningly, 'I have quite a bit of
work to do before the end of term.'

'Ah, end of term. I've been meaning to talk to you about

that. My wife and daughter are going away, and I'll be at a loose end. I wonder if you'd like to spend a few days away, out in the country somewhere? You'll be going back soon, and you've not seen much of England. I was thinking of showing you the Cotswolds, or even the West Country.'

Emmeline looks up from her work and raises her own eyebrows suspiciously.

'We're two tired colleagues badly in need of a break,' Clem goes on, winningly. 'It'll do us both good.'

'Sorry, Clem,' Emmeline dismisses him and turns back to her desk. 'I'm going to France for the Easter break.'

Clem swears to himself. He may as well join Celia and Eliza at his mother-in-law's in Somerset, he thinks sourly. At least there is that accommodating shopkeeper in the village post office, bored with her life and her husband and always ready for a bit on the side.

The thought cheers him. He jumps off Emmeline's desk and at last settles down to work himself.

'*Bonjour, ça va?* I can't believe you're here, you're really here!'

Marsha, clad in a printed cotton dress, white sandals, and a pristine white cardigan, swoops upon Emmeline and Daisy as they get out of the car. 'How was the crossing? How is dear old England? Em, you look *formidable* – do you dye your hair? I love that light brown but I'm jealous as hell. The rest of us got lighter, whiter, greyer as we got older, and your hair went darker. Where is all that blonde? *Mon dieu*, what is it now, eight years, seven years? Your fortieth birthday in the States was the last time I saw you. Or is it longer? You're not fifty yet, are you? No, you can't be. I am, of course. *Oh la la!*'

As they carry their bags into the house, admiring the new

furniture, the new décor (Marsha is forever redecorating the spacious modern house which is built along the lines of an ancient château, complete with turrets and a couple of towers), the three women frankly eye each other, take mental notes. Marsha is now totally grey, her hair severely pulled back in a French bun very like the way she wore it all those years ago on the *Castel Felice*, except of course for the colour. She looks exactly like who she is: the provincial wife of a French dentist in a pleasant, not very large town in the middle of Brittany.

Marsha notes with pleasure that Emmeline is still slim, still elegant, and that Daisy is, rather oddly, less grey than she was when she saw her last, the copper colour shining healthily in the French sunlight. This Marsha innocently attributes to the English rain and thinks no more of it. Daisy is still slim too, which is good as she is so tiny, her bones seemingly so fragile, that any excess weight would threaten to crush her. Marsha herself looks much older than the other two and is much plumper, though she does not mind in the slightest, and indeed slightly pities her two dear friends. She, after all, lives in this most salubrious area, in her beloved France, with the most dynamic and sexiest man in Brittany.

'Ah, my friends, welcome, welcome!' The sexiest and most dynamic man in Brittany ambles out to greet the new arrivals, kissing them twice on each cheek, effusively chattering to them in very good English. He is short and podgy and quite hairless, but he has magnificent teeth and his eyes are deep green and merry. Marsha adores him, as she adores her life of shopping in the marketplace (as well as at the big new Intermarché), gossiping with all the shopkeepers, cooking sumptuous meals for her husband and any family or visitors who happen to be about, and giving English lessons for the many French who wish to speak impeccable American-English.

Although it is still only the end of March, the weather here is fair and soft and mild, auguring well for the Easter break. On the ferry coming over Daisy was slightly melancholy, in a confusing turmoil of emotions, feeling guilty about leaving the Northgate Hostel, but not at all guilty over leaving Leo with his lambing. This did induce a twinge of remorse, which in turn angered her. Compounding all this was a desperate pining for Barnbaby, which hit her before the white cliffs were even out of sight.

Emmeline, unwilling to judge either Daisy or Barnaby, but very unhappy about the situation, had told Daisy about Clem's conversation. 'Do be careful,' she had warned. 'Do be circumspect, whatever you do. If the time comes when Leo has to be hurt, you must do it yourself. You cannot let him find out through someone like Clem Todd.'

On the ferry trip, and then on the long drive to Brittany, Daisy vacillated between remorse and euphoria, between hope and despair, between lugubrious silences and irrepressible giggles and high spirits. Emmeline, noting the signs – having seen them often in her students – of a reckless, intense infatuation, humoured Daisy, letting her mention Barnaby as often and as freely as she liked, and tried not, at this stage, to inject too much cynicism or dire predictions, knowing wisely that Daisy would merely switch off.

'I do worry about you,' she let herself say, as they were approaching Marsha's village. 'And about Leo. You've been married so long—'

'It's all right, Em. I'm in love with Barnaby, but I won't hurt Leo, or Marjorie, or any of our assorted children. He won't either. We've talked about it, you see. We both feel the same.'

Emmeline's heart dropped like a stone in deep, dank waters. How many times had she heard that before, from various friends and confidantes, only to be faced with the shards of a broken relationship a month, a year, later.

'Daisy,' she began warningly, knowing she could not let this go.

'Hush, Em. Please hush. We're almost there, okay? I've got ten days away from both of them, Leo and Barnaby. I'll try to get my head together, I promise. Just don't lecture me while we're here, all right?'

Emmeline had smiled. 'No lectures. But you do your bit, okay? Think about Leo and the kids. Think about your years together. Think what loving Barnaby can do to that, no matter what you believe now, in the headiness of the moment.'

And now they are in France, unpacking their cases in a spacious bedroom crammed with Breton antiques which once belonged to Jean-Luc's family. Two single beds stand in opposite corners, and in between is a door leading to a luxurious modern bathroom where there is plenty of steaming hot water for them each to have a leisurely bath. Daisy, looking around her, forgets her promise to Emmeline and longs for Barnaby, wishing it were he sharing this comfortable room, this idyllic holiday, with her. The thought makes her feel disloyal to Emmeline, her dear friend, but not at all to Leo. Wondering if she is too far gone to be saved, and not caring in the slightest, Daisy soaks in a hot bath for a good half hour, and flagrantly fanatasizes about Barnaby.

At dinner that night, seated at the dark heavy mahogany table enjoying a delicious seafood meal, there is a sudden imperious banging at the front door and before anyone can answer it, there are loud shrieks and cries in French, Italian and English as Sojourner and Giorgio rush into the dining room and delightedly embrace everyone in sight.

'*Sorpresa!*'

'Are you pleased to see us?'

'*Bienvenue en France*! But you're late, I've been worried.'

'A slow journey, tourists everywhere this weekend. You didn't let on, did you, Marsha?'

'No, I kept it a secret.'

There is more embracing, and a profusion of exclamations. Emmeline, who has not seen Sojo for at least fifteen years, recognises her from her book jackets. Sojourner Truth Fioravanti, wife of Giorgio Ubaldino Fiorvanti (though she has dropped her last name for literary purposes), is now a renowned and popular international writer of romantic fiction which features, always, a black heroine, and a wide diversity of heroes who have, in the past, been black, white, yellow, and of just about every nationality. Sojo and Giorgio live in a splendid luxury apartment in Florence, with various other houses tucked away in the countryside. Giorgio has long since retired from the sea and is Sojo's manager. He contents himself with owning several little boats and has taken up fishing.

They look fantastic, Emmeline thinks, then she says it aloud. Sojo's hair is dyed red again (it has been many colours since they last met, including her own rich black occasionally), but it is a brighter, more crimson, more assertive red than it was before. It is shorter, too, but still stands tough and resilient all over her head. Her arresting face is heavier, and her great bosom more maternal these days than Amazonian, but it is still Sojo even though she now wears flowing sarongs instead of hotpants and mini-skirts, and rich embroidered velvet waistcoats instead of the see-through muslins and cheesecloth she favoured in the sixties.

Giorgio too looks good. Though his hair is completely white, it is thick and sleek, and his skin, though weathered and lined, is tanned, his body wiry and hard. He embraces Jean-Luc warmly; the two families are good friends, spending holidays together either in Italy or France whenever they can.

'So, you like my Giorgio?' Sojo says to Emmeline. 'He looks terrific, no?'

'So how come you have an Italian accent?' Emmeline laughs. 'You're American, have you forgotten?'

Sojo laughs also. 'By birth maybe, but not in spirit, not in soul, honey-chile.'

'I love your books. They're so wild and bizarre for romantic novels. I can never figure out if you're writing them dead straight or having everyone on.'

Sojo looks momentarily offended. 'Dead straight, of course. You know I was always a romantic at heart.'

The ten days are idyllic. Everyone is in a sunny, holiday mood, and the weather obliges. They take easy comfortable walks around the tiny town and surrounding villages, or along the canal that slithers through the valley. They eat copiously; they drink, they talk. Sometimes Jean-Luc and Giorgio go with them on their little excursions, but mostly the four women are on their own, for Jean-Luc has his practice to attend to, and Giorgio is addicted to fishing for carp along the prolific lakes and canals.

On the third or fourth day, Marsha takes the 'girls' as she calls them to a local café for lunch. Emmeline looks warily around as they enter, for the outside is not particularly welcoming. It looks, as a matter of fact, rather squalid, with its old torn plastic curtains, its wooden door with the peeling paint.

The owners, a corpulent middle-aged couple, greet Marsha with effusive kisses, and the other three with hearty hand-shakes. Then the man goes off into the steamy kitchen to get on with his cooking while Madame leads them to their table, one of about eight long tables, four on each side of the room. It is the only one empty, and is covered with a shiny oilskin cloth printed with lurid roses, but it is scrubbed clean and the plain place settings are immaculate. Succulent cooking scents permeate the air, mingling with an unobtrusive odour of French tobacco: several of the diners, who are mostly men looking as if they have come right off the farm, are smoking copiously between courses. Looking around, Emmeline takes in a small makeshift bar, no more than a wooden plank set up in a corner with a dozen or so bottles on an unpainted shelf behind. Dotted around the large room are great burlap sacks of grass seed for sale as well as a selection of early spring vegetables on offer.

'Could you ask for a menu, Marsha?' Sojo asks, feeling hungry. They have had a longish walk around the lake of a nearby château, and they are quite ready for their meal.

'No menu, it's set every day.' Even as Marsha says this a huge tureen of soup appears, with a butter mountain and a towering basket of fresh bread. 'I shouldn't eat too much, there's four more courses to come.'

Two hours later, they are at last replete. On all the tables are bottles of mineral water and a red wine which is quite palatable. After the soup Madame and Monsieur bring out platters of sliced cold meats and pâtés from the *charcuterie*, then lamb cutlets with an assortment of vegetables, and finally an enormous cheese board with a good half-dozen different cheeses. For those who can manage it, there is a basket of fresh fruit and Breton gâteau, though everyone admits it is now sheer gluttony to carry on.

As they eat they have several impromptu visitors to their table: the owners sometimes plopping down enquiring about the food, opening more red wine, gossiping with Marsha; the other diners who wander over, sit for a time, then amble back to their own tables. After several glasses of the strong red wine Emmeline asks for the loo, and is amused to find she has to walk over the worn but shiny linoleum floor to the kitchen, then through that and across a tiny living room where an ancient grandad sits watching television. The room is so small that Emmeline has to walk between the man and the screen, but he is obviously used to it: he barely notices her profuse apologies and does not take his eyes off whatever it is he is watching. The loo is outside the back door; it is about the size of a mousetrap but spartan and clean.

When she returns to the dining room, she sees that Jean-Luc and Giorgio have arrived and are seated at their table, deep in conversation with the owners. Another bottle of wine is produced and opened and consumed, and coffee called for. Finally – and it is about half-past three – they decide that lunch is over, and after settling the bill, which is ridiculously cheap, there are kisses and handshakes once again all around before finally the six of them are out in the street.

'Oh, bliss!' Daisy says. 'What a meal.'

'So well-prepared.'

'I'm so full!'

They all decide that they are now exhausted and can barely manage to meander back to the house, a mere ten-minute walk away, before collapsing into their respective beds for a civilised nap before the evening begins. All but Giorgio, who maintains

311

he is full of vigour and energy and needs a brisk walk, and would anyone like to join him?

No one does, but he does not seem disconcerted. Marsha says politely, like the charming hostess she is, 'May I suggest a visit to our local château? It is not far, and the grounds are excellent for a stroll. If you go around the lake, may I recommend investigating the tiny old graveyard tucked away behind the high, crumbling brick wall? It is quite peaceful, and there are some remarkable species of wild flowers growing amongst the tombstones.'

Giorgio, who after all these years has learned enough English to understand this, thanks Marsha and jauntily takes his leave of them. The others walk slowly to the house, where the three visitors retire to their bedrooms for a snooze while Jean-Luc goes back to face a broken tooth, two fillings, and an extraction.

Not all the women go to sleep. Marsha, humming an Edith Piaf song to herself, silently goes out the back door and nonchalantly walks along to the outskirts of the town, through the great iron gates of the château, and along the lake until she gets to the little graveyard hidden and obscured by the high ivy-covered brick wall.

Giorgio is there, behind a tall, chipped, moss-covered tombstone. He has gallantly spread his jacket on the ground, taking care to remove any large stones or jagged bits of twig before doing so.

'*Che sogno rivederti, amore,*' he says with delight to Marsha, his plump passionate plaything, his adorable angel. 'How lovely to see you, my darling,' he repeats in English, of which he is very proud.

Marsha, with a sigh, goes to him. They lie back on the jacket and it is, for them both, as it is each time, every bit as intense and passionate as it was that very first time on the *Castel Felice*. How odd, she thinks fleetingly, as Giorgio discreetly pulls away for a moment to make some necessary adjustments: we seem to have come a complete cycle. First we used condoms, then discarded them for the more sophisticated Pill. Now we are back to them again, only instead of protecting us from babies, we use them to protect us against other, more sinister things.

She is suddenly overwhelmed by a warm flush of love for Giorgio, for protecting her in so many ways for all these years. The love diffuses into lust, and soon the earth is heaving with pleasure, or so it seems, so it seems.

It never in the slightest occurs to either of them that they might be getting too old for this sort of thing.

'What a holiday!'

'Wasn't it fun?'

'How fantastic Sojo looks. And who'd have thought she and Giorgio would be so happy together? I'd have predicted their marriage would last a month, no more.'

Daisy, driving, carefully overtakes a yellow postal van and says, 'And look at Marsha. She positively radiates health and happiness and contentment. Why can't I be like her? She's so placid, so wifely, so demure at Jean-Luc's side. Why, she's turned into the little innocent we first met on the boat, only a married one now.'

'Well, so are you. A married innocent. You've been faithful—'

'I don't want to be any longer! Oh God, why aren't I contented like Marsha, why do I yearn for more, why do I yearn for Barnaby?'

'Hormones, darling.'

'Oh, do shut up, Emmeline! How's the time, are we running late for the ferry?'

'No, lots of time.'

'Marsha has hormones too, always has had. They used to ooze out of her like cream from an éclair. Remember how she blossomed, ripened on the boat? How that boy from Bible college followed her all over the place, the last couple of days? And look how quickly she leapt into Jean-Luc's bed.'

'No quicker than you into Leo's.'

'I suppose. We were all so wild then, so daring, or so it seemed. You and Hal were the only ones that showed a bit of restraint.'

'Oh God! You call that restraint? It was goddamn hell.'

'I know. Sorry. You know, I really regret sometimes that none of us knew what you were going through. We didn't suspect anything was wrong. Perhaps if we had, we could have helped.'

'How could you help when Hal and I couldn't help ourselves — wouldn't even admit there was a problem? I couldn't talk about it. I wouldn't even let myself believe there was something wrong. If ever I got uneasy, I'd tell myself that it was all my fault anyway and that with perseverance, experience, whatever, I would eventually get it right.'

'Self-blame again. Guilt that we're somehow responsible for everything that goes wrong. We women are great on that.' Daisy spots a parking area and says, 'Should we have our flask of coffee? And the *pain au chocolat*? You can drive the rest of the way, if you don't mind.'

They pull over, get out of the car and stretch. 'The rest of us were too wrapped up in ourselves, in each other, to notice anything wrong with you and Hal,' Daisy murmurs, still reminiscing.

'That's not true. How could any of you have noticed when I didn't myself? I hid it until it stared me in the face, till it exploded in my face. Only then did I acknowledge it.'

Daisy knows the story, knows it by heart, and so she is silent. 'Come on, love,' she says gently, putting her arm through Emmeline's. 'Let's have some coffee. We're in the nineties now.'

'Oh, sure. Terrific. We're older—'

'Wiser—'

'Smarter—'

They both smile, and Emmeline rolls her eyes. 'I've got Chester to sort out when I get home. Such a choice, carrying on with an unsatisfying relationship or being alone.'

'I've got Barnaby to face. Give him up and be totally desolate or carry on, have an affair, destroy everything Leo and I have built up.'

They both take a bite of their *pain au chocolat*, catch each other's eye, and giggle. 'Why is this so funny?' Emmeline says. 'Why are we laughing over ruining our lives?'

'Because we're in France,' Daisy says with a grin, showing chocolate teeth. 'Because the sun's shining.'

'Because we're immature and irresponsible?'

Daisy nods. 'Daft.' They laugh again.

In a few more seconds the moment passes. 'Em,' Daisy says seriously, her tiny face suddenly pinched, strained. 'I don't want to go back to England. I'm frightened. I don't know what to do.'

'I'm scared too. I don't want to go back to the States.'

They look at each other sombrely before slowly packing up the flask, getting back into the car.

On the ferry they are quiet, contemplative. Even the sunlight on the water, promising fine weather back in England, does not cheer them. It is, after all, April, Emmeline thinks. Before very long her year as co-ordinator for the junior year abroad will be over. Before very long it will be necessary to walk away from her past for the second time and face, once again, her uncertain future.

Chapter Fourteen

*E*mmeline and Daisy come back to an England revelling in an early spring, as if to make up for the hard bitter winter. It is April and the woods are covered with primroses. Shortly after the French holiday, Tony comes out to the farm and he and Emmeline spend a balmy Saturday afternoon dawdling in the woodland where the world seems upside-down, the primroses coating the ground with yellow as if the sun were shining from the earth instead of the sky.

'Such a profusion!' Emmeline exclaims. 'Even more than I remember.'

'You were here at the farm in spring, then?'

'Oh yes. Hal and I came to see Daisy and Leo right after our Easter break in Italy with Giorgio and his family.'

They walked in these woods on a day just like today, Emmeline remembers, but though the memory makes her thoughtful, it doesn't sear her like other memories have since her return. I have exorcised so many things since I have been here, she thinks, so many ghosts. She feels less fragmented than she has in years, and knows that much of this is because of Tony. Through him she has learned how to relax with a man, how to accept tenderness without being afraid, how to be friends, mates, instead of always an active participant in the war between the sexes. Had they had an affair, which seemed likely in the beginning, she would never have learned this, for she would have fallen into the same old sexist role and the relationship would have been doomed. This way, though they never became lovers, they are still very close, and will part as friends.

'I used to dream of these woods when I returned to America in the sixties,' Emmeline muses now as they walk along. 'It's so English somehow.' They both look around them. They are surrounded by oak and ash trees, by chestnut and birch and beech. As well as the primroses there is a scattering of wood anemones. 'There will be bluebells next,' Emmeline continues. 'I used to love them. You know, sometimes after my dreams of this place I'd wake up and find my face wet with tears. I never thought I'd see it again.'

Tony is silent, remembering his talk with Leo, thinking that if Leo has his way, the woodland won't be here this time next year. Leo has still not told his family, nor anyone but Tony, yet he insists he is going to go through with it. Tony has made numerous enquiries to see if the land could be purchased by some kind of a nature trust, to preserve the woodland, but these are hard times and there is just not that kind of money around.

He turns his attention away from Leo and the conundrum and says to Emmeline, 'And this time? Won't you miss it all a second time around?' His voice is casual but his feelings are not. Occasionally he makes himself talk to Emmeline about her eventual return to Georgia, so as not to fool himself that she is here for ever.

The easy, nonchalant tone of Tony's voice hurts Emmeline slightly; she wishes he cared more that in a few months she'll be gone. 'Of course I'll miss it,' she says with some asperity. 'I'll miss everything, Bella the Beautiful and Alan Lamb and the primroses. I'll even miss your bats! But I've got to get back to my own life, my own work, and I'm afraid bats play a very minor role at the university.'

Tony doesn't answer at first, and they walk a few yards in silence. The day is warm and sunny and smells of earth and early spring. You can almost hear things stirring and moving underfoot. Blossom is waddling along behind them, sniffing the air happily. Her sense of smell is about the only one of her senses that hasn't atrophied.

At last Tony says quietly, 'Don't make fun, Em. The bats may be a joke to you, but they are as important to me as your work is to you. You teach your students about theatre, I educate people so that they won't destroy things which have been on this planet as long as, longer perhaps, than we have. It's not just about bats, Em. I thought you understood that.'

They have stopped walking and are facing each other. Emmeline, distraught, says contritely, 'I'm sorry, Tony, and I wasn't making fun, I do understand. Perhaps if bats and owls and primroses and bluebells were more a part of my life, my work, it wouldn't seem so sterile sometimes.'

As Emmeline says this, she knows it to be true. What does she know of life, of the basics of it, of love and hate, birth and death? She knows of it second-hand, through the theatre and drama she studies and teaches. Her social life with Chester revolves entirely around people exactly like themselves, ambitious and successful, and her relationship with him is more need-fulfilment, now, than passionate. Though the sex is still good, it has, she admits to herself, become purely technical, lacking the intensity of love. Her work, though satisfying at a certain level, is in the end based on illusion and fantasy, on recreating myths and presenting them as truth, as reality.

And she's not even doing what she longed to do — act in that fantasy. Instead, she's teaching others how to do this, inspiring others to create. Writing about acting, about directing, about the theatre, instead of doing it herself. Tony, with his guitar and his music, is much more creative than she is, with her degrees and her publications, her lectures and her prestige. Suddenly, she does not want to go back to Atlanta; suddenly, she wants to be near where she was thirty years ago with Hal: still hopeful, still full of energy, still thinking that she would make a mark on life, on that glittering life so tantalisingly full of promise then.

'You don't need to go back to America,' Tony says gently, as if reading her mind. 'You have friends here, you can stay, you know.'

This is so outlandish that Emmeline smiles. 'I can't just turn my back on everything, drop out, do what I want to do, Tony. That sort of attitude belongs to Gemma and Baz. They haven't learned yet that there's no getting away from the system, or they haven't accepted it anyway. Good for them, I admire them for it. But it always gets you in the end.'

'Does it?'

'It got me, it got most of us. We all settled down and became respectable. Look at Marsha, look at Daisy. Even Sojo gave up searching for her romantic courtly lover and ended up writing romances herself. Giorgio plays golf now, did I tell you?'

'I don't feel very respectable,' Tony objects. 'Sometimes I feel downright seedy, only working when I need the money, messing about with the band or spending hours, days, grubbing about looking for bat droppings.'

Enmeline looks at him thoughtfully. 'I'm not sure about you,' she says at last. 'Maybe you're the only one who doesn't fit in. Maybe that's why you intrigue me so much.'

Tony laughs. He loves her frankness, her transparency. He always feels refreshed when he has been with her, like he's drunk icy well-water after a long sweaty day.

'And what about your Hal?' he says after they have walked through the primroses in silence for a few more moments. 'Hasn't he done what he set out to do in the sixties? I've seen his films, the ones he's both acted in and directed, and they're not only artistically fine, many of them also make strong political statements. You said he wanted it all; hasn't he done just that?'

Emmeline is quiet for so long that Tony thinks she has not heard him. Finally she says, softly, 'Yes, you're right. Hal went straight for what he wanted and let no one, nothing, stand in his way. He never compromised, not like I did.'

'But was it compromise? Maybe you just changed directions, began to want different things. Realised that other things were important as well. That's all right too.'

'Hal didn't. He held on to his vision. I used to want it all too, you know, even more than Hal. I wanted both him and a glorious life in the theatre, but it had to be with him; we had to do it together. After Hal, I gave up. He never did, and I guess that was the big difference between us.'

*

'Emmeline, do you always want more? We have today — these woodlands, the primroses. We have this amazing morning, this moment, the sun. So what if it rains tomorrow, so what if the flowers are beaten down, washed away? We will always have this: we'll always remember this perfect moment before the rain. Why isn't it enough for you?'

Emmeline shook her head, watching the sunlight fall golden on Hal's yellow hair, on the yellow primroses. It had been so perfect in Italy, she and Hal together for almost all the twenty-four hours in each day. And here also, at the farm, having Hal virtually all to herself, sharing the bedroom and the big brass bed . . . Impetuously, she had said that to him, that she hated going back to London now, that she wanted it to be like this for ever. 'I know we're both busy at drama school, you especially, but just lately it seems we've hardly had time for each other,' she had said. 'I've missed you, Hal.'

She was not usually so outspoken, so plaintive, but it was true that she had not seen as much of Hal in the winter term as she had in the autumn. He seemed elusive somehow, not just physically but mentally as well, and she sometimes felt he was drifting away from her. But it was not something she could quite put her finger on, and she often upbraided herself for imagining it. When they were together, she could not fault him, for he was still as caring and solicitous here in Kent as he had been during their stay in Italy.

Hal had replied to her outburst by saying that she should be thankful for what they had, for the moment here and now, instead of always projecting into the future, and he was right, he was always right, she knew that. And yet she was uneasy, troubled. He had not mentioned marriage for a long time, and when she tried to bring it up, even in the vague faraway future, he always said they had plenty of time and changed the subject. Emmeline, again, knew he was right; they were young, they were in London together, studying together: they were happy as they were, they were right as they were. When she longed for more, when she wanted Hal in her bed and at her side always, she chided herself for being too greedy, too grasping.

And really, she thought, sitting in shadowy bed-sits in Earl's Court or Chelsea or West Kensington, under huge life-size posters of Che Guevera or Marilyn Monroe, candles in Chianti bottles lighting everyone's faces, making them soft and glowing and luminescent – really, what more could anyone want than this? She listened to the eclectic conversation around her – Andy Warhol and Pop Art; David Hockney; Rita Tushingham in the film *The Knack*; Ian Smith and Rhodesia; troops in Vietnam escalating in just six months from 23,000 to 184,000 and what can we do about it? And her mind buzzed trying to keep up with it all.

Sometimes, though, her thoughts drifted away from the passionate discussions and she would gaze surreptitiously at Hal, Donovan on the record player somehow saddening her as he sang about trying to catch the wind.

But these were the good times, the wild times. It was official now. London was 'The Swinging City' – *Time* magazine in America had put a name to it. Life was as psychedelic as the new art, and Emmeline couldn't believe her luck in being part of all this with Hal, for in many ways he summed up the times for her with his energy and sheer creative force. He drew other people in as well – not only Daisy and Leo and the others, but also the students at drama school, for he was generous in sharing his many ideas, his imaginative vision, with others less gifted. For this reason he was loved and revered by many of the students, rather than envied and disliked for being so much more talented than most of them. He excelled in everything – acting, directing, even playwriting and set design, and though he was always magnanimous with his talents, there was also a certain hardness, an embryonic ruthlessness in him which, in truth, would be an asset in the tough profession he was embracing. This side of Hal came out only occasionally, when he was frustrated or thwarted in some aspect of his work. Hal had one goal, one direction, and he was determined to get there whatever it took, whatever it cost.

'Em, he's terrific,' Daisy said one evening down at their favourite pub in Earl's Court.

Leo agreed. They had come up to London overnight to see Hal in a one-act play by Edward Albee, in a converted warehouse by the river. Leo was impressed by Hal; more than that, he was moved, touched, by Hal's performance.

So was Marsha. 'I've seen Hal larking about, being silly and theatrical, but I've never seen him act like he did tonight. He's brilliant, Em.'

Some of the other students were there, discussing the production, and they too were stunned by Hal's performance. 'He not only can act, but you can't take your eyes off him when he's on stage,' one of them said. 'Even when he's just standing reacting to the other actors.'

Hal came in then, having stayed behind to strike the set. Joining them at their crowded table behind the door he shrugged off their praise, bought some drinks, and settled down beside Emmeline. 'You were fantastic,' she whispered. 'Just fantastic.'

But he brushed aside her praise as well, and changed the subject. He was not being modest, he just did not need to hear these things. He knew his talents, knew what he could do, and did not need constant adulation to confirm it.

Emmeline, of course, idolised him, as well as loved him. There was no way it could end other than disastrously.

*

Tony and Emmeline stroll slowly through the woods, enjoying the sensation of being outside after the difficult winter. The air is still, except for the occasional twittering of a bird – a thrush or a woodpecker. The ground, only recently so brown and sodden with the mud of winter, is pulsing with the pale yellow light of the myriad primroses. Blossom, her nose deep in some hole while her tail wags and wags, looks up at them suddenly with a primrose stuck to the end of her nose and they look at each other and laugh.

'I'll miss you when you're back in the States,' Tony says and then adds, 'and so of course will Leo and Daisy. And the kids.' He thus manages to dilute his own very real feelings.

Emmeline says, lightly, 'Why don't you come visit me sometime? You've never been to North America.'

Tony has never before had the desire to go, but suddenly he thinks it might not be such a bad idea. 'Perhaps. I might just take you up on that.'

This short exchange pleases them both so much that, superstitiously, they spontaneously change the subject, burbling on about inconsequential things, as if they will dissipate some kind of a promise made if they elaborate, try to commit the other further. Emmeline, with dismay, has begun to realise how much Tony's friendship means to her, how much she will miss his easy company.

Someone else is also thinking of friendship on this rosy Saturday afternoon. Marjorie has just phoned Daisy to ask if she is coming into town, and if so, to call in for a pot of tea and some cakes she and the girls have just made. Daisy was vague, evasive. 'Uh, yes, I *am* going into town as a matter of fact, but I'm not exactly sure what I'm doing. I have to pick up something from the vet's for Leo, and then there's the shelter . . . I'm not quite sure if I'm on or not, you see.'

She was over-apologetic, and said if she could she'd drop in, but Marjorie knows she won't. She hasn't seen much of Daisy lately, and misses her. Sometimes she thinks Daisy is avoiding her for some reason, and feels hurt, but then tells herself briskly to pull herself together and stop imagining things.

'Auntie Daisy is exceedingly busy at the shelter these days,' she tells her daughters, who love Daisy and are disappointed that she is not coming. 'We mustn't be selfish, nagging her to come here all the time when she has so much to do.'

Marjorie, saying this, believes it, and chides herself for demanding too much of her friends. 'Well now,' she cries, 'what are we all doing inside on a beautiful day like today? Chop chop, troops, put on jumpers — it's not summer yet, you know — and we'll go for a jolly nice walk, clear the cobwebs.'

The girls, grumbling, do as they are told, looking longingly at the television as they do so. Marjorie jollies them up heartily, and by the time they leave the house, all four of them are back in good spirits, cheerful and giggling as they set out on their walk.

Daisy is disconcerted after her phone call from Marjorie. She broods about it all the way into town, off and on between thoughts of Barnaby. She is no longer kidding herself that the intensity of feeling she has for him can be ascribed to a mere infatuation stemming from close proximity. In Italy she missed him so unbearably that it frightened her. She not only wanted to see him, she wanted to go to bed with him. It is the first time this has happened since she was married.

In spite of the fact that she was the first to advocate free love for all in those heady days of the sixties, Daisy is actually quite straight when it comes to her own sexual life. This is not some acquired prudery, or even anything to do with morals. Several of her married friends are having tumultuous affairs and Daisy neither approves nor disapproves: it is their life, and it is up to them how they handle it.

Daisy also prides herself on knowing how to handle her own life, or she did until the discord and despair of the past year. Her longstanding marriage with Leo is the kingpin on which the rest of her life revolves, and this marriage, to her, is maintained and oiled by the fact that Leo is her only lover. She cannot, she knows, be married to Leo and sleep with someone else; this is nothing to do with marriage vows or morality, it is to do with Daisy's own emotional pysche. She does not see this as any particular virtue, and indeed now, thinking about Barnaby, she sees it as more of a flaw. But the fact is, if she goes to bed with Barnaby, she would eventually have to leave Leo, for she would stop loving Leo, if indeed she hasn't already by the very fact of loving Barnaby.

It is around about here that her thinking becomes muddy, confused. She is in love with Barnaby, she is sure of this – but she hasn't quite stopped loving Leo, nor does she want to. She also does not want to lose him, though by this time she isn't sure if it is just him she is afraid of losing, or her children too, for they would never forgive her if she leaves their father.

At this point her mind collapses, splinters into shards. It is all too awful even to contemplate, yet crazily, irrationally, one message keeps flashing its blinding light in her mind and in her heart: Barnaby loves her, and she loves him. Like mad, like crazy. She loves his fuzzy bald cherub head and his little round glasses, and longs to take them off and lay them on a pillow somewhere. She loves the way he looks at her, all lovingly and lustingly, as Leo hasn't looked at her in ages. It makes her body lust too; it makes mockery of logic and rational thinking.

Perhaps deepest of all, and this is, to Daisy, the most dangerous, is how she loves to talk to Barnaby. It began with their work at the shelter; they were both so struck, so terribly moved and bewildered by what they encountered there, that the only way they could come to terms with it was to talk about it, endlessly. Through talk came love, not surprisingly perhaps, given the lack of communication in her own marriage.

And so now Daisy, suddenly thrown into almost daily contact with an articulate man such as Barnaby, who is made even more loquacious by his own stirrings of love, feels he is the man she has been waiting for all her life. In these few months her marriage, her children, her love for Leo which has spanned nearly thirty years, are as forgotten as a flash of lightning seen out of the corner of the eye on a stormy summer evening. She knows this is dangerous and unfair, but does not quite know what to do about it.

And so she does nothing, because it is early spring and the tulips are exquisite, and so is the feeling of buoyancy permeating her every step, her every action. She feels as if her emotions have become shrivelled over the years and are now plumping out like the buds on the trees down in the woods. She knows if she gives up Barnaby, she will have to give up this feeling of plumpness, of richness, of opulence of the spirit, and she can't do it, not yet, not in springtime.

Today he is not at the shelter. Though Daisy is putting many more hours into her work there, Barnaby is now only doing the soup kitchen one night a week. Marjorie, rightly so, was beginning to grumble, saying that the girls hardly saw him when he was out for so many evenings. Barnaby, feeling he barely saw his daughters anyway because of Marjorie's rigorous regime for the children, nonetheless had to agree that his work at the shelter was an additional infringement of his time with them.

Although Daisy and Barnaby now only work one evening a week together, they see each other far more often. When Daisy finishes her daytime work at the hostel, she usually meets Barnaby for a clandestine hour in obscure tea-shops on the outer edge of town, or lately along the banks of the river where they throw crumbs to the ducks and swans and sit huddled together on rusty iron benches. There is a desperation in their meetings now, born of the knowledge that there is no going back for either of them.

Daisy tries not to think about Marjorie. Because she knows she is heading for an affair with her husband, Daisy has been avoiding her as much as possible. She senses the woman is slightly hurt by this neglect, but because Daisy is genuinely busy at the shelter, she uses this as an excuse to see Marjorie as little as possible. Daisy dislikes this deception, but understands that it would be wrong to carry on an intimate friendship with a woman whose husband you are intending to go to bed with. Though Barnaby and Daisy have not yet plunged into the treacherous waters of adultery, Daisy knows it is just a matter of time and place, and so avoids the company of Marjorie. The betrayal is bad enough, she feels, without the added injury of listening to Marjorie's trusting confidences.

And so the complications of her feelings for Barnaby are beginning to insinuate themselves into Daisy's consciousness, as she stops calling in at his home, stops popping over at odd times just to say hello. This saddens her, for she is very fond of Marjorie, and has a soft spot for her daughters. Daisy is beginning to see that there are prices to pay for this sort of liaison, but tells herself that it is all worth it.

'What's up, Daise? You look droopy today.' Josy, coming into the makeshift lounge of the hostel where Daisy is doing some clearing up, puts down her assorted bags and collapses into a hard-backed chair. 'Whew, I'm beat. Bad night last night.'

Daisy doesn't ask, for she knows Josy is reticent about her nights. Anything could have happened: an harassment by a drunk, an eviction from a prime sleeping spot such as a station lavatory or an accessible builder's yard by an over-zealous night cleaner or night-watchman.

'I don't know why you won't sleep here, Josy,' she says automatically, having said this almost every day for months. 'You can have that mattress in the utility room. Eventually we'll have a women's shelter, I hope.'

Josy switches on the ancient black and white telly. Daisy notes that her arm is covered in a nasty, weeping rash, and makes a mental note to see if she can get Josy to consult a doctor. She is clad in a long corduroy skirt, once beige but stained indelibly with grease and oil and the passage of time, and a fairly new but hideous orange T-shirt, acquired from the pile of jumble which appears from time to time at the entrance to the shelter.

'It's so lovely and warm outside,' Daisy comments. 'We should be sitting in the park.'

'I've gone off parks, luv,' Josy grimaces.

'Of course. I don't blame you.'

For a few moments Josy glues her eyes to a vapid game show on the telly, while Daisy finishes dusting the dingy, stained furniture. Josy looks vacant, stupid, lethargic, but Daisy knows that she is, in reality, none of these things.

She has learned, through her years on the streets, that to show either too much emotion or too much intelligence is dangerous and counter-productive. Cunning, yes, the cold calculating kind, is fine, and indeed necessary. Josy knows the difference, knows it very well indeed.

She learned this difference quite young, at sixteen, when her mother died in an unnecessary accident, leaving her the damp and rather sordid flat they shared, a pile of unpaid bills, and no assets but a fistful of O-Levels that she hadn't a clue what to do with. With no money and no relatives, Josy found a job at a ridiculously low hourly wage as care assistant in an old people's home, where she stayed for almost ten years until, as she put it to Daisy, she went 'funny in the head'.

'It was seeing nothing but them old folks,' she tried to explain. 'I was the shy type then, scared as a bleedin' mouse, grateful for the peanuts they paid me even though I worked my arse off and was barely able to pay the rent, let alone feed myself. You know, I lost two stone in the couple of years after me mum died.'

Josy began to hear voices, which would have been all right if after a time she didn't start answering them, sometimes loudly. The owner of the nursing home, who had ignored Josy for ten years, suddenly took notice and fired her. She spent the next couple of months listening to her voices and chatting amicably to them in her flat, until her money was gone and the landlord evicted her.

There then followed several years in mental hospitals, where Josy lived in a vegetative drugged state that got rid of her voices, but also every vestige of human personality. When the hospital finally closed down, discharging her and the other patients into the care of the community, she moved in with a man called King who picked her up in the park one day, took her to his seedy but warm digs, and made love to her coarsely but not unkindly. Then he fed her and told her she could stay as long as she cooked and cleaned and fucked; he wanted nothing else from her.

King was a petty criminal, or so Josy assumed, for he never told her what he did, where he got the handfuls of cash he sometimes brought home. When he was in the money, he was effusive and generous, buying fancy things to eat and new clothes for Josy, and when he was broke, he beat her. She accepted this like she did most things in her life until one day he went out and never came back.

'To this day I swear I don't know if he's dead or alive,' she confided to Daisy. 'After a week, when there was no sign of him, I panicked. I had eaten everything left in the house and had no money, and the rent was due. I was sure King was in trouble, bad trouble, and that whatever had got him, would get me as well.'

She left King's place on a rainy day in April, about eight years ago. She had been with him four years, hardly moving out of the house, for he did most of the shopping, kept hold of all the money. She walked out with all her clothes on, layered one item on top of another, for she was afraid the landlord would see her and confront her if it looked as if she were moving out. In a couple of plastic carriers she took two thin wool blankets belonging to King – 'the only thing I've ever stole in me life,' she said ruefully to Daisy. She needed them, too, for that night she spent curled on a bench in one of the many city squares, relieved that at least the rain had stopped, though the night had turned icy and cold.

'Was that the last home you had, with King?' Daisy asked.

'Yup,' she answered matter-of-factly. 'I've been in squats, with others, but they don't count as homes, they were only temporary. Made some friends, though, for the first time ever. Still see them round and about.'

Daisy, staggered by all this, said, 'Don't you ever wish . . .?' She trailed off, not knowing how to go on.

'I don't wish nothing,' Josy said flatly. 'Not having a home made me into something, and I like that something well enough. I learned I could live on me own skills, didn't have to rely on nothing or nobody. I'm not afraid any more, like I was all them years. I'm *somebody*, Daise, and it took being homeless to find out who that is.'

Daisy thinks of this now as she stares without seeing at the television. Josy goes up again and fiddles with the knobs but she doesn't notice. Josy knows who she is, Daisy is thinking, but I don't. What have I ever done on my own, since I was eighteen and went off to America for that year? I've been Leo's lover, his wife, the mother of his children; I've been a farmer's wife and a housewife; I've been Emmeline's friend, and Tony's friend, and the friend of many others. Now I am about to be Barnaby's lover, just to add to the string of other people's acquisitions.

She is still brooding about all this later, in Brackenbury's Bookshop, rummaging through the health and fitness books outside Barnaby's office. He is closeted inside with a sales rep, and when the man finally goes Barnaby joins Daisy, clasping her hand first, then, glancing around to make sure that they are really alone, taking her into his arms and kissing her soundly. Her response is so intense that they barely have time to break apart as a young man darts up the stairs and says, breathlessly, 'They sent me up here to find the shiatsu books.'

'Oh. Right. Yes. Right here, as a matter of fact.'

Daisy, her cheeks burning, mutters some excuse and rushes

to hide in Barnaby's office while he points out the shiatsu books. She wonders if they broke away from their embrace before the customer witnessed it, wonders also if he is someone she vaguely knows as his face seems familiar. It could be one of her children's friends, she thinks distractedly: he is just about the same age as Paul.

Trying to look inconspicuous amongst Barnaby's papers and files (she doesn't have the nerve to shut the door to the office), Daisy sneaks an oblique look at the young man and wonders if she has really seen him before, or whether she is imagining it. She realises that she is nervous, stressed, and nagged by an emotion she doesn't recognise at first, until she identifies it as guilt. One kiss, and her life is suddenly filled with danger. Is this what is supposed to turn people on? she thinks disbelievingly. The customer's sudden arrival did just the opposite, quenched every spark of passion inside her as surely as if she had stood under an icy fountain on a bitter cold day.

Suddenly, she does not want to wait for Barnaby; suddenly, she wants to be back in the safety of the farmhouse, far from the world and all its sudden pitfalls. Waving a hasty goodbye to Barnaby, who is being lectured on the virtues of shiatsu massage, she quickly runs downstairs and out of the shop. Shaken and confused, torn between trepidation and intoxication (she was not unmoved by Barnaby's passion, uncircumspect though it was), she leaves the shop, nodding a guilty goodbye to Jim, the assistant. She is assailed by a sudden sadness, feeling that she has lost, or is about to lose, something dear, something precious. Yet perhaps, she thinks, it is necessary. Perhaps it is time to grow, change, move on.

Driving home slowly she suddenly wants to see Leo. Running into the kitchen she finds him alone with a cup of tea, preoccupied and uncommunicative. She tries to talk, tell him about her day, about Josy, and though he listens politely, it is obvious he is not there.

Leo is, as a matter of fact, absorbed in his own thoughts, his own schemes. Having told Tony that he is definitely going to sell the woodland, he has let himself believe that everything is now all clear for him, that the way is smooth and straight and easy. In his head he is making plans, totting up figures, drawing diagrams. He has not exactly forgotten that he still has not told Daisy, he has just not found the right moment. There was the lambing to concentrate on, and that is not yet quite over. Then she and Emmeline left for Italy. And Daisy has, of course, taken on all that daytime work at the shelter . . .

Daisy, desperate to talk, has changed tactics. She is teasing him now about his preoccupation, pulling out old worn jokes as married couples do, but that doesn't work either. Leo smiles, but distractedly, and when questioned, will not admit that anything is wrong. He almost tells her – almost. But he remembers that he has a difficult sow farrowing soon, and a number of chores still left undone. Soon he simply walks out, saying that he must get back to work.

Daisy, staring at his back at the kitchen door, watches him walk away from her. She watches for a long time, until he is lost behind the sheds and contours of his farm. *Fine,* she says to herself, lingering for a moment in the spring sunshine before going back into the house. *If that's how you want it, that's just fine.*

She doesn't know if what she is feeling is bitterness or relief. Lifting her face to the warm sun she hears a skylark in the field in front of her, and accepts this as an omen.

Chapter Fifteen

*L*eo, leaving Daisy and going to the farrowing shed where he once again checks his heavily pregnant sow, has forgotten his wife by the time he is out of the house. It is not because he does not love her. On the contrary, she is his life, and he is only able to concentrate so wholeheartedly on the farm because he can forget about her, for she is, has been, will always be, *there*.

The fact that he has not told her about his decision to sell the land is perhaps typical: he has always mulled problems over in his mind for days, weeks, before finally discussing them with her. Daisy knows of the financial setback accrued a couple of years back because of the fiasco with the pigs, but because Leo has not spoken of it recently, she assumes he is content with the way they are slowly pulling back from a precarious slope onto firmer and steadier ground. Indeed, she is correct in this assumption: if Leo did not have other plans, larger plans, then they could weather this financial hiccough without much of a problem, without selling the woodland, despite what Leo told Tony.

What Leo would like to do is to give up the pigs and increase his sheep flock. The pig enterprise was his father's venture, for it was the old man who had built up the unit into the profitable and successful pig farm it has become. But since Leo went to New Zealand, where he managed a sheep station of 3000 ewes, his own dream has been to emulate this one day, albeit on a smaller scale. He knows sheep, his heart is in their thick lanolin wool coats, their plaintive newborn cries. But Woodland Farm is geared to pigs; the buildings are specially designed, the contacts are established, the money, in spite of the awesome ups and downs, is generally more than adequate. It would be financially disastrous, at this point, to sell the pigs and put all his eggs in the sheep basket, and Leo knows this.

This is why he really wants to sell the land, that piece of old English woodland so cherished by Daisy, by the children, so loved by all their friends. What he told Tony was only partially true; he is in some financial straits, but if he keeps on with the pigs (the prices have picked up now and the future looks good), he will come out of it without too much loss. The trouble is, he's had enough of pigs. He dreams instead of building the sort of sheep run he had in New Zealand, so that one man and a dog can handle thousands of sheep a day; he dreams about early winter lambing, converting the hay barn into an indoor lambing area. Heading towards sixty, instead of dreams of retirement, Leo fantasizes about making a thirty-year-old vision come to life.

He can't do it unless he has money, and the only way he can get that kind of money is to sell the land. The enormity of this haunts him, keeps him awake at night. The fact that he is capable of selling the family's beloved woodland, to be destroyed, built on, decimated, simply to satisfy his own selfish whim to change from pigs to sheep, disturbs him, yet he is doggedly going ahead with the sale.

If Gemma had stayed on the farm things would have been

different. For her, he would have sacrificed his dream, kept on with the pigs, helped her expand the unit so that together they would have been the largest pig farmers in Kent. There would have been no dilemma then, no wracking soul-searching trying to decide whether to risk the anger and dismay of his family by selling their beloved woodland and using the money to convert the farm, or just plodding on with the pigs.

Leo finishes checking the sows but suddenly finds he cannot face doing any of the other chores. Instead, he begins walking slowly towards the woodland. He doesn't often go into the woods these days, he is far too busy on the farm. As a young lad he used to walk here with his father, shoot pigeons, but when Daisy came along with all her friends and all that talk of making love not war, pigeons were somehow included and he wasn't allowed to shoot them any more. Not that he minded; by that time he had gone off killing things, even damaging pests like rabbits and foxes. He wondered how much of that was Daisy and how much the process of merely becoming older, more aware. Right now he wishes he were not so bloody aware, so conscious of the land that he is walking through with its profusion of plants and wildlife that have been part of the woodland for generations. He would like to get rid of it without another thought, without another twinge of conscience, so that he can get on with following his own life, his own dreams.

'Dad, wait for me!' Gemma's voice snaps him out of his reverie and he stops while she runs towards him, Blossom puffing like a wheezing old woman trying to keep up with her. When she reaches him she gives him a warm kiss on the cheek and says, 'Oh, it's so beautiful! I told Baz I had to come up, to see the primroses. Do you know it's my earliest childhood memory, these primroses? Walking through them with you and Mum, all that yellow every-where.'

'Hm,' Leo says laconically. Then: 'Where's Baz?'

'He's working on the caravan. Painting it here and there, getting it into shape after winter. Getting it ready to go. I was helping him but I had to get away, get my fix of primroses.'

'When are you off?'

Gemma is sitting on the ground, oblivious to the spring dampness, and is bending over, smelling the flowers, feeling their silkiness against her face. Her hair is the same colour as the primroses, and the green velvet ribbons wound around her plaits could be leaves, Leo thinks. The bells on her ankles tinkle lightly as she moves, blending harmoniously with the birdsong. Gemma is as colourful as a wild flower herself this lovely afternoon, in a short cotton dress of patterned patchwork, each patch different and unique. Long silver earrings dangle from each ear, and wooden things hanging from thin cord necklaces bounce on her chest. As she straightens up and smiles at him Leo catches a whiff of her scent, patchouli oil, which is so reminiscent of the sixties, of Emmeline and Hal and Marsha and the others on their weekend trips from London, that Leo's heart contracts.

'We're not going until June,' Gemma says, standing up slowly, taking huge breaths of the fresh spring air like a swimmer emerging from deep waters. 'Baz's didge workshop doesn't finish till then. We want to make sure we have some money saved to get us going before we set off. I'm making quite a bit on my candles; several shops are taking them and they're going like mad, and busking's been quite good lately with all the tourists, especially the Americans. I don't think they've ever seen a didge before.'

'Gemma, if you need any help—'

Gemma turns to Leo, hugs him impulsively. 'Thanks, Dad. Mum's already offered. We'll be okay, honest. You've already fed and looked after Bones all winter.'

They walk slowly together out of the woods, Gemma exclaiming constantly about the primroses, much to Leo's discomfiture. When they get to the farmyard they pass the stable where Bones whinnies at them demandingly. 'He's eager to go, Dad, can't you tell? He's a real gypsy horse, eager to be on the road again now that spring's here.'

'How is Jonnie?' Leo asks, scratching Bones' head. The owner of the horse and caravan was up at the farm once or twice this winter to visit Bones, but Leo has not seen him lately. 'He's not had to have another operation, has he?'

'No, thank God, but he's still weak from the first one. If he hadn't promised us the caravan for the summer, I'm sure he'd be on the road again himself. But he's staying with his brother, who won't let him go until he's one hundred per cent fit.'

They are walking away from the stable now towards the orchard, passing the field where Alan Lamb stops his grazing to gallop up to the fence for a scratch on the head and a nuzzle in Gemma's hand for some titbits. Leo is about to turn and head back to his pigs and his chores but instead says, 'Gemma, are you and Baz really going to go around sharpening knives for a living? Where will you go? What do you know about that kind of life? It all seems so precarious somehow.'

'Jonnie has been a scissor-grinder for years, Dad, and his father was before him. People expect him every spring, every summer. We know exactly where to go, how to go about it. Besides—' she breaks off, for a moment not knowing how to continue.

'Besides,' she says, struggling to find the right words, 'it's a kind of a continuity, you know? Jonnie's way of life, now ours . . . We're holding on to it for him, you see? Keeping the chain unbroken, until he gets well and can go back on the road himself.'

Leo is quiet for a few moments. Alan Lamb baaas imperatively, seeking attention. Behind them in the sheds a piglet squeals, a sow grunts. 'Jonnie's old, Gemma,' Leo finally says. 'He's ill. He'll never make it back on the road.'

Gemma looks so stricken that Leo wishes he could cut his tongue out. She raises her head and looks defiantly at him. 'There will be others, then,' she says with all the idealism and naivety of Daisy at nineteen.

Leo only smiles, and this time has the wisdom to keep quiet, not to voice what he is thinking: that Jonnie's way of life is finished, died out long ago, and that Baz and Gemma's determination to keep it alive is as misplaced as it is romantic.

As they part at the orchard gate Gemma says softly, 'Do you mind very much, Dad? That I'm not coming in on the farm?'

Leo, who has minded very much in the past, now is not so sure. Gemma's question has forced him finally to look into his heart and ask himself exactly why he is not that distraught that none of his children will carry on with the farm. He knows his reasons are breathtakingly egocentric: he wants to make a name for himself by building up from scratch the best sheep flock in the South. If Gemma had gone in with him, there would have been no question of gambling, giving up the steady and predictable, embarking on the elusive unknown of a totally different venture. Gemma had been good with the pigs, working well with them. Leo would not have even contemplated changing Woodland Farm so drastically if Gemma also, and later perhaps a husband, a family, were relying on the place to support them. Her departure has, in a sense, freed him.

But he does not say these things. Instead, he says, 'I minded at first, I think. But not now. I'm too old and set in my ways. We'd have probably fought like wild sows over everything.'

'You're not just saying that, Dad?'

Leo stops and crosses his heart solemnly, like he did when Gemma was a child. 'Promise, love. I'm not just saying that.'

Gemma grins, hugs him fiercely, and runs off to her Baz. Leo, watching her go, feels an odd contraction, a fleeting quiver somewhere inside him. Shaking his head determinedly to get rid of the sensation, he wonders why the deeper you love, the more painful it seems to be.

He turns to go back to his chores, but glances contemplatively one more time at the vanishing figure of his daughter, her plaits flying, her bells tinkling. He watches as Baz comes around from the side of the caravan, puts his paintbrush down, and gathers Gemma into his arms. Turning quickly, Leo walks away from them and back into his own life. In spite of his dream it suddenly seems harder, bleaker. He wonders if he is just an old fool after all.

'A heart-to-heart with your dad?' Baz asks.

'Sort of.'

'He okay about us?'

'I think so. It's so hard to know what Dad really feels about things.'

'Well, your mum's come around, anyway.'

'Yes, she's been ace. And I think Dad's sound about it as well. I hope so.'

343

Baz sits down on the step of the caravan, pulling Gemma down on his lap. 'So what's wrong?'

'It's just . . . I was walking around the woods, and before that, around the farm, and it's all so beautiful now, in the spring, in the sunlight. The lambs running about everywhere . . . oh, you know!'

'And you're thinking you're going to miss it all.'

Gemma feels tears welling up and buries her head in Baz's chest. 'Do you think I'm crazy?' she wails in a muffled voice.

'Not at all. I think you'd be crazy if you didn't miss all this. I'll miss it, too. But we're not going for ever, you know.'

Gemma extricates herself from Baz's bosom and looks at him sombrely. 'Do you know I've never been away from home?'

Baz smiles. 'You won't have to be. We'll take our home with us. That's the nice thing about caravans.'

'The trouble with spring,' Clem Todd is saying to Emmeline the very next day, in the car driving along the road to Rye, 'is getting the students to do any work. They're all out in the countryside frolicking with newborn lambs or rolling in the primroses.'

'You said that in November – that they'd all be out throwing snowballs.'

'Well, they were.'

They drive along in easy silence for a few minutes. Clem, taking advantage of the sudden spring weather which he hopes will stir up Emmeline's hormones at last, has offered to take her to Rye for the afternoon, thinking that if anything will seduce an impressionable American, Rye will, with its ancient cobbled streets and marvellous Tudor buildings.

It is a Saturday, and though the sun is out, a rather strong cold wind, which started earlier as a pleasant breeze, whips from the sea and chases them through the town which is unfortunately teeming with rather harassed people. Instead of the charms of Elizabethan England, coachloads of American tourists imprint themselves on their expectant vision. On their third attempt to find a tea-shop that is not overflowing with vociferous foreigners, Clem gives up, hustles Emmeline into the car, and announces that they will go for a walk along an unspoiled piece of coastline he knows further along.

The coastline is indeed solitary, but that is because by this time the wind is howling so nastily that no one in their right mind would even think of walking along the sea on such a day. After twenty minutes or so, with sand in their teeth and their eyes streaming with the cold, Emmeline suggests, in a strident shout which is the only way she can be heard above the wind's roar, that perhaps it is time to go home now?

Clem agrees, albeit grumpily. He had intended a peaceful idyllic walk in the sun, Emmeline replete with a full English tea of scones and jam and cream, her head and heart crammed with the beauty of England's antiquities. They were to have walked, faces turned to the sun, and then stopped at a grassy sheltered isolated spot further on to lie back, feel the sensual warmth on their skin, feel the presence of the other only inches away . . .

'Fuck the weather,' Clem spits viciously into the wind as they struggle through it on their way back to the car. The sun has gone now, and gloomy clouds are lugubriously promising rain. It is too early even to suggest dinner. After the long, languid seduction by the sea, there was to be another walk, arms twined around each other, then dinner at some intimate tasteful place to cement the start of their brief but passionate affair. Instead, since by the time they get to the car the rain has begun and they are soaking wet, Clem stops at the first place he comes to, which unfortunately is a Little Chef, not the most romantic of venues. There, at a table with a view of the dual carriageway, they drink several cups of strong tea and eat a teacake each, Emmeline quiet and rather shivery, and Clem badtempered and monosyllabic.

Celia is at home that day, so Clem cannot ask Emmeline to his house, but his one hope as they drive back in the now torrential rain is that Woodland Farm might, by some miracle, be empty, and that Emmeline will invite him in, and then, and then . . .

Unfortunately, the farmhouse is crammed full of Dillards. Daisy and Leo are there, of course, and what looks like just about all the children and their various mates and partners. All up at the farm to celebrate the rites of spring on the old homestead, Clem thinks with disgust. The rain has brought everyone inside, and they are sitting around a roaring fire playing various instruments – God, how he hates musical familes! – and Daisy is passing around fat golden scones which he has to admit look rather appetising.

'Oh, you here as well, Tony?' he says ungraciously as he accepts a cup of tea from Emmeline.

Tony looks coldly at Clem. 'I've been checking on the bats,' he says to Emmeline. 'I had a feeling they'd be waking up after the last week of warm weather. They've survived the winter, at any rate.'

Clem bites into a warm scone and says, with his mouth full, 'You really get a kick out of bats, don't you?'

'Yup,' Tony replies caustically. 'Like you do with your fantasy life.'

Clem munches angrily on his scone, not sure whether Tony is referring to his life in the theatre, or to Emmeline. For a horrible moment he is convinced that Emmeline has told this philistine all about his attempted seductions, that the two of them have been laughing at him behind his back, but he catches Em's eye and she smiles vaguely at him. Clem's natural arrogance reasserts itself and he stops brooding to raise his eyebrows intimately at her.

'More tea?' Emmeline asks.

Both men decline. 'We've just been to Rye,' Emmeline offers brightly. 'Interesting place.'

Clem says, with a smug smile, 'I'll take you there again, my dear. When the weather is a bit better.'

Emmeline does not look overjoyed at this, much to Tony's delight and Clem's annoyance. He drains his mug, then turns to Emmeline. 'You said you'd show me the gypsy caravan; I hear it's a work of art. Should we look at it now?'

'Of course,' Emmeline says politely. 'Will you excuse us for a minute?' she asks Tony, and then, to Clem: 'I'll just check with Gemma and Baz if it's okay to go inside.'

Unlike the house, the orchard is damp and empty. Some older lambs, orphans who are still being bottle-fed twice a day, come running up, baa-ing loudly and demanding a feed. The caravan door is, as usual, open and Clem and Emmeline go in.

'Isn't it beautiful?' Emmeline enthuses. 'Look at all those mirrors.'

'Hm.'

'And that wonderful mahogany wood. It's not just a perfect gem to look at, it's functional, too. Everything is so comfortable, like this sofa here.' She plops herself down on the plush velvet cushions, to demonstrate.

Clem, unfortunately taking this as a hint, also sits down, and far too close to her. He is heady with triumph, thinking that Emmeline has taken him to this empty caravan for one reason only . . . and without any more ado he takes her in his arms and begins wetly kissing her just below her earlobe. Encouraged by Emmeline's sudden absolute motionlessness, her apparent acquiescence, he charges on ahead full steam, the pent-up hormones of months unleashing themselves in dazzling relief.

Emmeline is motionless because she is stunned, frozen, disbelieving. Knowing Clem wanted an affair with her at the beginning, she cannot now believe that he is still persisting, after all the turn-off signals she has given him. Simply, she cannot believe that a man can be so dumb, for she has made it impeccably clear that she does not get involved with married colleagues.

The second reason Emmeline does not, for a moment, move is more basic. It has been a long time since she and Chester made love, and something physical in her is shouting, *Hey, this is great, enjoy it!* But then, after no more than a second or two, she remembers who it is that is doing these things to her, and her passion dries and dies like an unwatered pot plant.

'Clem, please, I don't want this,' she says, struggling away.

'Oh, come on,' he says, well into it now. 'You know you want it as much as I do.' He begins some process of unbuckling and unloosening.

Emmeline tries to get up, but she is rather pinned down. 'Get up, Clem,' she insists. 'Let go of me, stop it!'

His grip on her tightens: the struggle is exciting him. 'Don't worry, no one's going to come out here, they're too busy being all homespun around the fire. Relax.' His face looms in front of her, lewd and eager.

'Get off!' With an effort Emmeline pushes Clem away, eludes his attempt to get her down again, and manages to get out of the caravan. 'I said no, and I mean no,' she says forcefully when she is well away from him. 'I'm going back to the house; I suggest you zip yourself up before going home.' Rather shakily, she marches out of the orchard and begins to walk towards the house.

Before she gets there, she stops to compose herself. There is something in her reaction to the scene that puzzles her, and she needs a moment or two to think what it is. That she is furiously angry with Clem somehow surprises her, though she knows it is justified. She had made it plain to him that it just wasn't on, yet he had remained obtuse and arrogant. She is right to be angry, the way he came on her like a bull at stud, ignoring the fact that she gave him no encouragement.

And yet . . . there is something about her rage that is slowly, like the sun coming out on a misty day, cheering her, comforting her. In a moment or so she realises that she is proud of it, for it is pure, simple, justifiable anger, something she should have felt long ago with more than one man who insisted on having sex with her when she wasn't quite ready, wasn't quite sure. When Clem began to make love to her, for the first time since Hal she did not feel *gratitude*, that a man desired her, wanted her, found her attractive enough, womanly enough, to go to bed with. All she felt was a righteous indignation, a fury which is still making her tremble as she stumbles through the insistent drizzle back to the house.

Emmeline, going inside, joining her friends, her surrogate family, knows with a kind of tenuous but deep peace that some bridge has been crossed, some hurdle conquered. What loving Hal did to her all those years ago, has finally been exorcised. For the first time since she was eighteen, she feels whole, self-contained, herself, and she knows that it will never again be necessary to have a man's approval to justify her existence as a woman. *But how long it took*, she thinks sadly, brushing the raindrops from her face. *How very long it all took.*

'Are you all right?' Tony asks as she joins him in the living room, noting her dishevelled hair, her abstraction. 'Where's Clem?'

'Gone home, I hope.'

Tony, though curious, wisely says nothing except, 'Odd, but I could swear I just got a whiff of patchouli oil. Reminds me of the sixties.'

Emmeline turns to him and smiles. 'The gypsy caravan. Baz and Gemma burn the stuff constantly in their aromatherapy burner.'

'How nostalgic it makes me feel! All the girls used to wear it as a scent, do you remember? Did you?'

Emmeline nods her head. She too can smell the faint aroma on her clothes now and it is so evocative that she closes her eyes for a moment, transported back once again to that other world, that other time. 'Yes,' she murmurs, her eyes still closed. 'I wore it all the time, then. My bed-sit in Earl's Court reeked of it.'

*

'Emmeline, God, can we open a window? I like that patchouli stuff, but you do tend to overdo it sometimes.'

'Sorry, Hal.'

'That's better. Look, is that the time? I've got to go, Em. Sorry I can't stay this evening: I didn't realise you were cooking a meal. Larry wants to talk about this play we're doing.'

Emmeline, silent, watched as Hal gathered together his

books, the Chekhov script they had been reading together, his scraps of paper littering her bed-sitting room. She wanted both to shout at him and plead with him to stay, but there was something about Hal which forbade nagging, something that made him seem above that sort of human triviality. It never occurred to Em to say, 'But you promised,' never occurred to her to complain that she saw very little of him these days, mostly at college where he was usually surrounded by a cluster of acolytes hanging on to his every word.

Occasionally, when they spent a rare evening together and it was too late to catch the tube home, he would spend the night with her in Earl's Court, but when he did so, Emmeline was ripped apart by a combination of sublime joy and a dreadful, insidious unease. These nights were very like other nights with Hal: the one in Italy, and the times she and Hal shared the big brass bed in one of the spare bedrooms at Woodland Farm. First there was the talking: dynamic, inspiring, for Hal was always full of ideas and he sparked Emmeline off too. Then, when it was very late, sometimes near dawn, and the talking had petered out, they would partially undress, Hal crawling exhaustedly in his underwear beneath the blankets and Emmeline, in her chaste nightdress, following. They would embrace and then Hal would kiss her, those strange, almost chaste kisses that were so sweet to Emmeline, but that made her long for more.

But there was never any more. After a time Hal fell asleep, and Emmeline dutifully did as well. In spite of the sixties dancing and flashing and swinging around her, Emmeline remained inexperienced and virginal, as she had been on the day she boarded the *Castel Felice*.

She had begun that voyage with an odd mixture of sophistication and innocence: assured and assertive as a budding actress, she was vunerable and naive as a young woman, and knew very little of the opposite sex. Though she had had the odd crush on certain boys off and on throughout her early high-school days, she was too quiet and self-effacing to be noticed, and it wasn't until her junior year, when she discovered she could act and began appearing in all the school plays, that her confidence grew, radically and powerfully, as a person if not as a woman. For although by then the high-school boys were beginning to notice her, she had found a new high, something which gave her much more of a buzz than a temporary infatuation. The excitement of the theatre, of being on a stage, became much too heady to waste by squandering long evenings with gawky adolescent boys, none of whom attracted her.

Emmeline discovered that she had in herself ambition, that she could be single-minded in winning coveted roles, perfecting stage techniques, spending hours on her own learning lines, watching other actors on stage or in films over and over again so that she could absorb, perfect her own art. She was so obsessed by it all that boys became, to her, obsolete, unnecessary except on stage to take the male roles. By the time she left for England she was convinced that she could never love anything other than the theatre, and this suited her splendidly. Hal shattered this illusion like he did all her others. She discovered love, swiftly, shatteringly, and cruelly.

And so in London, while all around her nice young girls from safe suburban families the world over lost their innocence in a great whoop of joyful, guiltless fun, there was Emmeline, lying next to a sleeping Hal in her chaste bed, wondering what she had done wrong. She wracked her brains trying to remember schoolgirl conversations, but these were always horror stories about boys who wanted to 'go all the way', and girls who 'went too far'. Adults were no better; the women at church painted boys and men as 'wanting only one thing', and her mother's only comment, on the whole boy-sex-growing-up topic, was an enigmatic, 'Now that you are going out with boys, Emmeline, you must remember to be vigilant the whole time.'

Emmeline would have liked to talk about these things to someone, but both Marsha and Sojo still assumed that she and Hal were lovers and Emmeline had not been able to bring herself to tell them the truth, had been unable to reveal things that she herself was confused about. It was Daisy she would have really liked to talk to, but they were rarely alone these days. When Emmeline went to Kent the farmhouse was always full, and Daisy came to London only for special events, like demonstrations.

'Are you and Hal sleeping together yet?' Daisy did ask one rainy late-winter day at the farm, during a rare half-hour when they found themselves alone.

'Sort of,' Emmeline had replied. 'That is, we share a bed sometimes, but we haven't had sex.' She then went on to tell Daisy all the things she had been telling herself, that they were waiting for marriage, that they had plenty of time. She was so busy justifying Hal's behaviour that she never got around to saying just how *she* felt, and the moment was gone.

Emmeline tried, that spring in London, to talk to Marsha, who seemed the height of sophistication these days, with her Sassoon haircut that looked like a complicated geometry problem, and her smart copies of Mary Quant clothes that she made herself on an ancient Singer sewing machine she had bought in a junk-shop. She was still teaching, illegally, at the suspect school of journalism, and writing long copious letters in French to her darling Jean-Luc who was soon to take his dentistry exams.

Emmeline and Marsha and Sojo were gathered in Hyde Park, at some impromptu anti-Vietnam war demonstration. Sojo was back again from Italy and living with Les the Australian while Giorgio was away at sea. She was extravagantly buoyant that day, for it had been a hot dry spring, and Sojo thrived on sunlight.

'Hey, isn't this kinky?' she jiggled, doing a little dance there and then. Some hippies lounging on the grass nearby laughed and clapped their hands, and one of them pulled out a harmonica and began to play an Irish folk-tune. Several people joined in the dance, but Sojo was indisputably the star, and when she finished she was given a hearty round of applause and offered a freshly-rolled joint.

Sojo was into her Flower Power phase, wearing a mixture of suede and buckskin and fringes and beads, American-Indian style, and Asian sandals and a rope of prayer beads around her waist. Her hair stood out around two feet all over her head, the red dye growing out now leaving her two-toned: rich black around her scalp snaking out for several inches, then that deep vivid red.

'Sojo, that was wild,' Marsha said as Sojo collapsed next to her. Around them a few people were still holding up anti-war banners and chanting, but mostly the speeches and protests were over for the day and everyone hung around, not wanting to leave with the sun still so hot, the day not nearly over.

'So am I, girl, as wild as a polecat! And man do I love it!' Sojo, passing around the joint, shook her head, her shoulders, her bosom, in a spirited exuberant movement, as if to prove her point; then closed her eyes and began to meditate. Marsha and Emmeline, knowing she'd be beyond reach for about twenty minutes, moved a few yards away from her to give her space and settled back down on the grass.

'She really misses Giorgio,' Marsha said.

Emmeline turned her head to look at her questioningly, the fresh sweetpeas she had pinned all through her hair that morning emanating a delicate fragrance. 'How funny you should say that. I was going to say the opposite, that she doesn't seem to be missing Giorgio one bit.'

Marsha looked wise, and Emmeline felt humbled.

'She's acting extra crazy and wild because she's pining for him so much. She misses their sex-life especially.' And Marsha smiled secretively, knowing exactly what it was that Sojo was missing.

Innocently, Emmeline said to Marsha, 'How can she miss Giorgio when she is living with that Australian?'

'How sweet you are,' Marsha replied placidly, 'and how young. You can love one man and still occasionally have sex with another,' she stated, thinking of Giorgio.

'I would imagine it's more than occasionally, if she's living with him, for goodness sake,' Emmeline said with some asperity.

Marsha took out a small compact from her handbag, opened it to look in the mirror, and began applying fresh kohl to her already blackened eyelids. 'Em, do relax about things. You're taking sex too seriously. Just because you're dotty about Hal, and can't imagine sleeping with anyone else but him, you think you'll never want to go to bed with another man. Believe me, it just isn't true.'

Emmeline closed her eyes, telling herself that this was Marsha speaking, that scared and trembling convent girl she had met in the cabin of the *Castel Felice* only eight or nine months ago.

'Look, Marsha,' she said, 'about this sex thing. I mean, just because everyone is doing it, that doesn't mean everyone wants to. I mean, not before marriage and all that.'

'Oh dear, you're not giving me the religious bullshit, are you?' Marsha asked in horror, with the zeal of the newly fallen-from-grace.

'No, no, I don't believe in all that any more. I just – well, I just wondered if maybe there are other reasons, like wanting to save the, uh, experience for, well, you know . . . To make it special, to make sure it's a real commitment.'

'Oh, hell's bells, Emmeline, what crap you are spouting. If you wait until you've made a real commitment, like getting married, before you sleep with a guy, then you can't get out of it if it all goes wrong, and you never know all the things that can go wrong until you do start going to bed with someone.'

Emmeline did not know what to say to this. Miserably, she rolled over on her back, not caring whether her new white embroidered Indian top would get covered in grass stains.

'Anyway,' Marsha went on, 'I shouldn't feel any guilt over you and Hal going to bed together, if that's what all this is about.' She laughed, poking Emmeline in the ribs. 'I'd only feel guilt if he *weren't* screwing me.' She laughed again, feeling sophisticated and daring. She had known life would one day be like this, knew it unconsciously as a child and later an adolescent, when her parents dragged her to Mission Sundays and Special Novenas and the sun was hot in the un-airconditioned churches and hormones raged like demented dragons inside her, making her long for unspeakable things.

Not quite knowing what was happening to her, Marsha had armed herself with a mendacious, insincere piety and prayed even harder. Others, noting her sombre hair and clothes and demeanour, commented favourably on her sobriety and decorum and saintliness, and even Marsha began to believe them, so well had she drowned the hot breath of the dragons inside her. She even, at one stage, thought of becoming a nun, and once on holiday with her parents in Florida, claimed she saw the Blessed Virgin Mary sitting in a mango tree.

Thank God for that boat, Marsha thought now, rolling over on her stomach and laying her head in her arms. Thank God for those ten days at sea, and then Europe, and this wonderful, crazy, incredible time!

Emmeline, the sun on her face, lay very still, knowing she could never tell Marsha now what was troubling her. She wondered sadly where she had gone wrong, wondered how she could remedy things. She had to believe Hal still loved her – after all, they were still engaged: he hadn't tried, ever, to break anything off, even though they were seeing each other less and less as he became more and more preoccupied. She loved him more than ever, if that were possible; she thought of his dear sweet face, the skin turned golden in the weeks of spring sunlight, outlining his blue eyes which seemed older these days, wiser somehow. His hair, much longer now than it was on the boat, had lost, this winter, its baby-like softness; it was thicker, more untamed. He was growing up, she thought suddenly, changing, she could see it clearly now. But where did that leave her? Was he leaving her behind, outgrowing her? The feckless boy she had met on the boat had disappeared, become the man he was destined to be, yet here she was, still young, provincial, unsure, afraid.

I needn't be, she said to herself. Hal loved her, and that was all that mattered. She was becoming wiser every day herself, always learning, gaining experience. The times were ripe for change, for promise: she would change too, become the woman Hal needed her to be. She wouldn't lose him, for how could you lose a part of yourself, a slice of your own soul?

Emmeline lay in the spring sun and felt hope awaken in her once more. Nearby, people chanted, talked, laughed, made music. She could hear the harmonica again, pleading, insistent. A Beatles song, and someone singing along, something about following the sun before the rain came.

The words ran around and around in Emmeline's head as she dozed in the park. Hal was her sun, and she'd follow him always.

She refused to contemplate the rain.

Chapter Sixteen

*B*lue and Flack walk away from the Primrose Café carrying knapsacks and an old brown suitcase. The rest of their possessions are already stored at Woodland Farm, where they will be living until they can find a place to rent. Daisy offered to put them up as long as was needed, but they refused, asking instead if they could pitch a tent in the orchard, not far from Gemma and Baz.

'It was a fucking good place,' Flack says, squeezing his eyelids tightly shut for a moment to stop the tears spilling over.

'It was a fucking *brilliant* place,' Blue says fiercely. 'And you are one ace cook, Flack. You've proved it now.'

'Fat lot of good it did,' Flack mutters, walking faster, not daring to look back.

Gemma and Baz are waiting for them in the orchard. They have set up the tent, a massive two-bedroom one that Marjorie Brackenbury has lent to Blue and Flack, insisting they keep it for as long as they need it. The two couples embrace wordlessly, tearfully.

Inside the tent Gemma has placed jars and jars of wild flowers, wood anemones and primroses and bluebells. Baz has made neat, compact wooden shelves for storage, and filled them with some basic provisions. Gemma's candles, her finest and most colourful, decorate them. 'This is for you both,' she says, handing them an object wrapped in old newspaper. 'Baz carved it.'

Blue opens it. It is a unicorn, beautifully carved in oak: tiny, delicate, perfect. 'Oh Baz,' Blue cries.

Flack is too moved to speak. He embraces Baz, then Gemma.

'C'mon,' Gemma says at last. 'Come into the caravan, I've made a huge meal.'

'Maybe we should eat it outside,' Baz says. 'Should I get a blanket?'

They agree this would be a good idea, and soon they are sitting on the grass between the tent and the caravan, under an old apple tree covered in blossom. The faded blanket between them is laden with bottles of wine, a nut roast, garlic bread, a salad. Baz opens a bottle, pours each of them a drink into a small tumbler, and says, 'Here's to the future.'

'Sod the future,' Flack says.

'The past, then?' Blue asks, raising her glass.

'Sod the past too.' He looks at her and gently clinks her glass. 'Here's to *now*, okay? Here's to this very minute, may it last for ever.'

They drink and eat, enjoying the early evening sun, the blossom, each other, as if it will indeed never end, as if the rain will never finally fall, as if winter will never come. It is very late, and very dark, before they finally go inside, into their separate homes, the night misty and eerie around them.

On campus the students are lying about indolently, like sleek young slugs. 'How they are enjoying this weather!' Emmeline says, looking out of the window of the office she shares with Clem.

'Hm,' Clem says, not looking at her.

Em, annoyed, says, 'Look, this is ridiculous. You've spoken to me in nothing but monosyllables ever since that day on the farm. Whatever you feel, we still have a few more weeks to go, working together. Can't we just forget about what happened, Clem, and be on friendly terms again?'

Clem thinks how simple Americans are, always wanting to patch things over, make up after quarrels – 'best friends' again like seven-year-olds. He is about to turn away from her, snub her as he has for the past fortnight or so, but then he remembers that she will be writing a report back to the university, on her students' – and her own – year here. Though the chances are slight that he would even be mentioned, it is best to be cautious: making enemies is never wise in academic circles, as Clem knows only too well.

And so he says, with a forced smile, 'Of course we're friends, Emmeline. It was just an unfortunate misunderstanding.'

Friends with a woman? he thinks sourly to himself. Impossible. But there are only a few more weeks, if that, and then the students will all be gone, the university year over, and he can forget about her. He is sure, at any rate, that she is frigid, or possibly even a lesbian. Yes, it certainly *was* a misunderstanding. She should have made it quite clear from the beginning what her proclivities were.

Emmeline waits for Clem to apologise for his behaviour in the caravan, to show some contrition. But Clem is busy at his desk again, looking at essay papers, no doubt expecting *her* to apologise for refusing *him*, for not being grateful that he fancied her, wanted to take her to bed.

She smiles to herself as she turns back to her own papers. Once no doubt she *would* have apologised, would have simpered with all sorts of excuses for not wanting to go to bed with him, to protect his ego, soothe his irritation.

Not any more, she thinks as she takes one last amused look at Clem's rigid back. *Thank God, not any more.*

Happily, she goes back to her work, forgetting Clem Todd immediately, to his eternal annoyance.

Leo, checking the sows and litters, is deluged with a profound weariness of the spirit. He goes through the motions of filling the creep-feeds for the piglets with deadened arms and a deadened heart. He knows, he feels, that he is not only ready for a change, but that it is imperative that he makes one before his soul cracks. Leo is not used to thinking of souls and hearts and spirits, and the fact that he is doing so now makes him realise the seriousness of this mid-life, or, he supposes, more accurately late-life, crisis.

Going from pen to pen, noting with a practised eye a blind teat, a weak runt, he knows that his depression, for that's what it must be, is rooted in the simple fact that he has had enough of pigs: he wants out, and soon. *Now,* he thinks, checking a sow which has just farrowed, producing fifteen vociferously squealing youngsters frantically searching for a spare teat. *Now.* He must sell the lot, buy sheep, realise his ambition before it is too late. His mind whirls round and round. He thinks of two of his five children in college on ever-decreasing grants, and another, Julian, an impecunious playwright. He thinks of Gemma, off soon in her gypsy caravan and sure to be needing help eventually, in spite of what she says. He thinks of Daisy to support, and himself, and the huge farm overdraft.

Leo leaves the farrowing unit and looks towards the

woodland, now shimmering in what seems like a luminous green haze, the new leaves on the trees soft and promising. It is as if those knowing, ancient woods have made a special effort to look especially beautiful this spring, to taunt Leo, to haunt him with guilt. Such whimsical thoughts startle him, make him feel that he is indeed going mad. He tells himself harshly not to be so sentimental, so idiotic. It is, after all, only land – and land is money in the bank, money he needs to have in his hands, to spend freely if he is going to attain his goal. With the money he will get for the sale of the land, he can pay off his overdraft, buy as many ewes as the farm can handle, get rid of the pigs, and have ample cash to support the whole bloody family if necessary until the sheep begin to show profit.

Without glancing again at the woodland, Leo hardens his heart and walks away from it, towards the far field where the ewes and lambs are grazing. He will contact the university next week and tell them he is prepared to sell. He decides, suddenly and firmly, not to tell Daisy or the children until he has informed the prospective buyers, and until he is irrevocably committed. He wants to be sure his family realise that he is in deadly earnest and do not try to change his mind.

As Leo walks towards his sheep, his spirit lightens, his steps lose their heaviness. Nonetheless there is a shadow hovering; he feels it following, lingering in the clear air around him. He will do what he has to do, what he wants to do, but he recognises that there will be a price. He will lose something in the end, by getting what he wants, and he can only hope that it will all be worth it. Whatever happens, there is no going back. Leo may take a long agonising time over a decision, but once it is made he will stick to it.

* * *

The woods are a busy place these days, what with first the primroses, then the bluebells and the first shimmer of green on the trees. The warm still weather holds, and on a light spring evening just as it is getting dark, Tony, unnaturally restless, decides to walk across the fields from his house to Woodland Farm. When he reaches the woods a full, mesmerising moon appears over the trees and Tony, bewitched by the beauty and enchantment of the evening, slows his pace. Several times he stops, looks around, listens, all his senses alert to the nightlife he knows is active around him. Growing up in the country, Tony has been sleeping outdoors since he was nine, has always been as comfortable with the creatures that live in meadows and woodlands as he is with his own friends, his own mates. He often thinks now that if it hadn't been for the lure of the times, the beat of the sixties, combined with his love of music, the need to be where the exciting new sounds were being made, he would have stayed in a forest somewhere, living like a wild animal himself, self-contained and contented.

The woods are especially compelling tonight, the earthy heat of the day having given way to a cool spring evening. The stars are coming out, large, riotous, bright. Tony, unhurried, stops to sit on a fallen log and stays there, motionless, for about five minutes, thinking of nothing but the peace of the night, the magnificence of the woodland. Then, like a flash, something moves: something barely seen out of the corner of his eye running up the bottom branch of a low-slung tree. It is as fleeting as a speck in the eye, but years of practice have made Tony alert to the mysteries of the countryside. He doesn't move but remains watching, waiting. What he saw was tiny, insubstantial – a movement, a bit of colour, russet, orange-brown . . . but he has a feeling, an instinct, and so is prepared to sit patiently and wait.

Nothing happens. The woods are still, silent. Tony notices the dense bracken, the honeysuckle and hazel copse growing coarsely in front of him and at last gets up, goes over to the young dwarfed tree and investigates the branch a few feet off the ground where he saw the flash of movement. In a moment he sees it: tiny, about the size of a cricket ball, made predominantly of honeysuckle bark and so well-camouflaged that he never would have been able to see it if he hadn't spotted the movement and known what he was looking for. It is a nest – domed, ball-like, and in it, about the size of his thumbnail, are two newborn creatures. They are bald, blind, helpless and pathetic, but definitely alive, and thriving.

Tony runs all the way up to the farmhouse. Leo and Daisy and Emmeline are in the kitchen, enjoying a second cup of coffee and lingering over a late evening meal.

'What's up?' Emmeline says. 'Are you okay? You look kind of flushed.'

'I ran,' Tony gasps. 'From the woods.'

Leo hands him a drink. 'You said you might walk over. I didn't know you meant run. Is this a keep-fit exercise?'

Tony shakes his head, catching his breath. 'Dormice,' he pants. Then, loudly, 'DORMICE.'

For a fraction no one responds. Then Gemma, who, with Baz, walked in on the last exclamation, shrieks, 'In our woods? You've found a dormouse?'

'Truly, Tony?' Daisy asks with excitement.

'Oh, where, where? Take us there, I want to see it!'

Leo, rather more sharply than necessary, says, 'Don't be silly, Gemma, it will be gone by now.'

Tony, trying to suppress his excitement, says, 'I found a nest. I saw the dormouse first, just a flash out of the corner of my eye, but I knew, *I knew*. Then I found the nest, with two babies in it. It must have been the mother I saw, out foraging for food. They're nocturnal creatures.'

'Tony, how can you be sure?'

Tony looks at Leo, who said this, and for the briefest of moments their eyes meet. Daisy says, 'Oh Leo, Tony's a naturalist. If he says they are dormice, of course they are.'

Leo is silent. Tony, looking at him, says, softly, 'I'm sure, Leo. Absolutely certain.'

Gemma is dancing around the kitchen, delighted and enthralled. 'A dormouse, our very own dormouse!'

Emmeline, who has been listening to all this in bewildered amazement, says, 'Uh, is this anything to do with *Alice in Wonderland*? I mean, did you find the creature asleep in a teapot? You're carrying on like we do in the theatre after a good review.'

Tony smiles. 'They're rare, Emmeline. They're wonderful creatures, tiny, quite pretty, elusive. Unfortunately they began to disappear, with woodlands being cleared, and new methods of farming destroying their usual habitats.'

'I didn't think we had any here,' Daisy says.

'I always used to want one!' Gemma cries. 'When I was little, I read a story about a dormouse, complete with pictures. Such sweet tiny things! They have this orange fur, and a long fluffy tail, and big eyes. Oh, I used to spend hours in our woods, looking for one.'

'And now you've got one – more than one if Tony's found a nest,' Baz says with a grin.

Emmeline looks at them, their faces pleased, buoyant, and wonders again how she could have strayed so far from Atlanta. How will she remember this when she is back in her own habitat? With amusement, perhaps? Incredulity? She has a feeling it will be with great nostalgia. 'Well,' she says with a smile. 'I suppose I ought to say congratulations?'

They laugh, all but Leo who has not said much, who is now sitting at the table, apparently oblivious to all of them. But suddenly he lifts his head and says carefully, 'The point is, Emmeline, that dormice are a protected species in this country.'

'Oh? You mean like bats?'

'Something like that. Only dormice are much, much rarer. If evidence of them is found in a field, or a woodland, that field or wood cannot be destroyed or demolished. The habitat of a dormouse must not be tampered with.' Leo looks at Tony as he says this, and Tony nods, almost imperceptibly.

'I should think not!' Gemma exclaims indignantly.

'No clearing of the land,' Leo goes on. 'No building.'

'Well, that's fine,' Daisy says. 'We wouldn't touch that bit of woodland anyway.'

'Never!' Gemma agrees reverently.

Tony, going up to Leo, tries to speak. 'Leo,' he begins softly, for the others are talking amongst themselves now and cannot hear him. 'I had to—'

'Not now, Tony,' Leo says, his head in his hands. 'Not now.'

It is several hours before Tony and Leo get a chance to speak to each other. Tony deliberately stays on, long after Gemma and Baz have left. When Daisy begins to yawn, Leo says, 'Why don't you go up to bed? Tony and I will just finish this bottle of homebrew.'

Emmeline, taking the hint, goes upstairs with Daisy. 'What was all that about?' she asks. 'Leo is acting very strangely.'

'God knows,' Daisy says. 'Something's been troubling him

for months, but he won't bloody talk about it. Maybe he wants to confide in Tony. He ought to talk to someone.'

She marvels that she can still feel hurt because Leo will not talk to her. Determinedly, she thinks of Barnaby, and of tomorrow when she will see him again. She puts Leo firmly out of her mind as he has all these years with her.

Leo has drunk much more than he usually does, but he seems no different; his speech, perhaps, is slightly slower. Tony also has had a considerable amount. He was offered a bed for the night by Daisy, but prefers to walk home. The moon outside is making copious light, just right for walking.

The two men drink another half-pint of beer without speaking. Finally Leo says, 'Did it not occur to you to tell me first, Tony? About the dormouse?'

'Yes, I did think of that, as I was running up to the house. But only fleetingly. I didn't see any point. And besides—' Tony breaks off suddenly.

'Besides,' Leo goes on for him, 'you were afraid I'd ask you to keep quiet about it.'

Tony hesitates. 'Yes,' he says finally.

'And then you'd have been in a right dilemma. Lose your friend, or lose your conscience.'

'Something like that.'

'If you kept quiet about the dormouse, no one would ever have known. I would have sold the land to the university. They would have built on it, extended the campus.'

'Yes.'

'And the dormouse would have become even rarer. Another little creature closer to extinction. What a sacrifice to help a friend.'

Tony says nothing.

'You wouldn't have done it, would you,' Leo states flatly. 'If it were a choice between me and a dormouse, you'd have chosen the dormouse.'

Tony sighs, stirs in his chair. He hates making explanations like the one he is about to give to Leo: they are so arcane and inadequate. How can you explain a feeling, something you know to be right and true but which is like the mist, as elusive as the tiny dormouse he saw tonight?

'You see,' he begins slowly, 'I don't think there is a choice, Leo. I think you and me and the dormouse, we're all one thing. If I wilfully destroy the dormouse, I destroy you as well. And me. And all of us.'

It is the best he can do. He gets up, finds his jacket, and says, 'I'm sorry, Leo.'

Leo also stands up and says, musingly, 'I don't know if I *would* have asked you to keep quiet about it. I'd like to think not. But I'll never know for sure.'

'None of us knows how we're going to act, in any given situation. It's probably better that way.'

'I suppose it is.' He grimaces at Tony ruefully. 'It was all against me anyway. Spring, and primroses and bluebells, and Gemma waxing lyrical about her childhood, ambling through those bloody woods.'

'And then dormice,' Tony says with a tentative grin.

'Yeah. Fucking dormice. I never had a chance.'

The men look at each other and smile, and then briefly, spontaneously, embrace. When Tony is gone Leo stands outside for a few moments, looking out at the field in the front of the house, at the old oak tree silhouetted by the moonlight. Instead of the anger and despair he had felt initially, when Tony had burst in with the news, he feels curiously relieved, though totally drained. Perhaps it is the absence of hope, he

369

thinks dispassionately. There is now absolutely nothing I can do. The land cannot be sold, not for building at any rate, and that was where the money was to come from.

At least there is no more agonising, he says to himself, shutting off the lights and closing up downstairs. No more choices to make.

Slowly he climbs into bed next to Daisy, who is sleeping soundly. He supposes he will wake up tomorrow profoundly disappointed and bitter, but tonight, at this moment, he feels oddly at peace.

Daisy, peeling potatoes, also feels at peace, though she is wry enough to understand the irony of it. It is because she is peeling the potatoes at the hostel rather than at home that she is feeling so contented. Part-time kitchen staff have been employed to prepare the evening meal now, but they are shorthanded today and Daisy has stepped in.

'Want a hand?' Kelvin, wandering in, looks rather lost so Daisy hands him a vegetable knife.

'Yes, you can slice those, please.'

Kelvin is looking healthier these days, Daisy notices: plumper, not quite so gaunt. Miles has moved him and three other permanent residents to another, smaller, room, where they have more privacy and more independence.

'How's the work going?' Daisy asks as Kelvin awkwardly tries to slice potatoes.

'Great. Off early today because of the weather.' Wind and thunderstorms have been pounding the area for twenty-four hours.

Kelvin is on a training scheme, working with local builders on various projects a couple of days a week. Yesterday he had a letter from his mum saying how proud she was of him. He still hasn't told her he lives in a shelter for the homeless, and decides he never will. Soon, he hopes, he'll be out of it anyway, in a job, in a place of his own. Sometimes, when he sees the likes of Clifton and Arnold, he thinks it's all a pipe dream but that kind of thinking frightens him, so he goes to find Daisy or Miles or someone who cheers him up again, makes him feel like he's in there with half a chance.

The cold wind has driven more people than usual inside and the massive table in the makeshift kitchen is full up. The meal is substantial, more than just palatable, with tasty stir-fry chicken, just past its sell-by date, donated by one of a large chain of department stores which sell food.

After Daisy has helped to clear up, and talked to some of the others she hasn't seen for a while, she is surprised to see Barnaby standing in the door just as she is walking out. 'I was hoping to catch you,' he says. 'I've got my car, so leave yours here for a bit.'

Barnaby drives out of the town for a few miles and parks the car at the start of a public footpath. 'Do you mind walking? I'd like to see you alone for once, not in a pub or in the bookshop or roaming the streets of Canterbury with people everywhere.'

The wind is bitter, but the storms have died out and at least it is dry. The sun has not yet set and there is an orange twilight glow in the air. The footpath goes along a narrow path with trees on one side and a grass field filled with ewes and lambs on the other. Barnaby and Daisy walk slowly, arms around each other, sheltering from the wind on the narrow path.

'Aren't you supposed to be at home with your wife and children?' Daisy asks, her voice raised against the wind.

'Marjorie has taken them out to something suitable and

371

worthy. A dance concert, I believe. It will be a very cultural evening for all of them.'

'You didn't want to go?'

'It is a ladies' evening, I believe. She is going with another mother and two daughters.'

'Marjorie is very good with the kids,' Daisy says conscientiously.

Barnaby stops walking and looks at Daisy with despair. 'I don't want to talk about Marjorie. Or the children. Or Leo and your kids. We do that a great deal lately.'

'But we have to,' Daisy says miserably, carrying on walking. 'They exist.'

'We've established that, all right? What about us? What about what we feel for each other? Doesn't that exist?'

Daisy brushes her windblown hair from her face as she says unhappily, 'It hasn't any right to exist. It shouldn't.'

'Oh, bollocks. Don't talk such rot. Right, right, right – who are we to say what has a right to exist and what doesn't? It's happened, Daisy. It's too late to say it shouldn't have.'

They have come to a stile, and instead of climbing over it, Barnaby sits down, pulls Daisy on to his lap, and begins to kiss her furiously. 'There,' he murmurs between lip contact, 'how can you say this doesn't exist?'

They kiss for some time, totally forgetful of the fact that this is what they insisted, at the beginning, they did not want. Indeed, they soon forget everything as they warm their cold wind-frozen hands inside each other's jumpers, on the hot skin of each other's bodies. Soon their thawed fingers, becoming bolder, begin searching further, and liking what they find, begin tearing away at the bits of clothing so maddeningly in the way.

Before they totally succumb and are about to lie down beside the stile and make love, a sudden roaring of a tractor alerts them and they jump apart. A farmer is bringing some salt licks up for his sheep and the tractor's lights sweep over them as they hastily rearrange themselves. The farmer, suspicious, lingers until he sees that they have got up and are slowly walking back to the car.

'We need some time alone together, Daisy,' Barnaby says as he drives her back into town, to her own car. Their hands cling tightly, letting go only when it is necessary for Barnaby to change gears.

'I know. I know.'

'I'll try to arrange something. I don't know what. Marjorie is going to take the kids to her brother's home one weekend. Perhaps . . .?'

'Yes? Perhaps?'

'We could go somewhere.'

'Where?'

'I don't know. Anywhere. Maybe France for the day, a couple of days.'

'How could I get away?'

'You have to try. You could be visiting someone there.'

'Yes. Marsha, I suppose.'

They are at the shelter and Daisy gets out, in a rush now because it has got quite late. 'Daisy.' Barnaby stops her, takes her hand for a moment. 'I love you, you know.'

'I know. I love you too.'

She runs off, into her car, frightened and excited, euphoric and unnerved. *This is it*, she thinks as she drives away, knowing Barnaby is watching her, waiting for her to drive safely away before pulling back onto the road himself. *This is when my new life starts*. She waves at him through her open window, and it feels like a promise. She carries on waving until he is out of sight.

Midsummer: another promise, pagan and ancient. 'Oh, how I love this eternal daylight,' Emmeline exclaims as she wanders with Daisy from the house to the big barn next to it.

'You should be in Scotland. It never really gets dark up there.'

'No, I'm happy right here.'

A party is going on in the big barn next to the farmhouse. The animals have all been moved, the concrete floor swept and cleaned to make room for dancing, and Tony and his band are playing. Straw bales line the sides, for those who want to sit, and a long table stacked with beer and wine rests near the entrance. In the farmhouse kitchen there is a mass of food, pizzas and quiches and sandwiches.

It is a going-away party for Gemma and Baz, for they leave tomorrow in their bright red gypsy caravan, heading westwards. Forty or fifty people mingle in the barn, and another twenty or thirty are in the house. Blue, her assortment of long beads and baubles bouncing rhythmically on her chest, is dancing frenetically with Flack, whose pony tail bobs from side to side as he bops. He executes a particularly flashy step as Gemma walks into the barn.

'Nice one, Flack,' Gemma says.

'Gemma, you can't go, I'll miss you!' Blue stops dancing to embrace her.

'I know. I'll miss you, too.'

'You'll be back,' Flack says, not missing a beat of his dancing. 'Unless you find some idyllic spot in Devon or somewhere and decide to stay.'

'No chance. Baz has his didgeridoo workshop to come back

to one day, and we have our friends. We wouldn't leave for good.'

Emmeline, who is standing nearby, says to Gemma as the other two go back to their dancing, 'You should tell that to your mom, honey. About not leaving for good. I think she's feeling kind of low about your going.'

At that moment Daisy, dressed in a long flowered skirt with slits up the sides, dances by with Barnaby, both of them looking so wildly crazy and happy that Gemma and Emmeline laugh.

'Well,' Emmeline says, 'maybe she's not as doleful as I thought.'

'She's okay. She's low, sure, but it's understandable. It's the first time all her kids have been away from home. But she's not resenting me for it any more.'

'I still think you should have a talk with her.'

Gemma hugs Emmeline and runs into the middle of the barn, begins to dance, slowly at first, then faster, till the bells in her hair twirl and tinkle and whirl like mad demented hummingbirds.

Tony, playing his guitar, glances over the scene with pleasure. Emmeline, who loves watching him play, hearing him sing, looks at him fondly, smiles at him when she catches his eye. Experienced musician that he is, his fingers nonetheless tremble for a moment; try as he has, he is still more than a little in love with the woman. Unrequited love has never been Tony's style, and he feels foolish, gauche, gawky. The trouble is, he's fond of her company, wishes he could enjoy it for what it is, what she can offer – a happy, deep, stable friendship – and not wish for what she cannot give him – an intense, passionate love affair.

The band finish their number, then decide to take a break. Tony goes to Emmeline and they get another beer, wander outside where the night is warm and clear, a perfect Midsummer evening. There they are joined by Daisy and Leo, who says, 'The hay will be ready to cut soon, if the weather holds like this.'

'Need a hand, Leo?' Tony asks.

'Could always do with a hand bringing it in,' Leo says gratefully. The two men nod, catch each other's eye for a moment. Leo seems to hold no resentment of Tony, for finding the dormice, for officially letting it be known that the woodland was a site for a dormouse colony. *For chopping up all my dreams into little pieces*, is the way he puts it to himself, before he gets embarrassed at his own theatricality. He wonders why he feels only a sad resignation. It is probably because he is too tired, he reflects. Life is tiring, these days. He feels improbably old.

Daisy leaves the three of them and goes to check the food. She meets Marjorie on the way, who shouts, 'Great party, what? I've just been talking to Gemma in the kitchen; she's very appreciative. Lovely girl, that one.'

The kitchen is surprisingly empty for a moment except for Gemma, who is nibbling the edge of a pizza. 'It's a great evening, Mum,' she says softly. 'The food is terrific. Thanks for doing it all.'

'It's not anything fancy.'

'Yes, it is. You made those special pizzas I've loved ever since I was a kid. I won't half miss those pizzas when we're gone.'

Daisy smiles. 'I'll miss *you*, love. I'll miss not having anyone to make those special pizzas for.' She says it matter-of-factly, without a tinge of self-pity or gloom. Gemma is immeasurably grateful for this.

'We're not going for ever, Mum. You do know that? You're not going to go all miserable on me?'

Daisy shakes her head. 'The hard time was last autumn. That's when you really went: when you left the house and moved in with Baz. I gave you a hard time then, I know. I regret that very much.'

Gemma hesitates, then says, 'I love the farm, you know. You and Dad must never think I don't. But there are so many other things I want to do.'

'And now I hope you're going to do them.'

'I am, I am.' Gemma picks up another bit of pizza, begins nibbling again. 'I've done so much already this year. The work at the shelter, helping Blue in the café when Flack had that job. Making all those candles, busking with Baz and the didgeridoo.'

'And now you're going travelling.'

'Hm.' Gemma munches thoughtfully. 'I'll miss you though. And Dad and the rest of the family, not to mention dear Blossom, and Alan Lamb, and Tony's bats – and Tony – and Emmeline, even though she won't be here very much longer. And naturally our friends, Blue and Flack and the others. Oh, and Bella the Beautiful of course!' She giggles. 'Have I missed anything? Oh yes, the dormice which I've never even seen yet, and the woods of course. Did I say the sheep? I'll miss the sheep. I love working with them.'

Daisy laughs, and begins chewing on a bit of pizza herself. 'You missed the pigs,' she chuckles. 'You didn't mention them.'

'Deliberately, I'm afraid. Don't tell Dad, but I can't bear the pigs.'

'What?'

'That's one of the reasons I couldn't stay on at the farm. I never liked working with pigs much. Sheep, yeah, but I never could get excited about pigs.' She licks her fingers. 'Hm, delicious. Oh, here comes Dad. Great party, Dad! Thanks for letting us use your barn.'

She gives Leo a quick hug and runs outside. The band has started up again, and the music pounds inside the kitchen. 'Good thing we haven't any neighbours,' Daisy says.

Leo picks at a bit of quiche. 'Gemma will miss haymaking this year,' he says. 'First time ever.'

'But Emmeline will be here,' Daisy says brightly.

'Em? What help will she be?'

'Oh Leo, you'll have plenty of help, you always do. I just thought how nice it will be to have Emmeline here, after all these years. She was at our first haymaking, remember? She and Hal, and all the others . . .'

Leo's face softens, remembering. 'So she was.'

'I had just found out that I was pregnant, with Paul. I'll never forget that day.'

'Nor I.' He grins mischievously.

'You! You hardly took any notice, not until the hay was finally all in. You were too bloody worried because the weather forecast was so unsettled. I was terribly hurt, you know.'

Leo, in a rare gesture, opens his arms wide and envelops Daisy in them. 'I'm a farmer, love. Always have been. It's not been easy for you sometimes, I know, and I'm sorry.'

Oh Leo, why now? Why now when it's too late? Daisy buries her head in Leo's chest, sadly wishing that he had said these things to her years ago.

They stand together like this for what seems to Daisy a long, long time, but for once Leo is not rushing out of her embrace, to race after a ewe, check on an ailing piglet, or just collapse into bed with sheer exhaustion.

Barnaby, coming into the kitchen looking for Daisy, sees

them like this and feels troubled. He has already booked a room for two in a tiny hotel in a secluded spot in Normandy in a fortnight's time. Daisy and Leo see him and move apart. Daisy is filled with guilt, but whether it is because she has upset Barnaby by embracing her husband, or whether she is about to risk damaging Leo and her marriage by going off with her soon-to-be lover on a clandestine weekend to France, she is not sure. The murkiness of her feelings upsets her, and she rather abruptly walks out of the kitchen and into the barn where she runs into Tony who is returning to the band after his break.

'Are you all right?' Tony asks, thinking she looks rather stressed and harassed.

'Oh. Tony. Uh, yeah, fine. The music's great, by the way.'

He looks at her carefully. He has just heard from Emmeline that both Barnaby and Daisy are going to France in a couple of weeks. By some coincidence they have booked the same ferry, but Barnaby is going over on business and will head in one direction, while Daisy is – supposedly – meeting Marsha somewhere in Normandy.

Tony understands what is happening. He has talked no further to Barnaby about Daisy since that one afternoon at the bookshop, but he has watched them both, and been troubled by what he has seen. He knows that both Barnaby and Daisy are about to embark on the most foolhardy endeavour of their lives, but he doesn't know how to stop them.

He hates having this knowledge. What in God's name can he do with it, in a way which would damage the least number of people? He wants to ignore it, to tell himself it is none of his business, to trust Barnaby and Daisy to know what they are doing, to be aware of the consequences.

But if not? he thinks despairingly. If they manage to blow the whole thing, destroy their lives, demolish two families — if they do this, and I have kept quiet, will I not wonder if I could have done something, anything, to have prevented it?

Tony leaves Daisy and joins his band, picks up his guitar. He dislikes this feeling of uncertainty, of confusion and impending disaster which looms over him every time he thinks of Daisy and Barnaby. Then he strikes a chord and the vibrations warm and comfort him, clear his head and his heart. Soon he forgets Leo and Daisy and Marjorie and Barnaby and lets the music work through him, become him, until he is no longer tentative and unsure but whole, true, sound, like the music itself.

Emmeline, watching, thinks with sadness that she could have loved this man, and wishes she had met him before Hal, when she was still innocent and believed in things like love, believed that passion could evolve from tenderness, intensity from kindness and caring.

Gemma dances by, her body a mass of rhythm and movement. 'Isn't it brilliant?' she shouts, high on happiness. 'Everyone here that I love, getting on so well together, being so good together. Oh Em, I'm soooo happy.' And she bounces away.

Emmeline, watching her, watches her own young self unning and dancing away from her one last time and closes her eyes, lets her go. Tony, glancing over, sees her brush away what looks like a tear as she opens her eyes and stares unseeingly at the crowded dance-floor. He would like to reach out to her, grab the hand still lingering on that enigmatic tear, hold it to his own face, his own heart. But a crowd of dancers vigorously twist and jump between them, and Tony plays on as Emmeline, oblivious, looks beyond all of them, at something only she can dimly, sadly, and finally, perceive.

Chapter Seventeen

'*Emmeline, grab my hand! There, up you come! Sit on my lap, love, there's not much room anywhere else.*'

Hal, sitting on the back of the trailer, pulled Emmeline on to his lap as the tractor began pulling it slowly down the field to where the rest of the hay-bales were scattered at random, like great lumps of giant's confetti. Leo was driving the tractor, and the trailer was crammed with people all eager to help bring in the hay. Apart from Emmeline and Hal, there were Marsha and her dentist, Jean-Luc, who had just passed his exams and was in England celebrating; there were Sojo and Giorgio, who was also in the country for a ten-day break between his stints on the sea; and there was an assortment of others. Some had come out from London with Emmeline and Hal, and many were local, friends of friends who had heard about Leo and Daisy.

The day before, Leo, baling his hay furiously before the rain came, had worried himself sick wondering if he'd be able to get all the bales in, and for once, he luckily worried out loud to Daisy. By a fortunate coincidence, Daisy was on the phone a great deal that evening, first to a friend in Canterbury, who volunteered to come up and help, bringing one or two others with him; and then to Emmeline in London, who promptly said that she and Hal, and whoever else she could find, would leave for Kent after their morning classes.

The next day was hot and sunny, with no sign of the heavy rain predicted for that evening. Leo, finishing his baling in the early afternoon, looked around him at the fields littered with hay-bales and still despaired, knowing he would never get it all in before the storms began.

At that moment the phone rang. Daisy, answering it, spoke briefly, hung up, and said to Leo, who was wolfing down a late lunch, 'That was Emmeline. She and Hal and nine others are at the Westgate Station. I'll take the van and collect them, but I'll have to make two trips.'

'Nine?' Leo asked, stunned.

'Come to help with the haymaking. Some of them have been down before, with Em and Marsha and Hal.'

The London crowd was just finishing a hasty snack Daisy had provided, calling in at the little shop down in the village for provisions between her two trips to the train station, when several cars began to make their way tenuously up the dirt track to the farmhouse.

'I made some phone calls,' Daisy's friend from Canterbury said, arriving in the first car with several people Daisy had never set eyes on before. 'Said you needed help, that you were the kind of people who deserved help. I think you'll find there will be quite a few more later this afternoon, when people finish work.'

In the end, about fifty or sixty people turned out to help get the hay in, if you included the children. Daisy, crazy with excitement, for she had just been to the doctor that morning and had her pregnancy confirmed, bought huge uncut loaves from the bakery, and ten pounds of cheddar from the local shop. Many people had brought food, cakes and scones, savoury pies and quiches, which they shared around generously. Quite a few brought beer, and Daisy drove down again to the shop to buy lemonade and cider, for it was hot work and there were hundreds of bales to bring in.

'This should be the last lot,' Hal told Emmeline as they jogged up and down on the bumpy trailer with the others. 'Everyone's worked bloody hard today.'

'All these people! Daisy said they didn't know half of them.'

'All ages, too. There are one or two old grandads humping bales, have you noticed? Put me to shame, too – they haven't taken a break all day.'

'And the kids! Daisy's gathered them together in the garden, to keep them out of the way of the tractor and trailer. It's a real kindergarten going on there. Somebody's grandmother has sorted out food for them, and with the help of a couple of the mothers, they're feeding the whole lot.'

Hal looked around him on the trailer. 'Quite a few of the helpers are students, by the look of it. I believe Daisy said her friend in town was at one of the colleges.'

'He must have spread the word around to his mates. What fun it all is! And Daisy's pregnant, too. Isn't that wonderful?' Emmeline turned around to look at Hal, but he was looking away from her. 'Hal?' she said, thinking he had not heard. 'You did hear Daisy announce she was pregnant, didn't you?'

Hal said, still not looking at her, 'Yes. Good for them.' His voice was taut.

'They want this baby,' Emmeline said softly. 'So much. I don't blame them.'

She wanted to say more, wanted to say how she longed one day to have Hal's babies, but something in his face had

383

hardened, become distant, out of her reach. Instead, she only said, 'I love you, Hal,' and luckily the tractor stopped then with a jolt, and everyone jumped off with a great deal of noise and laughter, so she never heard him say, in a low voice full of regret, 'I know you do, Emmeline. And I'm so sorry.'

There was a huge party that night. Emmeline and Hal and the others filled the trailer for the last time and trudged up the hill to the haybarn, where they helped to unload the trailer and stack the bales neatly in the barn. It was late evening by then but the sky was still light enough to see. It was just darkening when the last bale was in, and at that moment it began to rain, great relentless drops which quickly gathered force, became a downpour.

Everyone cheered, laughed, hugged, shouted, and ran for the shelter of the house. The assorted children who were still awake were running about silly with excitement, while others had been tucked to sleep in the bedrooms upstairs. There seemed to be masses of food, and beer, and Leo had brought out, along with his homebrew, gallons of his father's rich homemade plum wine that he had been saving for a special occasion. Moved and touched by the help he had been given that day, the spirit of solidarity and fun which had permeated the whole adventure, he knew that this was indeed the very special occasion he had been waiting for.

'Happy?' Daisy asked Leo, as they sat crammed into the huge living room, listening to a young woman playing a banjo while Jean-Luc, in his element, sang a rousing French folk-song which nobody understood, but clapped and whistled along to. 'Listen to the rain up there on the roof, and think of all your hay safe and dry in the barn.'

Leo nodded, put his arm around her.

'So now what about my news? Can we think about that for a minute, now that the hay's in?' she said teasingly.

'Oh God – the baby! I forgot about him.'

'Or her.'

'Either one. Maybe both, eh?' He smiled, and she knew he was as pleased, as overwhelmed, as joyous as she was. Wrapped in each other's arms, they let the music and ambience do the talking for them.

*

Gemma and Baz, flushed and laughing so hard they nearly fall off their perch on the caravan, leave the day after the Midsummer party. Bones is so excited to be on the road again that he has jolted them as they set off.

'Goodbye, goodbye!'

'Phone us! Reverse charges.'

'Don't worry, we'll be fine. Whoops! Whoa, Bones, easy, boy!'

'Look after Blossom and Alan Lamb and Bella the Beautiful.'

'Be careful.'

'Don't do anything crazy.'

'Write to me from America, Em!'

'I will. Visit me.'

'One day. Love you, Mum, Dad! Tony, look after the bats! And the dormice.'

'Just look after yourselves.'

'Goodbye, goodbye, see you soon!'

Daisy and Leo, Emmeline and Tony, wave and wave until the caravan is out of sight. As it goes down the dirt track they hear more shouts and cheers and greetings, for many of Baz and Gemma's friends have stayed all night, some crashing out in the barn, in the house, others not sleeping at all but celebrating the solstice. As Emmeline was drifting off to sleep at dawn, the last thing she heard was the mournful, haunting sound of a didgeridoo serenading the Midsummer sun, and sleep eluded her for a time while she listened, entranced.

Daisy is having a little weep in Leo's arms, and Emmeline and Tony tactfully walk away from them. 'Did you hear Baz playing his didgeridoo when the sun came up?' she asks.

'Yes. It somehow fitted the solstice perfectly.'

They begin to walk slowly towards the woods, enjoying the sun, enjoying the first day of summer. 'Can you show me the dormouse nest?' Emmeline asks. 'I promise I'll only look from a distance; I won't disturb the young ones.'

'They'll be quite grown by now.'

Emmeline and Tony begin walking lazily towards the woods. Emmeline, a city person, or so she thought, wonders at her new fascination for dormice, wild flowers, woodlands, bats. A couple of nights ago Tony took her up to the attic of the farmhouse at twilight where they sat on the floor and watched the bats getting ready to leave the roost for the night, stretching, grooming, flying around inside until finally emerging into the darkness outside. It was strangely compelling, plunging Emmeline outside of time and into somewhere ancient, mythical, mysterious.

She wonders, not for the first time, what Chester would think of all this: watching bats at twilight, being wakened by a didgeridoo at dawn, celebrating with excited euphoria the sighting of a dormouse. He would think them all simple, eccentric, and more than slightly foolish. Emmeline sighs, knowing there is *that* to sort out when she gets home. Although at this moment she feels confident and assured enough to sever the relationship, she is aware that old habits, loneliness, the

difficulty of making radical changes, may very well throw her
back into an unwanted partnership with him — that is, if he
hasn't found some other woman in her year's absence. Their
letters and phone calls to each other have become more and
more infrequent, distant.

'Thinking of home?' Tony asks perceptively.

'How could you tell?'

He smiles. 'You always get that same worried, preoccupied look.'

'Oh dear.'

'When exactly are you going back?'

'I've rented my house out until the end of August; it was
a year's tenancy. Originally I had planned to spend July
and August alternating between my summer house in the
mountains, and Chester's place in Atlanta.'

'Mm,' Tony mutters between gritted teeth.

'But somehow I just can't seem to drag myself back. It's so
beautiful here in England now, and I feel I'm only beginning
to rediscover it again.'

'Ah.' This is murmured with a broad smile that Tony simply
cannot hide.

'I really must return by the first of September. There is
always so much to do to get ready for the new term.'

'I suppose.'

She looks so dejected that Tony takes her arm companion-
ably and says, 'Cheer up, you still have two months. Your
students are gone, you're on holiday.'

'I know, and it's great. I want to do a bit of real sightseeing,
wander around London, explore Kent. You'll have to tell me
where to go, what to see.'

'I've got some favourite haunts. If you like, I'll take you to
one or two, when I'm not working.'

Emmeline likes this idea, and says so. They spend a pleasurable fifteen minutes discussing the places that Emmeline absolutely must visit, with Tony, of course, accompanying her. This conversation puts them both in a very good mood. Tony, because he is determined to enjoy the last remaining weeks of Emmeline's friendship without spoiling it by pining for more, and Emmeline because, simply, she can think of no one she'd rather be with than Tony.

'It should be a good summer,' Emmeline says with satisfaction after they have made their plans. 'And if yesterday and today are an omen, then it should be sunny and warm for us, too.'

'Don't count on it,' Tony warns. 'The weather here is erratic and changeable.'

'Yes, I remember. My only summer here, just before I went back to the States, was like a monsoon. The rain began suddenly one day, after that beautiful spring, and just didn't stop.'

She becomes quiet, contemplative. Tony knows she is thinking of that wet rainy summer and lets her be. They walk in silence until they come to the dormouse nest. Tony points it out to her, but they don't disturb it. 'Dormice are nocturnal so they'll be asleep, if they're there at all now,' he tells her.

Emmeline looks, listens to Tony, observes, learns. She hasn't a clue what use any of this knowledge will be back in Atlanta, then chides herself for being so pragmatic. Before long Tony's easy, laconic observations capture her, and she forgets Atlanta as she plunges with him into a world of honeysuckle bark and hazelnut copses, of hidden nests and the tiny creatures that inhabit them, of moss and fern and fungi and wild flowers. It's a beguiling world, perhaps because it is the first day of summer and the sun is out: whatever, Emmeline is lost in it. She finds herself wishing that she will never find her way out, that she and Tony will remain, enchanted, in this sunlit forest for ever.

Daisy and Leo, alone after waving Gemma and Baz off, walk back slowly, arms around each other, into the house. 'A pot of coffee would be nice before you go back to work, don't you think?' Daisy asks, blowing her nose on a mansize tissue. Saying goodbye to her daughter has shaken and saddened her, despite her acceptance of Gemma's new life, her independence.

Leo agrees and sits down at the kitchen table. He is still feeling lethargic these days, but the desperation which had been enveloping him over the winter months is gone. Resignation has taken its place. He is no happier, facing the prospect of many more years of working with the pigs, but he realises now how despairing and nihilistic his decision was to sell the land for building. He would have achieved his lifelong goal, but the price would have been his own self-respect, for in truth Leo has always known in his heart that to destroy that special ten acres of woodland would have been fatally, morally, wrong. He would also, and this is to him of greater importance, have lost the love and respect of his children, and of Daisy too, who never would have forgiven him for selling what she has always considered to be the most important, the lasting part of the farm. Those few acres, Daisy has always felt, connect them to a vanishing past which they have an obligation now to cherish and preserve.

Leo knows, and can only wonder why he was so blind not to have seen it before, that in the end Daisy is his life, his only love, and that without her, his dream would have been sand in his fingers. He is looking at her so intently that she stops pouring out their coffee and looks back at him questioningly. He is so full of love for her that he is sure it spills out all over him, like barley from a torn sack. It never occurs to him to tell her this, though she is waiting, expectant. The moment passes, and they sip their coffee in silence for a few moments.

'Oh dear,' Daisy suddenly exclaims. 'Do you realise your mother will be here any moment now? I'd forgotten all about her.'

On cue, the kitchen door flies open and Alma says, 'I must say, this is a fine welcome. Hippies up and down the track waving at me as I drove up, and no one to help me out of the car. Say hello to Winston, Leo.'

Leo, hastily kissing his mother, decides to first greet Gareth, the octogenarian who has followed Alma inside, before greeting Winston, the dog. Alma acquired Gareth at about the same time she acquired her fat, bad-tempered Jack Russell, several years ago now. As far as Daisy and Leo can see, Gareth and Winston both have the same function: to follow Alma around, express total reverence and devotion, and do exactly her bidding. Gareth does this with far more willingness than Winston.

'How are you, Gareth?' Daisy says politely. They have met him once before, on a visit to Leeds. He is a wealthy widower, a retired civil servant. He is quiet, never speaking unless spoken to, and is as dry and emaciated as Alma is lavish and buxom. His skin, his face, his eyes, his clothes, are all grey.

'I'm well, thank you,' Gareth answers Daisy, and those are the only words he speaks during the next half hour.

Gareth and Alma are off to Dover to catch a ferry to France where they are going to 'motor around the countryside' for a week. Alma loathes the French: their food, their language, their foreign-ness, and likes to holiday there so that she can complain endlessly when she returns home about how appalling everything was. She met Gareth at a bridge club social in Leeds, and likes to tell the story of how he was smitten at once by her youthful good looks, her well-bred charm. Indeed, she tells the story often, much to Gareth's discomfort.

Winston is being left at the farm during this week: Alma's sister-in-law, who had him the last time, having refused point-blank to do so again. 'Much more convenient, leaving him here, practically right on the road to Dover,' Alma says as they are leaving. 'My friends in Leeds are all threatening to drop in with their pets when they go abroad.' She bends down and waggles a finger at the corpulent dog. 'Now Winston, you must be a good baby. I know you'll miss your mum but you'll have Uncle Leo.'

Winston snarls. He eludes Alma as she tries to kiss him goodbye and snaps at Gareth who attempts to stop him from wriggling out of Alma's grasp. 'Dear Winston,' Alma says tearfully.

Blue appears, on her way to the barn to help clear up the remains of last night's party. 'Hello, Mrs Dillard,' she says cheerily. 'You missed Gemma. She and Baz have gone.'

'Oh?' Alma says suspiciously. 'Where?'

Daisy says, 'I told you, Mother. They are heading down to the West Country, doing some travelling and sightseeing.'

Neither she nor Leo have mentioned the gypsy caravan, deciding to leave it to fate whether Alma got here in time to witness the leavetaking for herself.

Alma gives detailed instructions on the care and feeding of Winston, makes a few caustic remarks about Leo's hair, which she compares to various birds' nests (it is slightly in need of a trim), and gets into the Volvo next to Gareth. Winston, loving car rides, snarls nastily when he realises he is being left behind. Blossom, hearing this, slinks off to hide somewhere, which she will do the entire week.

'Bloody dog,' Leo says, as Winston snaps at his ankle when Leo tries to prevent him from chasing the Volvo down the track.

'Blossom is terrified, poor thing. I wish we could just lock the revolting animal in a shed.'

'Stick him in one of your pig-sheds,' Blue suggests.

'It's a thought,' Leo broods.

Winston's behaviour deteriorates in the next few days. He steals food, is snappy with everyone, and finally actually draws blood from Blossom's jaw, attacking the old dog for docilely walking past his empty feed bowl.

'That's it,' Daisy decides. 'That vicious creature has to be locked up.'

'Where?' Leo says. 'He'd get out of the barn, there are too many holes his size.'

'Don't you have a spare pig-pen you can put him in? I won't have Blossom being attacked.'

Leo mutters something about not running a bloody dog kennel and goes out to look at the pigs. Blossom, her jaw still flaked with a few drops of blood, follows him mournfully. 'Poor sod,' Leo says. 'You don't deserve this in your old age.' He looks around him thoughtfully.

Leo spends the afternoon converting one of the small pig-sheds, which happens to be empty at the moment, into a kennel for the dog. The shed is perfect: Leo is able to make a long run for the dog with a cosy sleeping quarters. There would be room for several others just the same, he thinks, his brain whirling and leaping.

'Daisy, come and have a look!' he shouts, running into the kitchen. Daisy goes out with him and is suitably impressed. 'I used that fencing wire for the run, see? There's a perfect concrete floor. The shed is divided into units anyway, for the pigs, so I just used one of those. What I'd like to do is make an outdoor run too, for fine days like today. It wouldn't cost much at all. I could do most of it myself, or, even better, hire Tony to help out.'

'Just for a dog run?' Daisy asks. 'There's no point, Alma and Gareth will be back soon. The inside one will do, and if Winston behaves himself I'll take him out on his lead for a long walk every day.'

Leo's head is still throbbing, buzzing, filled with such ideas that, totally out of character, without thought or reflection, he blurts out to Daisy, 'Listen, I'm not just thinking of my mother's bloody dog. We could build a proper kennel here, a boarding one, for dogs and even cats. The pig-sheds are perfect for them, they could be easily and cheaply converted. They've all got concrete floors, plenty of light and air, and they're divided up just right – it'd be perfect!'

'But . . . why?' Daisy asks, bewildered. 'Where would you put the pigs?'

'Sell the bloody things, Daisy! If I could just get another steady income from somewhere, to tide me over until the sheep began to pay, I could sell the pigs, use a quarter of the money to convert the sheds into kennels, and the rest to buy ewes.'

Daisy looks at the newly-converted dog kennel, which indeed looks roomy and smart, and at Leo, whose face is flushed and young with excitement and hope. Something tugs at her, some long-lost memory. She says gently, 'You'd really get rid of the pigs? You'd rather run a dog kennel than a pig-farm?'

Leo is walking up and down the dog-run at a slow, measured pace that belies his excitement. He needs to think, and the walking steadies him. 'It won't be for long, having a kennel here,' he says at last. 'We just need to have some money coming in for a while if we get rid of the pigs. We're in a good spot here, not that far from Ashford and the Channel Tunnel, and of course Dover. People could drop their dog or cat here on the way to France or wherever, and pick them up on the way back. We need only do it for a few years, while I build up the sheep flock. We've got the land, we could have one of the best flock of sheep in Kent! Ever since New Zealand, I've longed to run sheep properly, to have a top-notch flock.'

'I never knew that, Leo,' Daisy says quietly.

Something in her voice stops his pacing. He looks at her, sees the sadness there, knows why it is there. 'I never was a talker, love, you know that,' he says, going to her and putting his arm around her. 'And you sometimes needed a talker, I know. I used to wonder, in the early days, if I'd ever be enough for you, if I'd end up being too boring, too inarticulate for you.'

He draws away from her for a moment, looks into the face that he knows like he knows his own soul, and says, with a half-smile, 'I'm only now getting used to the idea that you'll be sticking around with me.'

He kisses her, in the light familiar way that couples married for nearly thirty years have, and holds her tightly against his chest. Daisy, against the roughness of his worn farm shirt, feels the sting of tears. They stand there for several minutes, rocking slightly from side to side, then break apart, with arms still linked, to walk slowly outside the shed into the sunlight once again.

Leo knows she is crying, but doesn't ask why. He assumes that it is because of Gemma, now finally left home. He knows that if Daisy wants to tell him, she will. Living in his own self-contained world he assumes others do the same, and will never try to pry open something that is private and inviolate.

Daisy should know this by now. Indeed, this time she is, for once, glad that Leo is asking no questions. She is not even sure why the tears are streaming so copiously down her cheeks; she knows only it has to do with something lost, something irretrievable.

Later, after they have drunk a pot of coffee between them and have discussed in great detail Leo's new scheme to establish a boarding kennel, Daisy says, 'Well, I must say I'll miss the pigs a bit. They're nice creatures, really. Clean and intelligent, in spite of their pigsty image.'

'Hm,' Leo says. 'They're not bad animals, and it was all right working with them for a time, I suppose. I won't say I'll miss them.'

'You can't sell Bella the Beautiful!'

'Oh Daisy, come on now. We can't keep one sow.'

'We can and we will. If she goes, I go.'

Leo rolls his eyes. 'And I suppose you'll want to keep one of her grand-daughters, just so that we can always have a Bella here.'

Daisy laughs. 'For sentimental reasons, okay? For the kids.'

Leo's face clouds, and he says slowly, 'That's the one thing that worries me. Gemma. What if she changes her mind one day and wants to come back on the farm? I feel as if I'm cutting her right out, selling the pigs.'

Daisy looks at him and says mildly, 'She'll be more ready to come back with the pigs gone, Leo. She told me last night that she's never liked working with them much.'

Leo is stunned, confused. 'But I thought——! She was so good with them.'

'She was good at everything she did on the farm. She never let on because of you.' When Leo doesn't speak Daisy continues softly, 'If you'd only told us, years ago. Things might have worked out so differently.'

Leo puts his head in his hands in a gesture of hopelessness. Gemma — feeling the same as *he* had done all these years? Perhaps, if he'd told her of his plans, she'd have stayed on the farm . . . For a moment, he lets himself think of what might have been: he and Gemma together, working side by side, building up the fine sheepfarm he had always envisaged. Because of his silence, his inability to share with others the secrets of his own heart, he has lost his daughter.

'It's all right,' Daisy says quietly, going up behind him as he sits at the table, putting her arms around his shoulders. 'She had to go away, Leo. I was wrong to ever try and stop her. She needs to go, see other places, meet other people, do a dozen different things. Then, if she wants, she can always come back. But not until then. It would be wrong, and I'd tell her so.'

Leo lifts his head, nods. He knows she is probably right, but for the moment all he can feel is loss, loss and a profound regret. Clinging to Daisy's hands, which are still resting on his shoulders as she stands behind him, he knows that if Gemma could go because of unspoken words, of dreams unshared, then Daisy could too. His whole life, which had seemed so solid, so sure, seems to totter precariously in front of him like a child learning to walk and he feels, suddenly, chilled and frightened.

Turning in the chair so that he can look at Daisy, who is still standing behind him with her arms around his shoulders, he realises that he wants, needs, to say these things to her but the words don't seem to come. Instead, they stick in his throat like a sweet swallowed the wrong way.

'Daisy?' he tries, sounding pitiful to himself, pitiful and pathetic.

Daisy walks around in front of him, sits in the chair opposite. She waits: she owes him that. *But no more,* she thinks. *I owe him no more.*

Daisy waits, and the hard lump in Leo's throat seems to grow and expand and elongate, threatening to choke him, gag him, immobilise him so that he will never speak again, never breathe again. The seconds pass, and still Daisy waits, willing herself not to move, telling herself again: *I owe it to him.*

A moment passes, then another. Finally, haltingly, and just in time, Leo at last begins to talk.

Chapter Eighteen

*I*t is not until a day or so later that Daisy has a chance to see Barnaby again. She does a few hours' work in the shelter first, talking to Clifton who is feeling depressed and unsettled.

'Why don't you go outside for a bit?' she finally says. 'It's such a beautiful day; it seems a shame to stay inside.'

Clifton looks doubtful. His friend, Arnold, has begun on the rum rather earlier today and so is now asleep and snoring on his bed, and Clifton seems lost without his now-inseparable companion.

'Go on, an easy amble through the town will do you good. Go into Westgate Gardens, have a snooze in the sun on one of the benches.' Clifton reluctantly lets himself be persuaded, first finding his navy-blue cardigan, faded and shapeless with age, and putting it on carefully. 'If it's pouring with rain tomorrow I'll have a game of backgammon with you,' Daisy promises, as Clifton suspiciously opens the door and peeks at the sunny day outside. Cheered, he shuffles out.

As he goes, Miles bustles in, stopping first to exchange a few words with Clifton on the steps of the shelter. Then he calls to Daisy, 'Do you mind coming into the office? I'd like to talk to you when you have a few moments.'

'I can come now.'

Miles, thin and frenetic with an explosive energy that he doesn't seem able to contain in his rather frail body, says, 'I've been talking to the council, and the representatives of a couple of charities. There just may be enough money to buy some permanent premises to get a long-term hostel going, instead of just a temporary shelter.'

'How wonderful. Well done, Miles!'

'It wasn't me, it was everyone. At least we've convinced the powers-that-be that there is a definite need for one in the city.'

'A women's hostel next, I hope.'

'Yes, that's definitely next on the agenda. Look, Daisy, this is all related to what I want to talk to you about, your work here.'

Daisy feels herself go numb, cold. Another loss, she thinks dully. To her surprise, she finds that this one pierces her much more sharply than the other one, the one that she has been preparing herself for since Midsummer Day.

'You won't need any more volunteers,' she says, anticipating him. 'Once you move, you won't have any more use for unskilled workers like me.'

Miles smiles kindly at her. 'Wherever did you get that idea? How much money do you think we'll have? It won't be that much, certainly not enough to employ all the staff we'll need. Volunteers will always be necessary here, I can assure you of that.'

Daisy's face lights up so openly that Miles says, 'You really do enjoy working here, don't you?'

'More than you know,' Daisy replies, relief flowing through

her like swallows soaring to the skies. 'More than you'll ever, ever know.'

'Barnaby, can we talk?' Daisy says, an hour or so later. She is now in Barnaby's office, speaking softly so that the customers right outside the door cannot hear.

Barnaby looks at her hot, flushed face, the circles under her eyes, and says at once, 'I was expecting you anyway, thought we could drive out of town somewhere for lunch. The shop's not very busy and Jim ate early, so he can manage on his own.'

They drive a mile or two out of the city to a small pub with a large garden, where they sit under a flowery umbrella with a glass each of white wine. Neither feels much inclined to eat, Daisy because of what she must say, and Barnaby because he intuits what it is going to be.

'You're not coming to France,' he says flatly.

'How did you know?'

'The way you wouldn't look me in the eye at Gemma's farewell party, after I saw you and Leo embracing in the kitchen.'

'It was awkward.'

'It's always been awkward. What has changed?'

Daisy looks away from him, into the rose garden at the side of the pub, shimmering with petals of yellow and pink and orange. 'Leo,' she says finally. 'Leo has changed.'

Barnaby looks at her questioningly and Daisy continues. 'The day Gemma left, he talked to me for the first time in years. Maybe ever. Properly, you see. It was like a dam bursting. He talked and talked. About the farm, about his plans for the future, about how he's felt in the past . . .' She trails off, feeling uneasy now, discussing Leo with Barnaby.

Barnaby does not speak. The disappointment he feels is sharp and painful, but mixed with it is, oddly, something almost like relief. This morning Marjorie had said, wistfully (or at least as wistful as her loud and imperious voice could manage), 'I'll miss you while you're away. I wish I were going to France as well.'

She looked harassed; the children were all ill with colds and she herself was feverish. Barnaby felt a stab of something he couldn't quite interpret: guilt, yes, and pity, yes. On his way to the bookshop he figured out what else it was: love, of all things. He remembered how much he loved Marjorie when she became human and succumbed to the mundane illnesses the rest of us were prey to, when she wasn't quite so capable, when her voice, instead of booming out with such hearty assurance, became, like this morning, slightly unsure, a trifle unsteady, even a bit hoarse and nasally. He had fallen in love with her when she was in the throes of a nasty winter cold; she had walked into his bookshop, sneezed, asked for one of the tissues he had in a box on his front desk with a voice so muffled and croaky with infection, that every protective instinct in him rose like an antibiotic and he fell in love with her then and there.

Barnaby looks at Daisy, at her sweet face, the tiny features sharpened by strain, and says ruefully, 'We weren't very good at all this, were we. This extra-marital stuff. We never quite made it.'

The flat statement, the use of the past tense, both relieves Daisy and makes her cry at the same time.

'Don't cry,' he says, inanely and helplessly. He wishes he could go to her, hold her, but he knows this is a public place; there could very well be people both of them know here, and they have learned now to be circumspect. How unsatisfying an affair is, he thinks to himself, even a poor pathetic one like ours turned out to be.

Daisy, also remembering where she is, stops crying and blows her nose. How messy this all is, she thinks, and wishes she could hold Barnaby's hand, tell him how very much she would have liked to go to bed with him.

Barnaby is wishing very much the same thing. They sit there frustratedly for a few moments, not able to touch, not able to say the things they would really like to say. Barnaby wants to say things like, I'll never forget you, Daisy; but he is afraid of being banal. So they both look foolishly at each other, and each thinks the other looks so forlorn — which of course is true — that for a moment they forget where they are and clutch hands across the white wrought-iron table. The gesture says all they need to say, all they need to hear.

'Bloody hell, it's those two again,' says Clem Todd, coming into the garden with his arm around a fair-haired woman, not his wife, who is smiling appreciatively up at him. He tries to sneak out again, but Barnaby has glimpsed them, so he nods and sits down with the woman at a table as far away from the other two as he can find.

Well, at least Barnaby won't be saying anything to Celia about *me*, Clem thinks smugly as he turns to his companion, a journalist from London here in Canterbury to do a feature on some forthcoming events at the Cathedral. He in return will keep quiet now about those two.

Clem catches Barnaby's eye and gives him a conspiratorial wink, much to Barnaby's discomfort. Then he turns to the woman in front of him and forgets the other two as he beams in on her with all the subtlety of an InterCity train diligently racing along the same, well-worn track.

*   *   *

'Are you all right?' Emmeline asks Daisy later that afternoon, when Daisy finally arrives back at the farm. 'You're very pale. I'm glad you're off to France soon; you need a break. You've been working too hard at the shelter.'

'I'm not going to France,' Daisy says, and Tony, who has just brought Emmeline home after a day visiting Dover Castle, looks up at her questioningly.

'Why?' Emmeline asks. 'What's gone wrong?'

'Nothing,' Daisy says, looking suddenly (unaccountably for one who has just broken off with her lover-to-be) radiant. As she says this she knows it is true, that indeed nothing has gone wrong; on the contrary, suddenly everything is right, as it should be.

Tony and Emmeline are watching her with interest. 'You see,' she says with a wide happy grin, 'I have a job. A proper job, all of my own. I can't go running off to France when I'm just beginning the first proper paid employment of my entire married life.'

'What?'

'Where?' Tony and Emmeline start talking at once, asking questions.

'What's all the excitement about?' Leo, walking into the garden where they are sitting to catch the late afternoon sun, looks at Daisy's animated face and seats himself down next to her.

And so Daisy tells them. She tells them how Miles called her into the office and how, instead of being made redundant as she had supposed, she had been offered a job in the new hostel.

'I'll be doing the same sort of things that I do now,' Daisy tells them, 'but as a proper staff member, I'll be able to do much more with the residents. Link work, helping them to acquire social skills, helping them to cope with adjusting to a different life.'

'Is it full-time?' Emmeline asks.

'If I want,' Daisy says. 'And oh, Leo, I *do* want.'

Leo looks at her, at her rapturous face, her shining eyes, and is, momentarily, frightened at the changes he sees ahead, even though he understands that the money Daisy will be earning could not come at a better time. The pigs gone, his own new enterprise beginning, Daisy away from the farm five days a week . . . It is all almost too much, too quickly.

'Leo?' Daisy is asking tentatively. She is not asking his permission, he knows that; she will do it whatever he says, and so she should, so she should. But she is asking him to understand, to accept. To be supportive of her work, as she has been supportive of his all these years.

He looks at her with love and with pride, happy for her even though he knows he will miss her constant presence on the farm. 'Well done,' he says with a warm smile. 'Well done, Daisy.'

The four of them stay in the garden until after midnight. Tony insists on going into town to buy some kind of festive bubbly to celebrate Daisy's job and, though this will always be a secret from Leo, to celebrate also the saving of the Dillard marriage. Tony understands that whatever happened between Daisy and Barnaby is over, and he doesn't want to know how or why: he is content to know the crisis is averted.

While Tony goes for the wine, Leo does his evening farm chores, for once doing the barest minimum so he can return to the garden and relax. Emmeline, left alone with Daisy, says, 'Quick, tell me what happened. Barnaby, the French trip – it's not really off just because of the job, is it?'

'Of course not. I could easily have got time off for that. It's a good excuse, really.'

'So what happened?'

Daisy, watching the lengthening shadow of the old oak tree in the field in front of them, says, 'I'm not really sure, you know, Em. I got cold feet, I suppose. Or maybe I just began to realise all I'd lose.'

'I could have told you that, smartie.'

Daisy smiles. 'I know, but I wouldn't have listened. Gemma's party started me wondering. All the kids there, all our friends, Marjorie included. I felt as if I wasn't just saying goodbye to Gemma and Baz, but to myself, too, only it was much more final.'

She is quiet for a moment, and so is Emmeline. Swallows are flying about the garden, catching the early evening insects, swirling like shadows themselves against the summer sky. Finally Daisy continues. 'You know, I fell in love with Barnaby at the same time as I fell in love with my work, the job I was doing in the shelter. I think I got a bit confused. I think the love spilled on him rather accidentally. Once I was offered a permanent job there, it made it suddenly much easier to break off with him. I feel amazingly unbereaved now that it's all sorted out.' She giggles. 'Oh Em, do you think I'm dreadful?'

'No, I'm just so goddamn relieved.' They look at each other and smile. Then Emmeline says, seriously, 'But what if you didn't get the job?'

'Oh, I'd still have split with Barnaby. It was Leo, you see. He suddenly started talking to me.'

Emmeline comprehends. As Daisy explains to her what happened on Midsummer Day, Emmeline understands that Leo, after all these years, at last looked into a mirror, saw there a reflection of a possible future without Daisy, and, blinded, reached out for her at last.

'Thank God it wasn't too late,' is all Emmeline says now.

'Yes. Thank God.'

Leo returns then, and shortly afterwards Tony, and they open the sparkling wine that Tony has bought, and raise their glasses in a toast to Daisy. They drink, and talk, and lie on the blanket on the grass looking up at the sun growing low and red in the sky. At one point Leo wanders into the kitchen, scrambles some eggs, and returns with a platter full of eggs and bread and butter and sliced tomatoes. They eat voraciously, and drink more wine, and as the long evening darkens, Daisy runs inside and brings out a dozen of Gemma's candles. 'She left me these to sell,' Daisy says. 'So many of my friends buy her candles. But I think I shall use the whole lot myself.'

She and Emmeline circle the blanket with the candles, which are deep purple and blue, and yellow and red and orange, and shaped like pyramids, or massive tall columns, or octagons, or short squat round balls. Tony lights them, and the four of them sit inside the circle as the stars come out and the night settles like a soft dark blanket around them.

'Look,' Emmeline whispers. 'Look at those two swallows circling us.'

Tony whoops with laughter. 'Once a city girl, always a city girl,' he hoots. Then, fondly, 'Those are bats, love. Bats.'

Emmeline is not at all embarrassed. She looks at Tony, sees his clear hazel eyes reflecting the candlelight, and says, 'It's a good thing I've still got the whole summer left to learn the difference.'

The candles flicker on the ground and the stars flicker in the sky, and Emmeline cannot tell which is which because she has reached out her hand to Tony and he has taken it, held it, holds it even now as they sit side by side in their enchanted circle. Daisy, sitting opposite with Leo, observes this and catches Emmeline's eye, and sees a look there that she hasn't seen since Em was eighteen, if indeed it was ever there even then for more than a fleeting, transient moment.

'Leo, shall we go inside?' Daisy says. 'It's late, after midnight. I'm ready for bed, are you?'

Leo agrees, and after a few cheery good nights, Tony and Emmeline are left alone. For a time neither of them moves nor speaks, but their hands, still gripping each other's, are all the eloquence they can bear, at least for these first few dazzling moments.

Chapter Nineteen

'*H*al, *there you are! I thought I'd lost you. I've been so frantic, so afraid, all these people . . .*'

Emmeline held on tightly to Hal as they were swept along Oxford Street with the others on the peace march. This was the largest crowd Emmeline had seen on a march, and the feeling of euphoria, of hope and optimism, was intense and exhilarating. STOP THE WAR banners proliferated everywhere, across the wide selection of the population: housewives who looked as if they had never heard of the sixties, yet were chanting anti-war slogans; middle-aged men in baggy cords and duffel-coats; young women in white boots and clothes straight out of Biba or the Apple boutiques, with long straight hair curled up at the edges; Flower Children in their hippie clothes and carrying white carnations for peace which they sometimes gave away, with a loving embrace, to strangers. There were children, too, hundreds of them, skipping along in the crowd, their parents holding tightly on to their hands to make sure they didn't lose themselves in the mass.

Emmeline and Hal, very shortly after the march started, became separated. They had set off with Marsha and Jean-Luc, both still in England before returning permanently to France.

There was a jubilant, festive air about the march, inflated by the sheer numbers and the sanguine hope that this time the powers-that-be would listen and take heed of what the protesters were saying.

They had congregated at the Embankment. The morning was clear and warm, the day promising to be hot and sunny. It was a week or so after the haymaking weekend in Kent, and the rain that had begun the night the hay was safely stacked in the barn had lasted a stormy couple of days, then the sun came out again and had been shining ever since.

Emmeline, though finished with her first year at drama school, was staying on in London for most of the summer, purely to be with Hal. She intended to fly home for a couple of weeks in September, just before the autumn term began, but since Hal planned to spend summer in London, she would be here too. She had hoped that they could do tourist-y things together, like visit the Tower of London, go on a boat-trip on the Thames, things they were too busy to do during term-time, but Hal had got himself involved in a play somewhere on the fringes of London and was spending every spare moment rehearsing.

'Anything for me in it?' Emmeline had asked casually, a month or so ago when Hal first told her about it.

When Hal was silent, Emmeline added, 'I don't mean just acting. I'd be happy to be part of it in any way, props or working on costumes, whatever.'

But there wasn't a place for her, it seemed. Hal had met the others involved in the production at a theatre pub somewhere, during one of the evenings, more and more frequent, that he spent without Emmeline. What he did during these evenings Emmeline was never quite sure and Hal was never very forthcoming. Trying not to feel hurt, Emmeline told herself he needed his space; she must not crowd him, stifle him. But she longed for him when he was away, desperately. And waited sadly, patiently, for him to return.

She had inexplicably panicked when she got separated from Hal and the others on the march. She had stopped momentarily, to help a little boy who had tripped over his mother's feet and landed next to Emmeline, and by the time she had straightened up she could not see Hal. It was impossible to run through the crowd and the feeling made her crazy, made her feel as if she was wading through deep water, and she had to stop herself from pushing and shoving and screaming until she finally got to him. She tried to stay calm, telling herself that she would find him eventually: if she just walked slightly quicker than the other marchers, she would soon catch up with him. But it took longer than she thought, and though the crowd was gentle, amicable, unthreatening, the more she tried to get through it to find Hal, the more frightened she became, the more claustrophobic.

Because he was tall, she finally spotted him some way ahead, his blond hair, even longer these days, shining in the bright sunlight. She made a superhuman effort to break ahead of the crowd, to catch up with him, though once or twice it seemed as if she had lost him, as if he had disappeared for ever in the great throng of moving, heaving, bodies.

As she reached him, finally, she grabbed his right arm, and he turned to her, surprised and caught unaware. For a full three or four seconds, he looked her straight in the eyes as if he didn't see her, didn't even recognise her, before he finally acknowledged her with slight nod, a brief but detached smile.

'I thought I'd never find you,' she panted, clinging to his arm.

Hal said nothing, and the blank look on his face told Emmeline that he hadn't even noticed her absence.

They walked on in silence for a moment or two, then Hal, on the pretext of finding a handkerchief, detached his hand from Emmeline's, at the same time saying something to the young man walking next to him, who nodded and lightly placed his hand for a fleeting second or two on Hal's shoulder before turning and slipping off into the crowd. 'Who was that?' Emmeline asked, as the man turned again to smile and wave at Hal before finally disappearing.

For a moment she thought Hal wasn't going to answer, but he said, after a few moments, 'His name is Larry. He's one of the actors in the play I'm working on.'

'Oh.' They walked on in silence for a few moments. Emmeline was aware of singing going on behind her, of Marsha and Daisy arm-in-arm in front, Daisy dressed in cut-off jeans and a white T-shirt with a suede waistcoat, the fringes swinging against her hips, and Marsha in a cotton summer frock, sleeveless and high-waisted and very, very short. Jean-Luc, walking slightly apart from them, carried a rucksack filled with delicacies he had brought from France: jars of the tastiest pâtés, a bottle of red wine and a corkscrew. He thought it all a marvellous lark, and a far cry from exams and the dentistry college.

Emmeline said, 'Hal, why didn't you introduce me to Larry? You've mentioned him a few times; I'd have liked to meet him.'

Hal didn't reply, and something in his face, some strange mixture of determination and regret, kept her from asking him again.

That night Hal, for the first time in weeks, perhaps even months, stayed the night with Emmeline in Earl's Court. After the march, they had all ended up at a party somewhere in West Kensington, arriving back at Earl's Court around three in the morning, exhausted but happy. Daisy had already caught a train back to Canterbury, but Marsha and Jean-Luc stopped at Emmeline's bed-sit to share a last grotty cup of coffee before finally climbing the stairs to Marsha's room.

Hal collapsed into Emmeline's bed, still fully clothed, and fell asleep before Emmeline had put out the lights. Though it was four o'clock in the morning, she was wide awake, unsettled. She lay there for hours, watching the early morning light come through the openings in the curtain, and watching Hal sleep.

When he opened his eyes she had still not slept, was still looking at his suntanned face, the cheeks and chin dark now with stubble, the golden hair tangled on his forehead. He woke slowly, and she thought he smiled at her, though later she knew he was smiling at something he had dreamed, something far removed from her. The smile encouraged her, gave her hope, stilled the panic that had kept her trembling the whole night long, and she reached out for him. Turning her body slightly towards him she laid the length of her own body against his and put her hand out toward him, letting it fall on his chest, then under his shirt so that she could feel the beat of his heart against the soft skin.

'Don't.' His voice was low, muffled. Then, stronger: 'Don't touch me.' As he said it, he turned away from her. In a swift, unpremeditated movement, he turned so quickly that her hand dropped away and on to the bed, and he was lying on his side facing the wall, his body rigidly pulled away from her as if even the slightest contact was unbearable. Emmeline, unmoving, closed her eyes, and the tears fell silently down her face as they lay there, motionless, as the world stopped and time altered for both of them.

She couldn't stop crying. Looking back, she was astounded at how normally they behaved, except for the crying. After a time Hal, getting out of bed stiffly, put the kettle on and made them each a cup of instant coffee. Emmeline, her tears momentarily dried, sat up and drank it, saying nothing but gulping the hot dark liquid as if it would save her, save both of them. She understood that she was in some kind of shock; understood that some damage had been done to her – a damage which was most probably emotionally mortal but which, as yet, she could not feel, for a numbness had come over her which she accepted gladly. It protected her in an odd, confused away and enabled her not to think. So she drank her coffee, as did Hal, and stumblingly, they began to speak – about the march the previous day, about the party they had been to, about mutual friends. Emmeline talked as if by rote, carefully, dully. Hal was kind, and even smiled at Emmeline in the old familiar way, but there was an abstraction, a chilliness about him that would have frightened her had she not been so numbed herself.

Years later, she was incredulous when she remembered how neither of them spoke of what had happened, as if the enormity of it had rendered them completely incapable. They were too young to face it as they should have; they were young in years, but younger also in experience. And so they drank more coffee, and Hal ate toast spread thickly with butter, and then because it was Sunday he went to the newsagent and bought the Sunday papers which they both read silently over the kitchen table, pretending not to notice the occasional tears which welled up like a swollen river in Emmeline's eyes, muddy and unbidden.

Emmeline wondered why Hal did not go, for he had not hung around her place for weeks: he was always rushing off either to a rehearsal, or to meet someone, or whatever. She was glad that he did not, for she knew that when she was alone, the shocked numbness she was still feeling would ebb, leaving her with a pain she was not sure that she could handle. As if knowing this, he stayed, solicitous and friendly, if in a somewhat detached manner, as if he were already long gone on the journey away from Emmeline that he had acknowledged by turning away from her so unbendingly that morning.

After breakfast and the papers, they found themselves outside, reluctant to stay too long enclosed in each other's circle, as if afraid the words they were unwilling yet to speak would burst out unbidden and suffocate them. So they wandered desultorily around London, walking, walking, walking, not talking much, still ignoring the tears which kept filling Emmeline's eyes. After an hour or two of this they found themselves on the Embankment, leaning over the railing watching the sightseeing boats floating by in the afternoon sun.

'Should we go on one, Emmeline?' Hal asked. 'Shall we be tourists, just for today, just for once like we used to?'

Like we used to. The words moved her as nothing else today had, the words and the quiet desperation in Hal's voice. She could not stop the tears from overflowing once again.

'Please, Em, don't do that. Don't cry, for God's sake . . . can we for one day forget everything, just enjoy London?'

It was a plea from the heart, and Emmeline realised, through the fog that was engulfing her, that Hal too was suffering. And like her, he did not know how to bring them out of this misery in which they were entrapped. She and Hal were standing only a foot apart, but the real distance was immeasurable. They were facing the river, leaning over the railing, watching the pleasure boats that they would never be able to take, not together; watching the light-hearted tourists that they would never be able to emulate.

'Tell me,' Emmeline said with a heavy finality, her eyes aching with the dazzling light on the water, the crying, the sleepless night. 'Tell me.'

And so Hal did, telling it to the river, the gulls flying overhead, the slight breeze beginning to stir across the water. He did not look at Emmeline, not once, not until he had said it all.

'I'm in love, Em,' he began, so softly that Emmeline almost lost the words to the river and to the gulls. 'I'm sorry, I'm so sorry. I thought I was in love with you in the beginning, I really did. I felt so close to you, and I cared – I still do care – so much for you. Nothing that I feel for you has changed, it's just that I now realise it isn't love. I wanted it to be, desperately, but it isn't, never can be.'

A gull flew dangerously close, hoping for a hand-out, bread thrown in the water. Emmeline looked out at the river and wished that she were in it, floating in the sun like a dead fish, unknowing, unfeeling. Hal was still talking and his words, drifting into the sun, fell like acid rain on her heart, on her life.

'I never understood this, never knew that what I felt for you was a mixture of affection and fondness and, later, a kind of passive desperation, for I did want to marry you, Em, and live a nice normal contented life with you.' He stopped, passing his hand over his eyes as if ridding himself of the impossible dream. It was a moment before he could go on.

'For a long time, I was able to kid myself. If I had any doubts, I kept them well hidden, even from myself. I was determined to make you happy, to show you how . . . how grateful I was that you could love me, how precious that was to me. And then—'

Hal broke off. Once again the gesture, the hand passing in front of his eyes as if he were shaking away what he was seeing there. 'And then,' he continued, 'then I really did fall in love. For the first time in my entire life, I knew what it was to be frantic with despair because the one you love is five minutes late, to have those five minutes crawl by like an eternity. For the first time, I knew what it was like to really want someone, to be so unbearably lonely when that person was not with you that you felt you could die with need, with want, with love.'

Hal paused again, and Emmeline, through a thick glass, through fathoms of deep water, saw that he was indeed trembling, and on the brink of tears himself.

She didn't want to know any more; didn't know if she could take any more without the glass she seemed to be under exploding into shards, cutting her to shreds; without the water that seemed to be surrounding her holding her down, drowning her. But Hal went on, in a strange voice she had never heard before, 'I'm in love with another man, Emmeline. And I've never been so happy, and so frightened, in all my life.'

'Frightened?' was all Emmeline could murmur, her mind not able to focus, not able to grasp anything but that one word. 'Why are you frightened?' Her words were slurred, as if she were speaking underwater.

'Only of losing him,' Hal said quietly. 'It's the greatest terror of my life, that now I've found him, I'll lose him.'

417

'As I've lost you,' Emmeline cried, and then the numbness lifted and she was lost, destroyed, and it didn't matter. Nothing mattered, except that Hal was lost to her irrevocably, and the radiant times, the golden times, were gone from her for ever.

Chapter Twenty

'So you ran away,' Tony says gently, holding Emmeline's hand as they sit side by side on the boat which is crowded with Americans and Japanese taking photographs of the approaching Tower Bridge.

'For ever, so I thought,' Emmeline replies, smiling at him. 'I thought the only way I could survive was to leave drama school, leave London, and never, ever come back.'

'But you did,' he says, kissing her on the mouth. It is so sweet, so erotic, so full of promise, that he kisses her again, and again, until he realises they are being photographed by some teenage Japanese lads, amidst raucous laughter and shouts. Tony feels too good even to frown at the boys, but he does stop kissing Em and settles for putting his arm around her shoulders.

Emmeline and Tony are on a sightseeing boat to Greenwich. 'Do you know,' Emmeline had said after they had been in Tony's bed for more or less two days solid, not seeing anyone, eating the food from his cupboard and from his fridge, emerging only to take fragmented walks around the footpaths near his house or to sit in his sheltered garden hidden by a high crumbling old brick wall – 'Do you know, Tony, that

I have never yet seen London properly? I lived there for a year, and I never saw Westminster Abbey. Or went on a boat down the Thames.'

'We'll go now, if you like. It's early enough. Though it will mean putting on our clothes, of course.' He looked so regretful at this that Emmeline laughed.

They had gone to Tony's house the night of the wine and the candles, the night Daisy had announced her new job and the four of them sat in the midnight dark not wanting to move, not wanting to spoil the rare summer evening by going inside. When Emmeline had reached out her hand for Tony, overcome by the night, by the moment, by the quiet realisation that she was in love with this man, she had done so without thought or calculation, trusting him to be there, not to turn away as Hal had done all those years ago. And he was, of course. He had been waiting for Emmeline's gesture from the beginning, since last September, and when it came he took the outstretched hand and held it with such fierce joy that Emmeline knew he would never willingly let it go.

When they were finally alone, when Leo and Daisy so tactfully left them and went inside, they still did not speak or move but sat silent, clutching the other's hand like a talisman. Finally Tony turned, took her in his arms, and kissed her as he had been wanting to do for months. The stars shone, the candles flickered, the bats glided in the dark between the stars and the candles, and Emmeline and Tony kissed, and kissed again.

'Will you come back to my place?' he said at last.

Emmeline nodded, ran inside to grab some clothes and a toothbrush, and to tell Daisy, who was not at all surprised, that she would not be home before morning. Then she climbed into the van beside Tony where neither of them spoke on the short drive to his house; nor did they speak as they went inside, climbed the stairs with their arms twined around each other, and lay down on the big wooden bed covered with a red and black fringed wool blanket from South America.

'I love you,' Tony said as he began taking off her clothes.

And still Emmeline couldn't speak, but her body did it for her, and before the dawn had appeared outside Tony's uncurtained windows he knew, with wonder, that she loved him too.

'So what do you think of London?' Tony says now as they watch the city glide past as the boat heads towards Greenwich.

'I had forgotten how beautiful it was in the sunlight,' Emmeline says contentedly. 'I remember it in the rain — wet, dark, miserable.'

'Do you? But you were just telling me about the haymaking, the perpetual sunshine.'

Emmeline looks at him, touches his face. 'I forgot the good things,' she says simply. 'Until I came back. All I remembered when I left was that summer of rain, after Hal told me he was in love with Larry, the actor I had seen briefly at the peace march.'

'Why didn't you go back to America then? There was no reason for you to stay.'

'I know.' Emmeline watches as another boat passes, and the passengers on both vessels wave and wave. 'But I had no will, you see, to do anything, make any decisions. I had already booked a ticket for the beginning of September, and I simply did not have the strength or energy to change it. I sat in that tiny bed-sitter, day after day, all summer, watching the rain pouring outside the window, wishing I could drown in it.'

421

Tony, moved, tightens his arm around her shoulders. 'Didn't Hal help?' he says. 'Didn't anyone?'

'Marsha and Jean-Luc left shortly afterwards for France, and of course Sojo and Giorgio were in Italy. Daisy was wonderful, left the farm often to come and see me in London, urging me to stay in Kent for the summer. But I couldn't move from London. I think I was waiting for Hal, you see. To come back, tell me it was all a big mistake, a joke.' She looks at Tony ruefully. 'Pretty pathetic, eh?'

'And Hal?'

'He came to see me a few times, but it only made everything worse. He looked so happy, he couldn't hide it. I finally told him to stay away, and I think he was relieved. I never saw him again.'

'Do you want to see him now?' Tony says. 'His play is still on, you know. We could take in the theatre tonight if you like.'

Emmeline looks thoughtfully at the water. She is surprised how little it matters to her, whether they see Hal in the play or not. She thinks that perhaps one day she'd like to, for the same reasons of curiosity and interest she feels when she sees an ex-student or colleague of hers achieve recognition in some way.

But right now she doesn't even care about that. All she feels is the need to be with Tony, and for the moment, everything else is unimportant. 'I think not,' she says. 'Some day perhaps, but not tonight. I don't think I could concentrate on anything else but you tonight.'

The boat puffs its way up the Thames, like an old man walking up a steep hill. Emmeline and Tony, like the rest of the tourists, settle down in their seats with contented anticipation, looking forward to the journey ahead.